NEW YORK REVIEW BOOKS
CLASSICS

ENGLISH, AUGUST

UPAMANYU CHATTERJEE was born in 1959 in Patna, India. He joined the Indian Administrative Service in 1983 and at present works as a civil servant in Bombay. He writes novels on the side—when no one is looking, as it were. His family comprises one wife and two daughters. He enjoys diverse solitary occupations.

AKHIL SHARMA was born in Delhi, India, and grew up in Edison, New Jersey. His stories have appeared in *The Best American Short Stories* anthology, *The O. Henry Award Winners* anthology, *The Atlantic Monthly*, and *The New Yorker*. His novel, *An Obedient Father*, won the 2001 Pen Hemingway Prize.

ENGLISH, AUGUST
An Indian Story

UPAMANYU CHATTERJEE

Introduction by
AKHIL SHARMA

NEW YORK REVIEW BOOKS

New York

INTRODUCTION

SALMAN Rushdie's *Midnight's Children* was the first Indian novel to be widely perceived as a vital contribution to literature in English. Since that happened many Indian writers have gone on to become household names not only in England and America but all around the world: Arundhati Roy; Amitav Ghosh, with his historical novels; Vikram Seth, whose *A Suitable Boy* is a marvelous thousand-page-plus social comedy about arranged marriage. These famous authors, though, only begin to suggest the range of excellent English-language literature being produced in India.

To me, as an American writer of Indian ancestry and an avid reader of Indian fiction, one of the most striking things about so much contemporary Indian fiction is the way it presents itself as being representative—of the historical moment, of the social situation, of the cultural climate, of, above all, India. And perhaps it is this strange, but not unusual, idea that every Indian novel is, or should be, THE Indian novel, that Upamanyu Chatterjee had in mind when he gave the subtitle of "An Indian Story" to *English, August*, his extraordinary first book. *A* story and not *the* story, even if *English, August* tells a story that could only be Indian. Whether or not that was Chatterjee's intention, there's no doubt that his book stands apart from other Indian fiction by virtue of being so attentive to the particular. *English, August* is a story about a young man in a small Indian town, who has a very particular job in the civil service. It's a book about doing paperwork (or avoiding doing paperwork), going to teas with your boss's wife, and overseeing village well-digging projects, as well as smoking pot, masturbating, and reading Marcus Aurelius. And if by the end of the book it turns out that *English, August* does indeed have much to say about India, that's almost a happy accident. Because it's the particularity of the book that makes it a work of art and gives such pleasure.

English, August does two things that are central to what novels have always done. It brings us news—about the way we live now; about the way others live now—and this is deeply satisfying. Almost as important, *English, August* offers us the pleasure of seeing what Upamanyu Chatterjee can do with language. Chatterjee is one of those rare writers who can be as funny as sad, as lyrical as plain. Let me quote a few passages:

Funny:

> Kumar remained adamant about finishing the booze while watching the [pornographic] films. They [two men traveling for work] settled down in bed, with mosquito-repellent cream on their skins and incense in the air. Kumar was giggling with alcohol and the promise of titillation. The first shot of the first film showed a thin American black man with painted lips and white bikini, gyrating. He was cajoled into stripping by five white girls, demented with lust. They all licked their lips and one another until the black, with horrendous coyness, displayed his penis. Then the girls got to work. "See, see," squeaked Kumar, trembling with adolescent excitement, "lucky black bastard . . ." Throughout the ogling he shifted in bed and intermittently muttered, ". . . this kind of thing never happens in India . . . Indian girls are too inhibited . . . bloody shame . . ."

Sad:

[The protagonist, a government official, goes to a distant village to examine complaints of a well that has become silted.] He was relieved to see more people around the well. But something was odd, and he realized in a moment that it was the muteness of the village, there seemed to be no laughter and no conversation. The village did have children, but they were all busy. Women were tying them to ropes and letting them into the well. After a while the ropes were bringing up buckets. He went closer. The buckets were half-full of some thin mud. The only sounds were the echoing clang of the buckets against the walls of the well, and the tired sniveling of a few children on the side. He looked at them. Gashed elbows and knees from the well walls, one child had a wound like a flower on his forehead. The woman who had come to the office was looking at him in a kind of triumph. He looked into the well. He couldn't see any water, but the children were blurred wraiths forty feet below, scouring the mud of the well floor for water, like sinners serving some mythic punishment.

Lyrical:

Then the rains came to Madna...Suddenly a roar and a drumroll, as of a distant war...The world turned monochromatic...Cloud, building, tree, road, they all diffused into one blurred shade of slate.

———

I said to a friend, also an admirer of *English, August,* that the book was, of course, a coming-of-age story. My friend countered, not at all, it was a slacker novel. Both descriptions are in fact true.

We meet Chatterjee's hero, Agastya Sen, at night in a car. He is driving down an empty street in New Delhi with a friend who is getting ready to roll another joint. Much is signaled and set up by this brief scene. To be a young man driving a car in India implies meaningful wealth, while the marijuana suggests rebelliousness and lassitude at the same time. These are children of privilege, young city sophisticates. We soon learn, however, that Agastya is going to be leaving Delhi: he has been accepted into the Indian Administrative Service, or IAS, about which he has very mixed feelings, and will have to start living in the sticks.

The town Agastya soon finds himself in is Madna, and Upamanyu Chatterjee's portrait of it is one of the great imaginative achievements of recent Indian literature. Probably American readers will have never seen a small town quite like this, one that by American standards would hardly qualify as small. The population could easily be in the high tens of thousands or more; the congestion and racket more akin to that of an American city. Its remoteness from the rest of the world, its claustrophobic self-containment, cannot be exaggerated.

Readers of this book will come to know Madna intimately. There is the dust, of course, which seems present in most books about India, but there is also the badly constructed statue of Mahatma Gandhi that is common to many town squares (often the statue is sculpted so blockily that Gandhi looks like a muscle-bound wrestler with glasses and a shaved head). The bedraggled country club that Chatterjee introduces us to is usually the social center of the town elite, a place where everyone seems aware of very fine distinctions in status. There is this and there are the local characters: the town doctor, the journalist who prints gossip, the police chief who loves pornography. Agastya is more at a loss in Madna than he ever imagined he'd be, and he soon finds himself devoting much of his time to hunting for wild marijuana plants.

Agastya is one of the funniest characters in Indian fiction and one of the saddest. His mother died when he was a child, which may have helped to make him the deeply lonely person he is. Part of the reason that he cannot bear Madna is that his isolation there makes that loneliness unignorable. Talking to colleagues, Agastya even invents a wife for himself, and this stupid, conceivably self-destructive falsehood is not just pointless but poignant. Because Agastya's life is littered with missing people: the dead mother, but also an absent father (off in Bengal, being the governor, it turns out; the father communicates with Agastya through letters that are both aloof and disappointed), a possible girlfriend gone off to graduate school in America, and a Hindu saint. Unsettled and restless in Delhi, Agastya is almost paralyzed with misery in Madna, where his colleagues repel him as grotesque, while such friends as he finds there strike him as even more to be pitied than himself. Because of all this, and for all his wisecracks, the question Agastya is struggling to put to himself is, Why am I so unhappy?

The way the question is raised and the way it is resolved connect *English, August* to the Western coming-of-age novel (it has been described as India's *Catcher in the Rye*) while also marking it as distinctively Indian. The sense of inauthenticity Agastya suffers from feels very Western (so much so that one might be tempted to dismiss it for a while as a citified affectation). This inauthenticity, by the way, is what is captured by the novel's somewhat puzzling title. Agastya is an old-fashioned kind of name—it comes from a mythological Hindu guru—which is why Agastya's friends have taken the liberty of Englishifying it into August, or even, going a step further, simply calling him English. Agastya, in short, seems un-Indian to them, and to himself as well at times. That hardly makes him English, though, as he is perfectly aware. Inauthentically

Indian, inauthentically Western: in Madna this crisis of identity comes to a head.

What feels oddly and specifically Indian to me is the resolution of the crisis. The resolution is not the breaking away that Agastya has been contemplating all along, and it's not a reconciliation. It's not a renunciation either. It's not even exactly a decision. In any case, Agastya does not surrender his independence or his native wit. But there is a change, an acceptance, that the reader cannot miss. An acceptance of necessity by virtue of which Agastya is set free.

———

There's an Indian saying that if you want to keep a secret you should put it in a book. It's all the more amazing, then, that when *English, August* was first published in India in 1988 it was an enormous best seller.

The reason *English, August* was such a popular success probably has to do with the Indian Administrative Service. In India to belong to the IAS is a little like being a movie star. Each year approximately two million people take the exam for eighty entry-level IAS positions. One of the lowest rungs of the IAS is district collector. Agastya is an assistant to a collector, though it is assumed that in time he will become one himself. A district is the equivalent of an American county, and the district collector runs or has great influence over the district's judicial, police, and administrative functions. The IAS is considered to be honest for the most part, though there is a joke that if you become an IAS officer you can earn so much money through corruption that your family will have enough to eat for seven generations.

The first time I read *English, August*, I was living in a small town in India and working with various IAS officers. The book was so spot-on that it didn't surprise me in the least that many of them complained about it. I read the book over and over and found comfort in Chatterjee's observations of the world I was living in, the sound of lizards plopping off the ceiling and falling to the floor, the squabbling among adults as to who gets to sit in the front passenger seat.

Chatterjee has followed *English, August* with three further novels (*The Last Burden*, which was published in 1993, *The Mammaries of the Welfare State* in 2000, and *Weight Loss* in 2006) while continuing to pursue his career in the civil service. A character in *English, August* talks about how each language has a "tang" and that it is hard to translate this very specific flavor. That, of course, is true of the work of our best writers as well. Upamanyu Chatterjee has his own "tang" and it is like nobody else's.

—AKHIL SHARMA

ENGLISH, AUGUST

To my parents

THROUGH the windshield they watched the wide silent road, so well-lit and dead. New Delhi, one in the morning, a stray dog flashed across the road, sensing prey. "So when shall we meet again?" asked Dhrubo for the eighth time in one hour. Not that parting was too agonizing and that he couldn't bear to leave the car, but that marijuana caused acute lethargy.

"Uh..." said Agastya and paused, for the same reason. Dhrubo put the day's forty-third cigarette to his lips and seemed to take very long to find his matchbox. His languorous attempts to light a match became frenzied before he succeeded. Watching him Agastya laughed silently.

Dhrubo exhaled richly out of the window, and said, "I've a feeling, August, you're going to get hazaar fucked in Madna." Agastya had just joined the Indian Administrative Service and was going for a year's training in district administration to a small district town called Madna.

"Amazing mix, the English we speak. Hazaar fucked. Urdu and American," Agastya laughed, "a thousand fucked, really fucked. I'm sure nowhere else could languages be mixed *and* spoken with such ease." The slurred sounds of the comfortable tiredness of intoxication, "'You look hazaar fucked, Marmaduke dear.' 'Yes Dorothea, I'm afraid I do feel hazaar fucked'—see, doesn't work. And our accents are Indian, but we prefer August to Agastya. When I say our accents, I, of course, exclude yours, which is unique in its fucked mongrelness—you

5

even say 'Have a nice day' to those horny women at your telephones when you pass by with your briefcase, and when you agree with your horrendous boss, which is all the time, you say 'yeah, great' and 'uh-uh.'"

"Don't talk shit," Dhrubo said and then added in Bengali, "You're hurt about your mother tongue," and started laughing, an exhilarated volley. That was a ten-year-old joke from their school-days in Darjeeling, when they had been envious of some of the Anglo-Indian boys who spoke and behaved differently, and did alarmingly badly in exams and didn't seem to mind, they were the ones who were always with the Tibetan girls and claimed to know all about sex. On an early summer afternoon, in the small football field among the hills, with an immaculate sky and the cakelike white-and-brownness of Kanchanjanga, Agastya and Prashant had been watching (Agastya disliked football and Prashant disliked games) the usual showing off with the ball. Shouts in the air from the Anglos (which increased whenever any Tibetan female groups passed the field, echoing like a distant memory, "Pass it here, men!" "This way, men!" "You can't shoot, your foot's made of turd or what men!" (Agastya had never heard any Anglo say "man"). He and Prashant had been lazily cynical about those who shouted the most and whose faces also contorted with a secret panic in the rare moments when the ball did reach them. Then some Tibetan girls had come together and taken out a fucking guitar. "The Tibs and the Anglos always have guitars," Prashant had said. Football had been abandoned. Then laughter and twanging. "It's the colour of the Anglo and Tib thighs," Prashant had said, "not like us." Agastya's envy had then blurted out, he wished he had been Anglo-Indian, that he had Keith or Alan for a name, that he spoke English with their accent. From that day his friends had more new names for him, he became the school's "last Englishman," or just "hey English" (his friends meant "hey Anglo" but didn't dare), and sometimes even "hello

Mother Tongue"—illogical and whimsical, but winsome choices, like most names selected by contemporaries. And like most names, they had paled with the passage of time and place, all but August, but they yet retained with them the knack of bobbing up out of some abyss on the unexpected occasion, and nudging a chunk or two of his past.

A truck roared by, shattering the dark. "Out there in Madna quite a few people are going to ask you what you're doing in the Administrative Service. Because you don't look the role. You look like a porn film actor, thin and kinky, the kind who wears a bra. And a bureaucrat ought to be soft and cleanshaven, bespectacled, and if a Tamil Brahmin, given to rapid quoting of rules. I really think you're going to get hazaar fucked."

"I'd much rather act in a porn film than be a bureaucrat. But I suppose one has to live."

"Let's smoke a last one, shall we," said Dhrubo, picking up the polythene bag from the car seat. "In Yale a Ph.D wasn't a joke. It meant something. It was significant. Students thought before they enrolled. But here in Delhi, all over India," Dhrubo threw some loose tobacco out of the window, "education is biding time, a meaningless accumulation of degrees, BA, MA, then an M.Phil. while you join the millions in trying your luck at the Civil Services exam. So many people every year seem to find government service so interesting," he paused to scratch his elbow, "I wonder how many people think about where their education is leading them."

"Yet you returned from Yale," Agastya yawned.

"But mine is not the typical Indian story. That ends with the Indian living somewhere in the First World, comfortably or uncomfortably. Or perhaps coming back to join the Indian Administrative Service, if lucky."

"You're wrong about education, though. Most must be like me, with no special aptitude for anything, not even wondering how to manage, not even really thinking. Try your luck with everything, something hopefully will click. There aren't unlimited opportunities in the world."

They smoked. Dhrubo leaned forward to drop loose tobacco from his shirt. "Madna was the hottest place in India last year, wasn't it. It will be another world, completely different. Should be quite educative." Dhrubo handed the smoke to Agastya. "Excellent stuff. What'll you do for sex and marijuana in Madna?"

BY THE fastest train Madna was eighteen hours away from Delhi, but of course the fastest train simply shrieked its way through it. As the train that did stop at Madna slipped out of New Delhi Agastya waved to his uncle and then locked himself in the toilet to smoke some more marijuana. His compartment had another traveller for Madna, an engineer in some thermal power station. Desultory train conversation began, and Agastya was soon asked to categorize himself.

"Agastya? What kind of a name is Agastya?" asked the engineer, almost irritably. He was a large unpleasant man, the owner of a trunk that wouldn't fit below the lower berths, but on which he wouldn't allow anyone to place his feet.

"He's a saint of the forest in the *Ramayana*, very ascetic. He gives Ram a bow and arrow. He's there in the *Mahabharata*, too. He crosses the Vindhyas and stops them from growing."

The engineer looked dissatisfied, almost suspicious, as though Agastya had just sold him an aphrodisiac. He interrupted Agastya again, almost immediately, squeaking with surprise. "Excuse me, IAS? You are IAS? You don't look like an IAS officer." He eyed him doubtfully. "You don't even look Bengali," pronounced Bungaali.

Agastya was only half-Bengali. His mother had been Goanese, a Catholic. He hardly remembered her, she had died of meningitis when he had been less than three. He was athlete-thin and

9

bearded. He had no devouring interests, and until he came to Madna, very little ambition.

Outside the Indian hinterland rushed by. Hundreds of kilometres of a familiar yet unknown landscape, seen countless times through train windows, but never experienced—his life till then had been profoundly urban. Shabby stations of small towns where the train didn't stop, the towns that looked nice from a train window, incurious patient eyes and weatherbeaten bicycles at a level crossing, muddy children and buffalo at a waterhole. To him, these places had been, at best, names out of newspapers, where floods and caste wars occurred, and entire Harijan families were murdered, where some prime minister took his helicopter just after a calamity, or just before the elections. Now he looked out at this remote world and felt a little unsure, he was going to spend months in a dot in this hinterland.

The train was four hours late, they reached Madna after dark. A small tube-lit station, stray dogs, a few coolies, a man selling rusks and tea, a family of beggars arguing in an unfamiliar tongue around the taps. A sweating swarthy man came up to him and mumbled something. He smiled and said in Hindi, "Will you speak Hindi, please. I'll take some time to pick up the language."

The man smiled, embarrassed, and asked in a harshly accented Hindi, "Are you Mr. Sen, IAS?" In Madna, "IAS" was always to be attached to his name; it almost became his surname.

In the jeep he realized how stifling it was. "Where am I staying?" he asked.

"The Government Rest House, sir," said the swarthy man from behind. He was a naib tehsildar, he had said. Whatever that was, Agastya had thought. "Accommodation for government officers is a problem in Madna, sir," said the man. For a year Agastya was to move from one room in a Rest House (a suite it was called, for some reason, and pronounced soot) to some other room in some other Rest House—homelessness of a kind.

Glimpses of Madna *en route*; cigarette-and-paan dhabas, disreputable food stalls, both lit by fierce kerosene lamps, cattle and clanging rickshaws on the road, and the rich sound of trucks in slush from an overflowing drain; he felt as though he was living someone else's life.

His education began on the first evening itself. The room at the Rest House was big, and furnished not like a room, but like a house. It had a bed, a dressing table, a dining table with four chairs, a sofa, two armchairs, a desk and chair, two small tables and a beautiful bookshelf. The room looked like the storehouse of a dealer in stolen furniture. "Why all this furniture? I don't need all this."

"Sir?" With the naib tehsildar was a grey-stubbled sullen man, the caretaker-cook of the Rest House. He spoke Hindi with great reluctance. There were children at the door, in various sizes; all seemed to breathe through their mouths.

"What's a sofa doing here?"

"For guests, sir."

"No, take it away. Far too many things in here, I don't need all this. Can't you remove some?"

"Remove some?"

They did eventually, their faces and forearms tense with disconcertment. They called others for help. They dragged the bed under the fan. Agastya sweated, directed them in Hindi, and felt the mosquitoes. "Isn't there any insecticide that we can spray?"

Vasant, the caretaker-cook, looked at him murderously over the back of a sofa.

"Yes, sir, horrible mosquitoes here," smiled the naib tehsildar. They sprayed the room with Flit.

Vasant brought dinner almost immediately after, on a tray. The naib tehsildar hovered at the door, never failing to show something of himself to Agastya, a shoulder, a shoe, a leg, and each portion of his body saying, There, I hope you continue to feel uneasy and strange. Dinner was unbelievable, the dal tasted like lukewarm chillied shampoo. The tang of Flit in his nostrils, he was awed by the thought of months in which every meal would taste like this. "Is this the usual way you cook?" He finally communicated the question to Vasant through the naib tehsildar. Vasant said yes. Then the naib tehsildar said that the Collector had told him to tell the cook to boil Agastya's drinking water as there was endemic jaundice and epidemic cholera in Madna, and that he had already done so and that may he now take his leave, sir.

Ten o'clock. Agastya was on the veranda outside his room. Around the tube-light wheeled a hundred different insects. The frequent plop of careless lizards falling on the floor. His room was one of two in a kind of cottage. The other room was silent, locked. Other similar cottages, and 200 feet away the large Circuit House. A few lights on in the compound, two jeeps outside the Circuit House. He was 1,400 kilometres away from Delhi, and more than a thousand from Calcutta, the two cities of his past.

Before going to bed he lit an anti-mosquito incense stick under the table and rubbed mosquito repellent cream all over himself. He slept under a mosquito net, but the mosquitoes got him anyway. He surfaced, struggling, out of sleep thrice that night, only to hear the mosquitoes droning in the glow from the veranda.

On his first morning in Madna he woke up feeling terrible ("feeling fucked," he later wrote to Neera in Calcutta, "like the fallen Adam"). He found opening his eyes difficult, then realized that the mosquitoes had reached his eyelids too. Some start to the day, he looked at the wooden ceiling and said to himself, if your very first emotion of the morning is disgust. He looked at the mirror. Two red swollen spots on his right cheek, above the beard, one below his left ear. Calcutta's mosquitoes seemed more civilized, they never touched the face. This place has drawn first blood, he thought, wasn't elephantiasis incurable?

He stepped out to ask Vasant for some tea. Beyond the veranda the other buildings were turning white with the glare. The sun seemed to char his head and neck. Eight fifteen in the morning and he could almost sense the prickly heat spring up on his skin.

And yet this was late summer. The year before Madna had topped the charts, as it were, had been the hottest place in India. It had a few traditional rivals in the Indian Deccan but every year Madna's residents were almost always sure that their town and district would be hotter than those. In salutation (and to be fair, to avoid sunstroke), the residents tied a towel or a napkin over their ears and head at eight in the morning and took it off after sundown. Later he tied one too, quite enjoying himself, even getting himself photographed in his hood. And later still, he would think, that those who saw menace in an Indian summer, and called the sun angry and pitiless, and enervating, and words like that, merely reduced the sun to a petty anthropomorphic jumbo. Of course the heat did weaken the calves and dehydrate the head, but the sun, like so many things in Madna, was educative. It taught him the aphorisms of common sense: don't fight the processes of nature, it seemed to say; here, stay indoors as much as you can, if possible turn nocturnal. The world outside is not worth journeying out for, and any beauty out of doors is visible only in the dark, or in the half-light of dawn.

If Madna had been Delhi, and the weather less hot, and if he'd woken up earlier, he would have gone for his run. He had been a competent long-distance runner in his college days. Running seemed to clear his mind and start the day well. But he returned to his room and wondered if he should smoke a joint. After all the jeep wouldn't come for him till eleven. While wondering he made one and smoked it anyway. Then he put on Tagore's *Shyama* on his cassette recorder and lay down to contemplate the room.

He had to get organized, unpack properly and think a little, maybe smoke less, because there was something dangerous in smoking alone, and in an unknown place. The room was at least big, he liked that.

High up on the wall facing him, amid the lizards, hung what he would later call the usual improbable Rest-House painting—a sunset, and water, and therefore two sunsets, a boat, a boatman in a Japanese conical hat, on the shore two trees, like giant mushrooms. As he went higher, he relaxed more, and grew more amazed, in an objective way, at the absence of imagination in the painting. He tried to visualize the painter, and couldn't. He thought, Had the painter been brushing his teeth or bending over trying to get his cock in his mouth, or what, when he painted this one? There wasn't a single thought behind a single brushstroke. Irritated, he got up, climbed a chair and took down the painting.

At the back, beneath the cobwebs and dust of years, he read, in ink turned brown, "Donated to the Madna Circuit House, my unwanted second home, by me, R. Tamse, Deputy Engineer, Public Works Division, 4 July 1962." Below this was a tremendous poem, again in brown.

> Away from my old life and my spouse,
> So many days at this Circuit House,
> Away from Goa, my dear home,
> On office work I have to roam.

Now the painting looked different, and a little less ridiculous; this was the Goa of an imagination forlorn, not perhaps accustomed to creativity, but compelled to it by isolation. Suddenly Agastya thought that he could see Tamse better. He would be short, plump, but not worried at all about his weight, and therefore very slightly complacent, gentle, and not quite relaxed in the company of people like Agastya. In a room and place like this, certainly not given to marijuana or inventive masturbation or hunting for sex, Tamse, what would he have done. Perhaps many had convinced him that he painted and wrote well; his father might have said, in the language of proud fathers, "You must always have these as a second string to your bow." Tamse had been lonely but had not given in, had re-created in his wilderness an image of home. Perhaps those mushroom trees and sunsets were a view from his window, perhaps boatmen really did wear Japanese conical hats in Goa.

He turned the painting over and over, relating the brush-strokes to the poem. He liked "my old life and my spouse"; at least Tamse admitted to missing his wife, some others would have been shy of this. He was sentimental too, otherwise he would not have donated the painting. Despite the nullity of talent, it was still an attempt to share a mood and an experi-ence. He smiled at the blue walls and thought, they just might grow on me too.

A rapid but timid knock on the door, like the scurrying of some rodent. A small black man in the white khadi of a peon. He was Digambar, the peon attached to Agastya for his stay. "Here," said Agastya, "just clean this painting and put it back."

At eleven, still stoned, he went to the Collectorate to meet R. N. Srivastav IAS, Collector and District Magistrate of Madna, his mentor and boss for the months of training.

DISTRICT administration in India is largely a British creation, like the railways and the English language, another complex and unwieldy bequest of the Raj. But Indianization (of a method of administration, or of a language) is integral to the Indian story. Before 1947 the Collector was almost inaccessible to the people; now he keeps open house, primarily because he does a different, more difficult job. He is as human and as fallible, but now others can tell him so, even though he still exhibits the old accoutrements (but now Indianized) of importance —the flashing orange light on the roof of the car, the passes for the first row at the sitar recital, which will not start until he arrives and for which he will not arrive until he has ensured by telephone that everyone else who has been invited has arrived first. In Madna, as in all of India, one's importance as an official could be gauged by how long one could keep a concert (to which one was invited) waiting. The organizers never minded this of the officials they invited. Perhaps they expected it of them, which was sickening, or perhaps they were humouring them, which was somehow worse.

And administration is an intricate business, and a young officer who lacks initiative cannot really be trained in its artifices. There is very little that he can learn from watching someone else; Agastya learnt nothing. For a very short while he worried about his ignorance, and then decided to worry about it properly when others discovered it.

The Collectorate of Madna was one building among many in a vast field (which could not be called a compound, for it had no wall or gate) near the railway station. He had missed them all in the dark of the previous evening. The jeep inched its way through people and cattle on to an untarred metalled road. He saw a few flags against the hot clean sky. The national flag, he presumed, was over the Collectorate. "What are the other buildings?"

"That's the office of the Superintendent of Police, sir," said the naib tehsildar from behind, "and over there are the Police Lines." Whatever they are, thought Agastya. "That's the District and Sessions Court, and behind, there, that big one, the District Council—"

"You mean, on which there's also the national flag?"

"Sir. And then that side, behind, the offices of the Sub-Divisional Officer, tehsildar, et cetera." While the naib tehsildar was pointing out the buildings the driver nearly ran over a child defecating beside the road, and snarled at her in the vernacular.

On their left was some kind of pond, with thick green water and the heads of contented buffalo. Scores of people, sitting on their haunches, smoking, wandering, gazing at anything moving or at other people. Most were in white dhoti, kurta and Gandhi cap (or was it Nehru cap? wondered Agastya. No, Gandhi cap and Nehru jacket. Or Gandhi jacket and Nehru cap? And Patel vest? And Mountbatten lungi and Rajaji shawl and Tagore dhoti?), some had towels over their heads. The jeep chugged through them, honking petulantly. The people sitting on the road stood up and moved away at the last moment, reluctantly, some scowled. For them the road was the one stretch that the rains of Madna wouldn't immediately turn to mud; therefore it was a place of assemblage.

"They cover their heads because of the heat, no?"

"Yes, sir."

It seemed wise, to bother not about appearance, but first about health. He tried his handkerchief over his head but it was too small. The naib tehsildar chuckled appreciatively. "Too small, sir. Napkins easily available in the market, sir. If sir wants I'll get one."

"Yes, thanks, please do that. How much will it cost?"

"Not to worry about price, sir."

"Rubbish," said Agastya, and offered him a twenty-rupee note.

The naib tehsildar raised his hands to ward off the horror. "No, sir, not to bother, sir, hardly must, sir." Agastya was momentarily distracted by the "hardly must." What could he mean? He reached over and, ignoring the naib tehsildar's giggles and soft shrieks, put the note in his shirt pocket, among the spectacle case, papers and pens.

In all those months he never got used to the crowds outside the offices.

"*All* these people have work here?"

"Yes, sir," said the naib tehsildar, a little surprised, perhaps at the stupidity of the question. They all looked patient, as though waiting for entrance to the political rally of some awesome demagogue, Nehru perhaps, or one of his descendants. To him they also looked stoned. Their eyes were glazed, probably with waiting, and followed every movement around them without curiosity.

Just near the Collectorate he saw cannabis growing wild. That was nice and, he smiled, somehow symbolic. He would have to return alone one evening.

The Collectorate was a one-storey stone building. Its corridors had benches and more people. The naib tehsildar led him to a biggish hall full of mostly unoccupied desks, and through another door. A fat officious man said, "Yes?" The naib tehsildar mumbled something and the officious man immediately turned servile. "Good morning, sir. Collector saab not yet come, sir. Myself Chidambaram, Reader to Collector. Kindly accompany me to RDC's room sir."

They moved through another door and down a central corridor, also crowded with people, benches and water coolers. Another door, with "C. K. Joshi, RDC" above it. There were three men inside, Chidambaram mumbled something. They all stood and shook hands, the two younger ones called him sir. All introduced themselves, Agastya didn't catch a single name, and didn't bother. Thank God for marijuana, he thought.

Formal pleasant conversation, someone brought in thick sweet tea, which the others drank from their saucers. After some slow haphazard guesswork he decided that the man on his right was Ahmed. Joshi was, or should be, the old jovial man behind the desk. On his right was what had sounded like Agarwal. Ahmed was immediately obnoxious, with blank eyes and a false smile. He never listened when anyone else was speaking, but always looked down at his thick forearms and flexed them. Both Ahmed and Agarwal were "Deputy Collectors (Direct Recruit), sir." Whatever that was, thought Agastya, but nodded with what he hoped was appropriate awe.

He eventually got to know, but by accident as it were, what a Deputy Collector (Direct Recruit) was, and where a naib tehsildar stood in the Revenue hierarchy. He himself made no effort to know his new world; as it unfolded, it looked less interesting to him; and later, even to see how far he could extend his ignorance became an obscure and perverse challenge.

Sitting with the three men, he was again assailed by a sense of the unreal. I don't look like a bureaucrat, what am I doing here. I should have been a photographer, or a maker of ad films, something like that, shallow and urban.

"How old are you, sir?"

"Twenty-eight." Agastya was twenty-four, but he was in a lying mood. He also disliked their faces.

"Are you married, sir?" Again that demand that he classify

himself. Ahmed leaned forward for each question, neck tensed and head angled with politeness.

"Yes." He wondered for a second whether he should add "twice."

"And your Mrs., sir?" Agarwal's voice dropped at "Mrs."; in all those months all references to wives were in hushed, almost embarrassed, tones. Agastya never knew why, perhaps because to have a wife meant that one was fucking, which was a dirty thing.

"She's in England. She's English, anyway, but she's gone there for a cancer operation. She has cancer of the breast." He had an almost uncontrollable impulse to spread out his fingers to show the size of the tumour and then the size of the breast, but he decided to save that for later. Later in his training he told the District Inspector of Land Records that his wife was a Norwegian Muslim.

He went on like this, careless with details. His parents were in Antarctica, members of the first Indian expedition. Yes, even his mother, she had a Ph.D in Oceanography from the Sorbonne. After a while the personal questions stopped. Later he felt guilty, but only for a very brief while.

Chidambaram poked his head in and said that the Collector had come. Joshi accompanied Agastya. Srivastav was short and fat and shouting at someone standing in front of him when they entered. He asked them to sit down and continued shouting. If you can tick off a subordinate in the language, thought Agastya, you're really fluent. On the far side of the desk stood a trembling black suppliant, weeping fresh tears, as though he had just been beaten. The other old man being shouted at turned out to be the District Supply Officer. Later Agastya would conclude that they all looked the same, the denizens of the Collectorate, ageing, with soft faces that hadn't seen much sunlight. They all wore pale shirts and loose pants. Their shirt pockets bulged outrageously with pens and spectacle cases.

Most smelt nice, of some very Indian perfume, or scented hair-oil, or paan. They could withstand, like placid buffalo, anything that an industrious superior could shriek at them. The District Supply Officer's face shone gently in the volley from the Collector.

Lambent dullness, Agastya remembered abruptly, now where was that? Suddenly he was back in his college English class three years ago, with *Absalom and Achitophel* open in front of him, stoned and watching the new female teacher perform. Nervousness had made her aggressive. Narasimhan, beside him, also stoned, had asked her some stupid question. "Your question doesn't make any sense," she had said, arching her back. There had been giggles from the gigglers. Narasimhan had laboriously scrawled a long note on his Dryden and passed it to him. "August, tell her, Yes, my lovely bitch, when my hands are full with your flat buttocks, my mouth on either breast, I shall give you lust-gnaws between your absalom and achitophel." His laugh had even woken up the back row. He had been sent out. The Supply Officer wiped his forehead with a many-coloured handkerchief. Yes, lambent dullness, definitely. That he could relate a phrase from an eighteenth-century English poet to this, a sweating Supply Officer in a Collector's office, in Madna, made him smile.

The Collector paused for breath, said, "Hello, you've to get used to this. An administrator's job is not easy," and returned to biting the Supply Officer's sweating head off. The shrieking stopped after a while and the Supply Officer left. At the door he again used his many-coloured handkerchief. The weeping man left too, after many namastes and two half-prostrations, forehead touching the Collector's desk.

Srivastav smiled at Agastya. His sideburns were like right-angled triangles, the hypotenuses of which looked like the shadows of his cheekbones. "So? Agastya, what kind of name is Agastya, bhai?"

When you were in your mother's lap, you ignoramus, he said silently, drooling and piddling, didn't she make your head spin into sleep with the verses of some venerable Hindu epic? "Agastya" is Sanskrit, he wanted to say, for one who shits only one turd every morning. But the Collector didn't really want any answer. Staccato conversation, while he rushed through his files. "Someone was there to pick you up yesterday at the station?"

"Yes, sir."

"How's the room at the Rest House?"

"Lots of mosquitoes, sir."

The Collector threw every finished file on the ground. They landed, depending on their weight, with dull thumps or sharp claps. Thus he eroded the mountains on his desk, and the files lay like corpses in a battlefield, perhaps giving him the illusion that he was victorious.

"Oh, mosquitoes, yes, I can see that from your face." A quick side-glance at him. "I tell you, Madna must be one of the unhealthiest places in India. Hot, humid, disease, everything. Are you boiling your water? I told the naib tehsildar to tell you."

"Thanks for that, sir. But I'm not quite sure whether the cook at the Rest House here understood yesterday what boiling means."

"Yes, you'll face the problem of language in Madna. They can't even speak Hindi properly." He rang the bell. "Get some tea." He suddenly leaned back and scowled. "You see, in North India and Bengal and other places, everyone can follow Hindi." Agastya was a little disconcerted by his Collector's scowls. Later he saw that that was his official face; at home, too, that face was occasionally donned, but only for office work, or when his wife or children behaved like his subordinates. "And now everything from the State Government comes in the regional language. They think this'll increase administrative efficiency." He wiped his face and forearms with a yellow hand-towel. "Rubbish, these fellows." He scowled at Joshi. "Joshi saab, arrange for some kind of a language tutor for Mr. Sen. And later you must subscribe to a vernacular newspaper, that'll also help, but not the *Dainik*, that just publishes nonsense." Joshi took notes, pen poised to record anything that the Collector might disgorge. Joshi's pad seemed to irritate Srivastav; it obliged him to emit noteworthy sentences. He rang the bell. "Chidambaram, get Mr. Sen the *District Gazetteer*."

"Sir, may I have a look at the map?"

"Yes please, while I finish some of this."

Agastya left his chair for the huge district map on the wall behind Srivastav. For the first few minutes nothing made sense. He finally located Madna town. God, the district was huge. The southern bits seemed heavily forested, that would be a good area to visit. Srivastav's voice penetrated intermittently. "I want to suspend this Supply Officer bugger. That corrupt cement dealer in Pinchri taluka has again been passing off bloody sand as cement and this Supply Officer can't haul him up because he's getting his cut too . . ." Agastya contemplated the improbable, that soon, in a few months, he would be mouthing similar incomprehensibilities and acting appropriately. Chidambaram touched his elbow with a huge black book. He returned to his chair with the *Madna District Gazetteer*.

"Don't read that now, take it back with you. It's wonderful reading."

Agastya opened it. "It's ancient, sir. It hasn't been updated since 1935."

Srivastav scowled. "Who has the time? Either you work, or you write a history. Those fellows never worked." He picked up his cup. "You'll soon see how the people here drink tea. Always from the saucer, look."

They watched a smiling Joshi pour his tea into his saucer. "Tastes better this way," Joshi said.

Srivastav, it seemed, had a lot to say to his protégé; he just didn't know where to begin, and bounded from one topic to another. "You have a copy of your training programme. For the last two months you'll be Block Development Officer and before that you'll be attached to various district offices. The first three weeks is with the Collectorate. And this first week you sit with me and try to grasp the work of the Collector. After all, in a few months you'll be Assistant Collector, doing in a sub-division what I do at the district level."

"Sir."

"There's an Integration gathering at the Gandhi Hall at twelve fifteen. We'll go for that."

"Integration as in National Integration?"

"Yes, but here it's called something else, of course." Srivastav rang the bell and said something to the peon. Joshi left. "You just see how many people come to meet the Collector every day, like they'll meet you when you're Block Development Officer later," scowled Srivastav at Agastya, and then at the villagers whom the peon had just ushered in.

Reverentially they unfolded and handed Srivastav a sheet of paper. Its black creases seemed to mark its tortuous journey, slipping off the hands of one unhelpful official into another's. A conversation ensued, Srivastav scowling less as he understood more, the voices of the villagers slowly gaining in confidence. Then while Srivastav scribbled the villagers waited, patient and passive, strong hands bent suppliantly. They had brought in a smell of sweat and the earth, but they weren't (thought Agastya irrelevantly, with a vacuous half-smile) remotely sexy, just sad, and then he felt vaguely guilty. Two of them looked at him now and again, he didn't fit into the Collectorate.

The visitors came all day. Agastya could eventually categorize them. Indeed, that was all he could do, since the conversations were beyond him. The petitioners always stood. Srivastav asked them to sit only if it seemed that they would take long; if they sat it was on the edge of the chair. The variety of complaints, from the little that Agastya grasped through instinct, gestures and the occasional tell-tale Hindi or English phrase, was bewildering, and the area of action spread over a district of 17,000 square kilometres (so the first paragraph of the *Gazetteer* had said). Someone had encroached on one petitioner's land, and the petitioner had received no help from the tehsildar. The police patil in a village had connived at a murder, and the entire police hierarchy seemed to be backing him up. Labourers on daily wages at some road site complained that the contractor paid them irregularly. A naib tehsildar somewhere seemed to be harassing a tribal's wife. A dealer in some village always adulterated his kerosene. Initially Agastya was impressed by the solidity and confidence in Srivastav's reactions; he seemed to know exactly what to do in each case. A few visitors after, he changed his view and thought, marvelling at the sideburns, that Srivastav *ought* to be confident because he had been dealing with such matters for years.

The petitioners partially explained the crowds outside the Collectorate. But there were others too, subordinate officers from various offices, who were summoned or came to report, and didn't sit until asked to. And then there were the gossips of the district, who were the most gluttonous about time, but whom Srivastav could not alienate, because they knew the pulse of Madna, and were also the politicians' groupies. Sycophants to the last, they wheedled like caricatures. Still others brought invitations, they would be honoured if the Collector and Mrs. Collector (and later in the year some included Agastya, "Sen saab, IAS," an afterthought in ink) graced with their presence the Sports Day of their school or the function to celebrate the eightieth birthday of some veteran freedom fighter of the district, who had perhaps had the overwhelming good fortune to have been jailed once with Gandhi.

Only a very few visitors breezed in before their names could precede them on slips of paper—the Member of Parliament from Madna, and two red-eyed Members of the Legislative Assembly. Agastya enjoyed his long speculative categorization, and placed at the apex the very select few for whom Srivastav moved forward in his chair to shake hands and to whom he offered tea—there were only two that day, the MP and the Managing Director of the paper mills somewhere in the district.

On the wall behind him hung a big teak board with the names of the District Magistrates of Madna since 1902. The earlier Collectors had been British, one Avery had been Collector for six years, 1917-23. He felt hungry and to dispel the pangs, thought of the horrors Vasant would feed him at lunch.

At twelve forty-five the Collector told the peon, "I'll meet the others when I return. Get the driver." Outside in the corridor the peons, the petitioners, the politicians' groupies and their groupies all stiffened and shut their babble when they saw Srivastav. They looked solemn and guilty, as though they'd been planning to strip him, thought Agastya.

The heat was terrible. The car began a slow furrow through the mass on the road. "This car has an emergency siren apart from the light. I've always wanted to use both together just to get to my office." They passed the wild cannabis and the pond. Children jumped from one buffalo to another. "When it rains the cattle camp in the corridors of the Collectorate. The same thing used to happen in Azamganj, where I come from. Earlier I used to think that a Collectorate with cows and stray dogs in its corridors could only be found in Azamganj, now I think it's a common story." A man poked his head in through the front window to gaze blankly at them. The driver snarled at him. "You're from a city. This place will initially seem very different. Then you'll get used to it." Someone thumped the back of the car in affection and boredom. Srivastav watched Agastya sweat. "If you think it's hot you should be here in May. The old residents say that on some afternoons in May, even birds have dropped from the sky, dead."

The car turned reckless as it left the field of offices. "And this Integration meeting?"

"Oh, there was a big riot here a few months ago, Hindu–Muslim. It surprised everyone because Madna has never been communally sensitive. The last Collector, Antony, was transferred, I think, because of the riots. They said he'd bungled there, but more likely the politicians who were actually behind the riots just wanted a scapegoat. These politician bastards, you'll really know what they are like when you're Block Development Officer. So we formed an Integration Committee, it meets once a month. Both Hindu and Muslim goondas get together and eat and waste time. Have as little of the food as possible, it'll be poisonous."

The brown curtains of the car couldn't keep out the town. Narrow streets and two-storeyed shacks, people and animals immune to the heat. Srivastav perhaps sensed Agastya's mood and said, "The population of the town is only two lakhs. Sometimes I think the development of Madna must be a representative Indian story. Once it was just another district, very rich forests, and made to feel proud of its tribal traditions, which is another way of trying to make you forget your economic backwardness. Then they found coal here, mica, limestone, one of the country's richest industrial belts, now oil, too. Factories soon surrounded this town, new ones come up almost every day." The car screeched its rage at a cyclist who cut across and darted down a side alley the width, or so it seemed, of a writing table. "Development is a tricky business. There must be something wrong with development if it creates places like Madna. But priorities is the problem, how're we to spend our money, will it be on coal and oil, or town planning, or forests. And the pressure of time, there is never enough time. But you'll see another facet of development when you're BDO, the insane race to meet targets." Srivastav talked on, with eyes half-closed, never looking at Agastya, as though he was speaking to a cassette recorder.

This bequeathing of wisdom was surprising, especially on first encounter; but the pattern was frequently repeated, with Srivastav and with the Superintendent of Police. Sharing the back seat of a car with a novice in administration, the senior officers always theorized, attempted to explain, to impress, to tutor, to justify.

The car was continually being trapped by cycles and rickshaws, which seemed to behave like out-riders who had suddenly decided to have some fun with the limousine. He saw snatches of other lives—veined hands on bicycle handle-bars, and behind them a man emptying a bucket into a drain, the tensed calves of a rickshaw-wala, sweat-wet shirts around a stall selling fruit juice. But in the months that followed he saw very little of the real Madna, the lives of its traders in wood and forest produce, the coal miners, the workers at the paper mills, the shopkeepers, the owners of cinema halls and restaurants. The district life that he lived and saw was the official life, common to all districts, deadly dull. This world comprised Collectors, District Development Officers, Superintendents of Police, and their legionary subordinates, many wielders of petty power, sulking or resigned if posted away from home, and buying furniture cheap and biding time till transferred to a congenial place.

Gandhi Hall stood beside the city police station, a three-storeyed building. For a moment he thought that it had been bombed, something out of a TV news clip on Beirut, broken window panes, old walls, an uncertain air, a kind of wonder at not having collapsed yet. A red banner over the door, and outside, a statue of a short fat bespectacled man with a rod coming out of his arse. He asked in wonder, "Is that a statue of Gandhi?"

Srivastav laughed shrilly. "Yes. Who did you think?"

"Phew. What's the rod, sir?"

Srivastav laughed even more. "That's to prop up the statue.

It fell off a few weeks after it was installed. Madna will have many more surprises, Sen." Then the goondas were upon them.

They enveloped Srivastav with effusion. A jumble of white khadi and red teeth, the scent of hair-oil distracting the nose from the stench of urine, a few black eyes glancing at Agastya oddly—he didn't fit. Srivastav introduced him to somebody, no one heard anything except "IAS," then they began fawning on him, too.

Wide stairs, the walls splotched maroon with paan spittle, like the scene of some frenzied killings (and abruptly he remembered Prashant at school, when life had been simpler, pointing to horseshit on a hill road, "English, I bet you can't lick that, I bet!" "Oh I can easily do it, if you give me something good for it, like enough money every month for the rest of my life"), the press of people and an alien tongue. On the second floor a huge hall and another banner, and below it a fat complacent policeman. With spectacles, thought Agastya, he could've resembled that travesty outside, of the Mahatma in stone.

"Sen, meet Mr. Kumar, the Superintendent of Police of Madna."

They all moved in, Kumar asking Agastya questions to which he could not hear the answers. Coloured paper decorations, mattresses on the floor with white sheets and cushions, the fans somehow encouraging the humidity. When Kumar sat down his knees cracked sharply. A hooligan joined them and spoke Hindi, "You are also IAS?"

"Yes. I'm here for training in district administration."

More questions. His lies were restricted by the presence of Kumar, but he did slip in that he had climbed Everest last summer. The hooligan left to arrange for their eats. Kumar lolled on his bolster, and patting the outside of his (own) thigh, said, "Hahn, Agastya, a very Bungaali name, yaar."

"Yes, sir."

"Bungaalis choose such difficult names for themselves, why, yaar?"

Agastya smiled. "The Collector was saying that they hold these meetings every month, sir. But what happens here?"

Kumar frowned and looked around, to see what everyone else was doing and how many were looking at him. There was a biggish gang around the Collector. "Nothing on the surface, we just eat some rubbish together, and nurse raw stomachs for a week. But it helps in many ways. We find out from them what's really happening in the district—gossip, the things that our police and Revenue officials won't tell us because they themselves might be involved." His voice turned dictatorial. "Effective administration really means meeting the people, and showing them that the Collector and the SP of a district are not uppity and high-handed, but like meeting them. This is India, bhai, an independent country, and not the Raj, we are servants of the people." A hooligan offered Kumar a paan, which he stuffed into his mouth. "Hahn, you look the English type—"

"The English type?"

"Any Indian who speaks English more fluently than he speaks any Indian language I call the English type, good, no?"

"Yes, sir."

"Hahn, so English type, do you want to watch English movies on video?"

"Yes, sir."

"You come over then, any time. I got new films, *A Passage to India, Amadeus, The Jewel in the Crown,* lots of others, you come." Kumar waved to someone across the hall, who salaamed him jovially. "But tell me, why do these English movies about India all have rape? Black men raping white women? Sathe, have you met Sathe? the joker of Madna, he says to be raped by a black man was a white woman's fantasy." Just then the one who had salaamed Kumar joined them and the two gossiped. A groupie provided Agastya with company.

ENGLISH, AUGUST

"What do you use this hall for normally?"

The groupie looked puzzled by the question. "Oh...
everything." He shrugged. "Family Planning vasectomy and
tubectomy camps, school table-tennis championships, bridge
tournaments, meetings of the Youth Club, marriage parties
...anything." All at one time, I hope, thought Agastya.

"Who built that statue of Gandhi outside?"

"An Executive Engineer called Tamse. He was here some
time ago, he's been posted in Madna two or three times." The
groupie's face creased with an unpleasant memory. "He's very
enthusiastic and untalented. He paints also, also very badly. I
was here when they installed the statue. Everyone was very angry, but it was too late."

An urchin handed Agastya a plate. On it were laddus,
samosas and green chutney. He could almost hear the chutney
say, Hi, my name is cholera, what's yours?

"No, not for me."

The urchin said, "Hayn?"

Agastya turned to the hooligan beside him. "I can't eat anything today. My mother died today." The man looked puzzled
again. "I mean, this is the anniversary of my mother's death,
and I fast." For a moment he contemplated adding, "In penance,
because I killed her."

The hooligan said slowly, face creased again, but this time
with perplexity, "But it's very tasty, try just a little."

"OK," agreed Agastya, and began eating rapidly. He was
feeling very hungry, and even finished a second plate, all the
while imagining the filth beneath the urchin's fingernails.

The conversation continued. Agastya ensured that the man's
perplexity never really disappeared. Both the Collector and the
SP were earnestly discussing matters. He was again besieged, as
he had been that morning in Joshi's room, by the sense that he
was living someone else's life. He looked at his watch. One
forty-five. In his old life he would've been with his uncle at

home, talking rubbish over brunch. He remembered Dr. Upadhyay, his head of department, and his words at their last encounter. Dr. Upadhyay was a small dissatisfied man. "I'm happy for you Agastya, you're leaving for a more meaningful context. This place," he'd waved his hands at the books around him, at the tutorials on his desk, "is like a parody, a complete farce, they're trying to build another Cambridge here. At my old University I used to teach *Macbeth* to my MA English classes in Hindi. English in India is burlesque. But now you'll get out of here to somehow a more real situation. In my time I'd wanted to live this Civil Service exam too, I should have. Now I spend my time writing papers for obscure journals on L. H. Myers and Wyndham Lewis, and teaching Conrad to a bunch of half-wits."

Anchorlessness—that was to be one of his chaotic concerns in that uncertain year; battling a sense of waste was to be another. Other fodder too, in the farrago of his mind, self-pity in an uncongenial clime, the incertitude of his reactions to Madna, his job, and his inability to relate to it—other abstractions too, his niche in the world, his future, the elusive mocking nature of happiness, the possibility of its attainment.

On the way back Srivastav asked, "So, what did you think of our SP?" Agastya smiled stupidly. "You must call on him formally at his office this week, also on the District Judge and the District Development Officer. No one else. Normally this meeting lasts much longer, some idiots make speeches, but I have a lot of work in office, so I cut it short. How many meals do you have a day?" Srivastav was again pogo-sticking topics.

Agastya wondered at the question. "Three," he said, thinking, Perhaps Srivastav knows people who have fifteen.

"When you start working you must reduce it to two, before and after office, that's my advice. Take my case. Office starts at ten thirty, I reach at eleven sharp." He made it sound like a virtue. "But no going home for lunch. Now, our SP followed quite another pattern earlier, but I fixed that. He reached his office at ten thirty but would go home for lunch at one and would sleep till four! and then come back to office at five. I fixed that." Srivastav smiled in memory of the triumph. "For one whole week I telephoned him at office at about three for some work or the other. His office would say, he's at home. They couldn't lie, no, because Collector was asking, and say he'd gone out. So I used to ring him up at home. His constable couldn't say he was sleeping, not to the Collector, so he was woken up. And when he talked he couldn't pretend that he'd been sleeping. One week of this. You have to straighten out these people, who think they're being paid to sleep in the afternoons. Kumar is an interesting fellow. He talks real big, about serving the people, that you'll soon find out, but he's a hopeless policeman. Do you want to go back to the Rest House for lunch?"

"Uh . . . yes, I think." An unwise decision, because the Rest-House room was much hotter than the Collector's office, but he wanted to get away from his Collector and his job, to his other life. His secret life that year was lived in his hot dark room in the Rest House, or in other hot dark rooms in other Rest Houses. His secret life became much more exciting and more actual than the world outside. In the afternoons the rooms were dark because the windows had to be closed against an incandescent world, and the window panes were painted an opaque pink ("Against the glare," explained one Junior Engineer. "For privacy," said another). There would be marijuana and nakedness, and soft, hopelessly incongruous music (Tagore or Chopin), and the thoughts that ferment in isolation. There would even be something vaguely erotic about the heat, about watching his own sweat on his bare skin.

"OK, relax after lunch, no need to rush things. You'll take a few days to get used to the heat. But tomorrow you come home with me in the evening."

At the Collectorate Agastya switched from the white Ambassador to the jeep. The naib tehsildar sweated and beamed at him. At the Rest House he said, "I shall take your leave, sir."

Agastya said, "OK, thanks, come tomorrow."

The naib tehsildar handed him a huge white napkin, with a blue border. "This morning, sir."

"Oh, of course." He tried it on. The driver and the naib tehsildar chuckled appreciatively. He asked the driver to call Vasant. His room looked quite welcoming, with its high ceiling and Tamse's picture. He wasn't hungry but he wanted milk to delude himself that he was careful of his health. "Vasant, is there some milk?"

"Milk?" asked Vasant, as though Agastya had just asked him for his wife's cunt. Vasant looked more insane with a green towel wrapped around his head, but he seemed in concert with Madna. Agastya asked for tea at five thirty and sent him away. He had three hours to himself, and was looking forward to them. He closed the door and prepared a smoke, contemplating to which music he should change his clothes. He smoked very slowly, till time, and most other things, ceased to matter. In Madna funny things happened to time. Outside the room its passage was wearisome, but in his secret life Agastya was to savour the seconds. No action was automatic: changing clothes, even the brushing of teeth, they were to become sensuous acts. He decided on Keith Jarrett, a valedictory present from Dhrubo.

He went up to the mirror on the dressing table, bent forward till his nose pressed against the mirror and asked himself silently what was happening to him. Not even twenty-four hours over and he felt unhinged, without the compensations of insight or wisdom. He lay down and looked at the wooden ceiling. He could masturbate, but without enjoyment. What is it? He asked himself again. Is it because it is a new place? Yes. So do I miss the urban life? Yes. Is it because it is a new job? Yes.

The job is both bewildering and boring. Give it time, not even twenty-four hours. He waited for the mosquitoes. The ventilator was open, the room filled with the stench of the excrement of others when the wind came his way. My own shit doesn't smell like that, he thought randomly. He absent-mindedly fondled his crotch and then whipped his hand away. No masturbation, he suddenly decided. He tried to think about this but sustained logical thought on one topic was difficult and unnecessary. No, I am not wasting any semen on Madna. It was an impulse, but he felt that he should record it. In the diary under that date he wrote, "From today no masturbation. Test your will, you bastard." Then he wondered at his bravado. No masturbation at all? That was impossible. But then the marijuana really hit him and even that ceased to matter. He lay down again.

He could sleep perhaps, but he would wake up dulled, and with a foul mouth, and it would somehow be wasted time.

Jarrett played on, soft and alien piano sounds. Music, he realized, was going to be important in Madna. When he'd been packing he'd thought that forty-two cassettes would be far too many. Suddenly a loud knock on the door, startling. The room all at once seemed a place of refuge, precious and secret, threatened by that incandescent world.

A fat, unshaven man, eyes red with drink, smiling. "Myself Shankar," he slurred in Hindi, "I stay—" He lifted a listless hand towards the wall that displayed Tamse's painting. He meant the next room, with which Agastya's shared the veranda. Agastya looked at his watch. Drunk at three in the afternoon, he liked Shankar immediately.

"Hello, I'm Agastya Sen."

"Agastya, a good name. Quite rare, means born of a jar. The jar is the womb, and thereby the mother goddess, but the jar could just as easily have contained Vedic whisky. Soma-type, good quality Scotch, bottled for twelve years." Shankar leaned against the door and yawned, exuding the effluvium of whisky and snuff. "You were playing Tagore this morning. I like. So I came to be friends."

"It's very hot, should we go to your room and chat?" He liked the idea of whisky with a stranger in a strange place at three in the afternoon.

Shankar's room, though identical, smelt awful—heat, booze and closed windows. He had retained all the furniture. A wizened man, lolling on the sofa, waved to Agastya. "My younger brother," said Shankar, "not to worry. He's insane, but very pleasant."

Agastya thought of getting some marijuana to ignite the whisky, as it were, but desisted. He felt unequal to the exertion, for one thing. Besides, he wasn't sure how Shankar and his brother would view it. He remembered with a smile his uncle's last words at Delhi railway station. "If you have to smoke that ganja, smoke in secret. It is not an addiction for display." He had then looked away. "Write as soon as you settle down." His uncle had been so scathingly cynical when he had discovered Madan and Agastya smoking in their first college year. A winter Sunday, they had been on the roof, Madan filling a cigarette. "You generation of apes." His contempt had not been outraged morality or a concern for their bloodstream. But Madan had argued and swept the conversation into the absurd. "But everyone in India smokes, in villages at sunset and so on." And watching Madan defend them, ugly face above a left palm cupping marijuana and dust, Agastya had felt his stomach contract with silent laughter. "My servant brings lots back from his village every year. And August has been smoking since school, so he told me."

At which his uncle's cynicism, as usual, had turned to rage. "The greatest praise you mimics long for is to be called European junkies. And who is August? In my presence, call him Ogu."

"Drink?" asked Shankar, poured him a stiff peg, and laughed shrilly. Agastya soon saw that he laughed a lot. "What are you doing in Madna, Sen saab?"

"I'm in the Revenue Department. Training."

"Oho, you're IAS. And I hope you're not looking for a BDO." Shankar laughed enough to slop a large swig on to his trousers.

"No, I'm not," said Agastya.

"Mr. Sen has not followed your foolish and confused remarks," said the man on the sofa, and continued, "When did you arrive here?"

"Last evening."

"A female Block Development Officer in Nurana committed suicide a few days ago. Yesterday a local newspaper the *Dainik* said that she had been having an affair with Collector saab and that she committed suicide because he wasn't divorcing his wife to marry her."

"You mean, Mr. Srivastav?"

"Yes." The man on the sofa yawned loudly.

"I'll get some cold water," said Shankar, who seemed to be sulking at his brother's last remark, and waddled unsteadily towards the door. He pressed the bell, which didn't work. He thwacked the switch board, it came off instantly and dangled on one nail. Debris on the floor and dust in the air, and a huge enraged spider scuttled off towards the ceiling. Shankar went out.

"The *Dainik* says Mr. Srivastav's been having an affair with a BDO?"

"I never lie."

Hmm, Peyton Place, thought Agastya, and again smiled, for he again remembered that his uncle, on a single theme, expounded with varying degrees of contempt, angles of face, tones of voice, in a thousand different situations. They had been watching a profound TV serial in which an anxiously expected guest didn't turn up before the final commercials. "Godot," Agastya had said, but Pultukaku hadn't laughed.

"Why is it," they had been on a walk to see the new stadium for the Asian Games, and while Pultukaku had been talking, he had stepped on some shit, and been very angry, "that the *first* thing you are reminded of by something that happens around you, is something obscure and foreign, totally unrelated to the life and languages around you?"

"My younger brother is nice, but a little stupid," said the man on the sofa, whose name was Shiv.

"But he said you were the younger one."

"Well, he *is* stupid." Shiv got off the sofa to get a drink. He was small and very shabby, shrunken, with the greyish eyes of age. "Shankar is a Deputy Engineer in Minor Irrigation. So he makes about 30,000 rupees a year extra, because he's only middling corrupt. I have an arrangement with him, that give me one-third of your annual illegal money, and I'll in return pretend to be your personal servant wherever necessary, when we're away from home and so on, so that you can puff yourself up and be an even better government servant. Then I cook for him if required, wash his clothes, go out to buy his whisky and paan. When he's away I sleep with his wife."

He is lying, of course, thought Agastya, or maybe he really is insane. Perhaps it was the form of insanity that was preluded by extreme boredom. Or perhaps Shiv just liked fantasy, because he found it both impossible and unnecessary to express accurately the mild horror of the tedium of his life. Agastya sensed something of this himself when, on his next visit to Delhi, he attempted to answer questions about Madna from Dhrubo and Madan.

"We arrived about a week ago. It'll take months to get a flat. Shankar's been transferred from Koltanga. The family's there." Koltanga, Agastya remembered from the map, was an adjoining district.

Shankar returned with a jug. "Oof, this weather." He pottered and warbled for a while. Then, comfortably seated, he smiled beatifically at the sofa. "So, Shiv, happy?"

"I'm never unhappy."

"He's a little insane," explained Shankar to Agastya, twiddling his index finger against his temple, "but happy. Have you met Sathe? The joker of Madna. He told me that he has seen a Japanese film in which the young in a family take the old to some mountain and leave them there to die. I was shocked I tell you," he paused abruptly, concentration narrowed his eyes until the eruption of an explosive belch, then the beatific smile. "In India we treat our old parents and other people so well, they always stay with us, and help out in the house and everything, like my younger brother here, we don't send them to mountains."

"But I read in an article somewhere that some of the inmates of the Ranchi Asylum are perfectly sane, they're just unwanted at home, and it's just cheaper to keep them in the asylum. Then the widows at Varanasi—"

"Ranchi Asylum?" asked Shankar, his face displaying the irritation that arises out of bewilderment.

"You know, Ranchi, in Bihar."

"Ahhh... Bihar," said Shiv, as though that explained everything, and turned to his brother, and said, "Bihar." He pushed his glass out for a refill. "I also read that article. It said that one person in the asylum went mad out of jealousy because his brother used to sleep with his sister and they wouldn't allow him to sleep with them."

This didn't seem to be a remark to which anyone could add anything. Shankar refilled the glasses. "Shankar saab," said Agastya, "you know Mr. Tamse?"

"Ohhh! Tamse!" He yelled in a mix of triumph and anger, and raised his hand in the first movement of some gesture of contempt, but it rapped against a bedpost, and the mosquito net collapsed with a soft rustle. "That joker of an artist. He's a buffoon. He's ruined many rooms with his paintings, I tell you. There was one in this room," he pointed to one wall, "but I said, either I stay in this room or the painting, that Vasant took it away somewhere, a horrible painting of sunsets and some boatmen. He writes foolish messages behind every painting. Tamse is a government artist. Do you know that phrase, a government artist? One who works happily at a desk in the week and paints trash on holidays, who is appreciated only by people who put up paintings like Tamse's in Rest Houses, and whose criterion of great art can be found in our drains. Most people think art is some kind of joke, that one can write a great poem when one is drinking tea or farting, you know, casual. Tamse is rubbish." Shankar ended virulently, and looked around the room with angry eyes. "I don't look like an artist to you?"

"No." He looked like a seller of cinema tickets on the black market.

"Yet I've been on the National Programme many times. If I had more will I could've been a legend." His face took on the solemn expression of one about to perform. He then sang the first few lines of an unfamiliar thumri exceptionally well.

"He sings very well," said Shiv from the sofa.

"Why do I drink? Because every singer in India is supposed to drink, it's part of the image, and because drink gives me an excuse against my lack of will. It's much easier, no, to get drunk than to discipline one's will."

On the next drink Shankar asked, "Do you believe in Jagadamba?"

"Uh..."

"You must, because she brought us here together. This is not chance or Fate, the goddess arranged for our having adjacent rooms, for our meeting. Otherwise, why should we have met? The only thing in common is that both of us are governed by Saturn. We have different backgrounds, have been brought up differently, in different places. Why, the age difference must be twenty years. Sometimes I know these deeper things. Music and astrology, they are in my veins." He lifted up his fat hairy forearm and neighed with joy. "They say," he brought his chair forward and enveloped Agastya in snuff, sweat and whisky, "that all engineers are corrupt. They make money, but not me," he leaned back, shook his head and enlarged his eyes, "not me. I have my music and my astrology. What is your date of birth?"

"4 August 1958." Agastya was lying again.

"And the day?"

"Friday."

"Do you remember the time?"

"Eight fifteen in the morning. My mother told me that I caused her a lot of pain."

Shankar placed his hands on his knees, contemplated the effort of getting up, sighed, and finally moved unsteadily to a side table to look for a pencil and paper. "I saw you this afternoon and loved you because you need the help of Jagadamba. You need lots of help." Yes, I certainly do, thought Agastya, was he a homo?

"At the moment what do you want most?" asked Shankar, as he slouched to his chair.

I want, decided Agastya with a silent shameless smile, to fuck Dhrubo's mother (who had been an adolescent fantasy for almost all of Dhrubo's schoolfriends, and for Dhrubo too, they insisted, only that he couldn't admit it, she had been slim and warm and inaccessible). "Well, what I want changes from moment to moment."

Shankar was most dissatisfied with this answer and shook his head drunkenly. "You must be true," said Shiv suddenly.

Oh well, what does it matter, thought Agastya, and said, "At the moment I want to know what my future will be like...not in any vague sense...but what am I *doing* in Madna, will I get to like this sort of life...I miss my old life, I think, mainly because I was attuned to it, and it was, well, comprehensible ... Of course, it's only been a day, but it seems much much longer, and I just feel strange..." he smiled, feeling ashamed of himself.

"Oh, Madna," gurgled Shiv unexpectedly, "everyone feels wretched in Madna," while Shankar scribbled and calculated at the table. "You should go to Koltanga, a lovely place." Another dot in the hinterland, thought Agastya.

"You will leave this place after August for a place you want to go to," Shankar tossed this over his shoulder.

"You mean I'll go to Delhi or Calcutta for the Puja holidays."

"Whatever it be, you shall be happy after August." Shankar looked up and disliked the amused disbelief on Agastya's face. "You don't believe? But you must believe in Jagadamba."

"What d'you mean, happy?" God, thought Agastya, could this thlob be oracular? Again ashamed of himself, he asked, "Jagadamba says so?" Suddenly he wanted desperately to believe.

"Yes, yes, Jagadamba has told me so."

"Godlessness, or a better future, or money, or unreason, we all do believe in something or the other."

His father had said that, most unexpectedly, at their last meeting, three weeks before Madna. "Most of us, Ogu, live with a vague dissatisfaction, if we are lucky. Living as we do, upon us is imposed a particular rhythm—birth, education, a job, marriage, then birth again, but we all have minds, don't we?" His father, as usual, had spoken with the caution of a humourless taciturn man. "For most Indians of your age, just getting any job is enough. You were more fortunate, for you had options before you." They had been strolling on the lawns at dusk in Calcutta, with the roar of traffic in Dalhousie Square (now Bengalified, Binoy Badal Dinesh Bag) beyond the walls. "These sound like paternal homilies, don't they, but you've always had surrogate parents, your aunts, and then in Delhi, your Pultukaku, and we've not really spent much time together."

They finished the bottle. Shankar belched and said, "Sen saab, can you lend me some money?"

"How much?"

"About a hundred rupees," said Shiv from the sofa.

Agastya and Shankar went out. Past five, the veranda was still very hot but much cooler than the room. The fresh hot wind surprised him, titillated his skin. Shankar left with the money, mumbling, "I think we should all sleep now." He pulled a chair out to the veranda and sat in the heat, still stupefied by the stuffiness of Shankar's room, and wondered whether they would ever pay him back, whether the money was an indirect payment for the booze, whether the afternoon had just been a long con to get some of his money.

He felt like sleep, but also too inert to leave his chair. Across the gravel, he watched the main Circuit House, pink and lifeless. Under the pipal tree in the car park a stray dog worried its tail. He remembered how, in their last school year, they had been asked to write a "frank" essay on "My Ambition" by the new English teacher, who himself had been a novelty because he had claimed to have a degree in Education from somewhere in Europe. It had been his first day, and he had irritated everyone by trying to be different and young and friendly. He had first talked about himself. Everyone had listened with the silence of the totally uninterested.

Their silence had only been broken when Dhrubo had begun with, "What I want to know—" Then everyone had smashed him up with, "No one wants to know," "Intellectual fart," and "You get your mother first." But beneath their voices Dhrubo had persisted, "—is what you are trying to prove with your degree from Europe." Then Dhrubo had been sent to the Principal, but everyone had disliked him the more for missing the essay. In his essay Agastya had said that his real ambition was to be a domesticated male stray dog because they lived the best life. They were assured of food, and because they were stray they didn't have to guard a house or beg or shake paws or fetch trifles or be clean or anything similarly meaningless to earn their food. They were servile and sycophantic when hungry; once fed, and before sleep, they wagged their tails perfunctorily whenever their hosts passed, as an investment for future meals. A stray dog was free; he slept a lot, barked unexpectedly and only when he wanted to, and got a lot of sex. But to his indignation, the stupid teacher had made him read out his essay to the class. The class hadn't heard him, and had instead yelled, "He's lying, his only ambition is to be an Anglo-Indian." The teacher had made Prashant read out his essay too, which had nonplussed everyone, because he, for reasons never explained, had said in it that he wanted to be a Tibetan.

A figure turned the corner—Vasant in his green towel. Agastya's tea. Refusal would mean conversation. Vasant left the tea on the floor beside the chair and for a while he watched the skin form on the surface. He tried to visualize the contents of his stomach. Twelve cups of different kinds of tea, the morning's crêpe-omelette, unvanquished despite his teeth and his saliva, the laddus, samosas and green chutney of the Integration Meeting, the afternoon's whisky, all fermenting and bubbling inside in a steadily churning mass. Every day every stomach was similarly assaulted, except those which didn't get enough to eat, and in those, acid gobbled up the warm red stomach lining. He marvelled at the human body. When Vasant returned for the cup he refused dinner and slept uneasily till two in the morning, when the mosquitoes woke him up.

Through the open ventilator the veranda light diffused a blue romantic glow. He was wet with sweat. The room looked mellow, as though readied for passion. He got up, took off the mosquito net and threw it in a corner, and lay down again.

Now the fan could dry him off. He couldn't sleep because his mind was too active, a mêlée of images. He got up again, washed his face, and went out and switched off the light. Two in the morning and Madna had finally cooled. The moon was bright, swollen. The buildings looked soft and surreal, huge creations of cardboard. He wandered on the veranda, but did not near Shankar's door. Just the memory of the stuffiness of Shankar's room still seemed to suffocate him. He wanted to smash the doors and windows of that room to let some new air inside. Impulsively he put on shorts and shoes and did push-ups on the veranda. Then, before reason could dissuade him, he went for a run.

Beyond the Circuit House lay a huge field, its purpose unexplained. Shacks of the homeless on one edge, timid encroachments, on the other side a few decrepit buildings.

Running felt splendid, clockwork movement, the criss-cross of arm and leg, rhythm and balance, the steady, healthy panting, the illusion that the body was being used well. The mind wandered pleasantly, yet not into chaos because the physical strain provided the leash. If anyone saw him, if he woke up one of those sleeping outside the shacks, it would be impossible to explain his running at two thirty in the morning, he grunted a laugh at the thought. On one building, by the light of the moon, he read "The Madna Club. Established 1903." He felt happy when he returned.

Drying off on the veranda he told himself, If you don't exercise every day you'll—and paused to think of something truly dire, you'll get elephantiasis; but that sounded too remote. If you don't exercise every day, unless you're ill, you'll never leave Madna. That sounded much better, and he wrote that in his diary, below the entry of a few hours before.

AT ELEVEN the Collectorate looked even more crowded than usual. There were many more jeeps. "Revenue Officers' Meeting, sir. All the four SDOs and ten tehsildars have come," said Chidambaram, "Collector saab said you should attend," and handed him a sheet of paper.

"I can't read this. Don't you have an English version?" Chidambaram handed him another sheet of paper.

On the top of the cyclostyled sheet was, "Agenda for Monthly Review Meeting of Revenue Officers, Madna." Below it he read some of the topics, "Revenue Drive," "Recovery of Government Dues," "Misappropriation of Government Money by Patwaris," "Revenue Case Pendency," "Agricultural Census," "Pending Pension Cases," ... "Hmm, nice topics," he said to Chidambaram.

"Sir, Menon saab wants to meet you. He's waiting in Collector's chamber."

"Who is he?" asked Agastya conspiratorially.

"Sir, he's IAS, sir," Chidambaram sounded outraged at his ignorance, "two years senior to you, Sub-Divisional Magistrate of Rameri."

Menon was large and fair, with a loud shrill voice. Later in the year Agastya was to conclude that Menon's smugness was endemic in IAS officers in the district. In its best form it was exhibited in Srivastav, as a confidence and an undemonstrative pleasure in the job (an attitude obscurely irritating). Rajan, whom Agastya met one November evening at the Collector's with his egregious pomposity, was its worst example. He was compelled to infer that the job was responsible. Kumar corroborated his views during the weekend they spent at Mariagarh. "I don't know how it is in other countries," Kumar said, "but in India from washing your arse to dying, an ordinary citizen is up against the Government. And your senior IAS bastards swell up because of the power they fool around with, especially in a district. To be able to play god over say, 17,000 square kilometres is not—what's the word?—conducive to humility. You see, Sen, India has had a *tradition* of bureaucracy."

"Aha, Sen," said Menon, "glad to meet you. When did you come?" They sat down. Again Agastya was asked to categorize himself, and again he lied, although cautiously.

"I see," said Menon, "so you're from Calcutta. Good. Education?"

"Yes, I'm educated."

"No, no, I mean, of course, you are. But where were you educated?"

"Uh...Cambridge."

"You don't say! I was there myself—Trinity. Went there for my BA."

Oops, thought Agastya. "Uh...Cambridge, Massachusetts."

"Oh, yes, of course, they have one over there too."

A peon scurried in, "Collector saab's car has been seen, sir, near the pond," and began building his skyscrapers of files.

Menon picked up his papers from the table. "Have you read this?" He handed Agastya a large green book, Ruth Prawer Jhabvala's *Heat and Dust*. "I borrowed it from the Collectorate Library because I was told it was about an Assistant Collector's life in the British days. But it's not really about that." Agastya flipped the pages. Many passages were underlined; all of them seemed to be about an Assistant Collector touring in the early morning to avoid the title. Comments in red ballpoint in the margin: "Not necessary these days to wear sola topee. Relic of the Raj. The bureaucracy to be Indianized," and "Difficult question. An officer's wife *should* mix with others, but without jeopardizing the dignity of office."

"Someone's been scribbling in the book," said Agastya.

"Yes, I thought I should put down what I feel strongly about so that other readers have at least a choice of opinion. Otherwise they might think that even now this is all that goes on in an Indian district."

The Collectorate hall was large and shabby, with pigeons on the ventilators and portraits on the walls. Gandhi, Nehru, Tagore, Tilak, and a Tamsevian mutilation of what could have been either Sarojini Naidu or a turbanless C. V. Raman. All the seats directly under the fans had been taken by soft middle-aged men. An orange standing fan, terribly new, had been placed behind the Collector's chair. It was going to be, thought Agastya, at least six hours of shifting one's buttocks on wood and clandestinely flicking one's sweat on to other people out of boredom and incomprehension.

The Collector came in, scowling. He usually put on his official face in the car. Everyone stood up. He sat down and began shrieking. Agastya opened his file, rearranged some papers in a suitably official manner, and wrote letters for about an hour. To his father first, a long descriptive letter, cautiously funny, concealing his sense of dislocation. His father perhaps would have understood, but he would also have been saddened. Life for him was a serious, rather noble business, a blend of Marcus Aurelius and the *Reader's Digest*, and on occasions, Agastya felt quite apart from him.

He did wonder at times what his mother would have been like, but more out of curiosity than deprivation. The aunts of Calcutta had substituted sufficiently well. In her photographs his mother looked plain, but happy and somehow irresponsible, ready for oddities, for marrying a Bengali Hindu, for dying of meningitis.

A letter to Dhrubo, of vile amusing anecdotes about Madna, the majority concocted, the rest exaggerated. Even to Dhrubo he felt shy of revealing his real feelings. Perhaps he was too embarrassed, or his feelings too confused, or too secret. But some of his self did seep through the words he used, like a stain. A third letter to Neera, in Calcutta, and a fourth to his uncle Pultukaku in Delhi, much like the letter to his father.

The meeting continued. The Collector continued too, to exhort his subordinates in the Revenue Department to greater efficiency and competence. They all nodded, seemed to take notes and wiped their sweat. Theirs was an admirable strategy for meetings. By seeming to take notes they could while away the time, could keep their heads down and thereby avoid, for brief intervals, the Collector's attention, which meant wrath, could cover the blankness of their minds—some could even get letters done.

Twelve fifteen, and the Collector hadn't yet reached the second topic. Agastya marvelled yet again at Srivastav's fluency in the language and watched his scowls and sideburns. I can't waste my day like this, he thought suddenly, listening to an alien tongue on alien topics, and then smiled. Certainly "waste" was the wrong word when he was doing what he was being paid to do. From behind Ahmed, the Deputy Collector (Direct Recruit), said, "Sir, Collector saab is looking at you." He stopped smiling.

He left soon after, very purposefully, as though he had much work to do elsewhere. From Chidambaram's cubby-hole he rang up the Superintendent of Police. "Sir. I wanted to call on you formally at your office."

"Arrey, I shall be honoured bhai, honoured."

"When, sir? May I come now?"

"Arrey, any time, yes, of course, come now."

On a sheet of paper he wrote, "Sir, I wanted to call on the SP and he asked me to his office at twelve thirty sharp. I shall return to the meeting after finishing there." He gave the note to Chidambaram, "Just take this to the Collector a little later."

The road to the SP's lay past the wild cannabis. He casually pocketed a few leaves. On the road, he watched the road to avoid the holes and the varieties of excrement. He tied his new napkin over his ears. A buffalo passed by, and with a casual whisk of its tail, deposited some dung on his forearm. Oh, you bastard, said Agastya. He scraped the dung off on a tree and smelt his arm. The stench remained. He began to laugh, oh how insane his existence was, it even included getting shit off his arms.

An old and mean constable at the door, suspicious. "The SP asked me to meet him at twelve thirty." Even to Agastya it sounded unlikely. Maybe I should shave my beard, he thought, and my head, grow a paunch, and wear a wig of short flat oiled hair.

"Hahn, Sen, come in." Kumar's fat forearm waved him to a chair. There was another man in the room. He was large and soft, as though he had once lifted weights with gusto and one day, abruptly, realized the foolishness of all exertion. A red face, blood, booze and joy. On his lap, a copy of the book of the BBC TV serial *Yes, Minister*. "Sen, meet Mr. Govind Sathe." Agastya shook hands.

"You are the IAS trainee."

"Are you the joker of Madna?" They all laughed. "Where did you hear that?"

The room was panelled entirely in wood. One whole wall had things written on it. Lists of the SPs of Madna, the number of dacoities, murders, thefts in the last year, the names of police stations. "Sathe is a yellow journalist. See, he looks it." Sathe laughed. He laughed fully, with his whole body. He said, "Mr.

Sen probably hasn't yet seen a small-town newspaper. Some of them are just one sheet, a little bigger than my palm. The dailies come out on the days when they can cook up some scandal or gory story, the weeklies on the Sundays when there's some gossip to report."

Kumar ordered coffee. "These newsmen live on blackmail. You see, each one of your lower officials has—what's the phrase—skeletons in his cupboard. The goondas here, when they aren't rioting, go to the bigger newspapers and say, Make me your reporter, I'll be stationed in Madna. No salary, just—what d'you call it—accreditation. He makes enough through blackmail."

"Of course, some are bold enough to attack the highest officer. Our Collector..." said Sathe and began laughing boisterously.

"Sen, do you know this?" asked Kumar, his torso jiggling with joy, "what the *Dainik* said, about the BDO?... You must try and follow the *Dainik*, it's the best way to pick up the language." He turned to Sathe. "But the Collector has written to Government for permission to prosecute. A good move. The case will be defamation against the post of the Collector, then Government will bear the charges of the case—that is, if anyone ever replies to his letter. If he sued personally it'd be expensive."

"And he just might lose." More laughter.

"Today's *Dainik* has a few new pieces against the Minister."

"Yes I saw that. Nothing new. But it's a disgusting newspaper." Kumar suddenly turned virulent, "It says highway dacoities have increased because the police don't patrol roads. What do they mean? What do they *know* of what they write, sitting in small smelly offices blackmailing people? Can any police patrol *highways*? Bastards, they always go on about our responsibility, what about theirs?"

"But these dacoities and murders have been increasing. You

know, the one that happened a week ago down the lane from the hotel." Sathe turned to Agastya. "Four dacoits killed three people, parents and child. They bashed the child's face in with one of the clocks in the house. At about twelve in the afternoon, yes. The kind of case that you only read about in the papers, that happens to someone else, in some other colony in some other part of town."

Agastya felt a little sick, as though someone had lightly snicked his testicles. They could visit him too, one kick in the balls, they could crush his face with his cassette recorder before they took it away. He thought of his room without music.

A knock on the door. Another constable, whose boots detonated on the floor as he saluted. He handed Kumar a file. Kumar read it for a minute or two, and then, with his elbow on the table, swivelled his hand and forearm in a gesture of utter incomprehension. The constable mumbled something. Kumar got up, said "Excuse me, hayn, just a minute," straightened his shirt over his lard, and went out.

"He's gone for some shady deal," said Sathe, "or a bribe."

"Which newspaper do you work for?"

Sathe laughed. "I'm not a yellow journalist at all. You've probably never met my kind before, they are a small disrespectable breed. I'm a cartoonist." Sathe had large, rather sad eyes. "I crack dull jokes every morning in four Marathi dailies, all published from Bombay and Pune, Poona to you."

"Then what are you doing in Madna?"

"Why, I *like* the place." Sathe laughed and had to put down his cup because he couldn't restrain himself. "With a question like that you really reveal yourself, Mr. Sen, your past, your bewilderment and boredom. Aren't you surprised at seeing me in Madna, I wear Levi's and read *Yes, Minister*?" He touched the book. "Riffling through it to see if I can steal some jokes, but their bureaucrats and politicians are so civilized and dull."

"No...uh...I'm just new to this place, that's all."

"To a whole world. Are you very busy? If not, why don't you join me for lunch?"

He thought of the Revenue Meeting. "Sure, thanks."

Sathe finished his coffee. "There's a Forest Service officer here who knows you. Says you and he were on the same floor in the hostel in your college days. Mahendra Bhatia."

"Oh, yes, of course." Bhatia was just an acquaintance, to whom Agastya used to nod on the stairs or in the college dining hall. But he knew that in Madna, they would meet effusively, claiming from their pasts an amity that had never been. In a strange place meeting an acquaintance was somehow worse than meeting a stranger. An acquaintance was neither stranger nor friend, with him one had to make adjustments. He was unknown, yet familiar, like the hinterland; he brought back the old life and its memories, but none of the consolations of remembrance.

"He told me about you. You must beware of the grapevine of a small town, by the way. Don't do anything here you wouldn't do in front of your mother."

The SP returned, with incoherent apologies. "I have to go, yaar. Something important has come up. Why don't you two have dinner with me tomorrow, eightish?"

Good, thought Agastya, that's one more meal away from Vasant. Sathe said, "Something more shady than important, Kumar saab."

"Not in front of innocents, Joker," Kumar patted Agastya's shoulder avuncularly, "one day, Sathe, some constables might pay you a late-night visit." He neighed a laugh and left.

Sathe's car was a red Maruti. "Cartoonists make a lot of money?" asked Agastya.

Sathe laughed, "No, it's not really my car. It's one of the family cars," and laughed again.

The car slunk away from the police station in low gear. "One of these centuries they're going to improve this road. So many offices here, and just two approach roads. Now they're building that TV transmitter here . . . Yes, TV's coming to Madna . . . oh, they say in three months' time. That could mean anything between tomorrow and the day when Darth Vader meets Jesus . . . TV's a good election stunt, hayn . . . please the oh-so-pitiable rural populace and place your faces in front of their faces for four hours a day . . . Elections, too, but there's a by-election here in Madna before that . . . you'll be watching a lot of that, won't you, as part of training. You should study your own Revenue gang during election time, how they puff themselves up." Impossible, thought Agastya, that Sathe spoke so openly about everything naturally. He sounded as though he was obliged to be unconventional.

The car moved beside the train tracks, slowly entangling it-self in the web of pedestrians and rickshaws. A monstrously overloaded truck struggled by, its speed belying its roar. Sathe stopped on top of the bridge. A beggar reclined against the rail-ing, studying his toe. He had the hairdo of some Western rock superstar. "I like the view from here," said Sathe, while Agastya wondered why they had stopped.

The train tracks aimed straight at the heat haze on the hori-zon, an enticing passage to another world. Five hundred yards away, the sad railway station and its yards with the hillocks of coal. On the left, the old and shabby office buildings that had ignored all the decades of an undramatic history. The flags, pa-tient in the heat. The pond, the buffalo with the dots of chil-dren prancing on their backs. The people who waited for Government to be kind to them, in white dhoti, kurta and napkin. On the right beyond the station yard, the town crawl-ing all over the ruins of the eighteenth-century fort of the ob-scure tribal king who had given Madna its name. The whole seemed to have been bypassed by all that had made history and news, had remained impervious to the Mughals and 1857 and Bande Mataram and the mid-century travails of megalopolitan

India. In the distance, cutting off the inch-line of forest, the futuristic structure of the new thermal power station, steel threatening the sky, beside the shrunken river, waiting for rain to flood the district and remind its people of the horrors that customarily lay beyond the orbit of their lives. "For all those who ever wanted to see the country, and sat around in the hotels of Bombay cribbing about the waste of a holiday, and for all those whose vision so far has been circumscribed by the smog of Calcutta," said Sathe lightly, and declutched.

Sathe lived in the newer part of town. The roads were still awful, but there was less of a crowd. New houses, somehow incongruous in Madna, sad imitations of the big city. "They are trying to make a metropolis out of Madna. Idiots, as though metropolises are good things." Some had planned greenery around their houses but the ubiquitous cattle had taken care of the saplings. Sathe slowed for a one-storeyed pink house. "That's the one where they killed the child." He finally stopped at a house beside a hotel called the Madna International. "Absurd name, isn't it? We own that damn thing.

"My father was a forest contractor here in Madna. You don't know what that means, do you? He arranged for the sale of timber and forest produce. Certainly a soul-squashing job but he made lots of money. So I was educated in Bombay and my elder brother even went to Geneva for a course in Hotel Management, that kind of money. He runs the hotel. It was built out of the money my father left us, it makes lots of money too . . . Come, let's go in here, the drawing room is far too ugly for display to what I'm sure must be a very refined taste . . . Yes, I live in this bit of the house . . . I'm not married . . . too old for straight sex, ha ha . . . My brother has my father's money-making sense. He saw the development of Madna years ago and said a hotel here would be a good idea, to drag in the executive type who has to go to all these factories and mills . . . I don't need money. Now you see why I'm a cartoonist?"

The room was large and very untidy. Books and files even on the floor, an easel by the window, pencils and paintbrushes on the bed. "Just sit somewhere... Why don't you have a whisky..." Sathe switched on the air-conditioner.

"Do you really read a lot, or is it just that it's nice to work surrounded by books?" asked Agastya. Sathe paused at the door to laugh and disappeared.

On the easel was an unfinished sketch. Sathe drew well. It showed a man at a typewriter beside a window. Through the window the Statue of Liberty. Agastya tried to guess the punchline.

Sathe returned with a uniformed waiter. "This is going to be in real style. The hotel says today's fish tandoori and chicken shashlik, whatever that is, are very good. I said anything that doesn't give us food poisoning will do."

The waiter poured them their drinks. "I've been drinking quite a lot here," said Agastya. "Yesterday was my first day. I drank with a Deputy Engineer who seems to know you, Shankar."

"Laxman Shankar." Sathe threw a few things off the bed and settled down on many cushions with a sigh. "Tremendous fun to be with for an hour or so. He sings very well, by the way."

"He sang us a bit of a thumri, excellent, I thought."

"You're interested in music, beyond the noise of Western rock? I'm surprised, I thought you'd be part of our Cola generation."

"My father calls it the generation that doesn't oil its hair."

"That's a nice phrase." Sathe struggled upright to scout for pencil and paper. "I'm stealing it. I've used the Cola generation at least ten times." He looked at Agastya with his sad eyes. "I do this all the time, pick other people's brains."

"And what will the line be for that joke?" Agastya pointed to the easel.

"No, that one won't work. It's too ambitious. The best cartoon can only suggest pettiness and absurdity, very rarely something more complex." Sathe got off the bed and went to stand in front of the easel. Agastya didn't want to leave his chair but felt obliged to join him. "This is a very ambitious one. I wanted to suggest an Indian writer writing about India, after having spent many years abroad, or living there. There are hundreds of them—well, if not hundreds, at least twenty-five. I find these people absurd, full with one mixed-up culture and writing about another, what kind of audience are they aiming at. That's why their India is just not real, a place of fantasy, or of confused metaphysics, a sub-continent of goons. All their Indians are caricatures. Why is that. Because there really are no universal stories, because each language is an entire culture." Sathe moved to the table to put a kabab into his mouth.

"That *is* ambitious for a cartoon."

Sathe laughed, and sprayed masticated kabab over the window pane. That made him laugh more. Still gurgling, he went to the bathroom for a towel and a mug of water. "I live in anarchy. If I had spat kababs out like that in your absence I wouldn't have cleaned up at all. I would've watched the stains change colour and texture over the days and wondered about mutability." While slushing water haphazardly over the window pane, he continued, "And this place is a continent, far too heterogeneous. Great literature has to have its regional tang—a great Tamil story, for instance, whose real greatness would be *ultimately* obscure to any non-Tamilian. Haven't you felt that heterogeneity in Madna? I presume you know at least three Indian languages, English, Hindi and Bengali, yet you find it so difficult to communicate here. And three languages, you could be master of Europe."

They were quite drunk by lunch, which was lavish and slow, and the conversation desultory. While eating, Agastya planned how he could eat more often at Sathe's. "Do I look very drunk?"

"Yes, very. Why?" Sathe's eyes now looked maudlin.

"I have to go back to attend the rest of the Collector's Revenue Meeting."

They began to laugh helplessly. Agastya's fork dropped on the floor. He realized obscurely that he was to lead at least three lives in Madna, the official, with its social concomitance, the unofficial, which included boozing with Shankar and Sathe, and later, with Bhatia, and the secret, in the universe of his room, which encompassed jogging by moonlight. Each world was to prove educative, and the world beyond Madna was continually to interrupt and disturb him, through letters and the radio, and through ungovernable memories. When he was leading one Madna-life, the other two seemed completely unsubstantial. He couldn't believe, for instance, that a few minutes' drive away from Sathe's, the Revenue Meeting, from which he'd now been absent for four hours, was still going on. The transitions from one to either of the other two were not difficult, but that was only because he willed it so. But this volition would decline rapidly in the months and meetings that followed, and he would begin to fantasize about allowing his lives to merge; looking at Srivastav's scowls, he would want to interrupt a Revenue Meeting with, "If you will allow me to talk about a pressing personal matter, I feel that each one of you here should invite me home for dinner, because at the Rest House I seem to be eating Vasant's turds"; hearing Kumar on the difficulties of being a good policeman, he would want to ask whether his semen also came out like a weak trickle from a limp tap. Then his fantasies would make him laugh silently.

"I think it's a very bad idea," said Sathe, "to go out in this heat to attend a Revenue Meeting." They convulsed with laughter again. Agastya washed his face and tried to look sober.

Sathe dropped him to the Collectorate. "Thanks, that was a great afternoon."

"You still look drunk."

The Collector was still shrieking, dehydrating his throat and drinking lots of water. Most heads were still down, and some seemed to be swaying with sleep. Everyone just looked more hot and tired. In five minutes Agastya couldn't believe the afternoon—Sathe, the ambitious sketch on the easel, the chicken shashlik. The meeting continued to drift past his ears. It ought to have convinced him that he should set about learning the language if he was really to get into his job, but throughout those months he had the feeling that his situation was somehow temporary, that he just had to live out a few months and that was all. But that in less than a year's time he would be actually posted somewhere as Assistant Collector, behaving like Menon or Srivastav—that seemed just too remote.

He occasionally marvelled at how little attention he was paying. To hide his red eyes, he opened his file and tried to look official. There were bound to be countless similar meetings, he thought, so on a clean sheet of government paper (thick and yellow, with a left-of-centre blue line), he listed, very neatly, possible excuses for the future. He was dissatisfied with all except illness, and he wished to save that for more serious dodges. Besides, he thought, illness would work only once, unless he could convince Srivastav that his metabolism, too, followed a lunar cycle and that his bone-racking menstrual tension coincided with the Revenue Meetings. Then Srivastav caught him laughing to himself again.

Suddenly, a restlessness in the air, as in a class of schoolchildren minutes before the bell. The Collector was emitting his concluding shrieks. Then outside, everyone stretched, grouped together and chattered, and wandered away to their jeeps. Menon and Agastya followed the Collector to his room. Srivastav unwound over his fifteenth tea of the day. "Oof, these fellows. Shout at them all day and practically no work gets done. Don't shout at them and they'll do even less." He looked very tired. "Menon, you bring Sen over this evening. Dinner."

Rameri was seven hours away, so Menon was staying the night ("making a night halt," in officialese) at the Circuit House. He dropped Agastya to his room and said, "Why don't you freshen up and come over to my room in about an hour?" He pointed to the Circuit House.

Agastya was surprised at his hectic social life in Madna, flitting from Sathe to Srivastav, and not all of it was boring. Of course, the combination of Srivastav and Menon promised to be lethal. Later, when he reflected on his months in Madna, most of his meetings with so many new people blurred and merged into one single massive encounter—a mêlée of voices and opinions, angles of face, twists of mouth, vagaries of accent, of a single behemoth with a myriad tongues.

He washed his face. The sting of water further reddened his eyes. While looking at them and wondering whether their veins would burst and emit tears of blood like some ancient prophecy or myth (he would then, he decided, go to his father and say quietly, See what the job that you said was so fulfilling is doing to me), he heard music from Shankar's room, and for a moment another life beckoned to him.

Menon had really freshened up. Agastya suspected that he had shaved again. Beside his pinkness he felt secretly unclean, as though he hadn't changed underwear he had climaxed in. "Ah, Sen, sit down. I've just asked for some tea." Perhaps if every day, thought Agastya disconnectedly, he subjected his stomach to tea after whisky, in time it would begin to crave for the combination.

Menon's room was also furnished like a house. "Who chooses the furniture for Rest Houses? Engineers?"

"Or their wives. As in everything else they make a lot of money from furniture too."

"But their taste," whined Agastya. The curtains of Menon's room had small red aeroplanes on a green background.

"Oh, I don't think you should be critical like that," said

Menon solemnly. Agastya wondered if he could slap him, many times, grab his hair and jerk his head off his neck, and say, Don't apply a different standard of aesthetics just because this is Madna and you've been to bloody Cambridge.

Vasant entered with tea. "So you were at Cambridge, Mass., as they say. What was it like?"

"Nice," said Agastya cautiously.

"It's a very good thing to join the Indian Administrative Service after a stint abroad," said Menon, pushing three spoons of sugar into his cup, "It's the best job possible, in the Indian context, you'll realize that very soon, and having been abroad gives you a better perspective."

"Oh, yes, even on furniture."

Menon looked at him intently, but let the remark pass because it made no sense, and therefore perhaps he had misheard it.

Agastya laughed silently at the thought that if he had heard of Menon from someone else, he would have been curious to meet him.

THE HOUSE for the Collector and District Magistrate of Madna had been built in 1882, in a twenty-acre compound. After 1947, occasional magnanimous Collectors had donated a few acres here and there—for the district offices of the Rehabilitation Department, a housing colony for government servants, a co-operative bank. The house had twenty-two rooms; most Collectors used about seven. The rest were silent, and stored official furniture discarded by successive families. The smallest room (the office, and called, for some reason, the camp office) was the size of the government flat in Delhi which Srivastav would get if he was posted there.

Vegetation had thrived for a century in the compound, and on the stone walls of the house; acres of old banyans and pipals, inexorably burgeoning, rapacious for more space; groves of guavas and mangoes, even national treasures in the form of two sandalwood trees (of which fact the Collector had to notify Government). Some of the families tried agriculture too, but, of course, none of their sweat ever dropped on the soil. The gardeners on the municipality pay roll were summoned to the house and made to plant paddy and potatoes and cabbage. Some Collectors who did not carry the belief in the dignity of office to any pompous extreme, even made good money on the sale of rice ("In a developing country we must never waste food," they explained).

The first fifty metres around the house had been demarcated

for a lawn by an ambitious Collector who had had no idea of the difficulties of gardening in a vast oven. Usually the first ten metres looked sufficiently green even in May. But the next forty were a no man's land, as it were, between the lawn and the wild. It looked like no man's land too, an unsettling reminder of what Madna really was beneath the efforts of its residents and their Government.

Madam Collector liked to stroll on the lawn in the evenings with the children. The weather was almost pleasant after sunset; besides, she was a little scared of the house after dark. There were two foxes in the compound (so she swore), but she preferred the possibility of their company to that of the unknown. For she swore too that there was a ghost in the house, she had heard mysterious noises. No one ever disagreed with her, partly because the house was vast enough for flesh, blood and the spectral; partly because in a life ineffably dull, a ghost meant a little romance.

Srivastav's children quite liked the house, and were intermittently curious about the other rooms. Mrs. Srivastav liked the house in the day because it was cool. Srivastav himself was completely dead to its beauty, but liked its system for the supply of water; he was a practical man. Kumar, the Superintendent of Police, loved the house, for beneath his lard lay a squashed romantic, but he never admired it too openly, for he feared that his words would be misconstrued to be the envy of the police for the magistracy. Agastya liked it because it looked majestic. Menon admired it because it represented accurately the esteem in which a Collector should be regarded. When they reached it that evening, huge bats were drawing patterns in a twilit sky.

Mrs. Srivastav was fat, friendly and surprisingly sexy. Throughout the evening Agastya kept looking at her thighs. He thought he saw her marriage perfectly. It would've been about seven years ago. In Azamganj an IAS officer would be revered almost as much as Krishna, so Srivastav must have made about five lakhs on the deal. But she called him Ravi, and in two of the photographs in the drawing room he had his arm around her, so their marriage was tinged with modernity, wherein wife could call husband by name, though she probably didn't do so when they holidayed at home. In casual conversations over the months most of his surmises of that first evening regarding their marriage were proved correct, except that her dowry had been not five lakhs, but seven.

Srivastav turned out to be that ghastly thing, a teetotaller. He was in kurta and pyjama, and tickling his two children on the divan. The children were shrieking. They seemed to be insane with ecstasy—without ecstasy, too, since they shrieked (Clearly a hereditary trait, thought Agastya), romped, fought and bawled without cause month after month. Agastya could see the panties of the six-year-old daughter (rather pretty) and looked bashfully away at the thighs of the mother.

"Sit down both of you. Malti, this is Sen, the new IAS." And Srivastav returned to extracting shrieks from his children. Agastya had a faint notion that he was trying to create an impression—Look, by day I am the Collector of Madna, but by night I'm a family man. Menon was, of course, familiar to the house, but behaved all evening as if the ghost had gone up his arse, jumpy because eager to please, but not knowing how.

"Yes, I've heard about you. But I can't call you Sen, that's for my husband." Here a half-smile at Srivastav. Agastya was reminded of Joshi's room on the first day, and Ahmed's voice dropping to a hush to pronounce "Mrs."; to all the admission of conjugality seemed a cause for embarrassment. "What's your full name?" Mrs. Srivastav was wearing a black bra beneath a yellow blouse. Agastya sneered at Menon (startling him a little), that would be hilarious dress sense in Trinity, but it's OK in Madna, no?

"Agastya," half-ready to answer the next question with, "It's Sanskrit for one who turns the flush just before he starts pissing, and then tries to finish pissing before the water disappears."

"That's even worse. Most Bengalis have such difficult names." Mrs. Srivastav had a nice smile. "I'm sure your parents or friends don't call you that. What do they say?"

"Ogu, and August." He thought of lying but couldn't immediately think of anything but obscenities.

She laughed. "August. That's nice."

"August?" asked Srivastav, abandoning his children who scrambled off the divan and crowded around Agastya. Perhaps you would prefer another month? asked Agastya silently.

A menial with haunted eyes entered, carrying a tray of Campa Cola and nimboo-pani. Agastya wanted both but restrained himself to the latter.

The daughter hit the servant in the stomach and screamed, "I want rose sherbet."

Srivastav screamed too, "Ice, Gopu, ice. You've been told a thousand times that when you serve drinks, serve them with ice. Is there ice in the house?"

"Sir."

"Then why haven't you brought it?"

"Sir." Gopu left for the ice, looking a little more haunted.

"And you're from Calcutta?"

"Yes, ma'am." The boy, who was four, suddenly seemed excited by Menon's face and began laughing loudly, clapping his hands and racing around the room. Srivastav tried to shush him.

"What does your father do?" She's trying to be friendly and to put me at my ease, thought Agastya, so he decided to be charitable and not lie. "He's in the Government, ma'am."

"I see, in which department?" asked Srivastav, trying to prevent his son from taking off his (own) shorts.

"He was in the Indian Civil Service, sir. He's now Governor of Bengal."

"Madhusudan Sen?" squeaked Menon. "You are Madhusudan Sen's son?" The ghost had lovingly patted his balls. Surprise and awe had pushed him to the edge of his chair, and widened his mouth and eyes. "He's had a fantastic record, he's been Home Secretary and Chief Election Commissioner, and when he was made Governor, some people objected, but he was never an insider to Bengal technically—he's spent all his years in the Bombay Presidency and in West India."

To whom was he talking? Agastya wondered. But just the recital of the record of a successful bureaucrat seemed to provide Menon sufficient excitement. "So your mother was Goanese. He married late, she was the daughter of some subordinate of his, and there was a bit of a romance, wasn't there?" Now he'll tell me (thought Agastya) on which days in February 1953 my father didn't brush his teeth twice.

Of course, the officialdom of Madna came to know of his father very soon ("Sen saab is son of Bengal Governor," moved from many mouths to many ears), and its attitude slanted marginally towards the sycophantic. Agastya was an IAS officer *and* the son of a Governor, Madna seemed to consider itself fortunate that he was with them. When they next met, even Sathe said, "You didn't disclose your lineage to me last time," and laughed.

Menon was stopped only by the shrieks of the Collector for the servants, "Gopu! Ramsingh!" Now Srivastav had, to use officialese, reversed his decision, and was taking off his son's shorts. "He's urinated in his shorts. Shame, shame, Shekhar, at your age."

Free of the encumbrance of his shorts, the boy then raced around the room, emitting short shrieks of joy, and suddenly stopped in front of Agastya, pointed to his penis and explained, "Piddle comes from here."

"Gopu! Ramsingh! These bloody servants. I'm going to send them back to the office." Menon got up too, forced from the recollections of the career of an idol to the immediate concerns of his immediate boss.

"The servants always go and smoke bidis beyond the kitchen. And it's such a big house that they can't hear from there," said Mrs. Srivastav. In her voice was embarrassment at Srivastav's anger, pride in the size of the house, and relief that the servants did not smoke bidis *in* the kitchen.

The corridor was almost directly opposite Agastya. He saw the servants before Srivastav could. They strolled round a corner into sight, sharing a bidi, Ramsingh scratching his (own) balls, while Srivastav and Menon continued to shriek for them. Gopu trampled on the stub, then both began running, ending in a close finish in the room, panting like defeated marathon men. Srivastav shrieked at them in the lingo for a few minutes, Menon stood near them menacingly. The screaming, kicking child was handed over to them for a change of dress. His sister waved to him from her chair, and said, "Bye-bye, piddler" gravely.

Near the door the boy bit Ramsingh's cheek. "These servants are impossible," said Mrs. Srivastav.

They were actually peons from the office. Many peons, officially government servants, did the domestic chores of successive Collectors. Many coveted the job, preferring to clean the shit of the progeny of a Collector than to shuttle files in an office. Their priorities made sense, for in the office the Collector was a million rungs away, but at home while they were bringing him his shoes or taking away his slippers, they were close enough to grovel for their desires, for a little land, for the expedition of a government loan, for a peon's post in some office for their sons. Their fathers and grandfathers had done much the same, but the skins of those Collectors had been red, and the accent of their English alien. Of course they shirked at home as much as they would have shirked at office; if any Madam Collector was unreasonably tough, they worked even less while waiting to be shifted back to the office. Yet not many were sent back because they introduced in the gossip there facets of the Collector's personal life: "Collector saab shat thrice yesterday, bad stomach." "Madam Collector sometimes wears (whisper) black panties, yes."

The contract was implicit but clear. The Collectors and their wives believed vehemently in the indignity of labour (so did most of Madna believe that one's social standing was in inverse proportion to the amount of one's own work that one did oneself), and it is easier to believe these things when one's domestic servants are being paid by the Government. The other party to the contract, the peons, believed in the indignity of labour too, it is part of the Indian story. But they also knew that the goodwill and help of superiors are much more important than beliefs.

"Antony, my predecessor, transferred one peon to Rameri because that fellow had refused to work at his house. He came to me a few days ago, saying, saab, bring me back to Madna, I'll work anywhere you like. You see, now he's feeling stupid because everyone is calling him a fool for having missed a chance to work at the house."

"No, Ravi, please don't talk about your office," smiled Mrs. Srivastav. "Why don't you instead ask Sen, no, August, what Kumar was like today?"

Agastya wondered how she knew, and said hurriedly, "Oh, he was fine. We talked a lot."

"Kumar's an Indian Police Service specimen, they are all jealous of the IAS," said Srivastav. "You must also call on the District Judge Mishra and the District Development Officer Bajaj. Bajaj is another specimen, a bloody promotee." A promotee was one who was not recruited to the IAS through the national Civil Services examination like Srivastav, Menon and Agastya, but promoted to the cadre from something lower, the regional Civil Service or the engineers. In Srivastav's vocabulary, "promotee" was a vile curse, ranking somewhere between bastard and motherfucker. "Bajaj behaves like a promotee, you will see. The Indian Administrative Service has a work ethic, these other fellows have none." Srivastav scowled a lot here. "If the country is moving it is because of us only." He meant exactly what he said, and Agastya felt very embarrassed.

"But not all of us are that good, sir," said Menon, beaming. "Mr. Antony, for instance..." Aha, thought Agastya, bitching session.

"Ha, Antony," scowled Srivastav and ruffled his daughter's hair, who pulled her head away with a "tch" of irritation. Srivastav turned to Agastya. "You know, this Antony fellow behaved like a promotee, took the curtains of this house away when he left. I wanted to complain, because at least an IAS officer shouldn't behave like this, otherwise where is the difference with the others? But I didn't complain because there must be solidarity in the cadre." Agastya wondered why Srivastav didn't change the shape of his sideburns.

"May I bring my books and study here?" asked the daughter sweetly, feeling perhaps that she should be paid more attention.

"Certainly not," snapped Srivastav, "you'll just mess up the room and disturb everybody. Just sit here quietly." The daughter ejected a few silent tears; when that didn't work, she ran bawling to her mother who asked her to shut up, otherwise she would be sent away to her brother.

Then Ramsingh came in with a clothed and beaming Shekhar. "Ha, the piddler has come," said a smiling daughter. Mrs. Srivastav took both away for their dinners, much to their dissatisfaction.

"What was your discipline, Sen, in college?"

"English, sir," said Agastya, and wished that it had been something more respectable, Physics or Economics or Mathematics or Law, a subject that at least *sounded* as though one had to study for its exams. Many times in those months, in a myriad forms, he was to feel embarrassed about his past, and wish that it had been something else. Sitting in Srivastav's drawing room, he remembered Pultukaku's objecting to his choice of subject in college, just as he had earlier, and for much the same reasons, objected to Agastya's schooling: "Chaucer and Swift, what are you going to *do* with these irrelevancies? Your father doesn't seem to think that your education should touch the life around you?"

"A useless subject," said Srivastav, "unless it helps you to master the language, which in most cases it doesn't." He scowled mysteriously at Menon. "The English we speak is not the English we read in English books, and, anyway, those are two different things. Our English should be just a vehicle of communication, other people find it funny, but how we speak shouldn't matter as long as we get the idea across. My own English is quite funny too, but then I had to learn it on my own." Agastya began to like Srivastav then; he was honest, intelligent and satisfied with his life; he was rare. "In Azamganj, where I come from, I studied in a Hindi-medium school. Now people with no experience of these schools say that that's a good thing, because we should throw English out of India. Rubbish, I say, many other things are far more important. I *know*, bhai. There's not a single good teacher in these schools in these smaller places. How can there be, when their working conditions are so bad, when they themselves pass out of such schools and colleges? When I went to college in Lucknow I felt completely stupid. So I began to read English on my own. I had to, because English was compulsory for the Civil Services exam. So I read Shakespeare and Wordsworth and people like that, very difficult. It's still important to know English, it gives one," he fisted his hand, "confidence."

Srivastav had the pride of a self-made man. Agastya had rarely met them. In his own world most people made it because of the people they knew. He could visualize Srivastav too, an obscure and mediocre college student, sweating with incomprehension but determinedly wading through *The Prelude* because he wanted to get on. "...You are what you are, just as English here too is what it is, an unavoidable leftover. We can't be ashamed of our past, no, because that is to be ashamed of our present. People curse our history because it is much easier to do that than to work." A bat flew into the room. Srivastav scowled at it. It left. "That a young man in Azamganj should find it essential to study something as unnecessary as *Hamlet*, that is absurd, no, but also inevitable, and just as inevitably, if we behave ourselves, in three generations it will fade."

They spoke of many things that evening; of course, most of the topics were selected by the Collector. He was a knowledgeable man, and neither at home nor in the office could he display his grasp of subjects beyond his work. He held forth on the Constitution, the reorganization of the states, the elections, drought relief, the nature of politics in the region, the democratic system. When Mrs. Srivastav returned (looking a little tired, because she had been putting the children to bed), Srivastav was letting them know his views on the importance and inadequacy of education in India.

"Ah, education," smiled Mrs. Srivastav, "you should ask me." No one did, so she explained to Agastya, "I teach in the Janata College here. I have done my M. Ed. from here too."

Mrs. Srivastav was one kind of wife to a Collector; their "further studies" depended entirely on where their husbands were posted. While the husband worked, the wife gathered degrees from the sad colleges of the small towns. It was not easy to refuse admission or a degree to the wife of a Collector, or a District Development Officer, or a Superintendent of Police, even if their previous degrees were from places that the Principal of the college was not sure existed. Indeed, he was hardly bothered by these petty matters, knowing full well that the earlier colleges Mrs. Collector had graced could not be worse than his own. Thus when Srivastav had been Assistant Collector at Lalchuk, Mrs. Srivastav had become a Master of Arts at the Lalchuck National College. And when the husband had been District Development Officer of Haveliganj, the wife had become Bachelor of Education at the Haveliganj Gandhi Graduate College. And now a Master of Education at the Janata College, Madna.

But these wives used their degrees well, for brandishing them with pride (justifiably, because the degrees indicated, if not their level of education, at least the force of their husbands' clout), they returned to those colleges to teach the rubbish they had learnt. It was even more difficult to prevent them from teaching, because that would mean depriving the Collector's family of a good monthly sum. One could say that these bright young officers invested well in the education of their wives. The wretched college gained too, people said, "It is a good college. Madam Collector teaches there." "So I have been busy wherever Ravi has been posted," smiled Mrs. Srivastav. "Come, let's go for dinner." At the table she asked, "How's the Rest House food?"

"Very bad."

"You must eat with us whenever you like. No formality. Just treat this whole place as your own house, OK?"

"Thank you, ma'am." He ate with them almost every day. He would walk across at about seven in the evening, down the long drive from the gate that was continually being threatened by the banyans, race with the children on the lawn, fascinate them with the contents of the other rooms in the house and the bloodsucking habits of the bats ("They particularly like children who piddle in their pants. It's the smell," after which Shipra the daughter cackled all evening), listen patiently to Srivastav, and chat inanely with his wife. They provided a welcome domesticity. He heard Srivastav rant against the methods of his predecessor ("That Antony fellow offered tea to anyone who came to the office. A silly populist measure, and a very bad precedent. The office tea bill just shot up"), and extol the virtues of their job. He sensed Mrs. Srivastav's pleasure at being First Lady of the district. He accompanied them to places, to an evening of ghazals (of course, the show didn't start until they had taken their seats in the front row), to the Club (after each visit Mrs. Srivastav would whine against those who had not got up from their chairs at their entry, and Srivastav would say, "What to do, Malti? It's the *culture* of the place").

Over dessert (a lovely kheer, which Mrs. Srivastav didn't have because she said, with a smile, that she was getting too fat, which was true), Srivastav said, "In your training you will move from office to office trying to learn what each office does. Most officers will tell you nothing because they are uninterested, lazy, incompetent, or just too busy. Just keep your eyes and ears open, that's the only way to learn." Later, "Do you play badminton? Helps to keep trim." (Srivastav was almost as fat as Kumar.) "We play every morning at the Club from six thirty. Come if you want to." And when he and Menon were leaving, "Tomorrow I'll come and visit your room, see what they have given you."

He did come, and scowled throughout the visit, it was official; but it was a shrewd and responsible move, to ensure that Agastya was treated well at the Rest House. "Where's the rest of the furniture? The sofa?"

"I asked them to take it away, sir. I didn't need it."

"But how will you entertain, bhai? When people come to your room where will they sit?" Srivastav stalked around the room, and Agastya wondered if he was looking for marijuana. "Do you want to shift to a flat?"

Agastya wasn't sure. He would be away from the Rest House phone and fridge, he would have to organize furniture and a kitchen, far too much effort for just a few months; but in a flat at least he would have escaped Vasant's meals.

Vasant's children were at the door. They had been drawn by the white Ambassador with its orange light but the driver had prevented them from crawling all over it. They were many and Agastya wasn't sure if Vasant had fathered all, but they did look similar, small, thin, black, with large quick eyes and open mouths, their liveliness transcending their malnourishment. Agastya interested them profoundly; whenever his door was open, they would peek in, giggle and scamper away.

Srivastav glared at them, and they looked at one another and giggled. "I have assigned a peon from the office to you. He comes every day?"

"Yes, sir." And, he added silently, sits outside, farts, smokes bidis and dreams up impossible requests for me to forward to you, all because I can think of no work for him.

Vasant appeared with tea. Srivastav blasted him in the vernacular for a while. "Just telling him to feed you well," he explained. "Pursue RDC about your language tutor. Without the language you will never survive. And you have to pursue these things because even RDC, like the rest of these fellows, would rather die than do any extra work, because to die means more rest."

INEVITABLE that Agastya's daily routine in Madna should fall into a pattern, however irregular; because mere living imposes its own cycle, of ingestion and excretion, of sleep and awakening. He eventually accustomed, or resigned, himself to the pattern of his days, to the insomnia, and the relief from it that graced him but fitfully, to the mosquitoes that dragged him out of sleep. He often exercised on the veranda in the half-light of dawn; if stiff with lack of sleep, he did his push-ups and his spot-running in the heat of his room before breakfast, while Digambar squatted outside the closed door, lazily marvelling at Agastya's foolishness in exerting himself so much more than was necessary. But he exercised regularly; it was a fragment from his old life, and it somehow seemed to imbue the day with a little meaning.

Vasant brought him tea between six and nine, some time; the precise time every day depended on when he, Vasant, pushed himself out of bed to fetch the milk; lives were led very leisurely in Madna. Agastya never complained, for guessing when Vasant would bring him his tea became part of the larger game, of identifying movements in the outside world through sound. He would lie in bed, stare at the ceiling through the mosquito net, feel the breeze from the window turn warm, and say to himself, Yes, that mad chatter is Vasant's children going to school, and that cycle is that senile bugger coming to clean the toilets, that mysterious thump is probably Shankar falling off his bed in a drunken stupor, that clink is perhaps Vasant and tea.

Some mornings, if the heat hadn't begun, he would take a chair out to the veranda, and in a daze, watch the trains screech by to Delhi. He noticed the colours on the trains, orange and cream, mustard, yellow and green, and decided that that would be a nice job, deciding colour schemes for trains. He wondered at the immensity of the Indian Railways, millions of people travelling thousands of kilometres every day—why they did so baffled him. On less calm mornings, he would think about his situation and his job, why he wasn't settling down, whether his sense of dislocation was only temporary, or whether it was a warning signal. But there was nothing specific that he wanted to do, no other job, and then with a smile he would retort, Yes, there was, design colour schemes for trains, be a domesticated male stray dog, or like Madan, even half-wish to be murdered.

"It's all over, then," Madan had reasoned with razor-edge logic, "and without your having done anything for it. Wonderful."

Digambar, his head swathed in a red towel, would arrive some time between seven and ten; Agastya saw no reason for fixing his time either. He washed Agastya's clothes, did the bed and the room in about six minutes, and then settled down outside to somnolence. Sometimes Agastya also envied him.

Breakfast from Vasant was unavoidable, so Agastya experimented with it. Bread, soft-boiled egg, sliced tomato, sliced boiled potato, tea, and his tin of condensed milk which was kept in the Rest House fridge, at the hole of which he sucked at the end of breakfast to get rid of the taste of all that had preceded it. He thought that he was being scientific about his food, and evading Vasant's cooking to the extent possible—all that actually happened was that he felt ravenous at eleven.

Food became very important in Madna, and he was soon to encourage and concentrate on his stomach pangs. For hunger was evidence of one's good health, and thinking about eating itself gave him something to do. It made him calculate which houses in Madna he could attack for lunches and dinners, and if compelled to eat Vasant's garbage, then the menu for it. A very few days in the district, and he was sick, even scared, of abstract thought—the problem of food gave him something concrete for cogitation. Lying on the bed, staring blankly up at the ceiling (his most characteristic position for all the months), he would ask himself where his next meal was coming from, and laugh helplessly at the clichéd question. Before Madna, he had always taken food for granted, like air. In his college days whenever the hostel fare had been inedible (but never like Vasant's creations), they had always gone out to some dhaba. Now he did hope that there were places in Madna where one could eat cheaply, but he didn't have the will to hunt for them, and consequently thought maybe he had to consider heterogeneity of taste, and maybe all over the town he would get only chewing-gum chapatis.

Mrs. Srivastav provided the largest number of meals that year. Otherwise while roaming through various government offices trying to learn the complexities of administration, he would surprise various officers by taking them up on their casual invitations. It was a good game, and he enjoyed it—while maintaining what Menon had called the "dignity of office" to extract an invitation to dinner, and to seem to accept reluctantly, but with grace, saying that he would be honoured (and actually feeling triumphant), while implying that the honour would be the host's. When Mrs. Srivastav also asked why he didn't shift to a flat and learn to cook for himself, it was difficult to answer, "Because scrounging is challenging and greater fun."

And in a perverse way, Vasant's food was exciting, full of hazards concocted to unsettle boredom. So was his ostensibly boiled water. "Let the water begin to boil, then let the water remain on the fire, boiling, for about ten minutes, and then switch off the gas. Boiling for ten minutes means counting ten minutes after the water begins to boil, not leaving the water on the gas for ten minutes." He said words like these to Vasant, slowly and carefully, as to an obstinate *and* demented child, almost every day, but in all those months he was never sure whether he really drank boiled water at the Rest House. Whenever Vasant brought the jug he would ask, "Is it boiled?" and Vasant would nod, sometimes dip his finger, and say, "It's hot." Defeated and amused, Agastya solved his doubt by drinking water everywhere he went, and patted his flat hard stomach in the mirror in compliment.

Once, out of boredom, he had wanted to go to the kitchen to demonstrate the boiling of water for drinking; he couldn't. Vasant at first didn't understand, and then seemed to pretend not to. Then he nodded his head vigorously, closing his eyes with each nod, and moved away. Agastya went after him, but Vasant stopped him with an outstretched arm and an open Buddha-like palm. Agastya said, "Fuck you," to his back. Vasant returned with a kerosene stove, which he placed on the veranda floor. Agastya said, "Yes, yes," and sent him away, thinking, Maybe he doesn't want me to see his kitchen, the mire out of which my meals emerge.

And lunch, which was really a second breakfast, also had its contingent perils, but they were sometimes as engrossing as a Sunday-paper chess problem. Once, while bringing the tray in, Vasant stumbled and upset the milk all over the rest of the food. He put the tray down on the table. Agastya retrieved the slices of potato and tomato from the milk.

"I'll go get another glass of milk."

"Here, take the tray with you." Vasant picked it up, a plate of milk in a tray of milk. He returned a few minutes later with a glass of hot milk with black dots in it. "What's that?"

"Tea leaves," said Vasant and removed them with his left index finger. It could have been pepper from the potato. Agastya suspected that Vasant had just filled another glass with the milk from the tray and the plate. He himself would have done the same. Then his cerebrations began. But the milk was hot. Well, Vasant had just heated it again. Perhaps I should ask him. But if the milk is actually fresh, with just a few tea leaves from the saucepan in it, then my suspicion will offend him. And give him ideas. He cooks your food, he could make you eat *anything*. And remember that Vasant looks mad anyway, with his grey stubble and the tumour above his right collarbone. Agastya left the tray to discuss the matter with the mirror. Now, you can't yell at Vasant because he just might feed you his turds. "Actually anyone who has a servant is completely at his mercy," his aunt in Calcutta (who had disapproved the most of his father's marrying a Goan) said all the time. Perhaps he should sneak up on Vasant one day, with stealth, in his running shoes. But if he was seen it would be very difficult to explain. Then he returned to the tray and dipped his finger in the milk too, to see how it felt.

On most days, the jeep came for him between eleven and twelve. Before its arrival there was time enough to smoke some marijuana, often against his will. On some mornings he didn't really want to. On those mornings he would go over to the mirror, absent-mindedly examine his beard, turn sideways and out of the corner of his eye try to look at his profile, an old habit, and ask his reflection why he should smoke, and, anyway, why he should smoke so much. Because there wasn't much else to do, he would answer, unless he wanted to masturbate. Sometimes he did both, laughing at the determined entry in his diary of the first day, and at the memory of Madan and their shared belief that fucking someone else was less satisfying and more tiresome than fucking your fist.

There *wasn't* much else to do. Reading was impossible, with his mind in its state of quiet tumult. And the titles that had accompanied him from Calcutta and Delhi were almost laughable in their remoteness: two Bengali novels, *Pather Panchali* and *Gora*, neither of which could hold him because the problems of their protagonists were almost unapproachable, he always wanted something with immediacy (Pultukaku had been scathing about this too, expectedly, when Agastya read them the first time, "Two seminal novels, in your language, and you can't even begin to appreciate them"); one literary curiosity, an English translation of the *Ramayana* by an American who, he gathered from the Introduction, seemed to have chatted often with Hanuman in the Himalayas; and a copy of Marcus Aurelius, his father's present on his last birthday—its first page said, in Bengali: "To Ogu, on turning twenty-four, hoping he makes you wise."

Sometimes, before the jeep arrived, he could concentrate on a few lines, especially when slightly stoned. The *Meditations* turned out to be (very incongruously, he thought) his only reading. The passages were generally short, so he wasn't asked to think for more than a few lines at a go. In those months he grew to like immensely this wise sad Roman. Marcus immediately made him feel better, because Marcus seemed to have more problems than anyone else—not the soul-squashing problems of being poor, but the exhilarating abstract problems of one immersed wholly in his self. Earlier, Agastya would have perhaps pooh-poohed him, life was to be enjoyed, not endured. But in Madna he could not dare say such a facile thing. Still, occasionally, he *would* say to the page, Seize the day, boy, and then smile, Imagine calling Marcus Aurelius boy. Yet again, the absurd, never far from him, would assail him—perhaps Marcus's meditations weren't really genuine, he could easily have whipped off a few on a marble writing table beside his couch while a beautiful Roman adolescent (exuding from behind his ears and his wrists the perfumes from the ports of Deccan India, which would have been a mere few hundred kilometres away from the spot where, sixteen hundred years after Marcus, a tribal would found a kingdom, and call it Madna) sucked him off, or while he was ejaculating into a guest's wine goblet, muttering *quo vadis* to the spirit of Caligula.

Like Marcus, he kept a desultory diary that year, for like Marcus, he meditated—but in the oddest of situations, while exercising, for instance. His exercise took about twenty minutes, and he quite enjoyed it, after he had somehow coerced himself to begin. I don't see a single person in Government who looks in shape, I don't want to be like them, he would say, as he lunged for a push-up. But the fad was Western—wasn't it a Western fad, to try to remain young? He would stop, pant, rush to his diary and note: "Is it a Western fad to try and remain young? Neera keeps saying so." Neera, his friend in Calcutta, did often say that the West worships youth; when they begin looking old, they get themselves face-lifts, but we in India are equally stupid, worshipping age (Neera herself was fat and lazy). He would return to his push-ups with his mind in chaos. He would again stop at his seventeenth push-up and watch drops of sweat fall on the carpet. Was it *wrong* to exercise and try to remain fit and young? An ant would perhaps scurry across the damp discs of sweat on the carpet. Well, did or didn't the ant feel the wet beneath its feet? Did an ant have feet? But if it didn't, then what did its legs end in, just dots? Get on with the push-ups, boy, but the strength would have left his mind. In his diary he would note: "NB Neera is a Marxist and talks a lot of shit," and below it, "Have you ever thought how embarrassing it would be if someone found out that you kept a *diary*?"

But not all the entries in his diary were frivolous; of course it was the seriously intended entries that he was more embarrassed about. Marcus Aurelius indirectly taught him the magic of catharsis, that writing assisted thought and clarity of mind, that it was good to be rational. The littlest things became significant. That a pen could move across a page and that its trail, as it were, could make sense—suddenly this seemed magical. A squiggle and a curve, they hold meaning. He wrote: "What are your problems?" and laughed, God, there were so many, and all so totally vague, but analysis helped, or seemed to help, that was why it was good to be rational.

The driver of the jeep that came for Agastya in the mornings was usually unable to differentiate one district office from another. So, for almost an hour on some of the (good) days, he would drive Agastya around the town, just trying to *locate* an office—of the District Inspector of Land Records, say, or of the Divisional Forest Officer. On the good days this was a strange and exhilarating adventure, racing down the narrow streets of an unknown town, braking dangerously to ask paanwalas and cobblers, searching half-heartedly for some office. Many hadn't heard of the place they wanted, some directed them wrongly, some were emphatic that the place just didn't exist. Looking at the people the driver asked, Agastya realized how little he knew of the real Madna beyond its offices.

And the ride itself was lulling. It was soporific to be mindlessly shunted about in a vehicle, to succumb to the marijuana, the heat, the rhythm and roar of the jeep.

Sometimes, when they finally reached the office on the schedule for that day, they would find that the officer was absent, was touring, was on leave. Sometimes he would be there, but with no idea of what he was to do with, or say to, Agastya. Sometimes Agastya's lack of interest was far outmatched by the officer's. Agastya would sit beside him and look around, at the decaying walls and the leaking water cooler in the corner, the fading map on the wall and the government calendar. The officer would ask a few questions, Agastya would lie without restraint. Then he would be obliged to ask questions in return. When he felt that he knew enough about that office to lie to the Collector that same evening about what he had learnt that day, he would announce that he ought to return to the Rest

House for lunch and add, with a smile, that it would be just too hot in the afternoon to return. The officer would beam his complete agreement. Sometimes he wanted to complain to Srivastav that no one was teaching him anything, but never did, because he felt that the fault might be his, that he would be reproached for his lack of interest, an accusation that he would be unable to deny.

He did learn a little in some offices, not about the intricacies of administration, but, broadly, about the ways of the wider world. The District Inspector of Land Records told him, for instance, that every inch of India was plotted on some map or other.

"Every inch?" He was somehow pleased and proud.

"Of course, sir. So much of government work depends on land records, who owns what lands, when land was transferred or inherited. If Government is to acquire land for something or the other, to build a dam or a thermal power station, we have to have proper land records, no, to decide whom to pay compensation to. After all land is everyone's most important asset." The Inspector was a worn apologetic man. He sat in a small noisy room, in an alley above a shop that sold plastic mugs and buckets and ran, on the side, a video library. He travelled on an old bicycle. "In the office we have maps of the entire district. We'll show you a few."

The maps came in with the tea. The Inspector drank from his saucer. The maps were on parchment or tracing paper and the Inspector unrolled them reverentially over the books on his table. (The books themselves fascinated Agastya. *City Survey Manual, Manual of Rules and Standing Orders relating to Land Records Establishments*—someone somewhere actually wrote such things, and there were people in this world who consulted these every day.) The older maps were in English, but still completely indecipherable. They all showed areas apportioned in a variety of geometric shapes, each with a number. Why, thought

Agastya, children could play games on these maps, and try and capture these squares and hexagrams through speed or deceit or both, and assign different values for each shape. "Land is important everywhere, all kinds of land," said the Inspector, "but you have lived in the cities. There you cannot sense the importance of agricultural land, it's the real wealth. Each of these squares and hexagrams could be worth lakhs." The Inspector had been sitting in that one chair for years. Every day he examined maps and their attendant ledgers and documents, drank his tea from a saucer to the noises from outside of cars and rickshaws and altercations. When he wanted to urinate he went downstairs to some hole behind the shop.

On rare afternoons Srivastav summoned Agastya to the Collectorate for some meeting or other; otherwise on most days he stayed in his room. He would spend some of the afternoon sometimes with Shankar, drinking, lying, listening to him on Madna, art, Tamse. "Don't you ever go to office, Shankar saab?"

"Speak for yourself, Sen saab," and neighs of joy, "we are very similar I tell you, governed by Shani, and loved by Jagadamba. We have similar habits," he lifted up his glass and neighed again, "neither goes to office after lunch, and similar views, we hate office and prefer the life outside, similar tastes, for music, similar situations, we have both been banished in Madna."

His afternoons stretched from his lunch to whenever he asked Vasant for tea. So he could, in a sense, control their duration. After the tea he had to contemplate the evening, but before it, he could doze a little, watch Tamse's painting, or the lizards race across the wall to copulate in a corner, listen to the music of Nazrul Islam or Vivaldi, daydream, fantasize, think of his past, reorganize it, try to force out of it a pattern, masturbate without joy, sometimes smoke some marijuana, read a little Marcus Aurelius, or just lie down and think of the sun shrivelling up the world outside. He liked the afternoons in his surreal darkened room. He felt safe while, to him, the world burnt. When he opened the door for Vasant, the sun would have weakened a little, and a few more hours would have elapsed in Madna.

He spent many evenings at the Collector's, but on some evenings he felt just too blown to go, his eyes looked too red, he felt too alone to talk sanely to anyone. Then he would wait for sundown and go for a walk. The town was too dirty and too crowded, and there was always the risk of meeting someone from the office and the tedium of consequent small talk, so he usually walked away from the town, along the train tracks.

On some nights he would listen to the nine o'clock radio news. Earlier, he had generally avoided newspapers and what they called current affairs. News had never interested him, unless it had been calamitous, in which case it had got to him anyway. But in Madna he began to listen to the radio carefully, sometimes just to have another voice in the room. It became a major link, the only objective one, really, with the world beyond Madna. For the Bombay and Calcutta newspaper came in late, and inevitably with stale news. In Madna he also became aware of the power of radio to disseminate doctored information, for millions relied on it, in micropolitan and rural India, for entertainment and information, and more than half of them were illiterate. The radio said that seventy per cent of the country would be covered by TV by the end of the year. Earlier he would never even have *heard* such a remark, but now it registered, made sense. TV was coming to Madna too, Sathe had said, and he could fully visualize its impact—it was much more powerful than radio, for it imprisoned the eye. Sathe had added cynically that TV in Madna was an election stunt, and that made complete sense too.

On most nights that he didn't eat with the Collector, dinner was early, at about eight, because Vasant liked to sleep early.

Then, after dinner, till about four in the morning, the insomnia. In Madna he could never take sleep for granted. He would repeat the activities of the afternoon, thinking that for more than twenty years he had always slept well, except for one or two nights when excitement had kept him awake, like the night before the class picnic when he was seven, when he'd roamed around the house all night, overwrought because he'd be wearing his new jeans for the picnic. But in Madna he seemed to have appalled sleep. When he finally dropped off, it was out of a weariness even with despair.

Thus he played out, in one day, one kind of life of the lonely.

"SIR, PHONE for you," said one of the Circuit House menials, at about six one evening, to him as he was sitting in the veranda with Marcus Aurelius.

It was Mahendra Bhatia from the Forest Colony. "Hello, Mandy, of course I remember you...Yes, must be three years since we last...Yes, Sathe told me too, about you...I was planning to ring you up, but you know how it is, new place, new job, am busy the whole day...Sure, we must meet ...What about this evening...? Yes, this evening, I'm free right now, got off early today...Yes, you come over, because I really don't know this town well enough yet...It's the fourth room in the Rest House, in the Circuit House compound...Oh, I came here about three weeks ago, I think...Yes, it *is* very different...(Whatever would they talk about when they met? They would have to drink together, otherwise the evening would be intolerable)...Listen, Mandy, why don't we drink this evening? Otherwise...Great, just bring that bottle along...OK, in half an hour...'Bye."

Despite the promise of whisky Agastya returned to the veranda not overly excited about Bhatia. He had been of a completely different set in the college days; a student of Physics or Chemistry, he had forgotten which, who had been, in Dhrubo's lingo, "just one more urban Indian bewitched by America's hard sell in the Third World." Bhatia liked T-shirts and Calvin Klein jeans, Delhi's fastfood joints, Indian motorcyles (because he couldn't afford a foreign one), girlfriends whom he "could lay anytime, man" (they proved elusive), marijuana, even a little cocaine, the singers who won the Grammy awards (and whom Indian TV, for his ecstasy, had begun, finally, to show), calling rupees bucks, and being called Mandy. His ambition had been to go abroad ("to the US of A"), perhaps to show it how well he fitted in with its lifestyle (Dhrubo had once said—they had been sitting on the college front lawn, stoned, and Bhatia had passed by, with some clones, two headphones and a Walkman—witheringly, "He's the sort who'd love to get AIDS just because it's raging in America"); instead, Bhatia had won Madna, Agastya found it delightful.

Agastya was even happier to see that the three years, and Madna probably, had subdued Bhatia. His clothes hadn't changed, Gloria Vanderbilt and a T-shirt that said "I don't want no Star Wars" (He meets the District Inspector of Land Records in these clothes? and Agastya laughed silently), but he was thinner, cleaner, and more sombre. Perhaps the job made him shave every day. His whisky, unfortunately, was only a half-bottle.

"Hello." They shook hands. They sat in the veranda. Agastya didn't want to sit in his room because visitors there looked incongruous; the room was really for the musings of the lonely.

Well, they eventually got a little drunk, enough for Bhatia to relapse into invective. He forgot that he and Agastya had been merely acquaintances in college; perhaps he remembered and didn't care, or perhaps to him it was enough that Agastya came from his old life and would consequently understand. Bhatia ranted against his job, the small town, the people, the boredom, the loneliness, the absence of sex. These cries of despair from an inarticulate mouth embarrassed Agastya profoundly; he would never have accepted that he and Bhatia could have anything in common, but now they palpably did: their dislocation.

"It's sick, there's no one to talk to, no place to go, nothing to do, just come back to your room after office, get drunk, feel lonely, and jerk off."

Bhatia made Agastya's secret life seem so ridiculous, he wanted to laugh. Its major consolation had been the possibility that it was a profound experience, something rare; now it seemed as common as a half-bottle of whisky, something he shared with Bhatia. Agastya faintly disliked him for this, for shattering one of his last consoling illusions.

But he could not admit to their similarity. He realized obscurely that the sense of loneliness was too precious to be shared, and finally incommunicable, that men *were*, ultimately, islands; each had his own universe, immense only to himself, far beyond the grasp or the interest of others. For them the pettiness of the ordeal was unrecordable, worthy, at best, only of a flicker of empathy. He was not really interested in Bhatia's life; later, Dhrubo would not be interested in his, and his father would not be able to understand it.

It was pleasant, however, to hear Bhatia, and to contradict gently and further incense him; time passed that way. "But, Mandy, all jobs are boring, and life for everyone *is* generally unhappy. You can't blame Madna. Maybe you should get married. Then at least you can solve two problems, sex and loneliness." Agastya soon began enjoying his facile and shallow (and shallow only because they were worn-out) arguments. "And I think whenever anyone shifts to a new place, initially he does feel a little weird."

Here Bhatia interrupted him, "What initially? I've been here for more than a year."

"But the world *isn't* a wonderful place full of exciting opportunities. It's generally dull and fucked everywhere. You just have to settle down, unless you want to commit suicide. Lots of people do, you know." Agastya rather liked his new theme. "There are many indigenous methods of suicide. You could change sex, kill your husband if he doesn't die on his own, and burn yourself on his pyre, but I think sati (suttee to you) is prohibited—they've killed a great Indian tradition, but there's a new one in its place—you could change sex and marry, and get your husband to burn you—the ultimate kink experience."

Agastya finished his third drink, and felt the whisky go down, move sideways and attack his liver. Bhatia hadn't been listening, was staring at the bottom of his glass. "What, Mandy, do you feel like a writer of ghazals over his empty glass?"

"No, there's some black thing at the bottom. It looks like rat shit. Have a look."

"Yes, it does look like rat shit." Agastya handed back the glass quickly. "Vasant, that insane man you saw, got the glasses from that cupboard in the Circuit House dining room. Have you seen that cupboard? A huge bugger. A tiger could stay inside, and no one would know. I thought the glasses were clean, the rat shit doesn't show through this green glass."

Bhatia held the glass up against the veranda tube-light. Agastya remembered a restaurant in Calcutta, whose pizzas Neera loved, where the bulb shades were green bottles. "What can I get with dissolved rat shit?" asked Bhatia.

"Plague?"

"Don't be silly, that's extinct."

"Extinct? Is that the right word for diseases? Nothing else, I think. It was stale rat shit, wasn't it?"

"How do I know?" asked Bhatia irritably.

"Who else will? You drank it." To which Bhatia said nothing, but mused over the catastrophes to come.

Then the electricity went off. Complete darkness, and shouts of joy from the servants' quarters behind the Circuit House. "That's probably Vasant's children, happy at not having to do homework, now they can even play ice-pice." It was nice, to see nothing, to feel the faint breeze, and to talk about ordinary matters to the dark.

"The electricity supply is really bad here. They'll begin soon, shutting it off regularly in the hottest parts of the day. Can you get a light from somewhere? There's a last drink left in that bottle." Agastya got a candle and placed it on the *Madna District Gazetteer*. He looked at the book affectionately. "This fat book's nice. As a paperweight, for placing candles on."

"You should open it some time. It's quite interesting." Agastya was surprised; he would never have thought that there were any facets to Bhatia. Bhatia lit a cigarette from the candle, and touched the *Gazetteer*. "From the office? Everyone treats government stuff like this. Really valuable stuff sometimes, furniture, old houses, old books, all treated like this. For keeping candles on."

"I think it's going to be plague. Are your armpits swelling?" The lights came on again, again the shouts of joy from the children. "Perhaps they are happy that the lights came on because it gives them a chance to shriek."

"What shall we do for dinner? I suggest we walk out and get another half-bottle, and stooge a dinner off Sathe."

That evening Agastya saw a little of Madna at close quarters. Bhatia wanted a rickshaw, Agastya wanted to walk, they took a rickshaw part of the way. They jolted in their seats and watched the calf muscles of the rickshaw-wala. He smelt of a decade of sweat and malnutrition. They passed garages, stalls selling sugarcane juice, shops. "Just notice the number of chemists in Madna," said Bhatia bitterly, "A clear sign how unhealthy this place is."

"Eight o'clock, but this place is far more alive than South Delhi is at six in the evening." Crowds on the road, the rickshaw-wala using both his bell and his hoarse voice against them, the smell of dosas and frying fish from a dhaba, and urine and mud from a police station, a transistor from a sugarcane stall deafening its surroundings with a Hindi film disco song, softer pseudo-ghazals from a music shop, the darkness of passing alleys. "It wouldn't be too boring, to get stoned and hang around here and watch all this."

"Impossible, Madna is just too small. Your official life would get to you. Some turd from some office will see you and talk to you, and it'd soon be all over the town, all over the other offices anyway, that this young Westernized type from Delhi just hangs around the bazaars. They'd disapprove—your Collector would, anyway."

They met Joshi the RDC almost immediately, when they were arguing with the rickshaw-wala over prices. "Hello, Sen, sir, what're you doing here?" He was with what looked like his wife, but he didn't introduce her. Be charitable, said Agastya to himself, maybe she's his mistress, maybe he has a harem of tribal women and dances naked with them every evening before dinner.

"Hello, Joshi saab, this is my friend Mahendra. He's an Assistant Conservator of Forests here. Mr. Joshi's at the Collectorate, he's RDC." And I still don't know what that is, he added silently. They parted after inanities.

Bhatia said, "Now, you wait and see. In a few days someone completely unrelated to Joshi will say to you something stupid, like, 'So you go for walks to the bazaar in the evenings.' You wait and see."

Three evenings later Mrs. Srivastav said, "I heard, August, that you get drunk and walk around every day in the market with some forester friends."

To which Srivastav scowled and added, "Sen, you must be careful of the company you keep in Madna. A small place, people talk a lot, they don't have much else to do. You be careful of people like that Govind Sathe, a scoundrel, a cartoonist. As an IAS officer you can't mix with everybody. It's not a job, bhai, where what you do after office is entirely your own private business, you're also responsible to Government in the after-hours. And that Govind Sathe, a really irresponsible type, thinks life is a big joke."

Bhatia and Agastya turned down an alley. Under the tube-light at the corner Bhatia nearly put his foot into a huge pile of fresh dung. "Watch it!" In the light the dung looked black-green, with small bubbles, reminding Agastya of Vasant's spinach. Probably tastes better, he thought. Did cows normally shit like that, or had the waters of Madna ruined them too? Or maybe this one had also eaten at the Rest House. On either side small ugly houses, old and unpainted—here in the alleys there seemed no one to clamour for beauty. Barred windows, a room with blue walls, a boy in a vest on a bed, studying under a tube-light. Madna had its life, too.

"Mandy, those are sculptures, aren't they?" Agastya pointed to a house. On the ledges on either side of the main steps sat two white goats, absolutely immobile.

"They don't smell like sculptures," said Bhatia. But in the light and dark of the alley they could have been statues in white marble. "Probably sleeping, or just stoned." Weren't white goats a good omen in Hindu myth somewhere? Agastya couldn't make the effort to scan his mind for the allusion, but he felt better just looking at them, so absurd and attractive, as though placidly waiting to welcome guests.

A blaze of light around a corner, a board depicting a gro-tesquely disproportionate Bharatnatyam dancer, and saying, "Welcome to Dakshin Bar and Restaurant." Bhatia said, "You order some pakoras here, we'll need them for the booze. I'll go and get it, the shop is just down the road. We'll save time." Agastya entered the restaurant, wondering why Bhatia wanted to save time.

Dakshin was huge, noisy and brightly lit. He sat nearest the door, facing the courtyard of rickshaws and scooters. He didn't want to be recognized, didn't want this world to be linked to the Collectorate. The speakers near the ceiling boomed out Hindi disco songs. He felt even better. At the next table a man with half his face altered by leukoderma gobbled up idlis from a sea of sambar. Agastya smiled at him, even my face should be like yours, he thought, my mother was fair and Christian, and then felt ashamed of himself. A Sikh entered, fat and powerful, in tight jeans and a T-shirt stretched across his huge firm breasts. He looked around murderously, with mean red eyes. A small beaked nose, thin lips, thin beard. I'd love to get to know this guy, thought Agastya, he epitomizes vice. The Sikh scratched his balls and left on a noisy motorbike. Agastya thought of the reactions if he took the Sikh to the Collector's house for dinner, roaring up the drive on his motorcycle, and introducing him to Srivastav: Sir, this is my best friend, almost my other half. Bhatia arrived with a packet, looking conspiratorial.

At Sathe's hotel the rickshaw-wala said, "Four rupees."

Bhatia said, "Rubbish, two." They argued for a while, lazily, almost perfunctorily. In the middle Bhatia turned to Agastya, "On principle, man. One always argues with any taxi-, scooter- or rickshaw-wala on principle. Otherwise the journey is not complete."

Suddenly the rickshaw-wala ended the argument with, "When next your father farts, push that two-rupee note up his arse," and left. Bhatia looked quite hurt. "No driver of any public conveyance in India ever leaves without his money. Why is that rickshaw-wala trying to be different, the bastard."

"I hope Sathe's at home." He was, and looked genuinely pleased to see them. "All three of us are a little drunk, I think," said Agastya, "we thought we should get a little more drunk and stooge a dinner off you."

In the corridor behind Sathe stood a haggard woman with large, slightly bulging eyes. "My sister-in-law, Geeti. Bhabhi, these are two young misfits from the Collectorate and the Divisional Forest Office." She seemed nice. "We're just sitting down to dinner. But perhaps you'd want yours a little later."

On top of the books on Sathe's bed lay an English translation of the *Bhagavad-gita.* The easel showed a new unfinished sketch, an easily recognizable Krishna on the battlefield at Kurukshetra, but a fat bald politician in Arjun's place, scratching his head, his face creased with incomprehension. "This one is the first of a series," smiled Sathe, taking out glasses from, for some reason, under the bed, "really ambitious ones. We'll need more soda. Just a second." He went out.

Bhatia picked up the book like an illiterate, or like a pragmatic government servant who disliked any printed word that did not further his career in any form; just because his hands were fidgety and the book was close by. The book could just as well have been a cricket ball, or Rubik's Cube. Sathe noticed it too. "That's not for Philistines," he said from the door, with a uniformed waiter behind him. Bhatia flipped through the pages like one shuffles cards, and put the book down.

"Tremendous fund of jokes, this book," said Sathe, evacuating a chair, "a real feast." He was again blasphemous as though people expected him to be so. "But I see you don't believe me." He settled down. "Have you ever read this?"

"Certainly not," said Agastya. The question wasn't even intended for Bhatia.

Sathe got up solemnly, took two steps, picked up the book and put it in Agastya's lap. "Read this. We are not discussing this until you read this. I'm quite shocked, I can tell you."

"You are also very drunk."

"I can expect Bhatia not to have read this, because he's a Punjabi, or an American born in Delhi—I doubt if there exists a translation of this in Punjabi, and, anyway, he doesn't read." Sathe turned a little, "You can see from his face that he doesn't read. But you," he walked over to assume an against-the-mantelpiece pose against his easel, "are a Bengali, the son of a Governor and an obscure Goanese Christian—yes the news has spread all over Madna—and, no doubt, in keeping with your race, your father did to your poor mother what all of you did to

Assam, but we only began to whine when the British did it to us—" Sathe pitched his voice high, in mimicry, " 'you're making us incapable of appreciating ourselves'—I mean, who cares?" He laughed with his body. "And so ignoring one-half of yourself you've grown up only a Bengali—dhoti, roshogollas and Tagore." He laughed again, almost toppling the easel. "Perhaps you haven't yet read the *Gita* because the Bengalis haven't yet been able to prove that it was written by one of them."

"Stop talking shit and get us some kababs," said Bhatia.

Thus, through happenstance, Agastya could place the *Bhagavad-gita* beside Marcus Aurelius on his shelf. Pultukaku, he knew, would have been displeased ("It is not written by Racine, you know, that you have to read it in English"). Agastya had always associated books like the *Gita* with age, when the afterlife begins to look important, and particularly with one orthodox uncle, who read old Hindu scriptures every day, still loathed his father for having married a Christian and for having become Governor of Bengal, bemoaned the decay of Calcutta and the exodus of the English (Pultukaku disliked him: "that senile confused Anglophile. Calcutta was kept pretty because people were prevented from moving around freely. Even Elliot Road would look clean if you remove the people from it. Is a city meant for people or for Hardinge and his gang"), and felt that the world would be at peace if everyone became a Hindu intellectual. Most passages were abstruse, but Agastya was surprised by some:

"The mind is restless, Krishna, impetuous, self-willed, hard to train: to master the mind seems as difficult as to master the mighty winds."

"The mind is indeed restless, Arjuna: it is indeed hard to train. But by constant practice and by freedom from passions the mind in truth can be trained."

"MAY I speak to Mr. Bajaj, please, the District Development Officer?...Yes...Sir, my name is Sen, I am an IAS officer, I...Yes, sir, I came (Just lie, said Agastya to himself, take the risk) about a week ago, sir...I've been ill, sir, and so couldn't call on you earlier...Yes, sir, uh, great stomach trouble, sir... May I call on you some time, sir?...Oh, right away?...No, sir, that'll be fine, I'll come over right away."

The buildings of the District Council were much newer, bigger and uglier than the Collectorate, with just as big a crowd loafing outside it. Agastya was distracted by a big jeep parked outside a side entrance. It was painted like some European flag, blue, yellow and white, and carried slogans in English and the vernacular: "Use IUDs," "Nirodh contraceptives are good for you," "Copper Ts ensure a happy family," "Have you been sterilized? Join the National Sterilization Programme." At the bottom was painted in red, "Official Vehicle of the District Health Officer, District Council, Madna." Maybe, thought Agastya hopefully, the District Health Officer took part regularly in the Himalayan Car Rally for the Insane. The door at the back of the jeep showed two deformed men wrestling, their faces ringed by drop-shaped squiggles, each the size of a tennis ball. With a sense of wonder he identified the drops as sweat. After scrutiny he decided that the wrestlers, with football heads and thighs fatter than torsos, weren't supposed to be deformed at all—it was just the work of an atrocious artist (Tamse!).

Through the wrestlers the Health Department seemed to be saying that sterilization did not cause impotence. Of course on the jeep they couldn't have painted a guy fucking with joy, the wrestlers were the next best thing. See, see, even after your crotch has been poked you can still be tough (and never mind if your head and thighs grow alarmingly), and can still wrestle with another guy who looks like you, and you will also sweat a little unusually, but then sweat has always been a sign of virility, no?

People wandering around in the corridors, relaxing on benches, more eyes glazed with waiting, a mean tough peon at the door, much like the constable outside the Police Superintendent's room, also suspicious. "I am an IAS officer," said Agastya. It worked.

Bajaj's room was furnished with taste, in complementing shades of brown. Two men sitting beside him, one woman, almost demented with nervousness, sitting opposite. "Ah, Sen, come in come in." Bajaj was very tall and worryingly thin, with large woebegone eyes and a receding chin, as though his progenitors had been a female spaniel and Don Quixote. Agastya had expected a fat complacent Punjabi. "Sit down and watch the fun. We're conducting interviews for the posts of teachers in the schools of the District Council." The giggling wreck opposite Bajaj was a candidate. "Twenty-three applied for the posts, we called eighteen for the interview, six turned up. All the candidates are tribals, the posts are reserved for them." With his elbow on the table and an immobile forearm, Bajaj flicked his wrist at one of the men beside him. "Meet our Education Officer." The other man seemed too unimportant to be introduced.

Agastya's entry seemed to have interrupted the interrogation. The Education Officer, solemn and enthusiastic, continued, "What is twenty per cent of eighty?"

She giggled, put the edge of her sari in her mouth, and asked in return, "Twenty-five?" Bajaj pushed over a sheet of paper to

Agastya and tapped his pen on one name. The giggler, Agastya read, had passed her Senior School Exam and even held a Diploma in Education from some hole. If she got the job, she would teach Maths, History, Geography, Civics and a whole lot of other things to ten-year-old victims.

The Education Officer, with the patience of one who believes that patience is a good characteristic to exhibit in front of a boss, explained the question.

"Fifteen?" Another giggle.

"Close enough," snarled Bajaj, and asked her to go.

"Last candidate, sir," said the Education Officer, as a small dark teenager entered. He was a BA. He mumbled the answers to the preliminary questions. Then Bajaj asked, "Who is called the Father of the Nation?"

"Nehru." A pat reply.

"I see, and what is Gandhi, then? Perhaps the Uncle of the Nation?" Later Bajaj said, "Select the third, reject the other five." The Education Officer assiduously jotted down the pronouncement, and said, "But these six posts have been vacant for four years, sir. And the politicians and schools have both been complaining for long."

"Well, then, appoint them all," and Bajaj shrugged and smiled at Agastya. He had a reputation for quick decisions. "You'll see, Sen, when you're BDO later this year, and dealing directly with these things, what development really is. Are you OK now?"

"Yes, sir," said Agastya, wondering what he meant (perhaps he was meant to have collapsed under the shock of those interviews), and then remembered, Oh, yes, his stomach trouble.

"Then join us for dinner. I'll ring up my wife and tell her." Bajaj seemed friendly enough. But Srivastav had warned Agastya, "He's like a snake, a promotee, remember, no ethics." Bajaj looked at least ten years older than Srivastav, but was the junior in the service.

The door flew open for a lawyer with a smile. He exuded confidence and paan spittle. "Aha, Bajaj saab." His daughter hadn't been admitted in the District Council College, she'd just missed the minimum admission marks by 0.4 per cent, just 0.4 per cent, Bajaj saab. "Tch, tch," said Bajaj. Now if Bajaj saab could telephone the Principal. "No," smiled Bajaj, "let the Principal decide. He has his job, I have mine." Arrey, but which Principal wouldn't listen to Bajaj saab? "You lawyers take such pleasure in burdening me with more than my share of work," smiled Bajaj. The lawyer laughed with innocent joy. So it's fixed Bajaj saab? "What is fixed?" smiled Bajaj. Bajaj saab, it just means a phone call, a girl's future is at stake. Agastya watched Bajaj refuse with his fixed smile and the unsmiling lawyer leave, banging the door. Bajaj smiled shyly at Agastya. With Srivastav, thought Agastya, a lawyer could never have banged the door. In the first place he could never have entered with such a request. A few evenings later, Agastya described the incident to Srivastav, who smiled in triumph. "Promotee! That's the problem of the promotee. People just don't give them the respect the post deserves."

Later in the week Agastya called on the District Judge also.

"Come at about five," said the Judge over the phone, "not for dinner, but for tea."

Agastya said, "Yes, sir." He was learning not to be surprised by Madna.

In front of the Judge's house was a garage of tin and canvas. The drawing room was dull-coloured and a little strange. It was bright and hot outside but the Judge had a tube-light on. From the sounds it seemed that a victim was trying to dissuade a murderer in the next room.

"I saw you a few weeks ago from my car," said the Judge, "near the Collectorate. You were rubbing your arm against a tree, and then smelling your arm and laughing." Nobody switched the fan on because, "I have a cold," said the Judge.

Agastya sat and sweated. They talked inanely for an hour, he lied dementedly. In the corner near the door stood a packed shoe-rack, above it a cracked mirror, beside it a noisy fridge. In the other corner a red plastic bucket. He's built that garage outside, said Agastya to himself, because he couldn't get his car into this room. Someone brought in karachi halwa. "Will you have warm water or cold water?" No, I'll have your piddle. The District Judge was a little deaf. Agastya had to yell out his lies. He was suddenly angry. If I was master of my time, he thought, I wouldn't have to waste it here.

"I'm retiring in a few months. I'll be very happy to get out of Madna. I miss my Belgaum," said the Judge. Agastya abruptly warmed a little to the old deaf man—so many people wrenched out of homes they never wanted to leave. "Will you take a little more halwa?" asked the Judge in a threatening tone, I'll leak the story to the *Dainik* if you do.

"Yes, thank you." The Judge's single remark about his homesickness had evaporated Agastya's irritation. Earlier the Judge had seemed a deaf and boring inmate of an insane house (the sounds from the next room now included occasional giggles), but now he seemed like Shankar or Agastya himself, just another person out of concord with the present. Everything fitted in, or seemed to. The invitation to tea (and not to dinner) was from one who loathed guests in a place he disliked. The mess of the drawing room indicated one who never invited people home and didn't care what they thought of him. In some ways the Judge was actually sulking, Agastya wanted to laugh.

When he said, "I'll take your leave, sir," (he had learnt a little officialese and quite enjoyed it), the District Judge got up, mumbling, "Yes, yes." Agastya wanted to pat him on the shoulder, console him, say, Don't sulk, boy, it is I who should be sulking at my age; then he saw the Judge's face from close and sensed that age was in no way connected with the intensity of a sense of dislocation.

"You must be bored in the evenings, Sen, you can always telephone me and talk to me over the phone, I'll try and dispel your boredom."

Two nights later, but the District Judge was in no way responsible, Agastya felt a fever creep up on him. About three in the morning, he had just dozed off—he woke up because the electricity had gone off. Without the fan the mosquitoes gorged deliriously. The room was absolutely dark, no light from the veranda. He wasn't sweating much because of the fever. He curled up foetally and licked his dry lips. The small of his back ached. He could have got up for a tablet but didn't have the will. He wanted to lie curled and accept, even encourage, the fever. The electricity returned. The veranda light again romanticized the room. The satiated mosquitoes were driven away. But the fan made him feel cold. He hid himself under a sheet. He could think of nothing. The mind is restless, Krishna. Where had he read that. He had read it but recently. He couldn't remember.

Vasant brought tea at six. "I have fever," said Agastya. Vasant looked at him with distaste, Well, don't give it to me. Digambar came at seven. Agastya sent him to the RDC's house with a note. Dr. MumbledName came at about eight.

He had a wonderful bedside manner. Agastya felt better just looking at him. He was small, squat and pink. What the hell are you doing in Madna? Agastya asked him silently. You should be making a fortune selling your arse to the Arabs in Bombay.

The doctor said, "Just a little viral fever, you mustn't worry. You'll be fine in two or three days. You mustn't feel that there is no adequate medical help in Madna, we're here to take care of you." Agastya was surprised: did his loneliness show on his face? Or perhaps the doctor said that to everybody, even to the Collector. It was just the kind of statement to irritate Srivastav tremendously—How can you take care of me when I have to take care of the district?—Srivastav would then laugh shrilly, through his nostrils.

"I'll look in again this evening, or tomorrow morning. Otherwise you can come to the clinic, if you like." He pointed to the prescription. His name, Agastya read, was Dr. Multani.

"Clinic? Aren't you from the Civil Hospital?"

"Oh, no, no, no," said the doctor, as though Agastya had asked him whether they could shit together. "I'm a private doctor." Multani smiled beatifically, "Joshi saab doesn't seem to trust government doctors. I've treated his family for years. I treat all the important people of Madna, Collector saab, SP saab, all the important people."

Later when Srivastav visited him he was to say, "If you weren't an IAS, Multani would never have come to your room."

Multani refused to accept any fee. "How can I expect fees from my good friends?"

When he was at the door Agastya remembered, "Oh, Doctor, I forgot to tell you another symptom, insomnia. I haven't slept for more than four hours a day in Madna, ever since I came here. Perhaps that could be connected?"

"Oh-ho, but why is that?" He returned to the bed. "What is preventing you from sleep?" Agastya marvelled at the concern on his face. Those Arabs don't know what they are missing.

"The heat, I think." As though I usually stay on top of Kanchanjanga. And, he wanted to add, my mind.

"Yes, this heat is very bad. But I hope you're not worrying about something, no problems or anything like that? You see, it's normally the mind that causes sleeplessness. I probably can't help with your problems if you have any, but you must sleep properly."

"No, no, my mind is fine." Agastya looked away, at Tamse's picture on the wall. What else could he say to a stranger.

Multani added something to the prescription. "If you sleep well, you'll get well even faster." He stood up, short and pink, but reassuring. "We must meet again, Sen saab, but unprofessionally. Most of my patients only remember me when they are ill. When you are OK, my family and I would be very happy if you come home and have dinner with us, no formality, just a family dinner." He smiled. "I always want to tell outsiders to Madna, especially those used to a different kind of place, that Madna is also nice, that you *can* make good friends here."

In the day a few dropped in to commiserate, perhaps to check if he was shamming. Joshi came first, with Lal, the Sub-Divisional Officer of Madna, a small jovial man; then Shankar, smelling of booze at ten in the morning (it must be last night's leftover stench, Agastya decided, not even Shankar could drink at ten).

Srivastav came in on his way to office, scowling, looking uneasy, even guilty. "You still haven't brought the sofa back into your room. Where will people sit? What did Multani say? Oh, viral fever. That's fine, I feared cholera. You're still boiling your water? You shift into my house after this, lots of room there. You'll eat good food and be more comfortable, you'll have company also." Vasant's children looked in, to giggle and scamper away.

Intermittently, over the next few days, he wondered how to evade Srivastav's offer. Staying at the Collector's would mean the end of his secret life. He wouldn't be able to smoke or evade office after lunch. The domesticity of Srivastav's house would be cloying when experienced in excess. He wouldn't be able to lie in bed for hours and stare at the ceiling, and wander around naked, talk to himself, fantasize without restraint. But direct refusal was impossible, and besides, would have to be accompanied with reasons. Perhaps Srivastav wouldn't mention the subject again, or maybe he would henceforth have to fall ill secretly, so that Srivastav wouldn't come to know, or he could sexually abuse the daughter (but the daughter looked highly unreliable)—he thus relapsed into fantasy.

The fever returned in the late afternoon, while Agastya was trying to read his English *Ramayana*. Srivastav had, before leaving that morning, eyed it in disgust, and shaken his head— imagine reading such a fat useless book, imagine wasting money on it, and luggage space, too. He put the book beside his pillow and returned to looking at the ceiling. A fever in the afternoon was less scary than at night. Suddenly he was laughing loudly in that silent, closed room. God, he was fucked— weak, feverish, aching, in a claustrophobic room, being ravaged by mosquitoes, with no electricity, with no sleep, in a place he disliked, totally alone, with a job that didn't interest him, in murderous weather, and now feeling madly sexually aroused. His stomach contracted with his laughter. He wanted to rebel. He said loudly, "I'm going to get well, shave my head, put on a jock strap, and jog my way out of here." His voice startled him. He didn't want to listen to any of his music, all his cassettes sickened him. When the electricity returned, he switched the radio on to the Hindi news read at slow speed. He had wondered for years why the news was ever read at slow speed. Now it suited his mood, one more act without explanation in the universe. Later the station played Tamil film music; he just left the radio on.

The antibiotic capsule was blue and yellow, and smelt like a stale-sweaty armpit, like a crowded Calcutta bus in summer. He wrote the name down in his diary, Ponomax, knowing that no one would believe that a capsule could smell like that. But no one would be interested either. How evil its contents must be, he thought, if, when cloaked in plastic, it stinks like this. Multani had asked him to try and not sleep in the afternoon ("Rest, but do not sleep"). When the fever slipped away he decided that being ill was not such a bad thing.

He laughed again, this time at his mercurial shifts in opinion. But illness *did* have its advantages. He didn't have to wash or bathe or brush his teeth or worry about the faint stench from his crotch ("rotting lizards and smegma," he had once thus described it to Madan) because no one was sharing his bed with him.

In a better mood, he switched off the radio and put on a cassette of Ella Fitzgerald singing Cole Porter, a present from Neera ("I don't like pop music, I can't follow it," he had said. She had rolled her eyes theatrically and said, "Ella Fitzgerald is *not* pop music, *please*"). Later he had liked the songs but had decided not to tell Neera. "I love Paris" came on. Her splendid voice warmed him. He felt vaguely deprived, he hadn't seen Paris, what a city it must be to have a song like this written about it. There was that song "Calcutta" too, but that was just a mindless army-type song, about whores in the war or something. He had never passionately wanted to go out of India (unlike Bhatia, he smiled), and he visualized Europe and America as madly expensive, strange, a series of minor misunderstandings with different kinds of people, a passage through clean beautiful places with faces looking through him. "I love Paris in the summer." He felt an upsurge of affection for Calcutta, and laughed, how Bengali, only Bengalis pined for Calcutta, stridently insisting that it had *soul*. Dhrubo had once said, "You'll like London very much. I think you should write to that lovely bugger, who loves us all, what's his name, Enoch Powell, introduce yourself as Nirad Chaudhuri's grandson, and grovel for an invitation." He had then switched to Bengali, "London is *nice*, bits of it are like a *washed* Calcutta, and all Bengalis will love it, being Anglophiles to their balls."

But certain places, thought Agastya, just *sounded* lovely, romantic, with a past. Calcutta did (and wasn't), Istanbul, Vienna, Hong Kong ("In Bangkok they even slice bananas with their cunts," Madan had breathed this information to him in their first week in college, after his fortnight's tour of South-East Asia with his parents, "then they offer the plate of sliced bananas to you, and you have to eat, otherwise they feel very hurt." "Who's they?" Agastya had wanted to know, thinking, maybe *everyone* in Bangkok behaved like that, bus conductors, chemists, ushers in a cinema hall, just *everyone*). Suddenly these names were no longer a Time-Life series, but palpable realities, fascinating only because unreachable. He had missed the experience of the world outside—what had that Thoreau said, that later I don't want to find out that I had not lived (but Thoreau was a little mad, and probably meant the exact opposite of what he, Agastya, wanted him to mean).

Vasant brought him tea, yawned, and asked him how he was. "I think I shall die by this evening."

Vasant sneered at him, "It's not so easy."

"Just boil everything. Not a single drop of oil. I'm supposed to eat only boiled food."

That evening Digambar brought him his first letter. "At last someone is writing to you, sir," he said. His father never used Raj Bhavan stationery for personal letters, but his handwriting was easily recognizable. He took letters like he took everything else, seriously.

My dear Ogu,

I am sorry for this delay, but I wanted time to compose my reply. I received your letter on the 4th, by the afternoon post. I read it immediately, and once again at night. I am unhappy at your unhappiness in Madna. You have not mentioned this specifically but it is palpable in every line of your letter.

At our last meeting I perhaps talked too much, but then I did feel I had a lot to say. I had suggested then that your job will provide an immense variety, and will give you glimpses of other situations and existences which might initially prove startling. Your dissatisfaction now seems to bear me out. I telephoned Pultu after reading your letter. He said that he had received the same impression from the letter that you had written him. He then, as usual, blamed both of us. Perhaps Pultu was correct when he, long ago, objected to my putting you in a boarding school. He said that a boy should always grow up at home. But he is so unpredictable that it was difficult to take him seriously.

But Ogu, remember that Madna is not an alien place. You must give it time. I think you will like your job eventually, but if you don't, think concretely of what you want to do instead, and change.

Your old Manik Kaka visited a few days ago, last Saturday, to be precise. He wants me to marry you off to his granddaughter. I told him that you were not contemplating marriage as yet, but he looked unconvinced. He took away your address. Do not be surprised therefore, if you hear from him on this subject. You wrote that you intend to take a break during the Puja. Will you come to Calcutta, or go to Delhi? Perhaps you could do both. Calcutta continues to be hot. Take care of yourself. Don't be despondent. Write regularly. I shall endeavour to be regular too.

With love, Baba.

Agastya read the letter again, with a half-smile on his face as he pictured his father writing it. In his months in Madna, well-written letters would always excite him, disturb him by bringing him other worlds and perspectives. He would get to hate casual letters, those in which not a single line contained a thought. For communication would become very important, and a letter one side of a conversation. He himself would take great care while writing, and preserve good letters, reread old ones, smiling at turns of phrase and recollections.

Multani had given him twelve sleeping pills in fancy packets of four each. They were called Somnorax and were made in

Ulhasnagar, near Bombay. There was a supine king on each packet, with hands beneath his head and eyes wide as chasms, and below him:

> —the innocent sleep,
> Sleep that knits up the ravell'd sleave of care,
> The death of each day's life, sore labour's bath,
> Balm of hurt minds, great nature's second course,
> Chief nourisher in life's feast,—
>
> Shakespeare, *Macbeth*

Agastya was moved as he had been by Tamse's painting; the packet was similarly so ridiculous as to be touching. Smiling, he put it into an envelope and addressed it to Dr. Upadhyay, his earlier head of department. "Dear Sir, Absurdity again, someone in Ulhasnagar has found some use for Eng. Lit.'s most famous insomniac. I thought you'd find this more interesting than L. H. Myers. Otherwise I move along, slowly, in second gear as it were..." He popped a pill almost with affection. But at eleven he was still fidgeting in bed, recalling that being unable to sleep after a sedative was what his father suffered. He felt unpleasantly older.

A plop, then a thump, behind the bathroom door. He hated closed doors. Perhaps a huge rat munching his soap and contemplating the plastic of the shampoo bottle. The sounds were repeated. He got up, warm more with tension than with fever, and switched on all the lights. His room looked so joyless. He picked up his white canvas shoe and checked it for inhabitants (one of his father's warnings). A flying rat, perhaps. Irritated at his nervousness he opened the door, almost simultaneously regretting his rashness. He groped for the light. Perhaps it's a scorpion, sitting on the switch. A flying scorpion, large and black, which settles on the back of your neck, and stays there. For ever. Not even twelve Somnoraxes then could get you a night's sleep. In the light at first there seemed nothing. Then he saw the large frog in the corner. He took a quick look around to see if there was anything else and then relaxed against the door.

How does one, he thought, get a frog out of the bathroom? The frog looked black-green and quite demure. Or is it OK to share one's bathroom with a frog? He couldn't decide, so he closed the door and went out to look for Vasant.

Vasant's entire family slept in the open. Their part of the compound looked like a relief camp after a riot; bed after bed amid chairs and pots and pans.

"Vasant. Vasant." He soon woke up everybody but Vasant. Three others got out of bed and shook Vasant awake. Maybe he stole some of my Somnoraxes, thought Agastya. "Will you come with me for a moment?" Much to his credit Vasant didn't ask any questions and followed, rubbing his eyes, rearranging his lungi, yawning.

Agastya showed him the frog. "There." The frog looked at complete rest, almost philosophic. "How do we push it out?" Vasant gave him a look. Agastya wilted. "You think it should remain there? But I don't want to share my bathroom with a frog...Isn't its skin poisonous?...A snake will follow it because snakes eat frogs don't they?...What d'you mean frogs bring luck..." But Vasant won. The frog stayed, off and on, for months. It was quite peaceful. Sometimes in those afternoons Agastya would shield himself behind the door and throw mugs of water at it. But it always moved only of its own volition, sometimes hopping into the room to look for a corner where it could immobilize itself into some amphibious nirvana. What a simple life the bastard leads, thought Agastya enviously, and after a few days gave it a name, Dadru.

Early next morning he sipped his tea on the veranda and watched the Ernakulam Express flash by on its way to Calcutta. Shankar emerged from his room, looking and smelling awful,

"Oh, Sen saab," and waddled towards him, gently fanning himself with a 100-rupee note. "For you." He leaned on the back of a chair, beckoned to Vasant, asked him for a tea, looked all around, exhaled heavily and said, "I was up all night, singing."

"Oh, I didn't hear you."

"Softly, controlled singing. Shiv has gone to Koltanga to get me my wife. He should have been back yesterday." He bent and breathed tunefully into Agastya's face, " 'The pearl has fallen from your nose-ring, my beloved.' Superb thumri, Sen saab, you have heard it?"

Agastya had, a lovely song. But Shankar never sang a song that did not ooze sexual innuendo. "Perhaps the falling of a pearl means the breaking of a hymen?"

"Chhee, chhee, chhee, Sen saab, Sen saab!" Shankar looked outraged and drunk. "What are you saying! It is a beautiful simple thought—the pearl has dropped from your nose-ring, my beloved. And I thought you could appreciate music." He sat down and slumped against his chair, occasionally shaking his head, ostensibly ravaged by Agastya's crudity. Suddenly he asked, "How's the fever?"

"No fever, yet. I'm still a little weak, though. There's a frog in my room." Shankar looked at him, red-eyed and uncomprehending. "It came in last night. It's still there, in the same corner of the bathroom. Vasant insists that a frog in the room is a good omen." Shankar yawned. Agastya couldn't believe the colour of his teeth. "How is Jagadamba? She said I'd be happy after August."

"But you mustn't be flippant about a goddess if you want her help. See, if the frog is going to bring you good luck you must at least first believe that it will. After all, everything around us," his forearm circled twice to encompass Vasant, the Circuit House and the sky, "is inexplicable, *fundamentally* inexplicable. What am I doing in Madna when I should be and want to be in Koltanga? I see it as a profoundly absurd question. You will say, because you have been posted here. But *why* should I have been posted here? There are engineers who are from Madna and who *want* to be posted to Madna and are willing to pay 30,000 rupees to the Minister for the transfer, and the Minister doesn't want more. *Then* what am I doing here. My reason cannot cope with this world, so I pray to Jagadamba and say, here, please, *you* arrange this world for me. Meanwhile I drink and sing. Similarly, how do you know that the frog is *not* a good omen? You will say, my *reason* says so. But the truer answer is simpler, that you have lived in the flats of Delhi and Calcutta and that a frog has never been in your bathroom before, so you don't know how to react to it, and *only* because it is the unexpected, you dislike it. A frog is a *good* animal, and wait and see, it'll eat up some of the mosquitoes in your room."

THEN THE rains came to Madna.

There had been a heaviness in the air for a few days. The electricity had gone off often. "It always does before the rains," Vasant had said wisely. He had sky-watched in the morning and announced oracularly, "It will rain today." One more hot afternoon, Agastya was naked in bed, lazily wondering if he had sunstroke. Suddenly a roar and a drumroll, as of a distant war. He took a few seconds to place the sound. Then he was off the bed, and fumbling with a lungi and kurta, and not being able to tie the lungi, and getting his head and arms stuck in the kurta, because of his haste. He rushed out. Outside there was nothing but rain.

The world turned monochromatic as the skies exploded. Cloud, building, tree, road, they all diffused into one blurred shade of slate. In minutes the gravel turned muddy, then bubbly. Vasant's children came racing round the corner, shrieking their ecstasy, naked and free. They writhed in the mud, gurgled, ran, shrieked, danced, infecting all those who saw them. The rhapsodizers were right, thought Agastya, there was something uplifting about the monsoon, and I don't mean the saris, ha, ha, as Vasant's wife, prematurely haggard with childbearing, came out to discourage her children. She had unexpectedly slim ankles and calves.

In the room the wooden ceiling began to leak at the corner,

every fourteen seconds an unsettling plop in the orange waste-basket. After a while Agastya found himself waiting for the next plop. He went out again. Madna was washed, the green on the trees was new. No dust, it gave one the illusion that one's eye-sight had improved. The rain had turned gentle and soothing. He opened his umbrella and went for a walk. His canvas shoes turned muddy in a dozen steps.

Some very unexpected women had wonderful ankles and calves, slim and blossoming up towards the knees, he remembered Vasant's wife. Mrs. Srivastav, he felt, would have stumps. The air of Madna smelt new, no excrement and exhaust smoke. Stepping carefully, he took fifteen minutes to reach the rail tracks. He wouldn't walk on those, people shat there all the time. He waited by the side of the level crossing and watched the trucks pass. The orange of the weakened sun glowed on the puddles, reminding him of a painting. He watched the rain pierce and attenuate the puffs of black exhaust smoke. Who-ever notices me, he thought, must think me insane, standing by a level crossing in the rain. Suddenly the crossing was down. The trucks began to queue, their drivers emerged for a piddle and a smoke, retying their lungis, scratching their thighs, turn-ing their faces up to the rain. He wondered, would the train be Madras to Delhi, or Hyderabad to Calcutta? If to Calcutta, he suddenly decided, then Jagadamba will be right, Dadru a good omen, I'll be happy, and if to Delhi, I shall be, well, just gener-ally fucked. He paused and added a postscript, for the rest of my life. He waited for minutes, smiling with the sudden ten-sion. It was a goods train, slow and heavy, with a few loafers at the mouths of the empty bogeys. The wheels were monstrous and wonderful, each one a killer. People were flopping down under them all the time. It would be a really quick way to go.

But it was nice, watching trains pass, as he moved down the tracks a little to pick some wild cannabis—yet somehow unset-tling too, the trains made him feel that the world was large and that it was moving, but without him. There were two tracks, one curved round the garages and seemed to disappear into the paan shop next to the church. That went to the thermal power station. The other one was really straight, it looked very businesslike, and at its end, seemed to touch the edge of the sky. Then he realized that he had seen these tracks from the bridge on that hot afternoon with Sathe. He looked away at the bridge in the distance, with its struggling toy cars and trucks, and patient pedestrians. He felt strange, without reason, at these linkages in perspective—I was there looking here, and now it is the opposite, this thought made him feel odd.

He began walking back, intermittently shifting his umbrella to feel the drops on his head. He moved off the road for the trucks. A wonderfully pretty tribal woman passed, tall and rigid. They exist, he shrieked silently, outside arty films about tribal exploitation and agrarian reform, they exist. She had large cracked feet and veined forearms. He wished that women were like this, instead of being soft-white-thighed and demanding of tenderness after coitus, and smiled wickedly at his adjectival phrases. He stopped, waited for the tribal's whiff. There was just a hint of sweat and tobacco.

From a distance he saw Bhatia turning in at the Rest House. He waved. Bhatia stopped. Shiv was walking towards him with a woman. She turned out to be Shankar's wife. Middle-aged and shabby, with lips that wouldn't fully hide her canines, she looked predatory.

"Lovely rain," said Agastya. Shiv winked in reply.

"Hello, Mandy, great rain."

"Yes, this place has at least cooled. But now the mosquitoes will really come out. I tried to get you on the phone but I think the lines are down." They began walking away from the Rest House. "There's this other Assistant Conservator of Forest I'm quite friendly with, called Gandhi. Did I ever tell you about him? He asked us to have tea with him. You too, he's heard about you and would like to meet you. A nice guy, simple, from Alwar. His wife's really sexy, too rural, though. Wish I could fuck her."

"What *do* bachelors do for sex in Madna, Mandy, apart from masturbating like adolescents?"

"I asked Sathe that once. He laughed as usual and said, 'Why do you think I go so often to Hyderabad.' You know, I think Gandhi's a very nice guy, but I wouldn't've dreamed of being friends with him in Delhi. I would've said, small-towner."

The remark irritated Agastya. He wanted, absurdly, to defend a city. "That's hardly the fault of Delhi. You and I weren't friends either, in college." He looked at Bhatia with dislike. He was wearing another T-shirt, it said, "Herpes is Forever." Again that unsettling feeling, that Bhatia was a funny-mirror image of himself.

"I don't want to go through life moving from place to place just making acquaintances. After a certain age I don't think anyone can make new *friends*. If you're in a job like mine you just stay away from old friends for long, they live a life you think you want to live, and when you next meet, everything is the same only on the surface, because you don't talk about the things that really matter. Communication is impossible and pointless, because you have to part again."

Just what is happening to him? wondered Agastya. They reached the gates of the Forest Colony. "I just want to show you something," said Bhatia, and took Agastya to the drain beside the road. There was a big light-yellow turd half-submerged in some green slime. "You wanted to show me this?"

"Look, I've been a year here in Madna and whenever, *whenever* I've crossed this place, I've found shit in this green muck. I pass this place almost four times a day, OK, and there's always a turd or two, as though this green scum wasn't filthy enough by itself. Someone shits in this mess *regularly*, I can't understand it, why can't he shit in a field or something? It's got so bad that whenever I pass this place I just have to check and see, maybe he hasn't shat today. But I'm always wrong. I'm going to photograph this one day and send it for a New Year card—Greetings from Madna. And I shall come here one morning and catch the shitter and ask him why he's doing this to me."

"Well, I've got a frog in my room. He came one of those nights when I was ill and he has decided to stay."

"Oh, frogs are OK." They entered the Forest Colony, Agastya wondering again why frogs were OK.

"Mandy, your Forest Colony is *nice*." The Forest Department had been in Madna long before the factories had invaded the district and wiped out vast chunks of what the Department was supposed to protect; it was a universal story. The foresters, as they were half-contemptuously called by the Revenue men, had built themselves a colony amid trees and hyena gangs, even the occasional tiger. That was a mere few decades ago; Madna's landscape was changing fast. The colony was a great expanse, demarcated by barbed wire that had long since decayed or been stolen, with once-pretty gates of bamboo that now showed that no one cared.

"These gates must've been lovely," said Agastya. Now both were off their hinges and had been propped against the posts. The bamboo had decayed and broken.

"Like your *Gazetteer*," said Bhatia, "government stuff, so made for neglect."

The drive was long and winding. The rains had given it a seductive romantic air, it looked like the walk for a couple whose relationship would never sour. Single-storey houses with false ceilings that ensured coolness and lots of living-space for rats, and as many trees as the earth would allow. It didn't look like a forest, for human hands had done the planting, but the trees still attracted monkeys and urchins who stoned them, and the occasional fox, who was a useful ally to the mothers who wanted to deter their children from exploring after sundown.

"Mandy, this really is a nice place. It's so quiet and different from the rest of the town. Must be a wonderful place for these kids to play around in."

One boy ran up to them, sturdy and sweaty, "Bhatia Uncle, Shalu says there's a snake under that tree."

"Don't go near it," said Bhatia. "They're planning a picnic for next Sunday. Everyone's going, Srivastav Uncle and Kumar Uncle also." The boy ran off to join his equally sweaty friends under a tree.

"My boss's son," said Bhatia. "It's disgusting, his energy. He runs around outside even on May afternoons. Just runs around pointlessly."

The sun emerged, meek and beaten, but the world shone. "Isn't it amazing, what weather can do to your mind?" said Agastya. "Was Sathe joking when he said he goes for his fucks to Hyderabad?"

"Probably not. He can't go to the whores of Madna because it'd soon be all over town. And they'd probably be as sexy as those whores some of us used to go to from hostel, remember? About as turning-on as trying to get a job. And we can't go whoring here, anyway, we'll probably meet a Range Forest Officer or naib tehsildar tying up his pants. Then they'll know you're hungry, and will provide you tribal women and booze when you go on tour." That didn't sound bad at all to Agastya. "It's sick," continued Bhatia, "they do do it for some officers on tour, but these officers are debauchees, and just don't care about their reputation or the job." Agastya thought fleetingly of Shankar. "If they're posted reasonably far from their bosses and their families, they even keep a tribal woman at home, for sex and scrubbing the floors—That's the Rest House. I share a suite of two rooms with Gandhi and his wife. Accommodation is one big problem in the colony." They turned towards the forest Rest House. Bhatia said "Good evening, sir" to a passer-by, then asked, "August, I've been meaning to ask you.

Sathe told me your mother was Goanese, I didn't know that in college."

"Well, my mother wore saris and ate fish like a Bengali," said Agastya lightly. He had no desire to reveal anything of himself to Bhatia. "My parents were married for about seventeen years, long enough for my father to really colonize her. I was born very late." His aunts had been triumphant, his father had said, when his mother had not conceived—this is what comes of trying to mix Goanese and Bengali blood. "I hardly remember my mother." He smiled to deprive his reminiscences of any hint of sorrow. "In my blood runs a little feni, or something like that, but that's about all." Bhatia kept quiet. He looked a little embarrassed.

Gandhi was quiet and stocky, self-possessed. Agastya liked him on sight. He had large peaceful eyes, much easier to respond to than Bhatia's, which were yellow-filmed and restless. His full name turned out to be Mohandas Gandhi. "Now why does the name sound familiar?" smiled Agastya.

"It's very embarrassing. I have an elder sister, my parents named her Indira. They do not care for confusing families and generations." They laughed.

Agastya smiled when he met Gandhi's wife, Rohini, for Bhatia's description of her came back to him. It had been very accurate. They sat in the veranda of the two-room cottage and watched the children play in the mud and their promenading mothers shriek their disapproval. A breeze began, tentatively. "I would never have believed that Madna could have a place as nice as this forest colony." Agastya stopped then, out of an obscure sense of shame. Somehow it seemed a terribly graceless thing to say. Over the months shame was to recur often, in the oddest circumstances, and for all kinds of reasons. "I must thank you, Mohan, for inviting me."

"Please don't mention it. We should've met earlier, but my wife hasn't been well." Mohan's voice also dropped a decibel at "my wife"; Agastya was distracted for a moment by a vision of the two writhing in bed. Later Bhatia told him that "my wife hasn't been well" was Mohan's euphemism for the early weeks of pregnancy. "Gandhi finds it embarrassing, see, to say that his wife is pregnant; because he thinks it's as good as saying, we've been fucking."

They chatted desultorily, and smelt pakoras frying. Mohan displayed none of Bhatia's rancour against the universe. He seemed not happy, but reasonably at peace, satisfied with his lot; a room in Madna, a bathroom that he shared with a colleague, a sexy and patient wife-cook, a surly servant, low voltage ("the tube-light works well only after eleven or so"), 1,800 a month, in a few weeks a posting to some black hole called Pirtana ("I'm hoping electricity gets there before we do"), a healthy body (but a mere well of blood for a million mosquitoes), a love for Sarat Chandra in translation ("Agastya, Agastya is a nice name, you must've read the original in Bengali, but I really loved a book of his called *The Man Without Character*"), and a future that would be a predictable extension of the present.

"I haven't seen any translations of Sarat Chandra in English." But you haven't seen many things, Agastya reminded himself humbly.

"Yes. I found it in Uttarkashi, in the College Library where I was teaching. A horrible translation, in a horrible place."

"I've been to Uttarkashi, we stopped there when we were on a college trek." Uttarkashi had been as dry as the skin of their guide; they had spent hours looking for illicit booze; curious yokels and ugly dhabas beside a silver-white Ganga. Agastya couldn't imagine teaching in an Uttarkashi college; no one could impart or imbibe wisdom there. "Did you stay there long?"

"Two years I taught there. It was horrible," Mohan smiled shyly. "The college was supposed to be postgraduate level, but the labs weren't even worth Intermediate. Everything broken or stolen. There were two old goondas claiming to be Principal, each had younger goondas as bodyguards. I used to wonder which of them was drawing the Principal's salary. When they met in the corridor they used to curse each other quite colour-fully, and most students would rush out of class to hear them. Even I learnt a few new curses by listening to them." Mohan turned in his chair a little to ensure that his wife was out of earshot. "Once one called the other, you cock of a diseased rat. Another time one of them said, your mother uses her turds as a dildo. The rival Principals of a college, remember. Actually, to be fair to Uttarkashi, the college wasn't worse than many other colleges elsewhere. For instance, it could easily be mistaken for a college in Alwar." They laughed.

The servant served tea surlily. Rohini joined them finally, shy and sexy. "These mithais are from the local shop here," said Mohan, "but you'd think they were made in Calcutta."

"Isn't that Gopalan?" asked Bhatia. "I think he's coming this way." Rohini scurried in to plead with the servant to arrange for another chair. They all got up as Gopalan came up. He was a Divisional Forest Officer and Bhatia's boss. Bhatia introduced Agastya.

"Hello," said Gopalan, "it's good to see another bearded government servant." They laughed. He seemed a pleasant in-formal man, and joined them without any excessive fuss.

"We're planning a picnic next Sunday, to Gorapak. Srivastav saab and Kumar saab have said yes. The wives are going to relax and the husbands are going to cook. I wanted to call Sathe also, but Srivastav saab negatived quite vehemently. He wants only officers and their families. You'll come of course, Sen?"

AN OBSCURE local holiday. "You come home for the day," ordered Srivastav. "Both lunch and dinner, you must eat well. Do you play bridge? You do? Good. We'll go to the Club in the afternoon, the SP's coming too. There's also a cultural programme there in the evening."

"Special lunch for you, August, now that you are well," smiled Mrs. Srivastav. "Fish for the Bengali."

The children raced around the room, screaming, "Piss for the Bungaali."

Kumar came in at about twelve, in another tight shirt. The bugger needs a bra, thought Agastya. "Hello, Sen," beamed Kumar. "I called you for dinner once, didn't I? Very sorry I forgot. But my house is in a mess until my wife returns, what to do."

At lunch Mrs. Srivastav said, "Arrey, August, you eat fish like a real Bengali. Look, his plate is so clean."

"A real Bengali," repeated the daughter, and leered at Agastya.

"Looks like your mother's side couldn't corrupt you," said Kumar.

Only Srivastav seemed to feel that the topic might irritate Agastya. He said, "Dhiraj, you are going for the foresters' picnic, aren't you?"

"Of course. Should be fun. And the district officers can get together."

"But these foresters," scowled Srivastav, because he was now talking about office matters, "seem to suffer from some inferiority complex. Why can't they gracefully accept the fact that their job and position is far less important than that of a Collector, or," he added, mindful of those present, "an SP? They always invite us for their functions and get-togethers, as though we have all the time for these things." He looked at Agastya. "You see in the picnic, how they behave. They will try and behave like equals, especially the wives." The picnic began to sound nightmarish.

"Oh, those forest wives. But August already has a few good friends among the foresters," slipped in Mrs. Srivastav.

Agastya wondered if he could slap her, and said, "I hope this weather lasts till then."

"Ah, yes, the rains. It should rain more, so that we don't face any scarcity of drinking water later in the year. But if it rains too much then that river will flood." Srivastav smiled with tired complacence (a Collector's job is monumental, but Government has been wise in picking the right man for the post—that kind of smile). "When you're Assistant Collector somewhere, Sen, you'll realize how, in a position of responsibility, you have to view things differently, in a practical way. Festivals, for instance, are not a time for relaxation and enjoyment at all." He half-closed his eyes and shook his head, "What we have to worry about then is law and order and the possibility of communal riot. The entire perspective changes. And we don't think of the rains as something romantic, oh, no." Oh Srivastav saab, said Agastya silently, oh, nobler than Atlas, the burden of the world rests on you.

Everyone watched Kumar help himself to a second bowl of dessert. Mrs. Srivastav even smiled. The daughter said, "Kumar Uncle will explode, then we can have him for dinner."

While her parents shrieked at her Kumar said, "Club in the afternoon, no? The others will be there?"

"Yes. Joshi telephoned to say they'd be there at two. Sen plays bridge, he says."

"Oh, very good. Bridge is very important for your career, bhai. You partner Srivastav saab and play well, see what a good Confidential Report he gives you." Only he laughed. "We must get the Club going again, Ravi."

"Yes, but not with Antony's methods." Srivastav neighed a laugh of disapproval, and said to Agastya, "That Antony. He gave the Club a licence for boozing. I cancelled that as soon as I took over. The Club is for families, not for lonely drunkards. In Antony's time no lady went there. It was not even safe! His own wife used to work and stay in Hyderabad, so Antony never bothered about other wives. The Club became a bar in a Hindi movie I tell you. Drunks reeling around and singing." He looked at Kumar. "We have to encourage bridge and other games and cultural evenings. A district is generally not an exciting place. If officers' families cannot go to the Club, where can they go?"

Kumar sprawled on the divan after lunch and belched gently. The daughter made no effort to hide her giggles. "So Kumar saab, when is Kum Kum returning," asked Mrs. Srivastav, "not that you seem to miss her?"

Kumar seemed to be mentally preparing himself for a siesta. "I'm going in Dussehra, spend two or three days at home and then return with her."

Srivastav came in from the corridor, jangling the car keys. "Shame on you, Dhiraj. What an example you set for Sen, sleeping after lunch. He has strange habits already, prefers the Rest House to staying with us."

Kumar struggled upright with effort. "He probably has his reasons. Maybe he has already managed to contact a female BDO who he..." Kumar winked. The others laughed. Srivastav said, "That rascal newspaper. Those buggers at the Secretariat are taking so long to reply to my request. But Joshi says that the *Dainik* is going to publish a retraction and an apology."

"Good, that is good. But these fellows should be even more punished for behaving like this." The three of them moved out to the car. Mrs. Srivastav and the children would join them in the evening for the music. "How's your wife, Sen?" asked Kumar.

For a second Agastya wondered what to trump up. "I'm not married yet, sir. I would've been married long ago, but my father disapproves of her, she's Muslim."

"You aren't married? I heard you were, that your wife is dying of cancer in England."

"Me? My wife? No, sir, there's some confusion. That's my cousin."

Srivastav drove, and Kumar sat in front. Agastya watched the backs of their heads. Kumar's was round, on a two-tier neck, Srivastav was balding. Suddenly he had had enough of Madna. He leaned forward and asked, "Sir, may I go to Delhi for a few days during the Puja?"

"OK," said Srivastav, "if you take Casual Leave you can go for a maximum of ten days. Those are the rules."

"We'll go together, Sen," decided Kumar, turning his head to its maximum of an inch. Agastya sat back, as relaxed as though he had just climaxed. The small of his back throbbed faintly, as with the passing of tension.

"Oof, this road," whined Srivastav, "these PWD engineers will never widen it." Ahead of them was the mess of traffic characteristic of the roads of Madna.

"But today the problem seems to be that truck," said Kumar, "look at the way the bastard has parked it." The truck squatted like a bully on half the road that was in any case far too narrow for the number of vehicles on it.

Srivastav got out of the car. "Come, Dhiraj, we'll go and teach that truck driver some road sense."

On the road Srivastav and Kumar looked a little odd, Agastya realized that he had never seen them walking. They looked like ordinary citizens who hadn't got a rickshaw, one merely much fatter than the other. They passed cycles and scooters and cars, and faces ugly with exasperation. A scooter grazed a car, the quarrel attracted a crowd that simultaneously increased the chaos and distracted the sufferers. But it felt good, thought Agastya, to walk through stalled traffic, it made one believe that one was somehow gaining on the world, and had been wise, in a practical kind of way. The truck was abandoned. "Where's the driver?" Srivastav scowled at a few passers-by.

The driver was finally located at a dhaba on the roadside, cross-legged on a charpai, chatting with a gang over tea.

"That truck is yours?"

A small crowd of the usual idlers had formed around Srivastav and Kumar, for both were used to command, and years of it had tinged each syllable they spoke with a sense of their own importance; an attitude that was mesmeric.

"Yes." He looked like any other truck driver, aggressive, in lungi and kurta, permanent blood-tainted eyes, dedicated to being mean and tough.

"You've parked in a very wrong place."

The driver looked at his friends and said, "Toughies, these ones."

"Not toughies, you are talking to the Collector and the SP of Madna." The driver left his tea, put on his slippers (and in his hurry, Agastya was very happy to note, right foot in left slipper), and ran clumsily towards the truck. His friends stood up. The truck moved off at great speed. "Good," said Kumar, "shall also catch the bastard for speeding on a narrow road." Then, while Agastya stood there impressed, Srivastav and Kumar lectured the disinterested assembly on the absence of road sense in Madna, and even, in general, in India. In Delhi or Calcutta, thought Agastya, this reaction from a truck driver is unimaginable, unless some constables beat him up and take away his money, his licence and his truck.

Back in the car, with the road in its customary chaos, Srivastav decided to continue the lecture, "You see, Sen, the power and the responsibility of the job?" He was like a king in ancient India, smiled Agastya, walking incognito among his subjects, revealing his identity to do good and punish evil, the bugger.

He had seen the Club before, on his late-night run. Then the moonlight had attenuated its ugliness. An old building, a long veranda with arches for entrance, yellow peeling walls, the electric wires painted a dark grey. Five tables set for bridge in the central hall, three games in progress. Joshi approached them, beaming servility. He was dummy at one table. "I expected more people," scowled Srivastav, stalking around. He liked crowds to greet him, even in a club. Some players scowled back their disapproval of the disturbance. They were from the Electricity Board and the thermal power station, some were businessmen—all beyond Srivastav's squeeze.

Kumar and Srivastav ganged up at one table against Agastya and an unknown. In minutes Agastya identified him as the Club type. In the halcyon days of Antony's reign he would have been integral to what Srivastav had called a scene from a Hindi film, drunkenly reeling and singing songs. Tall and thin, sleeves rolled up to just below the elbow, handlebar moustache, paan-ravaged teeth, small dead eyes. He was too used to the Club, and probably drank at home before spending his hours there. He would be ready for anything, bridge, tambola, gossip, billiards, table-tennis, badminton. He didn't "sir" either Srivastav or Kumar, so he was immune too.

"What convention?" he asked Agastya. "Goren, if that's OK with you." Srivastav and Kumar played Strong Club, and very badly. Kumar turned out to be a natural goof, and Srivastav a bad partner. In a few rounds Agastya was bored and Srivastav was controlling his rancour. He couldn't shriek at an SP, and Agastya felt sorry for any subordinate who ever partnered him.

He daydreamed about his Delhi visit in snatches, and he and his partner sailed two rubbers ahead.

The afternoon was intolerable. Srivastav's mood worsened. Their post-mortems after every game lengthened and grew more rubbishy. At last the partner was called away to help with the arrangements for the music. But Srivastav hadn't had enough. He summoned Joshi from the other table. "We want another partner for Sen. You join us." Fortunately Kumar refused to play, pleading exhaustion. Silent and grim they all went outside for tea.

Agastya was enraged at himself, for agreeing to the afternoon, for being in Madna, for a job that compelled him to be polite to Srivastav and his wife, for being in the job he was, for not having planned his life with intelligence, for having dared to believe that he was adaptable enough to any job and circumstance, for not knowing how to change either, for wasting a life. He watched the chairs being arranged in rows and the tables being hidden by bedsheets, and couldn't believe his future.

Outside, Srivastav and Kumar became officious and soon began bossing the preparations. In a short while they were quite enjoying themselves, arguing about the arrangement of the chairs, the carpets on the stage, the angle of the lights. Agastya wandered behind them, hating himself.

All moods are transient; thus his slowly improved. And besides, it felt good just to be outdoors, to be detached from the bustle under a pale-with-exhaustion monsoon sky. The memory of the bridge and his intense self-loathing were gradually eroded by the inadvertent humour of the confusion around him. He watched Kumar direct a peon to place a huge drum of drinking water on a side table. The table collapsed with a quiet crack. The drum slid off, in slow motion as it were, and landed with a great dull thump on a rug. The water gurgled out happily and endlessly, like some secret source of a river. Kumar shouted at the peon, hoping thereby to convince everyone that the fault was entirely his. The peon heard not a word, went to the edge of the cricket field, took off his wet pants, spread them on the grass to dry, and returned to the bustle in his long underwear. But this was a dress Srivastav would not allow ("Idiot, you want us to see your knees, hayn?"); he asked the peon to go away and not return until his pants dried. The peon wandered away towards the food. Suddenly the world seemed infinitely comic to Agastya, and he smiled at himself—Well, your mood has certainly improved.

He sat down on the edge of one of the last rows, away from Srivastav, Kumar, and their bossing. That men are at some time masters of their fates now seemed a seductive untruth, at best a half-truth. At what moments in time? he wondered, looking at Srivastav's mercurial profile (how could he gesticulate and scowl so much, his eyebrows were like worms in one's shit, real wrigglers) and speculating whether those cheeks beside the triangular sideburns would be soft if well-boiled and stewed. He felt that one saw significant moments in time only retrospectively, glittering mocking jewels of *past* time, that left in their wake only regret and consequent desolation, the first cause of a series of atonements and attempts at reparation. Most men, like him, chose in ignorance, and fretted in an uncongenial world, and learnt to accept and compromise, with or without grace, or slipped into despair. The human reason seemed so inadequate that afternoon. Agastya wanted his reason to show him the implications of an act before he committed it. I want to know in the present, he said to himself, I want my reason, and not even my intuition, but my reason, to tell me, here, you are now master of your time to come, act accordingly. But it seemed incapable of directing significant action. Once he had believed that it was good to be rational, but now it seemed that his reason could never answer the overwhelming questions, or grasp the special providence in the fall of a sparrow. One way out was to turn like Shankar to the extra-terrestrial, to

Jagadamba, and like Vasant to believe in that special providence, even in the arrival of a frog; another was to slink away from having to think, to wish to be that pair of ragged claws that had so tantalized him in his college years, scuttling over the floors of silent seas.

He saw Kumar looking his way, as though about to call him to help them increase the confusion. He didn't wish to return to his room, as he had done earlier. He went back into the Club and wandered around. Only the billiards room had people in it. He played for a while. The standard, like that of the bridge, was very good—thus he continued to be surprised by Madna.

People had begun to move in when he came out. The stage looked nice in the lights, a most unlikely outcome of the chaos of the late-afternoon preparations. There was a set of drums, two electric guitars, a harmonium, a set of bongos and, he was astounded to see, a small Moog synthesizer. Kumar was near the stage, fat and happy, surrounded by a group laughing at everything he said. Maybe, Agastya hoped, he wasn't saying anything funny, and they were laughing at *him*. Most people seemed to be dressed in their best ("looking like raw sex," he remembered Madan's phrase); the evening was apparently a great social occasion for the families of the officials of Madna. Later, when he had seen a little more, he would modify his opinion; *all* excursions—to the market, the bank, to someone's house, for a movie—were great social occasions in their arid lives; they dressed up and powdered their faces for all of them. He saw Ahmed before Ahmed saw him and ducked behind a woman, startling her not a little. The kids were all shiny and clean, and weren't allowed to touch their hair. They all looked a little dazed; some had Snoopy and Superman on their chests. The women seemed to have walked off the showcase of an emporium—one could window-shop by just looking around. His mood improved even more when he saw Sathe, Bhatia and

Mohan (Rohini couldn't come, he said, she was not well) in an inconspicuous corner, looking cynical.

"Idiot," said Sathe, pointing at Srivastav. Agastya began laughing helplessly, the afternoon draining out of him. "He's messed up the Club. Once it was a good place to have a drink, play billiards and waste time. But he's cancelled the licence— did he tell you that? He wants all the *families* to come to the Club and chat with him or something. I can't understand it, this move of his to keep what he calls the non-officials out of the Club. It's like the Raj, natives not allowed." Sathe laughed loudly, attracting a few glances. "And in this case the natives of Madna not allowed. You officers are birds of passage, anyway, Srivastav will leave in a year and a half. *We* are the ones who stay here with the Club. If we want to drink here we should be allowed to. Anyway, Antony used to drink with us. Antony was OK, no pretensions to maintain Srivastav's silly dignity of office. What does he think the Club is, anyway, a kind of haven of refuge from the wild town? If his family wants entertainment, why can't they hit the town? No, the Collector mustn't be seen too often at movie houses and restaurants, he would be compromising his position." The peon who had taken off his trousers to dry had put them on again and was now carrying around a tray of soft drinks. Bhatia finished one glass in a single gulp and picked up a second.

"Don't be so angry with Madna, Mandy," said Mohan.

"Tell me, August, do you know anything about the bureaucracy?"

"No."

"What is this British India chip on the shoulder that people like Srivastav have? That's what he's trying to do, isn't it, with the Club, it's going to be a place where officials who think they've worked their cocks off for the district in the day can go and relax in the evenings, away from the heat and dust, and meet other officials with similar delusions. They should leave

Madna alone, to grow as it wants to, and that includes the Club. Always interfering. I used to like the Club once." Just then, a flurry of sycophants at the gate. Mrs. Srivastav had arrived.

Hers was the only car allowed into the Club. "As though her arse would break if she walked from the gate," said Sathe. Joshi and Co. trotted beside the car, like modern out-of-condition versions of some eighteenth-century runners (Agastya smiled at the image) accompanying a queen's palanquin. Mrs. Srivastav was in a pink and gold sari—looked rich enough to be Kanchipuram silk. Under the light he again noticed the black bra beneath the pink blouse. With her make-up her face looked a pale equivalent of a Kathakali mask. The kids followed, the boy whining. His new T-shirt lied and said, "I am a Good Boy."

"How can anyone dress up like this for a club like this? She must've waited all week for this moment," said Sathe. He *was* in an awful mood. "That bastard told Gopalan, Sathe shouldn't be called for the picnic. But notice at the picnic how the wives behave. Gorapak's a lovely place, incidentally, especially the temple and the place where the sadhu stays."

A man began cracking jokes over the microphone. Everyone moved towards the chairs. The musicians took their places. One guitarist cracked a few other jokes against the joke-cracker. Fittingly a child began to wail. "Do we have to see this rubbish?" asked Agastya.

"It won't be rubbishy, not all of it. I've heard them before, the standard's quite good," said Sathe. "The choice of songs will be rubbishy, probably aimed at the highest common factor of this crowd. They'll have to include Hindi film songs to please people like Mrs. Srivastav."

Then even Mohan said, "I think we should go somewhere and get drunk. I hardly get an opportunity like this."

What decided them was Kumar's coming their way. "I can't

take that rhino," said Bhatia, and they all moved towards Sathe's Maruti.

"Oh," Agastya remembered in time, "I was supposed to have dinner with the Srivastavs. Will you wait a little? I'll go and say I have a headache or something, that I'm going to my room." The lights had dimmed, and the first song had begun, a Hindi film disco song. The crooner seemed lost in his gyrations and leers, but sang well. Agastya noticed then that the men and women were sitting separately, separated by a central aisle and a few vacant chairs.

Later Sathe tried to explain, "That's been the tradition in Madna. In other small towns too. The men sit apart from the women and children. I really don't know why. Maybe because no one wants to see a man and a woman enjoying anything together."

"But why?" Agastya said. "They aren't fucking in public. This happens even at movies?"

"No, not at movies, not anywhere where they have to buy tickets."

Srivastav was in the front row with Kumar. Kumar's eyes were closed. He was jerking his head to the beat. Agastya moved up to them bent, as through a low tunnel, and began, "Sir, I've got a headache—"

"Where have you been all evening? The SP and I have been looking for you."

He explained, with the appropriate face of a victim of migraine, and felt vaguely guilty when he said, "Please excuse me from dinner, sir, I'll," a half-smile, "come tomorrow to finish my share." Srivastav was too engrossed to argue much. He scowled at him, and then scowled for a while at the stage.

They moved out in the Maruti stealthily, as though guilty of some vile act. Suddenly Sathe asked, "So how's the *Bhagavad*?"

"Yes, I've been reading it. Most of it is very remote. And the bits that aren't—'But if one merely sees the diversity of things, with their divisions and limitations, then one has impure knowledge. And that steadiness whereby a fool does not surrender laziness, fear, self-pity, depression and lust, is indeed a steadiness of darkness'—they make me feel small and foul, like a used-pantie-sniffer, you know, a case out of Krafft-Ebing."

Sathe laughed and laughed and nearly collided with a rickshaw. "I really feel religion only begins to make sense when our cocks have ceased to stand." That was the mood for the whole evening, boisterous and blasphemous, against officialdom, their own situations, the world.

Agastya returned to his room late, to find a letter from Dhrubo that Digambar had slipped under his door.

Renu, that Punjaban I was fucking, has gone to America [So began the letter, without date or hello. But that was Dhrubo's style, abrupt and ashamed of emotion]. She said that was the only way to break our relationship, some First World stance she's adopted before she's even got there—"independence" and "discovery of self," she even used those phrases before she left. Beneath her tears she seemed to half-enjoy everything. Quite probable that creating a mess made her feel mature and adult. "Look, everybody, please, I'm breaking a relationship, so I'm adult, aren't I, it's not the same thing as eating an ice-cream, is it?" Her behaviour has made me feel like a child-molester. Come to Delhi for Puja. If you go to Calcutta the Governor will take your arse for treating the bureaucracy like your pants, letting them down. The police are being very unreasonable with the dope peddlers here. So get some if you can. Dhrubo.

Not a word about Madna. Another universe; yet he had been part of it just two months ago; now disturbing in its complete difference. Agastya wandered around the room, letter in hand, trying to fit Sathe and Renu the breaker of relationships, Mohan and Dhrubo, into some coherent whole. He didn't want the friends of the different stages of his life to meet. Their encounter would almost be between facets of himself, face to face. Whatever would they say to each other? he wondered, and then immediately answered himself. Don't be melodramatic, if they met they would converse ordinarily, about politics and the weather, and India's débâcle in the last cricket Test; and it would be unnecessary for them to discuss anything less ephemeral; because no one reveals himself more completely to others than to himself—that is, if he reveals himself at all. The frog was squatting near his shoes. "Hello, Dadru." We are all cocoons, thought Agastya, with only our own worries and concerns; Dhrubo should have sensed that I'd be as interested in his world, more or less, as he had been in mine.

PICNIC day. They were to convene at the Collector's house at six thirty and leave by seven for Gorapak. Gopalan had wisely decided that venue; for the venue itself would ensure that everyone was on time. If they had decided to meet at any other place Srivastav himself would have been late—his position would have demanded it. Agastya set his alarm for five because he wanted to exercise that day, too.

He had become almost manic about his exercise. The day seemed much more awful than usual if he skipped it. His exercise was something he felt he must hold on to, some anchor of stability, without it the day would slip into anarchy. And only after its completion was he ready for anything, for any acts of illogic and unreason. But without it, he felt black, almost as though the push-ups and the panting were a duty, a good deed for the day.

After he had begun he even enjoyed it, and his distracting conversations with himself during it ("At thirty-five I don't want to look like Srivastav or Kumar." "But why would you want to look twenty when you actually *are* thirty-five? That'll be deception, won't it?" "Well, I also exercise because then I feel nice, and that kind of self-confidence helps a lot in sex." "And just where is that sex in Madna?" "I exercise because then I can eat like mad." "Yes, that's true. You *do* eat like mad. Like a Bengali, as Madan says." "Women don't seem to exercise. They just diet. The soft option." "Neera doesn't even diet."); and after he had finished, he glowed with an unreasonable sense of accomplishment. He glowed even more on the day of the picnic because he managed to exercise *and* set out for the Collector's by six fifteen; the glow of a mission accomplished, a target achieved.

"Begin each day by telling yourself: today I shall be meeting with interference, ingratitude, insolence, disloyalty, ill-will, and selfishness—all of them due to the offenders' ignorance of what is good or evil." Fun, of a kind, to remember Marcus in the morning, on the morning, as he walked along beside the citizens of Madna who were out for their stroll. Marcus's sorrow was always soothing, the world never seemed as bad for Agastya as it always seemed to have been for Marcus. "At day's first light have in readiness, against disinclination to leave your bed, the thought that 'I am rising for the work of man.'" That would never get anyone out of bed, thought Agastya, as he passed a group of children chatting and shitting by the roadside, no one, not even Menon. "Is this the purpose of my creation, to lie here under the blankets and keep myself warm?" From Menon that would have sounded like turds falling in a commode, but from Marcus it sounded, and he smiled, it sounded *cute*.

The compound of the Collector's house seemed still asleep. The gloom of the banyans was undisturbed, even by the snake-catchers in loincloths, lean and sharp-eyed, moving as silently as wraiths from shadow to shadow. A monkey masturbated unselfconsciously on the lowest branch of a pipal. The air was still and fresh. Agastya wanted to inhale it deeply, so he began to run, lightly and easily, startling the monkey into stopping to leap on to a higher branch. He felt vital, running on a road through what could have been primeval forest, silent but for the sounds of the forest, the cawing of birds and the rustle of animals perfectly at home. He stopped for breath before he reached the front of the house.

He was the first to arrive. Mrs. Srivastav was having tea on the lawn, looking sleepy, bad-tempered and sexier than usual. "How fresh you look," she said disapprovingly. Srivastav emerged, looking faintly shy in his jeans and tight T-shirt. He also needs a bra, thought Agastya, maybe he should wear his wife's black ones (and he remembered, in school Dhrubo had said, of fat and loose-skinned Prashant, "When he squats to shit he has to flick his boobs over his shoulder, otherwise his nipples tickle his balls"). The children were behind him, whining with sleep. Then the picnickers all came in together, the roar of their vehicles annihilating the last of the morning's peace—Bajaj and his wife, a fat reticent woman, Kumar in jeans, kurta and goggles, the Forest gang, a few of whom Agastya hadn't seen before. All at once the lawn seemed full of shrieking excited children and wives smiling politely while sizing one another up. The wives looked like TV announcers very late at night—cosmetics and smiles couldn't quite hide their desire for sleep. Mohan seemed to be torn between looking after his wife and planning with Bhatia and Agastya when to smoke the first joint. Srivastav, Kumar, Bajaj and Gopalan fussed, bossed over the peons who were packing the enormous amounts of food into the jeeps, and argued the formation of the motorcade. "Food, women, children and peons first," so two cars and two jeeps left, with giggles, breathless shrieks, shrill laughter, and disregarded injunctions to the children.

A car and two jeeps left for the men. Suddenly all wanted to be macho and rugged and travel by jeep. The false protests of Agastya, Bhatia and Mohan were ignored and they were pushed into the car, along with two others from the Forest Development Corporation. Their names were Reddy and Prabhakar. Prabhakar had a few opinions to voice. "This is not a real picnic, this is like officers going on tour. I am very disappointed. We were supposed to cook ourselves, then why are we taking so many peons with us? These people . . ." but words failed him, or his vocabulary did.

Agastya's first journey out of the town, and into the district; his education continued. They took half an hour to struggle through the town. They passed Gandhi Hall, he remembered the Integration Meeting of his first day. The rod was still there, pushing up the statue's arse. "No one could believe that this was a statue of Gandhi," he said.

"What else do you expect in Madna?" snorted Bhatia.

"Well, it's hardly the fault of the town or the district," Agastya replied, remembering that earlier he had similarly defended Delhi against some accusation of Bhatia, but he couldn't recall when.

"But it *is* the fault of the town. If they had any respect for themselves, or for the Mahatma, they wouldn't allow that statue to stand." Bhatia's retort silenced Agastya. He was usually amazed by and faintly contemptuous of Bhatia, and would normally have disbelieved that a remark from him could make him think. But what Bhatia had said was true, that no one in Madna really cared for what the town looked like. That a statue like that was *also* an insult to their taste never troubled them. At that Integration Meeting that hooligan had said that the installation of the statue had angered everyone, but that it had been too late, which was really saying that no one had been angered enough. But of course apathy was not singular to Madna, he thought, it was just that in a bigger place, Delhi or Calcutta, he would never really have *seen* the statue. If he had, it would have been only in passing, through a bus window, or out of the corner of his eye; a dim perception that his senses had just been assaulted by a travesty in stone; but the assault would have had nothing of the immediacy that it had had in Madna. He wondered why, the reason wasn't that his eyes had less to see in Madna—then he realized, that in Delhi and Calcutta his mind was much more busy with *trivia*, talking rubbish with someone, filled with impatience to get somewhere in time for something, trying to remember to say something to someone when they next met. There, his mind was just too cluttered up for him to notice anything.

Two and a half hours to Gorapak. Throughout the journey Bhatia, with the lip-licking obsession of an addict, whispered that they should smoke a joint in the car itself, and balls to these two Forest Corporation types. Agastya was game for anything, but Mohan dissuaded them both, all in whispers and mumbled code.

Fifty years ago one end of the town of Madna had been the walls of its fort. Beyond the gate had been a dry moat (now used for dumping the town's refuse), a few furlongs of cleared land and then the miles of forest, teeming with its sporadically disturbed life. But the population had long since burst the confines of the fort, and spread out like a flood to the edges of the forest, and then attacked the forest itself—another universal story. Through this East Gate the elephants of a tribal king had once moved in single file; now the Ambassador squatted at the mouth of the gate and honked its impatience at two embroiled rickshaws, while a truck, swaying drunkenly under its overload of timber, tried to edge past. The paanwala in a niche of the gate was surrounded by loafers eyeing the Ambassador without curiosity. Roadside vegetable and fish shops, sugarcane juice stalls being set up at seven thirty in the morning. From the gate shacks seemed to stretch to the horizon, where glinted the silver of the river. The shitting children got up to thump the car as it passed, as if egging it on at a rally.

The car could only speed up near the forest. "Young teak trees," said Bhatia to Agastya, "another few decades before they mature, all planted by the Forest Department." The trees were thin and gaunt, the forest scraggy.

"One of the biggest areas for teak smuggling in India," said Reddy from the front seat, "very difficult for us."

"These are our plantations," said Mohan, perhaps sensing

Agastya's disappointment at the density of the forest, "the really great teak forests are in the south, in the sub-division of Rameri, but even they are now being denuded. That's a largely tribal area, and lots of Naxalites there, trying to organize the tribals to rebel against exploitation."

They passed small villages, the bus-stops for the district buses, bridges being constructed across small nalas. The car disturbed groups of villagers relaxing on the road in the shade of huge old trees, sitting, sprawling, scrambling up when they heard the horn. "Do you think they sit on the road because there are less chances of snakes?" asked Agastya. No one seemed to know. "Do you think they *prefer* sitting on the road to sitting on grass or packed earth? Obviously *all* of them don't, because then there'd just be many more of them on the road." Again, no one seemed to know. No one seemed much interested either. The others all looked a little dopey, perhaps the effect of yet one more long car journey on too-familiar a road. Then the answer struck Agastya. "Of course, it's not the road that attracts them, it's the shade." The discovery excited him, and he spent much of the rest of the journey trying to unravel the minor mysteries of rural India. "Why are some roofs flat and some sloping?" "Are they digging those trenches to prevent accidental forest fires from spreading?" "That strange shoot, bush, tree, whatever it is, is that bamboo?"

To the last question Mohan said, in chaste Hindi, "You make such a fetching virtue of the display of your ignorance." After which Agastya quietened down.

They crossed the river just before they sighted the temple of Gorapak. The river lay huge and swollen, but smooth, like a dormant beast. Its bridge was, however, quite an arsebreaker.

Agastya was surprised by the Shiv temple of Gorapak. (Mohan said, later the same day, in a mildly irritated voice, "Why're you always being *surprised* by Madna, by this temple, by that statue of Gandhi in the town, by the beauty of the Forest Colony? How did you come to the district with such low, or such distorted expectations?")

The sign of the Archaeological Survey of India outside the temple compound announced that the temple was a protected monument, and that its desecration was punishable with imprisonment and a variety of fines. "I wish it would tell us who built it and when," said Agastya.

"Arrey, August, you seem to have a very *intellectual* attitude to temples," smiled Mrs. Srivastav. Some wives giggled.

The gang of four was bossing the removal of the provisions to the Forest Rest House. Mrs. Bajaj was asking everyone, "Should we see the temple before or after lunch?" No one was answering her.

"I don't think we should hang around here," said Bhatia, "We might be asked to help."

"I think we should smoke first," said Mohan, "then everything will be in perspective." They slipped in through the gate.

The temple was on a hillock, overlooking the now-majestic, distended river. A descent of 400 feet on uneven rock steps which the villagers of Gorapak traversed with the grace and speed of felines. Almost ten in the morning, under the sun and the faint breeze the water a vast ribbed sheet of gold and glass; a few boats, still as a painting, birds on sandbanks; from below the moist sucking sound of water lapping on a shore, and murmurs of conversation, from the village women who were washing and carrying away water. "Eyeing the women, hayn?" gurgled Kumar from behind.

The entire gang had come in. They were being guided by a priest, talking feverishly to Srivastav. Bajaj was being pestered by a swarm of beggar children. They would pull at his forearm skin, whimper for alms, then smile at one another slyly. The priest guided the gang around the ruins in the compound. The compound wasn't big or crowded, though the chant from within the temple was quite loud; about the size of four tennis courts, and just a few stragglers, mostly tribals.

Kumar and Agastya moved towards the group, Agastya wondering just where Bhatia and Mohan were smoking. Kumar asked, "When is your Police Attachment starting?"

"In about ten days' time, sir."

"Good, we'll have some fun then." He pointed at the temple walls. "Have you seen all that? Sexy sculptures, just couples having sex in impossible positions." The serrated walls of the temple were covered with intricately carved figures of different sizes, all of whom seemed to be having a good time.

"If you'll excuse me, sir."

"Where are you going?" Agastya lifted up his little finger. "Or have the sculptures excited you—need a little hand practice?" Kumar laughed till his goggles slipped down his nose.

Agastya finally located Bhatia and Mohan behind the ruins of a wall. "Where have you been?" asked Bhatia, handing him the smoke. Mohan was sitting on a granite block, head against the wall, smiling cynically. "August," he said, and then laughed, "what a name, August. I'll call you Agastya."

Mohan looked at him with something like contempt. "Agastya, your ignorance cannot be *more* shocking than Mandy's. It has to, just has to be less."

Bhatia said, "Mohan becomes a Hindu fanatic when he is stoned. In Alwar apparently he and his rustic gang smoked chilums and then asked one another tough questions on Hindu myth, whoever lost seems to have given his arse to the others."

Mohan laughed the laugh of the stoned—lazy and uncontrollable. "Tell me, Agastya," he said slowly and mockingly, intending to irritate, "you child of the Christians, what is that?" He pointed to the ruin of a magnificently sculpted wall opposite them, but these carvings were of both animals and men.

Agastya saw a fish, a tortoise, a few men. "Oh, the ten

incarnations of Vishnu." He settled down beside Mohan to look at the wall with more attention. "These are very well done."

"And Bhatia said that if we had the full wall, it would've shown a great bestial orgy. He said it seriously." Mohan smiled soothingly at Bhatia, "How does it feel to be a national shame?"

"Let's smoke a last one," said Bhatia, "before we join that horde."

"This temple was built in the second half of the tenth century, I read a second plaque down there somewhere. By Dhanga of the Chandela dynasty. You, of course, have never heard the name before." Mohan apparently was going to sneer at each of them in turn.

"Oh, Khajuraho." If Agastya hadn't been high he would have been more excited. "The Chandelas built Khajuraho. No wonder." He looked at the opposite wall with even more interest.

"I'm very impressed," Mohan patted his shoulder. "Of all these idiots at the picnic not a single one will know this. Some like Kumar will be titillated by these wet-dream women. Some like Rohini, who thinks sex is dirty, will think all this is OK because it's a temple. Didn't Mrs. Srivastav tell you just now, you have an *intellectual* attitude to temples. For her very little could be more disgusting. What she meant was, how *dare* you come to a temple and *think*? She couldn't say so because she is an inarticulate cow."

"But sexy," said Bhatia. "I think we should go down, otherwise someone like Kumar will come up."

"Have you ever seen how women behave in front of a shivaling?" asked Mohan.

"No." Agastya didn't particularly want to move.

"Oh, it's like a blue film. So what if the cock is Shiv's, it's still a cock. Come, let's go."

The others were at the mouth of the temple, taking off shoes and slippers. "Pity I'm wearing good shoes," said Bhatia, "otherwise would've stolen a better pair." The chant was much louder, but still melodious, "Great Shiv, I bow to thee." Kumar winked at him, then came up and breathed, "Was it satisfying?"

A corridor led into a biggish room where sat about a dozen devotees, singing. Their voices boomed. The priest seemed to be tonguing the ear of the Collector, perhaps enacting something from the walls, hoped Agastya. He felt the walls with his fingers, the life that had been created out of cold stone. There was a tube-light in the innermost sanctum directly above the black stone phallus of Shiv. There the wives came into their own.

They took turns to gently smear the shivaling with sandalwood paste, sprinkle water and flowers over it, prostrate and pray before it, suffocate it with incense, kiss their fingers after touching it. Agastya found the scene extraordinarily kinky. Kumar beside him was breathing a little heavily.

But Agastya was not conscious of any blasphemy. Religion was with him a remote concern, and with his father it had never descended from the metaphysical. One cannot prove the intrinsic superiority of any one religion, his father had loftily said to his brothers and sisters when they had asked him, conspiratorially, to get his wife to convert—I remain Hindu and she Catholic because we were born such and see no reason for change. Yet he had wanted his son to be a Hindu, for which his arguments had seemed sophistic. He had said that it would make the least demands on his time. "You can think and do what you like and still remain a Hindu." Consequently Agastya had rarely been to a temple, and when he had stood in front of any idol, it had only been Durga, and the occasion always the autumn Puja—a boy, and later an adolescent, in the tow of his aunts in Calcutta, with everyone in new clothes, inhaling an air heavy more with festival than with religion, ready for magic shows and all-night open-air movies.

His Pultukaku had had, as usual, original objections to his

elder brother's marriage with a Goan. "Your children will culturally be mongrels. The past makes us what we are, you will deprive them of coherence." But no one ever listened to or bothered with him. Over the years he had objected to a million family decisions, but his stance on Agastya had not changed. "You are an absurd combination, a boarding-school-English-literature education and an obscure name from Hindu myth. Change your name officially, please, to any of those ridiculous alternatives that your friends have always given you."

Kumar pulled at Agastya's sleeve. They went out. "I always go with my wife whenever she goes to a Shiv temple. She thinks I'm very holy," and Kumar exploded into laughter, goggles down his nose, one eye closed against the sun. "And everyone comes to Gorapak, even the British Collectors did."

A man in a hat came up to them. He said "Good morning, sir," to Kumar and shook hands with Agastya. "I'm Dubey, the Assistant Conservator of Forests here at Gorapak." He turned to Kumar, "The snacks are ready, sir, at the Rest House." Later, Agastya found out that he was wearing a hat not to avoid sunstroke, but to hide his shaven head, because his father had died a few days ago.

Dubey had been driving the peons hard at the Rest House, setting up a camp fire in the yard. Before they began cooking they sat down for breakfast on the lawn, and ate and drank, in order, some fried dal, grapes, lukewarm colas, very sweet tea, parathas stuffed with potatoes, curd, omelettes, mangoes and fried rice. Agastya was too stoned to refuse anything. After this chaotic meal everyone felt too lazy and too sick to cook lunch. Srivastav said, "We magnanimously allow the wives to direct the peons what to cook for lunch," and laughed shrilly. So everyone else also laughed. The wives moved away towards the fire to boss and argue. Mohan sent his wife with them ("It doesn't look nice, Rohini, if you and I stay together while the other wives work"), then pulled Bhatia and Agastya away for another joint. But while they were walking away Gopalan yelled for Bhatia.

"Bastard," muttered Bhatia and went off. When they returned he was with Gopalan near the wives. Mohan went to join Rohini. Everyone else seemed somnolent in easy chairs, except Gopalan's son Ashok, who was running around with a cricket bat and ball, looking for someone to play with. He rushed up to Agastya.

"OK," said Agastya, "but I'll bat first."

The boy giggled with excitement because at last someone was talking his language. "No, I'll bat first."

"Then fuck off," smiled Agastya.

"OK you bat first," said the boy, and rushed off to get the wickets. He preferred bowling in the heat, it seemed, to not playing at all.

They put up the wickets in the drive outside the gate. Dust and no shade. "No hitting," said the boy, "if you hit you're out." Agastya patted ball after ball back to the boy. Soon even the boy lost his energy. "Now let me bat."

"But I'm not out yet."

"No, now it's my turn to bat." The boy was about to cry.

"OK one last ball," said Agastya. The boy scampered off to his bowling run. Agastya hit the ball to the moon, watched it parabola over the trees. "Lost ball," he smiled, and thought, now at least the fucker will cry, now at least I shall tear this universe, hear it scream.

"I've brought many balls with me. I'll just get another one." The boy ran off, jumping occasionally. "You wait, huh, no running away." Agastya swung the bat hard at the wicket, but neither broke.

Bhatia appeared. "They want you to help cut onions. It's pretty good fun, to be stoned and cut onions."

The boy returned running, his face flushed with heat and joy. "I have to go and cook," said Agastya. But he wanted most to destroy the boy's energy, his joy.

The boy's face crumpled. "But you have to give me my batting."

"Here, Bhatia Uncle will do that. Mandy, just break this fucker. Remember, he is your boss's son."

There was much frolic and laughter around the fire. Everyone was there. Sweat coursed in rivulets through the make-up of the wives. He was aroused by the sweat patches under Rohini's arms. Bitch, he said silently, for being inaccessible. "Arrey, Sen, where have you been? Join us," shrilled Srivastav. The men were on a white sheet, cross-legged, with knives and onions.

"He was very moved by the sculpture on the temple walls," winked Kumar. Everyone shrieked.

He sat down, cross-legged. Gopalan threw a knife and four onions at him. "Start crying." Everyone laughed. He put his finger against the knife edge and pushed down. A short sharp pain. He watched the blood well up and smear the onion. His blood looked false, he had expected it to be thicker and more maroon.

Srivastav was the first to notice. "Tch, you've cut yourself." He sounded more irritated than concerned.

"I'll just go and wash it." He walked away.

Extra beds had been dragged into one room of the Rest House so that the children could sleep together. A peon squatted at the door, trying to hide his bidi. In the bathroom Agastya unzipped his trousers and touched the tip of his penis with his bloodied finger. But he felt nothing. The mirror blurred his face—he looked distorted, faintly comic.

That evening he wrote to his father.

Dear Baba,

I'm sorry but what you read into my last letter was

true. I just can't get used to the job and the place. I'm wasting my time here, and not enjoying the wasting. That can be a sickening feeling. I'm taking a ten-day break during Puja but I'll go to Delhi because of one or two things. I think I shall also meet Tonic. Could you phone him or write him a letter, because if you don't tell him he'll never believe me, that I might take up the job he offered. I'm sorry. With love, Ogu.

PS Write back to Delhi.

THE POLICE Attachment began with a weekend with Kumar at Mariagarh in the sub-division of Rameri. Kumar went to Mariagarh ostensibly to inspect its police station. Agastya accompanied him to see how he did it.

So his second journey into the district, but this time at dusk, to the hyperboles of love of Urdu ghazals from the car stereo. Kumar sighed with ease and luxury and took out his tin of paan masala. He shovelled four spoonfuls into his mouth and offered the tin to Agastya. "Here." Agastya took some. Kumar smiled. "I thought you'd refuse. Your addictions would be too English-type and refined for paan masala."

Kumar scratched his armpit and looked out at the miles of paddy. "So what did you think of our picnic?"

"Nice, sir."

"But throughout that tambola session in the afternoon you looked dead bored."

"I was, sir."

Kumar laughed, jiggling his breasts.

The car quickened as it slipped past a village. "Can't you smell the paddy?" asked Kumar.

Oh, thought Agastya, so that's paddy, and fleetingly wondered why paddy sounded so frivolous, like a pet name, or a college-christening for an originally sober name, Padmanabh perhaps, or Padmaja. "Yes, sir."

"You know, Sen, as you grow older in the service, you will

realize that these are the only real consolations of the job, this sitting in a fast smooth car, on a smooth road (the engineers made lakhs for themselves off this road, by the way), at twilight, none of those horrible town smells that we always get in Madna, just the lights of an occasional village, and these fields of paddy."

"Sir."

"All else is illusion, bhai, maya." Kumar laughed again. "But your job is different from mine. I am a policeman, we just smell the sweat of criminals for thirty years."

"But someone, sir, I forget who, has said, that *everything* is maya except the feeling of completion at the ejaculation of semen and since this feeling itself is so transient it shows how ephemeral the whole world is." He had made that up; he wanted to encourage Kumar to talk dirty. Then he decided to legitimize the fiction. "If I remember correctly, sir, it's the opening verse of the *Kamasutra.*"

"Do you want to see a blue film this evening?"

"Yes, sir."

The car slowed down and stopped behind some trucks at a level crossing. Now a gaining dark, a few lights at the crossing. No moon, just a faint sheen on the miles of paddy, in the twilight the whistle of the approaching train. Kumar and Agastya got out to piddle.

To the patter of their urine Kumar said, "They should have a mini-video for a car. So much long-distance travel, that's another thing you'll have to get used to. I frankly tell everyone that if you like a lot of travelling by road, you are a good administrator. Three-quarters of your work seems travelling, bhai—these districts are so big, the divisions, the states, the bloody country is so big."

The train hooted as it thundered by. Lights on in the bogeys, silhouettes of a myriad heads, flashes of other lives. They stood among the truckers and watched the train. Kumar said,

"What's this rumour I heard that you're not at all interested in your training?"

"Rumour, sir?"

"I heard, bhai, I don't remember from where, that you sometimes don't go to office at all, and you never return to the office after lunch."

"Oh no sir, that's not true." In the dark Kumar shrugged a well-that's-your-problem in reply. By the time the level crossing was opened, the SP's driver had edged past the trucks and was off, the orange light winking like a huge firefly.

Kumar reached behind him for the wireless. "Hello, Mariagarh, Sugar Peter here, Sugar Peter calling, hello." Lots of static in reply. Kumar grimaced and switched off. "When it's working those buggers are not at their posts."

"Sugar Peter?"

"For SP, Superintendent of Police."

"Oh, why not Sierra Papa?"

The light from an approaching jeep lit up Kumar's puzzled face. "But why not Sugar Peter?"

Because it sounds obscene, said Agastya silently. Ever since the picnic and the letter to his father, though they seemed to have nothing to do with the change, he had begun to feel emptier than usual. He had begun to stone more. Earlier he had lain in bed and speculated, reached what had seemed profound conclusions, that loneliness was a petty and private thing, that the human reason was inadequate—now all that seemed puerile and dull, the desultory cogitations of a healthy mind. Now he seemed to have ceased to think and observe the world around him. When he woke up he hardly heard the sounds of the morning. On some afternoons he couldn't leave the bed even to roll a smoke. At night the insomnia remained, unvanquished by Multani's Somnoraxes. But now it was no longer an irritant. It had become just a part of the fact of being alive, to watch the surreal glow of the tube-light till three or four in the morning, to toss and turn, to mess the sheets with semen, to hear the frog flop from one corner to another. He had begun to masturbate more, but more mechanically. That he didn't enjoy it did not worry him. Nothing worried him. He met the same people and continued the rounds, but without his mind. He bothered no more to analyse himself. He would gaze for minutes at the nick on his finger that he had given himself at the picnic without seeing it. Sometimes he would press the scar with his thumbnail to relive the pain.

The meditations of the authors of the *Gita* and Marcus Aurelius were far away, and sometimes even false. For he came to believe that whoever could have made the effort to write down all those things could not have felt them with any intensity. Yet he had loved those lines once. "O, the consolation of being able to thrust aside and cast into oblivion every tiresome intrusive impression, and in a trice be utterly at peace." Now he felt that those were far too many words to use to express any genuine longing for emptiness. "In the dark night of my soul I feel desolation. In my self-pity I see not the way of righteousness." "But many-branched and endless are the thoughts of the man who lacks determination." And that was really all, he felt. The mind is restless, Krishna.

At the Club that afternoon, with Srivastav and Kumar, at the bridge and at the music, his future had bothered him, briefly, but darkly. But now he couldn't see his future at all, but that wasn't unnerving either; it was merely one more fact. Sometimes he would lie in bed and remember Prashant, his schoolfriend who had been perfectly ordinary and likeable, but who had opted out, one June afternoon five years ago, by stepping into the path of a truck, to be minced into the melting tar of the VIP Road, leaving behind only a note saying that he was sorry—an apology, but no explanation. Yet looking for that kind of a cessation was also too much effort.

He had never had any ambition, perhaps because he had

never before been unhappy. Now he was surprised by the memory of those earlier desires of what he felt had been his innocence—to choose colours for the bogeys of trains; such wishes had always been frivolous, now they became blasphemous. For life had suddenly become a black and serious business, with a tantalizing, painfully elusive, definite but clichéd, goal, how to crush the restlessness in his mind. That is why he began to feel that his experience of Madna was wasted time, the seconds ticked away as he saw his unhappiness etched even in the stains on the wall. That men at some time are masters of their fates was now no longer merely a famous quotation. The idea haunted him, continually taunting him to confront it, but his mind responded only dully, in slow ineffective spasms. He did not know whether he should resign himself to his world, and to the rhythm that, living as we do, is imposed upon us, or whether he should believe in the mere words of an ancient Hindu poem, which held that action was better than inaction. But he found all this impossible to explain to anyone, there was no one in Madna to whom he could say this, and no one elsewhere either. No one would be really interested, and the others would not understand.

From the bed he would look down at the carpet, watch two ants meet and converse, and say to himself, I want to lie in the winter sun on the roof of the house in Delhi, or that decaying mansion in Behala, smoke, read a little, listen to a little music, have sex with someone, anyone, who would not exist before and after the act, and work only so I can do all the rest. Then he would return his eyes to the ceiling without seeing the patterns in the wood. He had always wanted to be alone by choice, but in Madna he was lonely, there was a vast difference. The novelty of Madna had aroused his mind, but now no more. He didn't feel rewarded, only deprived, time was running out. And now and then even that didn't matter. Sometimes he looked back on his experience of Madna with wonder and faint self-contempt; how could his mind have been so alive to these new impressions?

Now he didn't even long for his earlier megalopolitan life, paradoxically he missed nothing. He felt no contempt for the world around him, Srivastav and his family, Menon, Kumar; only disinterest, a disinterest also in his father and Dhrubo and that world which came to him through letters and the radio, which he sensed when he saw the trains pass. He had written to his father that he wanted to change jobs but he didn't really want to—that had merely been a gesture, of the rage of despair imprisoned by impotence. He wanted nothing, it seemed—only a peace, but that was too pompous a word.

"That's the road to Jompanna," said Kumar suddenly, pushing a fat forearm into the darkness, "and to Marihandi, where Avery was killed by the tiger." He turned to Agastya suspiciously, "You know the story, no?"

"Yes, sir." He didn't know the story, but had no wish to hear Kumar's voice.

"So sad, no, what a way to go."

Kumar and Agastya reached the Mariagarh Rest House at about eight. The Rest House was on an artificial hillock. "This place caused a scandal a few years ago," said Kumar as the car stopped at a porch which was built like a smaller Gateway of India. "Some years ago the Government sanctioned the Madna River Dam Project. Crores and crores. The first thing the engineers did after siphoning off their own lakhs was to build this Rest House. Tomorrow morning you'll see it properly, looks like an expensive whorehouse from a Hindi film, the kind the villain hangs around in. Then a change of government, the project was shelved. Now just the whorehouse remains."

Their arrival galvanized the Rest House. Lights came on in the grounds sloping away from them. Shadowy figures brought chairs out to the veranda. The Rest House was one-storeyed, but hidden green lights lit up on the roof a Taj Mahal dome.

Subordinate policemen waited rigidly, with chests and paunches out, to be commanded. Someone had already left a video and two bottles of whisky for the Superintendent.

"We should sit outside, but the mosquitoes." Kumar turned to a shadow and ordered, with a chuckle, "We want to sit out. Get rid of these mosquitoes, will you." Someone lit incense, someone sprayed the entire Rest House with Flit, a constable humbly offered the Superintendent a tube of mosquito-repellent cream. Kumar set up his recorder in the veranda and played more ghazals. "Do you understand chaste Urdu, Sen?"

"No, sir, barely."

"Oh-ho, then it's pointless. You're missing such fine poetry I tell you. Such subtle complex love poetry. Kya yaar, Sen, you're really an English type. I'll try and explain some of these lines, but they're quite untranslatable."

From the veranda the necklace-lights outlining the large lawn below reminded Agastya of Diwali. The shape looked familiar. "Oh," said Agastya, "have the engineers built that lawn in the shape of India?"

Kumar laughed. "A Gateway of India porch, and a Taj Mahal dome. There's a Konarak wheel on one wall inside, but somebody broke a spoke, and no one is sanctioning repairs. And a small replica of the Char Minar between drawing room and dining space. Just three soots in the entire Rest House, but God knows how much they spent. This entire whorehouse was designed by a bastard of an Executive Engineer called Tamse, you haven't met him yet, I think." A shadow came up and whispered something. Kumar turned to Agastya, "Chicken or mutton for dinner?" then to the shadow, "Both." The shadow moved off. Kumar said to its back, "Is the ice clean? Otherwise we'll do without it," then to Agastya, "Soda is safer, no? With the rains we can't trust the water."

"Will soda be available here?"

"You're the guest of the police, bhai. The police can do anything." Silence while they accustomed themselves to the night sounds, the stars, the insects, the lights of the village in the near distance. "In government, you'll realize this over the years, Sen, there's nothing such as absolute honesty, there are only degrees of dishonesty. All officers are more or less dishonest—some are like our engineers, they get away with lakhs, some are like me, who won't say no when someone gives them a video for the weekend, others are subtler, they won't pay for the daily trunk call to Hyderabad to talk to their wives and children. Only degrees of dishonesty. But, of course, honesty does not mean efficiency."

Agastya wished that Kumar would shut up, so that he could unwind in the silence and darkness, and listen to the voice from the recorder sing of love and lamentation. The sodas arrived, but so did Menon, in a jeep that devastated the quiet of the night. A courtesy call, in the dark he didn't look so pink and enthusiastic. "Have a drink," said Kumar, but Menon refused and talked shop instead, and left soon, after which Kumar cursed him. "Clean and pink bastard. Now he'll tell the entire district that Kumar is making Sen drink with him. Wait and see, in a week Srivastav will ask you about this." Then the two of them began to drink. "When my wife is in Madna I come here more often, to drink and watch some hot films. The Inspector at the police station here is good in these matters and hopeless at his job." Kumar stopped to exclaim in ecstasy over a line of a ghazal. "Wah-wah-wahwahwahwah. Did you follow that line?

> Marriage would be an unholy act
> For I would then soil you with my palms."

Kumar wagged his head in rapture until the song finished. "When're you getting married, Sen?"

"Not for a while." He had forgotten which story he had fabricated for Kumar.

"You should get married young. Then in the district at least the problems of loneliness and sex are solved."

He had heard that before, but he couldn't remember where. By dinner they were pleasantly drunk. Inside, opposite the Konarak wheel, one entire wall was covered by a monstrous blow-up of the Eastern Himalayas, bright blue and white. "Oh, that's Kanchanjanga," said Agastya, "the view from Darjeeling." Suddenly the days of school returned with a rush, innocence before innocence, licking their lips at the Nepalese girls in their unbelievably tight jeans near the bus-stand, but steering clear of the Tibetan toughs ("They even exercise their balls," Prashant would insist, "strange secret exercises, you could crack your toes if you kick them in the balls"), but wheedling with them to teach them the guitar, in their last two years being rooked by them while buying their marijuana, drinking their chhang with them and trying to like its taste; long jogs on the mountain roads, passing Tibetan nymphets singing Hindi film songs in unrecognizable accents, waking up at an unearthly hour at least once a summer to accompany enthusiastic relatives to see the sunrise over Tiger Hill, getting stoned by the roadside to watch the undulating miles of tea, and always on the horizon this same Kanchanjanga. Agastya was again mocked by the glittering jewels of past time.

"That Tamse bastard," said Kumar, absent-mindedly engulfing bunches of grapes, "wanted to squeeze all of India into this Rest House, as though the Prime Minister spends every weekend here and needs to be reminded of national integration."

They waded through dinner. Kumar said, "You've got leave for Puja, no? Good, we'll go together. Have to go to Kanpur, but will go via Delhi, that is best. Friday's a holiday, see, so we'll leave Thursday afternoon. We'll go air-conditioned sleeper, what d'you say?"

That night they watched hard porn till three. The constables set up the video opposite the bed in Kumar's room, blocking part of a monstrous blow-up of the temples of Rameshwaram. There were a few fat grey four-inch insects in the room. Kumar found one beside his pillow. But the insects seemed quite docile, and didn't object to being swept out. Ants were eating into the corpse of a lizard near the bathroom door. "That Tamse bastard," said Kumar, in cream kurta-pyjama, checking cupboard and bed for other living things, "all his fault. He didn't want wire mesh on the windows, d'you know why, because of that Gandhi quotation from *Young India*, it's written outside somewhere—that my windows should not be stuffed and cultures of all lands should blow around me freely. Tamse's mind *is* like that. So cultures of all lands means mosquitoes and huge grey bugs. But equally possible that some Junior Engineer pocketed the money sanctioned for the wire mesh and then spread this story about Tamse. But the story fits in with this Rest House, doesn't it?"

Kumar remained adamant about finishing the booze while watching the films. They settled down in bed, with mosquito-repellent cream on their skins and incense in the air. Kumar was giggling with alcohol and the promise of titillation. The first shot of the first film showed a thin American black man with painted lips and white bikini, gyrating. He was cajoled into stripping by five white girls, demented with lust. They all licked their lips and one another until the black, with horrendous coyness, displayed his penis. Then the girls got to work. "See, see," squeaked Kumar, trembling with adolescent excitement, "lucky black bastard..." Throughout the ogling he shifted in bed and intermittently muttered, "...this kind of thing never happens in India...Indian girls are too inhibited ...bloody shame..."

THEN AT last the passage to Delhi. But it would be so fugitive, thought Agastya, it would provide no repose, would instead only salt his restlessness. A mere ten-day interlude, and one and a half days would go in the travelling. And he knew that in Delhi, because his mind would not be disciplined, he would be haunted by the images of Madna. While arguing with Pultukaku about where to plant the tulips, he would be thinking that next week this time I shall be exercising in the Rest House room while Digambar waits outside. While watching the planes land at Delhi airport with Madan, stoned at one in the morning, he would think, next week this time, I shall be in bed at the Rest House, eyes wide with insomnia, scratching the mosquito bites, waiting for the sound of Dadru's next hop. And in nine days he would be packing again and saying 'bye to his uncle, by which time his mind would mock him with the evidence for a belief, that the ecstasy of arrival never compensates for the emptiness of departure. Then someone on the train would again ask him to categorize himself, would not believe that he was what he was, and would never have heard of the name Agastya.

But despite himself, despite all that, on the morning of the departure, he was excited while packing with Digambar. Maybe I should pack everything, he thought, and go away never to return. From the shelf he picked up Marcus Aurelius, Sathe's *Gita*, and his diary.

Kumar and he boarded the train escorted by the station master and a dozen subordinate policemen. Kumar instructed them until the train moved, and even after, largely about himself and his personal matters. "...And ring them up and remind them to meet me at the station, hayn, we'll reach at about seven tomorrow morning...and remind them to book me on the night train to Kanpur, and if reservations are not available, then *any* train...You tell Bakhtiar that the fridge is still giving trouble and he should send another man soon, otherwise I'll give *him* trouble...that tailor will come with two shirts, tell him I'll pay him when I return—otherwise you pay him..." Seconds after the station the train passed under the bridge, on which, many afternoons ago, Agastya had stopped with Sathe for a view; and then the level crossing where on the first evening of the monsoon, he had sensed that the world was large and continually moving. He was on the tracks that reached the edge of the sky, in an orange and cream train, and then behind the church was a polygon of fading yellow, the Rest House, where he had sat over tea and watched these same trains pass.

Eighteen hours to Delhi. Kumar enjoyed train travel, as he enjoyed everything else. He put on his goggles and smoked a cigarette in celebration. Then he impressed his identity on the coach attendant, thereby ensuring for the two of them excellent blankets for the night. Agastya was getting stoned yet again in the lavatory. They got off at almost every station to eat and drink rubbish. A child shat in its shorts and happily wandered around in the bogey, disseminating its stench impartially, but nevertheless Kumar cooed to it. "Arrey, Sen, there's no pleasure like going home."

"But it's even better never to leave it."

"No, sometimes I think not. It is better to leave it because then homecoming is so much sweeter. Living is so full of ups and downs, anyway."

He was hurtling through the hinterland, and now he knew

what its dots were like. The train stopped unreasonably just outside Ratlam. Bits of the town were visible. That old and still-pompous building, with the flag, could be the Collectorate, he thought, and the grey decaying house with a red-tiled roof the District Judge's, and that ruin perhaps the Ratlam Club. These buildings would be in the quieter part of town, perhaps called the Civil Lines; a furlong away from them would lounge in torpid weather a life of which they and their inhabitants would be unaware—the world of paanwalas and shopkeepers and cobblers and rickshaw-walas; who in turn would be aware of a yet wider world only when they stopped at level crossings to see the trains pass—some of which would be coloured orange and cream.

Kumar had brought dinner; rather, some subordinates had reverentially left with the luggage, packets and tiffin carriers. "Can't trust the food of Indian Railways, no," said Kumar, and opened two or three. "These fellows," smiling and shaking his head with greed and affection at the feast, "they think I eat like a pig." Then he and Agastya proceeded to do so. "Indian food is supposed to be very unhealthy, hayn, Sen, lots of oil and chilli, but what is life without spice, yaar? What, at home do you eat English food, all boiled and baked? No, no, I remember, you eat fish like a Bungaali." After they had swelled up Kumar asked, "Whom do you stay with in Delhi? Alone?"

"No, with an uncle."

"And when your father retires, then? He must've built a house somewhere."

"No, we have a sort of family house in Behala, in Calcutta. A nice place, my father loves it." They then ate paan masala and Agastya smoked another joint.

At night he again slept fitfully, fretting under an anarchic mind. The deep rhythm of the train beneath him felt like a vast insensate beast, faintly arousing, but totally remote. The air-conditioning vent was directly above his head. He half-hoped that he would catch a chill, so that bodily discomfort could supplant his mind's restlessness.

Six in the morning, and Delhi's satellite industrial towns, whose ugliness even the morning light couldn't soften. But in them Agastya could sense the pulse, sounding louder every minute, of a big city. He went out to the door of the coach to catch the fresh chill of the morning and imposed on the factory chimneys and storage yards a grace wholly alien to them. He had sensed this often before, and it always thrilled him, this megalopolitan feeling; it had been most acute over Calcutta a few months ago, with a dying sun behind the west wing of the plane, and an orange glow diffused over the brown sadness of a great city. The train clattered on. Peculiar megalopolitan smells, of exhaust and sewage too voluminous for the city's drains; megalopolitan sights, of shacks and shanties, but some with TV aerials, and millions purposefully on the move.

No delegation of sycophants awaited Kumar at Delhi station. Smells of tea and pakoras, crowds slowly dissolving into coherent groups, sounds of suckers bargaining with coolies, and Kumar sulking. "These fellows, so irresponsible. Can't even make a phone call." He wasn't strutting any more; without his entourage he looked like any other fat grubby traveller. Agastya remembered his odd feeling when he had seen Srivastav and Kumar on the Madna road, walking towards the wrongly parked truck; they had looked insecure, a little shrunken. They waited a while, though Agastya was impatient to leave. At last, "OK, Sen, let's go. We'll take a taxi, you drop me off on the way."

At the taxi-stand they stood patiently while the hooligans fought over them. The victor looked like a Chambal dacoit, his leanness belying his monstrous moustache, his voice battering down all opposition. "All of North India is so crude," whined Kumar as the taxi bullied its way through the rickshaws. "I know it, I grew up in its cities. In Madna, didn't you notice, people are much more cultured, more soft."

The wide clean roads of South Delhi, but its traffic perhaps not quite honouring the face-lift that the Asian Games had given the city. But Agastya was happy, despite the assurance of the ache of eventual departure. He had no definite memories of happiness in Delhi; all he knew was that he had not been unhappy, and that seemed enough. Perhaps he was merely longing for the past in an uncongenial present, forgetting its petty unhappinesses, bewitched by it only because he was not its master.

Kumar stopped the taxi in one of the inner lanes of one of South Delhi's older colonies. The taximan got out to remove a suitcase or two from the boot.

"How much?" asked Kumar.

Agastya made a token protest, "I'll pay him at home, sir."

"Arrey, I can't let a junior pay for me, hahn, bhai, how much?"

"Fifty rupees," said the taximan, scratching his balls and examining his fingernails.

"Just what d'you mean, fifty rupees, hayn!" Then followed a long argument. "Fifty rupees!... what d'you think hayn, why don't you just hold us up with a gun and rob us, you'll find that much simpler... bloody dacoit... your bloody meter shows twenty-five, and actually it should be twenty..." Agastya wished that Kumar would shut up. The crookedness of taxi- and auto-rickshaw-drivers of all the North Indian cities was matchless, almost mythic. While Kumar tiraded the driver yawned, hawked, lit a cigarette and feigned boredom in a few other ways. "You don't know who we are, I'm an SP, an IPS officer, this is an IAS officer—"

Upon which, very unexpectedly, the taxidriver, looking at Kumar with his red hooded eyes, undid his pyjama and drawer strings, fisted his cock and said, "*This* is what I think of you Government types."

Agastya's first reaction was to laugh; so, surprisingly, was Kumar's. It betokened a wisdom, he was not in Madna, dealing with an erring truck driver. Then Kumar got serious and asked the driver to pull up his pyjamas and wait while he called the police. "Sen, get your bag out of the car," he said, and went up to the first floor of one house.

Agastya said to the driver, "You shouldn't have done that. It's not nice to show your cock to strangers. That fat man is really an SP. Now he's going to fuck you."

The taximan got into the taxi, "Tell him to get his arsehole stitched with the fifty rupees," and drove off.

Kumar appeared on the veranda. No one on that first floor seemed to know the telephone number of the nearest police station. Agastya gave him the number of the taxi and began walking towards the main road. "'Bye, Sen," said Kumar from the veranda, "see you in Madna." It sounded strange.

"Was the train late?" asked his uncle, dressed in his dhoti and kurta, and contemplating his lawn from its centre, as Agastya touched the gate.

"Hello, Kaku, no, I had to drop an idiot on the way."

Parthiv Sen was almost sixty and a bachelor. He was a free-lance journalist of the suspicious kind; no one quite knew how he lived so comfortably. Dhrubo maintained that he was a CIA agent. He was a little eccentric; his situation demanded it. He wrote a page or two of pedantic political commentary in quite a few Bengali and English magazines. He extracted astounding mileage out of the simplest political incident. The knack, he had often explained to his nephew, was to hide meaning in ver-biage. A decade ago, he had been to some obscure American university for a course in International Relations and Third-world Journalism, or something like that, some very *American* course (the course had helped, and he had subsequently hated all Indian universities for not providing it, all American univer-sities for the opposite, and occasionally himself, for finding it useful), in some place called Rapidwater or Flowingbrook; after which he had begun to write about the mess of Indian politics for obscure American journals. He seemed to thrive on obscurity and disapproval. The house was his, built almost thirty years ago with the money that Agastya's grandfather had left behind. "Dada telephoned a few days ago, and there's a letter from him waiting for you." Dada, Elder Brother, was Agastya's father. "You haven't had breakfast, have you."

The Garhwali servant, a cheerful teenager, appeared, said, "namaste" and took away Agastya's bag. Agastya had spent, off and on, almost six years in that house. When in the college hostel, he had spent weekends with his uncle, and his entire last year. It was a three-bedroom house, simple, but familiarity had bred a kind of love. The servant cooked well. Simple things, good food, a lawn shaded by neem, jacaranda and gulmohar trees, a luxuriant yellow bougainvillaea outside the east window of his room; in Madna his only ambition had grown to be to clutch these simple things.

"What is this rubbish, that you want to leave the IAS and want Tonic to give you a job." Agastya brought two chairs out from the veranda. He smiled at his uncle's directness, it was part of his eccentricity. "So Baba must have sounded worried over the phone," he said.

They sat down. One whole side of the house was bordered by thirty-year-old eucalyptus trees. "I'm not very happy in Madna. I can't settle down to the job—" He smiled shamefully. His uncle was a pale soft man, with a large nose and small brown eyes. He said nothing, but looked at Agastya distastefully, prompting him to speak, to defend and justify himself. "Of course, nothing is fixed. I'm in a sort of state of flux, restless." He shuffled in his chair. "I don't want challenges or responsibility or anything, all I want is to be happy—" He stopped, embarrassed. It seemed an awful thing to say. In that mild autumn sunlight Madna seemed light years away, yet he knew that it would return, perhaps after dark, or whenever he was alone. It seemed unreal, yet accessible, a sleepwalking eighteen hours away. He wanted to say much, but didn't know where to begin, or how to express himself. He wanted to say, look, I don't want heaven, or any of the other ephemerals, the power or the glory, I just want this, this moment, this sunlight, the car in the garage, that music system in my room. These gross material things, I could make these last for ever. If I have any grand desires, they are only grist for lazy fantasy—Vienna and Hong Kong and kink in Bangkok. This narrow placid world, here and now, is enough, where success means watching the rajnigandhas you planted bloom. I am not ambitious for ecstasy, you will ask me to think of the future, but the decade to come pales before this second, the span of my life is less important than its quality. I want to sit here in the mild sun and try and not think, try and escape the iniquity of the restlessness of my mind. Do you understand. Doesn't anyone understand the absence of ambition, or the simplicity of it.

"And why Tonic? Tonic is an idiot. You want to leave a good job to work in a publishing firm? Edit manuscripts on the forms of Indian dance and the tribals of Chhota Nagpur?" (Tonic was a second cousin, who had with great tactlessness refused to publish a book of Pultukaku's articles on something called *The Indian Renewal*.) The servant came out and said that breakfast was ready. Agastya opened his father's letter.

My dear Ogu,

I was a little surprised by your last letter, but I have done as you wished. Even Tonic was surprised by your decision. He said, "This is what comes of living in a city and not knowing what the rest of India is like," or words to that effect. I think that Tonic, as usual, exaggerated. It is true, however, that you have led so far, in Calcutta and Delhi, a comfortable big-city life, wherein your friends and lifestyle have been largely westernized. When we had last met I had said that your job was going to be

an immensely enriching experience. By that I had meant
your exposure to a different kind of environment. Madna
must have placed your Delhi and Calcutta in perspective,
it must have. The same happened with me when I was in
the Konkan, forty years ago. But I suppose my reactions
were different from yours. After Presidency College the
Konkan was a wonderful surprise. But here I repeat myself. I said all this to you when you last came to Calcutta.
At this moment Madna might seem dull to you and life
perhaps unsettling, but do not decide to leave your job
for only this reason. Ogu, do not choose the soft option
just because it is the soft option, one cannot fulfil oneself
by doing so. Yet it is also true that it is your life, and the
decisions will have to be yours. No more homilies. Try
and meet Tonic early, so that when I telephone Pultu
next, you can tell me how the meeting went.

With love, Baba.

"Tonic telephoned too last evening," said his uncle, "to find
out if you'd arrived." Agastya went to his room, to unwind and
unpack. He had been happy once, or so he thought, he was not
happy now, and his mind could analyse no further. He only
wanted to regress, deep into the autumn sun. I will feel regret
in the future, he wanted to say to anyone who would understand, but I shall face that when it comes. Please, only one
world at a time.

The bougainvillaea outside his room seemed to have thickened and was riotously in bloom. The dust danced in the light
as the servant swept the floor. The bedspread was the one he
himself had bought a few months ago and had left behind because he had wanted to travel light, a cream sheet with a huge
red dot in the centre, "What idiots who don't know the meaning of the word 'ethnic' would call ethnic," Dhrubo had said
when helping him to choose it. He unpacked slowly, wander-

ing around the room, trying to revive a sense of belonging. On the monstrous made-in-Japan stereo system ("Why does it pretend to be a computer," Madan had scoffed when he had first seen it, "all these flickering lights and dials, why don't you loan it to the *Star Wars* man for his next hero, and why the hell are you playing silly Bengali songs on it, these things are only meant to play Pink Floyd"), he put on a favourite song of Tagore. He had last heard it on the morning of his departure for Madna; he had been quite groggy then, after the previous night's stoning with Dhrubo, they had sat in the car outside Dhrubo's flat, watching the wide silent road through the windshield at one in the morning; a stray dog had at one moment flashed across the road, sensing prey. The song was slow, and romantic like almost all of Tagore.

> With the death of the day, a red bud burgeons within me
> It shall blossom into love.

The music that distant morning had been in tune with his mood; he had felt a little sad at leaving, and a little curious about the days to come. But now the song was defiled by irony; because of its associations it seemed to lament the inevitability of a thousand departures from the places one began to call home.

He looked out of the window. Beyond the bougainvillaea was the drive, then the low wall, the pale grey trunks of the eucalyptuses, like pillars, then a lane, and a field, where the Bengalis of the neighbourhood had set up the shamiana, the marquee, for Durga Puja, the worship of Durga.

On many nights he used to go out to look *into* his room from the window, it was an old habit, to see what it would look like to someone else, a voyeur or a thief. Beside the bed, and on the perennially untidy desk would be the twin lamps that he had bought years ago from the Assam Emporium. They always looked the best, made of bamboo and shaped like huts; and the room always looked cosy, waiting for inhabitants, and somehow romantic, a place for fulfilling assignations.

Later in the morning, he rang up Dhrubo at his office and reached him through two phoney-accented secretaries. They took some time to understand Agastya's name.

"Why don't you tell your whores at the phone that this is not your New York office and that they can therefore forget the accent?"

"No, I can't do that, they take lessons in the accent from the Indians who work at the American Center, spelt t-e-r."

"I was once called English, will they give me a fuck?"

"Only if your cock looks Caucasian, a white and mottled red. I'm going home soon, why don't you come for lunch? My mother's leaving for Khartoum in the afternoon."

"If she's free, may I have a quickie with her?"

He was tense with happiness as he drove to Dhrubo's house.

Dhrubo's mother opened the door, looking tired and sexy. "Oh hello Ogu come in...you've lost a lot of weight...I'm leaving for Khartoum this afternoon, to join your Kaka, hence all this mess in the house, just don't look at it..." Dhrubo hadn't returned. "...Dhrubo was to go with me just for a break, but now he can't because of the exam, a good decision I think, because even though Citibank pays well—"

"Which exam?" asked Agastya, picking up an apple from the table.

"He's taking that IAS exam, didn't he tell you. You must give him a few tips for it. After I go he'll be alone and sure to run wild."

Dhrubo arrived, dressed like what he was, a successful executive, black tie on immaculate shirt. Small talk while they tried to order the chaos of last-minute packing, questions about his life in Madna the casual answers to which Dhrubo didn't hear. Lunch eaten half-standing; then they saw Dhrubo's mother off at the airport. On the way back they smoked a joint in the car on the Airport Road.

"Madan around?" asked Agastya.

"Oh, yes, he came over last weekend to get stoned to watch the planes land. What enduring interests."

They watched, through the windshield, the traffic on the road, cars and taxis whizzing past the boards that read Speed Limit 60 kmph, around them miles of vacant flat land under a soft blue sky.

"So now you feel that the Government of India needs you more than Citibank," said Agastya lightly.

"Oh, Ma told you," and Dhrubo looked away. "Yes, I've been thinking of that, in a vague disorganized way." He rummaged in the glove compartment for a cassette and put it on, and revealed himself to the strains of Scott Joplin.

"I suppose you want to know why," said Dhrubo. Agastya didn't, really: to each his own, he felt. "Not if it's soul-searing and demands too much attention."

He looked at Dhrubo's profile, the small sharp nose and the thin double chin, and sensed that Dhrubo too wanted to say much, and didn't know how to begin, or how to express himself.

"Well, I *am* sick of Citibank. But not unbearably sick, really." Dhrubo spoke haltingly, which was unusual. Perhaps it was the marijuana, or reluctance, or the inadequacy of words to express an idea. "But ten years later I don't want to tell myself, bastard, you should've changed jobs long long ago. But it's not that, really." He leaned against the door of the car and spoke to the windshield, over the sound of passing traffic and teasing Scott Joplin. "I've...I think I've had enough of...this whole Occidental connection—why're you smiling, motherfucker?"

"Whose mother? What does 'Occidental connection' mean? You're just using the phrase because it sounds nice, like an international dope gang."

"I can't explain..." And Agastya suddenly wanted to ask him not to. You feel even more naked and alone, he said silently, when you reveal yourself, a gratuitous act, for the strength and comfort that you look for, any of those last illusions of consolation, can finally be only within you. "All those expense accounts, and false-accented secretaries, and talk of New York and head office, and our man in Hong Kong, it's just not *real*, it's an imitation of something elsewhere, do you know what I mean?" And Agastya again sensed the largeness of the world, and the consequent littleness of his own crises; while he had been in Madna, talking to Mohan or walking carefully to avoid a buffalo's tail from flicking dung on to his arms, Dhrubo had been where he, Agastya, had wanted to be, but struggling against the surreal. "And I wear a tie, and use my credit card, and kiss the wives of my colleagues on the cheek when we meet, and I come home and smoke a joint, listen to Scott Joplin and Keith Jarrett, and on weekends I see a Herzog film, or a Carlos Saura, it's... *unreal*."

"It sounds quite nice," said Agastya, but Dhrubo looked agitated, so he added, "Well, that's ironic, because I was toying with the idea of leaving this job myself." He tried to explain, half-heartedly, his dislocation and loneliness in Madna, and sounded flippant and shallow.

He enraged Dhrubo. "Just who and where do you think you are, an American taking a year off after college to discover himself?" He increased the volume on the car stereo, and they drove off, the lazy mocking notes of ragtime now loud as they whizzed with the other cars.

"When did you decide to be this foolish?" Dhrubo asked after a few minutes.

"At a picnic, by a temple, in a place called Gorapak." It seemed so far away. "I was playing cricket with the son of a Divisional Forest Officer. I behaved very meanly."

Dhrubo stared at him in incomprehension and nearly

rammed into a public bus. The driver snarled at him. Dhrubo snarled back, and said to Agastya, as they were moving away, "That dogfucker. No one in India has any road sense."

"Neither do you." They laughed. At Dhrubo's house they sprawled on the sofas and smoked another joint. "I've taken a few days off from work, for Puja and loafing around. The Governor must be insane at your foolishness."

"He is disappointed. But my uncle is the one who is angry, but I think that's more because he dislikes Tonic so much. If I said I was leaving the IAS to become a free-lance journalist, I don't think he'd mind." On the opposite wall hung a Jamini Roy painting that Agastya hadn't noticed before. Theirs was a government flat (which, Agastya realized with a smirk, Srivastav would get only after fifteen more years of scowling), but Dhrubo's mother had concealed the fact quite artfully under her decorations—brass vases and coir wall hangings. Dhrubo's father was in Khartoum on some UN assignment.

Dhrubo got up. "I want to show you Renu's letter." He returned from his room with a thin cream envelope.

"Renu is your Punjaban out to break relationships, isn't she? I don't think I want to read her letter, unless it's full of fond remembrances of your sexual technique. Why don't you arrange for some tea and put on some music?"

"No, you should read it you mongrel, get a glimpse of the First World—half our opinions come from there." Dhrubo began to prepare yet another joint. "Did you smoke a lot in Madna?" "No, not much." He was going to reveal his secret life to no one.

Renu wrote from Illinois, on small bright-white paper, a neat controlled hand.

Dear D,
["Dhrubo, she calls you D! God, D!! You two have really gone far beyond first name terms, haven't you, ha, ha!"]

It was really odd, on my first evening here, there was a get-together of the local Indian gang, and they were all talking about the Teen Murti Library and the University Coffee House and the M.Phil. Department, wallowing in nostalgia. One girl called Mrinalini said she knew you, or had met you once at some pompous Foreign Service party where you'd told her, "The US and the Soviets are in this nuclear arms race primarily to distract the rest of the world. It's all a game, they want to keep all our minds away from the real issue, which is the throttling of what they call the Third, Fourth and Fifth Worlds by Soviet Necessity and the American Dream." I hope you are squirming with shame? Mrinalini thought I wouldn't believe her. She said you were fat, pompous and very drunk, like the rest of the party.

I've been trying to write as few letters as possible because writing letters is the supreme indulgence for me nowadays. Communicating with people is difficult here and it's such a temptation to make up for that through letters. At least with letters you don't have to deal with immediate reactions—you can imagine that whoever you're writing to is interested and understands exactly what you mean. Writing letters is a wonderful way of copping out of everything—the lectures that go so badly, all the people in this place whom I can't talk to. It's so tempting to take the easy way out, to go on about how the people here are so dull, ignorant, smug and provincial. They *are* all that, but there's also something very wrong about my attitude to them. Because of my colour, accent, etc., I feel wary and strained talking to Americans—the moment I face one of them, I can feel the shutters going down in me, and I know my face looks blank, bored and closed.

In just a few weeks here I've managed to establish "a

circle of silence" around myself (as Ganapati used to say with great annoyance) which nobody would want to break into. To appear quiet and disinterested is the greatest defence, to convince yourself that nothing matters. And the "stay away from me" expression gets quite out of hand sometimes—the only American who's made heroic efforts to make me comfortable just asked me if I wanted a poster. Without thinking or even looking up, I said, "No, you can keep it." His warmth feels like a terrific obligation and a responsibility—it takes me such an effort to respond that I sometimes actually run away when I know he's around. I don't know why the hell I'm writing all this.

There was a real low last week—I have to make my class do an exercise called freewriting—they have to write nonstop for ten minutes about whatever is on their minds. Last week one student wrote, "I'm not paying big bucks to listen to an Indian telling me how to write English. And her fucking accent is giving me a migraine." I really wonder what I'm doing here, especially because academically this place really "sucks," the one American expression which covers all possible negatives. Some other time I'll write you a bright bitchy letter about the kind of absurdities one hears at lectures here. The worst is not having anyone to share the absurdity with. It's hard getting to know people. Everyone seems friendly at first, everyone stops and asks, "Hi, how ya doin'?" But after a while you realize that that's it, nothing ever follows up that "Hi, how ya doin'?" And to answer that with anything less exuberant than, "Pretty good," is a social outrage. The creed is to be bright, brisk and busy. You can imagine what a disadvantage my face is, and my voice— dull, gloomy and lazy as can be.

I share my room with a Mexican. She's OK. At times I hysterically wonder why people ever leave their own countries and go abroad. Why don't we ever learn that all changes of place are for the worse. It's not love for a place, it's the familiarity, like old winter clothes. Didn't you feel something of this at Yale? You were always so closed about your American experience. Yesterday another American asked me where I was from in India. I said, "Bombay." He thought for a while and asked me seriously whether I rode to college on an elephant. I said, "Yes, but I had to hire one, since we were too poor to own our own." That's entirely my fault, for not being where I ought to be, back home.

I can't transfer to another university within this Ph.D programme unless I'm willing to lose credits. My only experience of the US before this was of NY and I ought to have known that being in the heart of corn country will be very different from NY.

What I really didn't bargain for was the nostalgia—I have such a bad memory that the past usually becomes mere past for me with great ease. But here I take nostalgia to absurd extremes—watching Hindi movies, *Guddi*, *Barood*, etc., I don't think it works, to run away from a place when your relationships there get messy. For the first time now I feel I need some continuities. But then I don't know if anything lasts, except that I'm the same person wherever I go—and that certainly is no cause for joy! In the first few days I thought I'd get friendly with my Mexican roomie and ask her about subtle racist attitudes here. Fortunately I didn't, because I remembered in time how we behave with Africans in India, remember Mbele?

I don't know why I'm writing all this but now that I've missed a class already, I might as well fill up the page. Of course I'm being defensive again. I can't say anything to anyone without leaving an escape route for myself, prefacing everything with, "Don't take this too seriously" or "I don't know why I'm saying this." The only way to cope with things is to pretend that nothing matters.

Oh, there are some lovely things here too—the varieties of ham, books for ten cents each, Mrinalini, the underground radio station which plays hours and hours of old blues, the bars—but they're not nearly enough.

I can see you perfectly sometimes—perfectly composed in your tie behind your Citibank desk, drowning some client in bank jargon. I keep asking myself, why were you so cold and curt at the end? "At the end" sounds terribly dramatic but you know what I mean. It feels absurd to even mention it because that was in another country, and besides. For the last line you could consult your English Literature friend who, if that letter of his that you showed me is anything to go by, is enjoying going insane, in some backwater somewhere, what was it, Madna?

Please write back. With my love, Renu.

Agastya folded the letter carefully and put it back in the envelope. "What a naked letter. She sounds quite sexy. You should marry her on the condition that she communicates with you only through letters."

They went to the kitchen to make tea. It smelt of phenyl and washed rags.

"So you don't think I should leave Citibank?"

"You remember Madan's story about what the Japanese say when any Indian asks them for assistance,

Maybe yes Maybe no
Maybe I don't know—that's my answer.

Decide for yourself, it's your nightmare. Or just live with the indecision, everyone does it all the time, you'll get used to it soon enough. Then, when you ever take any snap decisions, you'll feel odd, like withdrawal symptoms or something." He wanted to sound callous; Dhrubo's question had irritated him, reminded him of his own incommunicable and secret inquisitions. "A friend in Madna routed all his problems and decisions to Jagadamba and boozed while waiting for her answers—just what are you doing?"

Dhrubo had been struggling for a while with the knob of the cooking-gas cylinder. "They're turning modern without warning, these bastards. This is some wretched new sealing system for gas cylinders. Only my mother and that servant know how this thing opens." He gave it a typical last-chance yank. The whole thing came off in his hand. "God, now it's leaking." Instantly they could both smell the gas. They stared at the lethal mouth of the cylinder for a while. Dhrubo began to giggle, "It looks like an arsehole."

"We should do something about this," said Agastya. "Shall we light a match? That would take care of your indecision." For one long apocalyptic second he wanted to explode, into twitching bits of blood and bone.

Dhrubo tried to jam the head back on to the mouth of the cylinder. "What a wretched typically Indian story for tomorrow's newspapers. Two inches of the third page: 'Gas Cylinder Bursts, Two Dead.'" They heard a soft but distinct click. The head seemed to have been fixed. They stared at it suspiciously. "It came off because I turned the knob the wrong way. I think it's OK now," said Dhrubo with great doubt in his voice.

"Really? Then why don't you sound more confident?"

They looked at each other and smiled, almost guiltily. "You loved science in school, why can't you fix this?" asked Dhrubo.

"Don't talk through your arse, since when has our education been useful. Why don't you check those *Reader's Digest* books you used to get your father to buy, *A Thousand Things To Do When You Are Not Reading Us*, they might have a column on this, with diagram alongside." They sniffed the air, cautiously. Agastya touched the head of the cylinder. "Listen, I'm going to light a match. We came here for tea, remember. If this is leaking we'll soon find out, ha, ha. You don't want this to go on leaking till tomorrow morning, do you?"

"We could call someone," said Dhrubo, again dubiously. "Who?" Agastya pounced with the question, like a debator scoring a telling point off an opposing speaker. He then smiled and picked up the matchbox. "Indecision will be your epitaph—isn't that a line in some very noisy song that Madan plays for us all the time? Or I could lose half my face or both my arms. Then I wouldn't have to return to Madna, or think about my future, or think about anything but half my face. Much simpler living." He grinned at Dhrubo.

"Wait," from Dhrubo, a squeak of panic, "are you sure you know what you're doing?"

"This is no time to ask profound questions, stupid," and Agastya lit the match and put the kettle on. He crouched and examined the head of the cylinder. "You bastard Dhrubo, the instructions are *written* on this thing! 'Turn knob north for flow of gas, east to seal cylinder, south to remove head to attach new cylinder.' Didn't they teach you Gas-Cylinder Operations at Yale or Citibank?"

"But why're the instructions in English? The language of the bloodsucking imperialists, they made our hearts weep, and crippled us from appreciating our glorious heritage. I object, and like a good Bengali I'm going to write to the 'Grievances' column of the *Statesman*, that the instructions on a gas cylinder should be in *all* the fourteen Indian languages recognized by the Constitution."

Again post-coital-exhaustion-postures on the sofas, tea cups trembling in their hands, they began to laugh. "Phew, that was *really* close," said Dhrubo, "I think we should smoke another joint in celebration."

"Of course, you know, you junkie, this would never have happened if you hadn't been so stoned."

Agastya telephoned Tonic at his office. "Hello, may I speak to Mr. Gopal Chowdhury, please... My name is Agastya Sen ... Uh—my name is August Sen... August, April, May, June, July, August, August Sen... Hello, Tonicda?" He switched to Bengali, because it would irritate his cousin. "Ogu here..."

Tonic said, "Just hold on a minute," and went off the line.

Agastya turned to Dhrubo. "You haven't ever met Tonic, have you? He's the most boring person in South Asia, you can only talk to him when you're stoned. I think Pultukaku hates him so much because he can bore a statue into crumbling."

"Has it never occurred to him to change his name?" said Dhrubo, lying abandoned on the divan with his head beneath two cushions.

"Apparently he loved tonics as a child. He's the only child in recorded history to have actually liked the taste of Waterbury's Compound. He used to steal extra spoonfuls—" Tonic returned to the phone. "Hello, Tonicda, I thought I'd see you tomorrow... Where, at home or at office?... Why don't we talk about that when we meet..."

A few hours later, refreshed, bathed and still stoned, they were at dinner with Agastya's uncle, who was uncommunicative that evening. His eccentricity required that he be phlegmatic at least twice a week. Agastya wanted to nettle him, for on his phlegmatic days his uncle's sarcasm was matchless. "Kaku, Dhrubo is also planning to quit his job."

His uncle said nothing for a while, and then, with his small brown eyes on Dhrubo, "And also planning to join Tonic's vast publishing network, I hope?"

"Oh, no, no," said Dhrubo hurriedly, "I might take the Civil Services exam this year. Aug—Ogu is stupid, I am not."

"Well, if you're really not stupid," said Agastya's uncle, trying to lean back in the straight chair, "why don't you try and transfer some of your intelligence to your friend here?"

Then the drums began to beat. From the Puja shamiana in the field beside the house, the thunder of celebration. The drummers carried on for hours, the drum hanging from the shoulder, moving steadily in front of the idol on calloused feet; they were specialists, had fanned out all the way from Bengal to thousands of similar shamianas all over the country; for four days the rhythm of revelry at the foot of a figure in apotheo-sized clay. The beat was inextricably linked in Agastya's mind with the mildness of October, late-night movies on a makeshift screen in the open air, with the mist of incense around the idol, with eating omelettes and meat pies at some dhaba at three in the morning.

"When my generation was young I don't think your father or I would've behaved with your flippancy. This was no land of plenty, and jobs were difficult to get—even for us who knew the right people for jobs. This certainly is no land of plenty now. None of us would have walked out of jobs like this, good jobs—a government job is so secure, you needn't work at all, and you can never be thrown out. And you want to leave the *IAS*, no less, after having been just a few months in the job. Disgusting. It would've been like your father wanting to leave the Indian Civil Service. For what? Not for a cause —Subhash Chandra Bose or somebody like that—but to be *happy*, you said this morning, all I want is to be *happy*. What you need is a whipping. I think your father is trying to be too reasonable. Sitting there at the Calcutta Raj Bhawan play-ing his silly games of Patience, he attributes to you far more sense than you possess. You don't seem to like your place of posting because it's not Calcutta or Delhi, and it doesn't have fast-food joints selling you hamburgers. You have always known security, that's why you're behaving so shallowly. You need to grow up, Ogu, you cannot remain an adolescent at twenty-four."

"That's what I told him this afternoon," said Dhrubo, his head seeming to nod of its own volition, "that in India he was trying to be the American trying to discover himself."

"Kindly do not interrupt me with rubbish." But Pultukaku didn't bother to look at Dhrubo to say this. "And you have asked that Tonic for a job only because it will mean that you will stay in Delhi. You don't know anything about publishing, you aren't remotely interested in it. But, then, you are interested in nothing, and you think that is a virtue."

Agastya and Dhrubo moved out to have a look at the Puja. "Lovely mood he was in," said Dhrubo. "Perhaps that cute servant didn't lend his arse last night to dear Pultu."

They were at the gate when Pultukaku called them from the drawing-room window. "Ogu, Manik telephoned this evening. I gathered from his incoherence that he wants you to marry his granddaughter. He's coming here early tomorrow morning. I told him that was the only time to catch you when you were in Delhi."

The drums were quiet. The plays and movies must have begun. The crush of parked cars and people determined to enjoy themselves; for the rest of the year the men wore trousers and shirt, but for a festival, white dhoti and kurta, assertions of their ethnicity. The ubiquitous paan and cigarette stalls around the shamiana, dhabas selling egg parathas and sweets, tube-lights on poles, covered in coloured paper to radiate a coloured glow, two sari shops, even a stall for Russian books. "The Soviets will overrun us," said Dhrubo, looking at a photograph of Gorky on a vellum edition of *My Apprenticeship*.

The shamiana itself was dark, and emanated occasional laughter. They strolled in, crowds sitting and standing, watching a mime show, heads of oil-flattened hair in silhouette against the glow of the outside lights. Agastya saw the audience and remembered Madna. "In Madna at a function of this kind the men and women would sit separately." But Dhrubo wasn't listening; he had stopped at the mouth of the shamiana to read the chart of the evening's programme. Agastya turned away towards the idol.

Durga had been put up, as usual, opposite the stage, about sixty yards away. The demon Mahishasur lay bleeding at her feet, the rictus of defeat on his face. She was surrounded by incense and silk, fattened eyes in a yellow face. The two drummers, small hard men, relaxed in a corner, smoking.

Year after year he had seen her tumid October face, and had involuntarily heard the chants in her praise from the radio at pre-dawn and from devout lips—"Give me beauty, Give me victory, Give me fame, You conqueror of evil." He looked up at her face, blood-lips and a third eye below a clay crown of gold. She had a thousand facets, but none had ever remotely touched him, or moved him to anything which could have had the dignity of faith. We all have to believe in something or other, his father had said, but for him faith had always been festivity—watching the women in eye blinding silk, and releasing balloons against the night sky, and when with his aunts he had joined his palms in front of Durga in the perfunctory gesture of devotion, the dust of marijuana had mingled with the moistness of sweat brought on by a Calcutta evening. "I bow to you, you immanent goddess, you exist in everything, in fame, in sleep, in shame, in all"—surely some devotees believed in miracles, but none seemed to importune her for peace, and he half-smiled at the idol, the eyes lustrous in vengeance. Please, Jagadamba, what about happiness, Jagadamba, please.

"You look very stoned," Dhrubo broke in. "Good news. After that mime idiot stops twisting his face for laughs, they're screening *Ajantrik* at ten. Films all night, but the other two are Bengali potboilers. Let's go out and get some tea." They moved off, Agastya a little startled at what he had done—he had half-believed in Shankar's assertions of his world view.

They sat outside a dhaba, beside the road, on aluminium chairs, two islands. An urchin handed them two half-glasses of sweet tea. Agastya felt exhausted. "I haven't seen *Ajantrik* before, have you?" prattled Dhrubo. "Actually this'll be my first Ritwik Ghatak. Of course, he was awful until the French said he was good, and now he's a Master—why aren't you listening to me, bastard?"

"Too stoned." Then Dhrubo too fell silent. They took in the scene around them, Agastya continuing to wonder at himself. Cars honking six feet from them, helpless in the crush, the babble of happy crowds, the stench of gas from the balloon-seller's stall, potato tikkas frying on a giant pan, the urchins being yelled at for dawdling by a fat man who combed his hair over his ears, a young girl, self-conscious in dazzling sari and painted face, escorting an aged couple across the road, a green glow from the nearest tube-light on a good-looking man at the next table.

"In America I missed all this," said Dhrubo suddenly, his hand drawing aimless circles. But Agastya didn't hear and continued to look around.

Then clapping from within the shamiana, the lights came on. The usual after-the-show stirrings, rustles and murmurs, then a voice over the PA system in Bengali, "We were to screen Ritwik Ghatak's *Ajantrik* at ten o'clock, but many of our friends have expressed a wish to see the other two films scheduled for tonight first. So *Ajantrik* is postponed to four in the morning..." A roar of approval from within the shamiana, some people outside clapped. The announcer raised his voice, "We'll start the first film at ten thirty, to give some time to those who want to inform others of this rescheduling."

The crowds moved out, the babble increased, somewhere a child bawled. "So much for the Master," said Dhrubo with a laugh.

"You want to stay till four?"

"No," said Dhrubo, "let's just sit here for some time, this whole noise and chaos is nice, maybe have another tea, then we'll move."

One in the morning, he was on the roof of the house, Dhrubo had left an hour before. Through the eucalyptuses he could see the Puja ground. The crowds had thinned. He could hear snatches of the film dialogue. The tops of the trees stood silent against the stars. One day gone, seven and a half to go. He didn't want to sleep, that would be six hours wasted. Perhaps it was raining in Madna, soothing night rain. The room would be silent, his cassettes on the table slowly gathering dust. He remembered Renu's letter, and half-smiled, she needn't have gone so far to suffer so much. The inhabitants of his world moved so much, ceaselessly and without sanity, and realized only with the last flicker of their reason that they had not lived. Endless movement, much like the uncaring sea, transfers to alien places, passages to distant shores, looking for luck, not sensing that heaven was in their minds. I was not born for this, said Agastya silently. He had said that all he wanted was to be happy. Now alone under the stars he could admit this to himself without embarrassment. His father and Dhrubo had prophesied that the experience of Madna would prove educative, but all that his mind seemed to have learnt was the impotence of restlessness. He had begun to be appalled by thought, thoughts that scurried in his mind uncontrollably, like rats in a damp cavern, thought without action. And Madna had tainted his old world here in the city, the crowds at the Puja had reminded him of the Madna Club, Durga had recalled Jagadamba. It was too much, to endure the load of more than one world in the head.

Three thirty in the morning, laughter on the roads, happy people going home after seeing two potboilers free. He sat in a corner of the roof, on the cold cement and brick, watching a blue-white austere moon.

He was woken up next morning by a man whom for a moment he didn't recognize. Bald and skeletal, a thin skin stretched taut across the face, large spectacles on a skull grinning with nervous glee. "Ah, Ogu," it giggled and said in Bengali, "your uncle was right, the only way to meet you is to catch you in the morning."

"Oh, Manik Kaku, hello, I—uh—" Agastya sat up, his head throbbing for more sleep, wondering whether he should display his morning erection to send the old man away, "slept late last night, you know, uh, Puja nights."

He followed him out to the lawn. Ten in the morning, his uncle was reading his own article in the *Statesman* with scorn. "I told Manik to wake you up, he's been here since eight, giving me details of his incomparable granddaughter. I told him it wasn't a good idea since you were about to leave the IAS to join a publishing firm."

Manik laughed shrilly, a sheen of sweat on his head. The servant brought tea. Agastya said, "Baba wrote that you met him in Calcutta." His mouth tasted foul, a mix of mucus and dung, and now tea.

"Yes, yes," said Manik, "I did, your father was as nice as ever. He doesn't forget old friends."

"What does your granddaughter do, Kaku? I haven't met her ever. In fact I met you last at least ten years ago."

"Yes, yes," said Manik, his head jerking in indecision, vacillating between slurping over his tea and beaming at Agastya. "Of course, my granddaughter was a mere child then."

"So was I," simpered Agastya, "I knew nothing of the world those days," except that if you unrolled a condom to find out how big adult cocks were, you could get very worried.

"Yes, yes," said Manik, again yellow teeth in a bespectacled skull. He would, decided Agastya, die right there, saying yes, yes. "My granddaughter is twenty now, doing her MA in Calcutta, English. A very fine subject, Keats and Tennyson, very good—for girls especially. She's—"

"You mean, it's a distinct advantage in the marriage market," said Pultukaku, smiling viciously, his torso hidden by his newspaper. "Then your advertisement in the matrimonial columns can say 'convent-educated, MA in English,' and when you exhibit her in the drawing rooms of her husbands-to-be, she can, after singing the mandatory Tagore song, recite 'The Lady of Shalott.'" And if she marries an IAS officer, at all district parties she can be even more condescending than the average Madam IAS, and when the 'prominent citizens' call on them in some godforsaken sub-division, while the husband makes them wait the obligatory forty minutes, she can talk to them about Lochinvar." The newspaper then moved up to cover his face. It was his day for misanthropy.

"I don't really want to marry now. Besides, I really might be changing jobs, Kaku, in which case you certainly won't be interested." He waited for the old man's protest but there was none. "Perhaps we could discuss this later or something." In his state of mind marriage was awfully remote—like a death in a road accident, it was something that happened to other people. It was inconceivable, sharing his room in Madna with some unknown—perhaps a twenty-year-old girl with an MA in English, and getting stoned in front of her to read Marcus Aurelius. While Manik chatted with Pultukaku and elicited from him a few misanthropic monosyllables, the familiar feeling of the absurd, as much a part of him as his names, overwhelmed Agastya, and he wondered whether, when married, he would be able to exercise in front of his wife, and what he would do if, just when he was lunging for a push-up she were to say, For someone who exercises so much you're in awful shape. And suppose she stole his money? And the all-important subject of kinky sex—she might not like sharing each other's used underwear, then?

Eventually, he knew, he would marry, perhaps not out of passion, but out of convention, which was probably a safer thing. And then in either case, in a few months or years they would tire of disagreeing with each other, or what was more or less the same thing, would be inured to each other's odd and perhaps disgusting ways, the way she squeezed the tube of toothpaste and the way he drank from a glass and didn't rinse it, and they would slide into a placid and comfortable unhappiness, and maybe unseeingly watch TV every evening, each still a cocoon, but perhaps it would be unwise to be otherwise. And his once-secret life would be entombed in a mind half-dead to an incarcerating world, and he would remember, with a sense of bemused embarrassment, and in epiphanic flashes, brought on by uncontrollable jolts to his memory through a smell or some unexpected sight (perhaps the view from a train or an ad on TV), his this experience of Madna, that once the restlessness of his mind had seemed the most important thing in the universe, and that he had once been shaken by the profundity of an ancient Hindu poem.

On the way to Tonic's office he dropped Manik Kaku off at some convenient point, with shallow promises to write to him from Madna. Agastya watched him cross the road, dhoti billowing around stick-legs.

Tonic's office was about fifteen kilometres away from home. At a red light he decided, while eyeing a neighbouring Fiat painted an impossible red, that he wasn't going to do this journey every day. He wondered why he was going to meet Tonic, he didn't particularly want to work with him. On the day of the picnic at Gorapak he had written to his father from an abyss, he had wanted to explode his irresolution once and for all, but now it seemed preposterous, to change one bridle for another. A bus overtook him, with office-goers hanging out of the door like tongues out of canine mouths. I'd be one of them, he thought, I certainly won't be paid enough for the amount of petrol this senile monster (he was driving his uncle's decayed Ambassador) guzzles; and then nine every morning, he'd be rushing for a bus, lunch packet or tiffin carrier in hand, he'd queue up sweating at the bus-stop, but still stand all the way, in the stench of engine oil and bus-sweat, like the stench of that antibiotic capsule he had had in Madna when he'd been ill. And his questions would contract to whether he would be able to catch his most convenient bus, and whether he would get a seat on it; and the bus timings would be down on a slip of paper in his table drawer and would be embossed in his mind; any unannounced change in them would be cataclysmic, and his wonderful days would be those on which he got a seat both ways.

Unlike many others of his age and in his time he did not have to job-hunt. Unlike them he had never known the suspense of financial insecurity. But he envied them the concreteness of their worries, these office-goers who had to hang out of buses like tongues, and felt guilt about the envy. Neera would have instantly demonstrated in her strident Marxist way that his envy was a symptom of a despicable something-or-the-other. There wasn't a single thought in his head, he smiled at the back of the bus ahead of him, about which he didn't feel confused. His mind was always coercing a pattern out of his past, but the attempts towards order led nowhere. Dhrubo, for instance, was as closed about his Yale experience as he himself was about Madna—but getting chaos to cohere in this fashion was really a fruitless exercise, just sport for the mind, like chess, or his father's games of Patience. His father's addiction to Patience was quite inexplicable—his mother had taught it to him. But his father always defended the game with great conviction. "It teaches us something important, Ogu, that order cannot be achieved without patience." Balls, Agastya had thought, but hadn't said so. Suddenly he didn't want to finish like his father either, alone, in his spare time reading the *Katha Upanishad* in the vast rooms of a Raj Bhavan.

He parked and walked. He passed Macmillan's and the Oxford University Press, huge show-windows proudly displaying lethally dull titles.

Tonic's publishing firm was on the second floor of a pink building in a side street. Tonic was in his cubicle, filling his pipe and ignoring his work, a slim but soft man, with a double chin and bulbous eyes. "Ah, you aren't serious, are you?" He always began directly, and thereby, for a few seconds, impressed those who didn't know him, with a sense of his efficiency.

"No, not really." Tonic frowned at his answer, perhaps it deprived him of a reason for talking non-stop. But Agastya wanted to provide him with a take-off point, and said, "Baba said you said that I dislike a small town because I've always lived in big cities and never knew what the rest of India is like."

"Ah." Tonic lit his pipe as though he was in an ad for something romantically masculine, aftershave or cigarette lighters. Perhaps he would suddenly change his clothes, wear something terribly sporty, and go off in a red car with some Bombay females to play golf. Then on the road hopefully a truck would eat up the arse of the red car, and the truck driver would beat up Tonic for lighting a pipe like that. "Ah. India lives in its villages, a terrible cliché that, but really very true, like all clichés. Wittgenstein, wasn't it, who said that India lives in its villages?"

"No, Gandhi."

A subordinate came in. Before he could open his mouth Tonic said, "Oh yes I remember I'll get that done it'll take me no time at all it's really very easy but it keeps slipping my mind I've been terribly busy don't worry I'll see to it." The subordinate left. Tonic blew rich smoke after him.

"Ah. You know, people like you, Ogu, really have no idea of what the real India is like. Especially you—South Delhi is such a *vulgar* place, and your only companion there is Pultukaku, you are bound to get an insane perspective on the real things—appalling poverty and even more appalling ignorance. But, then, look at our education system." Oh, how he loved to talk. He leaned back to pick up a manuscript from a side table. "Dr. Prem Krishen of Meerut University has written a book on E. M. Forster, India's darling Englishman—most of us seem to be so *grateful* that he wrote that novel about India. Dr. Prem Krishen holds a Ph.D on Jane Austen from Meerut University. Have you ever been to Meerut? A vile place, but comfortably Indian. What is Jane Austen doing in Meerut?"

"Or *Macbeth* in Ulhasnagar, and Wordsworth in Azamganj —no nothing, do go on."

"We're publishing Prem Krishen because he'll fetch us lots of money. His book is entirely in a question and answer form. Students lap that up." Tonic lit his pipe again. Agastya again thought of the truck driver beating him up. "Why is some Jat teenager in Meerut reading Jane Austen? Why does a place like Meerut have a course in English at all? Only because the Prem Krishens of the country need a place where they can teach this rubbish?" He jabbed dramatically at the manuscript with his pipe. "Surely they can spend the money they waste on running the department usefully elsewhere." Tonic fixed his bulbous eyes on Agastya to see whether he had understood, or perhaps to discourage his smile. "That's why education is a real challenge. And in the years to come, as a bureaucrat you'll be in a position to do something about these things, things that matter. And yet you want to leave the IAS, for callow reasons, just because in Madna you don't see the girls that you see in Delhi and Bombay, in their arse-hugging jeans and T-shirts with lewd one-liners."

Agastya was angry with himself for looking like the sort of person to whom such things could be said.

Tonic asked for tea. Another subordinate entered and exited after extracting from Tonic furious promises of immediate action. "Look, Ogu, I can give you a job any time, but you need to think a lot about this thing. You haven't really thought about this, I can see that on your face." Agastya felt angry with his face. "Leaving such a job is a ridiculously high price to pay for trying to regain some of the shallow pleasures of your past life."

Agastya left with his mind in a whirl. It confused him even more when people he held in affectionate contempt talked down to him and talked sense.

At home over lunch Agastya told his uncle that he probably wasn't joining Tonic. Pultukaku said, "Any person who is not insane would conclude the same, especially after one look at Tonic in his office. He functions as though he's paid to be a leaking balloon, emit hot air."

After lunch, contemplating a nap, the phone rang. Agastya picked it up, "Hello."

"Hello, is that Delhi, Mr. Agastya Sen?...Will you kindly hold on, please...the Governor wishes to speak to you..."

A few transnational clicks and short screeches, then "Hello, is that Ogu?" Agastya warmed to the voice, firm even when distant.

"Hi, how's the Patience? I met Tonic this morning. He gave himself a pep talk and sent me away."

"I see. So...?"

"I don't know anything, Baba. I'll go back to Madna and try and get used to things." A pause.

"Yes, Ogu, do that. At least see your training through before deciding anything. All these months you've just been moving from office to office. Now you are going to be Block Development Officer, and that is sure to prove more interesting."

"Yes, I suppose I should do that." He felt an emptiness well upwards from his scrotum, like blood that would not be stanched.

"And Ogu..." He could see his father perfectly, white hair on a thinning scalp, small golden spectacles, dhoti and kurta of cream silk, up since five in the morning, wringing out from each day its pith, the impress of Marcus Aurelius and the

Reader's Digest on his face. "...I wish I could be of help, but you must already have been so bothered by Pultu and his sarcasm, but try and ignore everything so that your mind is clear, and think and decide for yourself..." and a little later, "...will you put Pultu on, I want to quarrel with him about a few things."

Six in the evening, Agastya and Dhrubo went to meet Madan, an old college friend. On the way Dhrubo cursed the traffic of West Delhi. "You wouldn't think such a mess existed ten kilometres away from South Delhi's colonies."

Madan's father, who had just returned from another mysterious business trip to Singapore, continued the theme. "Singapore is so organized, I tell you. The traffic is so ordered, and no spitting and urinating on the road, and no restaurants with signs saying, Don't Wash Your Hands In The Glass—an Indian couldn't survive there. And this place, huh, my blood pressure goes up every time I sit behind the wheel." He was a jovial and extremely ugly man.

Madan looked different. He had cut his hair, and wasn't wearing his terribly faded jeans. "Because of this damn job. I have to look clean every day." He had recently joined a reputable firm of chartered accountants. "Come, let's shift to my room." Which was a college euphemism for smoking marijuana.

Later, suitably high, Madan said, "It's sick, I think, having a job, having to work. Your whole day is gone. The one thing worse than a CA firm will be a bank, I think." He looked at Dhrubo and laughed. "Bloody Oedipus Dhrubo, how does it feel, sitting all day behind a desk and counting other people's money? My sister's going to Oxford. She's got the Rhodes scholarship this year. She's already picked up an accent from somewhere, and says, 'Pardon,' and, 'Thanks awfully,' at everything. Bitch. Now she roams around looking for people who've been to Blighty—she's stopped calling it England. I'm deeply

ashamed of her. I told her to ring up the British High Com-
mission and find out how people shit at Oxford, whether in
vases or ladies' handbags, because all over the world people, I
said, have different habits. The stupid girl went to whine to my
mother, who stunned her by taking my side—because my
mother's been sulking ever since my sister refused to take two
huge jars of pickle with her." Madan lay down. "Every day in
the office I feel as though my head is being raped, like somebody's pushed his cock in through my ears and is moving it
around in my brain, mixing his semen in my brain matter. Do
you two ever feel like that?"

"Do you remember Bhatia, from college? He was on our
hostel floor, wore T-shirts which said things like 'I'm the best
lover in town' and spoke American slang all the time? Well, he's
in Madna, in the Forest Service."

"Serves him right. I hope he's feeling at least as fucked as he
looked," said Madan. "Well, what's Madna like, what're you
doing for sex there?"

"You don't know what a BDO is, but I'm sharing one with
my Collector. She's exhaustingly oversexed, like a case for
Krafft-Ebing."

Thus the three talked on, desultorily. Their mouths seemed
to work on their own, forming syllables seemingly independent
of their minds. None of them paid much attention to the other
two. Each wanted to talk, but not fervently. It was as though
some time had to be passed, and it passed least taxingly when
one talked, because to keep silent meant that one had either to
listen or to think. And Agastya didn't mind particularly. He
had no wish to expose the confusion of his soul. They wouldn't
be interested, for one thing. Then, like Tonic that morning,
they would demolish its nobility by a few careless words.
Already he realized that most of what he thought and felt was
rather trite and not remotely unique—Bhatia, for instance, was
out of place in Madna too, and Madan didn't like his job either,

felt he was wasting time in it, and knew of no alternatives. No emotion was sacredly his own, and he half-hoped that his restlessness would thus succumb to attrition. Perhaps his mind would finally realize that its disquietude was merely an index of its immaturity, as inevitable a sign of growing-up as the first emission of semen, as universal as excrement, and about as noteworthy.

"There's an American woman staying with us for a while," said Madan. "Christine Something, she says she likes being called Christ. She's the daughter of some shady business connection of my father. Thirtyish, damn sexy. She's fucking a Kenyan called Hungu. He studies Management at the University. He looks as though he has a big cock. I think he hates me, but he also hates all Indians. Your Krafft-Ebing reminded me of them. Skin fetishism. She's quite hateful. Goes on and on about the *real* India, and how people all over the world don't know enough of one another, as though that was in any way important or desirable. My fault, I led her on to the topic the day she arrived. She comes from Chicago. How was I to know that someone studies Ancient Indian History over there? She says they do. All I knew about Chicago was Al Capone. That started her off. How ignorant I was, and how people from all over the world should meet to remove this ignorance of one another, and how there should be more interaction—judging from her behaviour I think she meant intercourse. She knows a lot about India too, the bitch. She's leaving tomorrow or day after for a place called Lothal for some research, and then she shrieked when I asked her where it was. Then she went on and on about Indians being blind to their own history, apart from being blind to the world outside. She says all the time that all we read in books about other cultures, et cetera, is just rubbish, and people in different countries get horribly distorted views of one another through books and films. I think she works for the CIA. She kept using my Al Capone remark as an example, saying, 'see, see, that's all that you know about America.' Then I said, Lionel Ritchie. Now she doesn't talk to me much."

They went for a drive, after Madan went to the kitchen to buy some more marijuana from his servant. Dhrubo cursed the traffic till they stopped in one of the parking lots of Rajendra Place. Guarded by the dark blocks of offices, they heard the horns screaming at one another thirty metres away and felt safe, as on an island. Madan slowly rolled a smoke in the light from a street mercury lamp and Dhrubo changed Scott Joplin for Keith Jarrett. Outwardly it could have been almost any day of the past six years.

"Office warrens look nice only after dark," said Dhrubo. Every encounter with West Delhi seemed to sour him further. "Every morning, won't this place also get execs like me, who in their spare time browse through the *Wall Street Journal* and the occasional *Time*—I suppose *Business India* in their case, and *India Today*."

"You must always say *Time and Newsweek*, otherwise *Newsweek* will feel hurt," said Madan who, like a craftsman, was checking the shape of the joint against the street-light. "August, Dhrubo must've told you about how he's feeling unreal? He makes it sound awful. Stupid man, I wish I could feel unreal. Entirely his foolishness, of course, and varieties of foolishness. He's bothered that everything doesn't hang together—Yale and your damn Durga Puja—a real idiot, and because he can't manage by himself, he must make demands on someone else's life. And that Renu, you never met her, did you, she looked as though her puss smelt, and told me she was a 'very private person.' I thought that meant she was willing to hump, anyone would think the same at such a remark, but she didn't, amazing. Sex should be like male stray dogs, no hassles—with lots and lots of condoms. And Dhrubo shows his letters to all his friends, behaving like that American Lothal woman, as though the world's a *Reader's Digest* place, and everyone is dying to be nice to everyone else."

Jarrett played on, proximate piano against the cacophony of traffic. A constable walked out of the dark, beret, khaki-in-daylight overcoat and a thigh-high stick, and straight up to the car. Dhrubo didn't even have time to lower the joint. But, amazingly, Madan knew him, and chatted with him, cordially and obscenely, in Punjabi. The constable smoked that joint with them and left after Madan gave him another joint's worth of marijuana. Agastya drove on the way back, while Dhrubo communed with Keith Jarrett, and Madan fantasized aloud, "I'd like to be someone's mistress, I think . . . a flat, money, a video . . . nice underwear . . ."

The days passed so fast for Agastya. He woke up with the day almost half-gone. At brunch he would remember the food of Madna and then overeat, as though he could store up. He played chess with his uncle or listened to music in his room. He talked to his father almost every evening, and told him that he'd take a holiday in Calcutta after his training. He met Dhrubo and Madan every day. They didn't go anywhere in particular or do anything, they just relaxed, mostly in Dhrubo's house and talked without listening. He jogged at odd hours of the day. The days passed so fast, but the nights were slower. At night he would lie awake and hear the clack of his uncle's type-writer and watch the dark shape of the bougainvillaea outside the window, and see in its twists and turns a million things, but never his future.

AND THEN he was again on the train for Madna, staring blankly at the hundreds of kilometres of countryside, at the moonscape of the Chambal Valley, the small towns, totally oblivious to the changes intended by the best-laid plans, the fields lush after a good monsoon, from the bridges the dots of people below, washing clothes and selves in the waters of swollen rivers, timeless. Madna and Delhi seemed two extreme points of an unreal existence; the only palpable thing was the rhythm of the beast beneath him, a wonder, that could link such disparate worlds together.

He lay down on his upper berth to avoid all human contact, and said silently, to anyone who would listen, no more journeys, please, no more. Living had become a simpler business, gliding from day to day and discovering more and more what he did not want. Now all he wanted, or thought he wanted, was one place, any one place, with no consciousness in his mind of the existence of any other. He could even make do with Madna, if his mind would not burgeon with the images of Delhi, or of Calcutta, walks with Neera in the Lake Gardens, long chats about life and books and sex, and her hesitant revelation of her virginity; and beyond that Singapore, where everything was ordered, and Illinois, with its infinite varieties of ham. It was convulsing, the agony of the worlds in his head.

He writhed in his berth, tormented by masochistic images of a myriad women, chastening phoenixes out of his past, some glimpsed but fleetingly—at cinema-ticket queues and chemists' shops—but their faces and thighs recorded by that part of the mind that sees catharsis in pain and a sexual release in agony. Their attitudes, like his entire past, blurred into a congeries of mockery, causing him to curl up in the berth in the postures of atonement, like the fingers of a paralysed hand.

Then Madna station, on time. The beggars squabbling around the taps, their language now no longer so alien, the arse-breaking jeep, the cigarette and sugarcane stalls, the bridge, Vasant's children swinging on the Rest House gate, waving at him, the stench of booze and stale air around Shankar's door (he had gone to Koltanga for a few days, but had left his fetor behind), Vasant with his jug of supposedly boiled water and a cup of sweet tea. Everything unchanged, as though time itself had accompanied him away from Madna.

Vasant and his progeny crowded him to watch him open the door. Vasant said, "Many people have come. Collector of Paal, and Deputy Secretary Industries, and the Englishman with his wife." They followed Agastya into the dark silent room. The frog, disturbed, hopped to another corner. Agastya went to the mirror. His reflection, like the room, was sullied by dust.

He took his tea out to the comfortable warmth of the veranda. While the children explored the room while pretending to clean it, Vasant followed him, to repeat the news. "Collector Paal and Deputy Secretary Industries are staying in Srivastav saab's house. But the Englishman is staying here." He pointed to the Circuit House. Agastya was determined not to enquire, and to see how long Vasant could refrain from divulging all his information without any display of interest from his audience. He was cynically amused at how easily he had slipped back into the Madna life, playing personality games with a caretaker-cook. Vasant lost that round almost immediately. "The Englishman came here two days ago. He's come to find out about his cousin." It made no sense, but Agastya let it pass. Dust billowed out of the open door. Through its haze he saw one child force the wastebasket over another's head.

"Tell them not to disturb the frog," he said to Vasant as he moved his chair away from the door.

Later, he unpacked slowly. He put back on the shelf the *Gita*, Marcus Aurelius, and his diary. He had hardly remembered them on his holiday. He spread on the bed the cover he had brought back with him, the cream sheet with the huge red dot in the centre. He yelled for Vasant, asked him for more tea, and gave him Tamse's painting to dust. He trimmed his beard slowly, with care. The lizards seemed to have multiplied greatly in his absence. The late-afternoon sun touched the cassettes on the table. He browsed through his diary. Now he had nothing to record. He picked up the *Madna District Gazetteer* from beside his canvas shoes on the bottom shelf. He read a paragraph or two, but the words didn't register. He then lay down to watch the ceiling.

Like an automaton he repeated familiar acts. The walk to the Collector's house at about seven. Through the Circuit House compound and past the yawning stray dogs. The huge field with its shacks at one edge. Near the Club they had put up nets, the cricket season had begun. Past the Madna Club. The crowds in and around the bus station. Scores waiting to get away from Madna. A green and yellow State Transport bus revving up at the mouth of the station. Passengers on its roof, tying down their luggage at their own risk. The board read, Madna to Jompanna. Dispirited faces behind the window bars. A woman was being sick at one window. He watched her white vomit crawl down the side of the bus. Someone called his name. It was Mohan, smiling and walking towards him. The whole scene clicked into focus. Bhatia was buying cigarettes a few yards away. With Mohan was a man with very short hair, who seemed familiar.

"Hello, August, how was Delhi? You've met Dubey before,

haven't you, he's Assistant Conservator of Forests at Gora-pak…"

"Of course we've met, you arranged that feast at our picnic."

They laughed and shook hands. Bhatia came up, looking happier than usual. "I'm getting out of here, a long Diwali break. I'm leaving this evening, in fact, just now. I'm rushing back to pack the last-minute things, then I'm moving."

"Don't look so excited," said Mohan, "you'll be back here before you can even brush your teeth."

"Well, it's better than not going at all," said Bhatia.

"I'm not so sure," said Agastya.

Bhatia only beamed in reply, said, "'Bye, we'll chat when I return," shook hands with the three, and left. They watched him scurry away through the traffic.

"You couldn't be going to any place that you couldn't go to a little later, let's go and have tea somewhere," said Mohan. "As Sathe says, no one does anything in Madna that couldn't wait."

They moved towards the dhabas on the far side of the sta-tion. "You like spending your free evenings here, watching the buses leave?" asked Agastya. "Perhaps you feel nice, seeing peo-ple leave Madna?" They laughed.

Dubey said, "I came up here for the day. I'm returning to Gorapak now, and Mohan and Bhatia came to see me off. I missed the six thirty bus, I've to wait for the next one."

They passed a small crowd around a crafty old man selling aphrodisiacs. The man's beard seemed grey more with dirt than with age. Exhortations and promises in a voice roughened by the years of yelling out his petty fictions. Agastya noticed, with a half-smile, his peon Digambar succumbing to buy a bottle.

All dhabas all over look the same, thought Agastya—kero-sene lamps, cracked tables, abundant bustle, urchin-waiters, a sweaty toughie yelling at them, crates of indigenous Coke sur-rogates, an enticing smell of tandoori rotis and chhole mingling with the stench of the drains. "Three teas," said Dubey to the urchin who wiped the table with a dirtier rag.

"Aren't you two going home for Diwali?" asked Agastya.

"Yes, I am," said Mohan, "the day after tomorrow. Rohini will stay back in Alwar. No sense in taking her to Pirtana."

"Pirtana will be worse than Gorapak, which is saying quite a lot," said Dubey, with a shy smile, "no electricity, remember."

Mohan smiled, "Exigencies of service."

A bus roared out of the station, filling the dhaba with exhaust smoke. Dubey scratched his head. He looked drawn and ugly, like a convict. His face convulsed occasionally as he spoke of the barrenness of his life at Gorapak. "There's no market, nothing. There's a small club where everyone just plays bridge, nothing else. After office I don't feel like returning to my room, where I just lie in bed and wait for dinner, but there's nowhere to go."

"What *do* you do then?" asked Agastya.

"I go and watch the river sometimes, or I go and watch them playing bridge."

Agastya looked away. He seemed to be enclosed by the unheroic and petty desolation of others in exile—the District Judge, Bhatia, now Dubey.

"I've asked for a transfer to a better place," said Dubey, "with my father dead, my mother and younger sister can't stay alone, they'll come and stay with me. I hope the transfer comes through."

"Transfer to?"

"Well," Dubey smiled again, "after Mohan leaves, there'll be a vacancy here in Madna. We're waiting for my sister to finish her school exams. She could do her college here in Madna." Under the able tutorship of the Collector's wife, said Agastya silently.

They finished their teas and went to enquire about the next bus to Gorapak. Crowds, and the smells of weary bodies around the ticket counters. Stained cement benches under the wan tube-lights. Infinitely patient village women, in incongruously gaudy pinks and greens, squatting on the floor, smoking bidis. Somewhere a transistor belting out a Hindi disco song, hopelessly dissonant with its environs. They watched Dubey get on to a bus and become another dispirited face behind the window bars. At least I get a jeep wherever I go, said Agastya silently, as the bus pulled away.

"Where *were* you going before we pleaded with you to grace our company with your presence?" asked Mohan, as they moved towards the gates of the bus station.

"To the Collector's, to sort of report that I'd returned from my holiday."

"Come, I'll walk you part of the way." Mohan sounded a little preoccupied.

They passed the Industrial Training Institute, a one-storey building in an acre of rubble, barbed wire for a boundary wall and gate posts without a gate. "It's Rohini," said Mohan abruptly, "she doesn't like being so far away from home, and living in places where there's nothing much for wives to do." Agastya made consoling sounds in reply. Mohan asked, "Where're you going for your BDO training?"

"I don't know yet."

They parted at the turn to the Collector's house. "I'll come over tomorrow to say hello properly," said Agastya.

"Yes, you must," Mohan smiled, "because who knows when we shall meet again?" He saw the faint perplexity on Agastya's face. "See, I'm leaving the day after tomorrow for Alwar. When I return you'll be BDO somewhere, probably in some other sub-division. And anyway I'll be going to Pirtana almost immediately. And then you could be posted as Assistant Collector anywhere in the state."

All the lights seemed to be on in the Collector's house, far more lights, anyway, than Agastya had ever seen before. There were lamps in the garden. Maybe in these ten days they went mad and converted the place into an asylum, he thought, and the other lunatics killed the nurses and the wardens and everybody else on the night of the full moon and are now celebrating, and maybe the whole district will turn up to drink blood jubilantly over the corpse of Srivastav, scowling even in death.

Chairs on the lawn, Urdu ghazals from two speakers on side tables, peons flitting, Kumar standing in front of two seated victims, pulling up his pants and describing something with a zest seemingly not shared by his audience, Srivastav was even serving booze, Joshi in flapping safari suit flitting with the peons, two bridge groups, the women sitting in one large formal circle, painted and perfumed, kids racing around, Shipra, Srivastav's daughter, saw him first. "Bungaali Uncle has come! Bungaali Uncle has come!" She ran shrieking to her mother. Her friends followed, repeating her chant. In some delinquent mouths it changed to "Pumbaali Kunkal has bum." Wondering how to strangle them all, Agastya went after them to say hello.

A round of namaste to the wives; he noted that Kumar's wife was also short and fat and that the wife of the Deputy Superintendent of Police was startlingly sexy; then on the way to the bridge tables he could not circumvent Kumar. "Hahn, Sen, when did you arrive, remember that bastard taxi-driver in Delhi? Well, he was beaten up and his licence confiscated." His seated victims were Bajaj and Rajan, the Collector of Paal.

Srivastav was dummy at one table, and scowling at his partner, who was immensely fat, bearded and placid; he looked like a maker of lethally dull art films. "Hahn, Sen, I'm glad you've come, I hope you enjoyed Delhi," surprisingly Srivastav took him to one side. "Look, go and talk to the Englishman and his wife. I don't know what to do with them. They are both very silent and dull, but someone has to talk to them, bhai."

"Where are they, sir?"

Srivastav looked around, scowling. I once read in an Enid Blyton, sir, said Agastya silently, that if the wind changes when you're making faces, then your face gets permanently fucked. "I can't see them. Perhaps they've escaped and returned to the Circuit House," said Srivastav wistfully. "Look, Sen, they are your responsibility. Are you going to drink?" Srivastav was scowling at Agastya's top shirt button.

"Yes, sir."

"Well, drink with them and keep them happy." Srivastav returned to the table with less of a scowl, to find that his placid partner had lost the contract.

The Englishman and his wife emerged from the house. Either his wife was Indian, thought Agastya, or he had gone to piddle with his Indian mistress. They were both young, definitely less than thirty. "Hello, my name is Agastya Sen." He didn't catch either name.

The woman said, "You've been our only topic of conversation for the past two days. All these district officials have been anxiously awaiting your return. They've been saying in practically as many words that once you return the two of us are going to have a simply lovely time in Madna. We are supposed to get on famously. Your mother was Christian, so we are meant to have a lot in common, and your father is Madhusudan Sen, and we are both very impressed, though I had to nudge my husband to ooh with awe at that time." Agastya was a little taken back. She was heavy and full, like the centre of an adolescent wet dream, in a dark blue salwaar kameez.

"Mr. Srivastav's been awfully nice to us," said the Englishman. Light brown moustache and small, rather timid, blue eyes. They sat down beside a lamp at some distance from the others. Kumar grinned at them from the right, and raised his glass in a long-distance toast. Agastya could hear Srivastav explaining to his fat partner, but in a surprisingly polite voice, exactly how badly he, the fat partner, had played the last game.

He was determined not to find out just what the English-man and his wife were doing in Madna; it was more interesting that way. "What will your drink be, sir?" A polite waiter, he spoke English, short brushed hair, thick moustache, could've been in a macho cigarette ad. "You aren't from the Collectorate?"

"Sir?"

"You aren't a peon at the Collectorate, are you?"

The waiter had apparently been tutored not to look baffled. "I work at the Madna International, sir."

Oh, Sathe's hotel. So Srivastav had enlisted professional help. "Where is Mr. Govind Sathe?"

"He left about half an hour ago, sir, for something. He should be returning soon."

"Uh...I'll have a whisky 'n' soda. Won't you drink?" Agastya turned to his two charges.

"We've been doing just that all evening," said the woman, "gin 'n' lime."

"A double whisky," said the Englishman.

Agastya quite liked the prospect of the evening; he would get drunk on official booze (Srivastav would certainly put down this dinner under any one of many expenditure heads: perhaps "working dinner with Collector of Paal to discuss law and order problems in border tehsils" or "working dinner with Deputy Secretary Industries to discuss problems of District Industries Centre, Madna"; Srivastav's office would be able to concoct a million things to explain the dinner away) on the lawns of the Collector's house, chaperoning an unknown Englishman and his outspoken sexy wife.

"You were away on holiday?" asked the Englishman.

Agastya wondered for a second if he should lie, then said, "Yes."

Shekhar, Srivastav's son, ran up, hit Agastya on the arm, said, "Pumbaali Kunkal has bum," and scuttled away, shrieking.

"What on earth did he say?" asked the wife.

ENGLISH, AUGUST

"It's a popular tribal prayer of this area," said Agastya. "It means, roughly, May God grant me fertility. It is used most often by those tribal groups in the district that worship snakes. These tribes practise esoteric fertility rites with cobras." For an instant he contemplated getting sexual in his fabrications; no, it was too early. "That's very Indian, you know," he said graciously to the Englishman, "like cattle dozing or chewing cud sitting in the fast lanes of the streets of Delhi, very Indian. The children probably learnt it from their ayah. I hope Mrs. Srivastav doesn't get to hear them. I should think she would be quite angry." The wife looked appropriately nonplussed at this unexpected information.

"You're in the IAS, aren't you?" she asked.

"Yes," Agastya turned to the Englishman, "that's the Indian Administrative Service."

"Yes, I know," said the Englishman, "approximately what the Indian Civil Service was before 1947."

"Don't let Mr. Srivastav hear you," said Agastya, "he'd be very angry." Predictably they didn't follow.

The waiter returned with the drinks. Agastya noticed Sathe's sister-in-law among the women, still haggard in a red and gold sari. The wife asked, "You also stay at the Circuit House, don't you?"

"In the Rest House, yes, that's in the same compound, but it's not as vulgarly finished."

"Yes, that cook, Vasant, pointed out your room to us. He cooks for us, too."

Agastya laughed, "Cooks well, yes?"

The Englishman and his wife laughed, too. "I don't know how you've survived on that food for so long," the wife said. "I stooge a lot of meals off others, mainly Mrs. Srivastav." "I keep telling John that Vasant's cooking is the exception rather than the norm."

Ah, so one was John. Perhaps she was Mary, and John and

Mary were going to live happily ever after. But more likely, and Agastya laughed silently, that they were going to get hazaar fucked in Madna; if one took those silly books and films to be even one-tenth true, then all those Englishmen who came to India looking for soul, any foreigner actually, who came looking for anything, soon found that both some native *and* his country had wrapped their thighs around him, and that he was getting it in the balls.

"What is the nature of your work here?" asked John.

Agastya looked at him suspiciously, to read on his face whether the question meant, exactly why is the Government of India paying a moron like you. "Uh . . . I'm being trained in the wiles of administration, moving from office to office, trying to learn what each office does."

The no man's land beyond the lawn, he noticed, was being used as a parking lot. A woman appeared from behind an Ambassador. Whatever had she been doing there? he wondered. Perhaps she was a fetishist, and could only piddle behind cars. Like Prashant's youngest brother, he remembered with a silent laugh, who till the age of three, would only shit behind the drawing-room sofa, about which act Prashant would soothe his mother with, "How can you worry, Ma, it's a sign of genius— like Einstein." Agastya had never seen the woman before. She looked around, half-waved to someone, and surprisingly, came towards them. She looked bossy, so Agastya got up from his chair.

"Hello," she said to John and his wife, "enjoying your-selves?" She looked at Agastya enquiringly.

"My name is Agastya Sen, madam. I—"

She smiled. "Oh, I've heard of you from Mrs. Srivastav. You seem to be under her wing in Madna. I am Vatsala Rajan. My husband is Collector of Paal. Wait, I'll get a chair," she said, and waited for Agastya to move.

He went off to get another drink first. Srivastav was again

dummy. When he rejoined the group with a chair, Mrs. Rajan was leaning forward and talking with mouth and hands, "—in Tooting, I have some friends there. And I think the Festival is to be applauded simply because it was such an *ambitious* effort." She finished and sat back, looking excited.

"Pity we didn't see much of it," said John, looking at his wife.

Mrs. Rajan leaned forward again, neck tensed, like a conspirator. "But it's so important for India to have the right *exposure* abroad. One must explode these wretched myths about India, you know, that it's the land of cringing natives, and snake-charmers, elephants and Tantric rites. It's ..." she unfisted her hand, like a bud opening in time-lapse photography; perhaps she had hoped to find the telling adjectives in her palm.

Agastya wondered if he could slip away to eye the wife of the Deputy Superintendent of Police; but, then, when he returned Mrs. Rajan would still be talking, but to two corpses; and then John's son, a toddler, perhaps, somewhere in England, an Anglo-Indian like those in school, would arrive in Madna thirty years later to unravel how his parents had died while listening to a woman at a party, and would not believe the post-mortem report which would read, "Death by Boredom," until John junior himself met Mrs. Rajan in Delhi perhaps, in the huge house that the Rajans would have built for themselves when Mr. Rajan had been Secretary, Culture, and had single-handedly fucked up the Festival of India in Iceland—Agastya realized that Mrs. Rajan had asked him a question.

"Sorry, ma'am, I didn't catch that."

"We were trying to define our positions, John and I," Agastya thought for a lightning second of sex, "and we've reached an impasse. John here insists that I use the word 'Indian' far too loosely. Now tell me, Agastya—you have a lovely name, really, so ethnic—how would you define the word 'Indian'? I maintain that India is too fascinatingly diverse a country for the word to have any precise definition."

Agastya's eyeballs flicked from left to right, seeking ways of escape. Just what had these fuckers been up to? No wonder Rajan was sitting there patiently listening to Kumar; compared to Rajan's wife, Kumar was Somerset Maugham. "Uh . . ."

"Your heritage is mixed," said Mrs. Rajan, "your point of view should be particularly interesting." A surprising adolescent giggle from John's wife.

"Uh, I don't know, I've never thought about these things—"

"That's a very important admission," said Mrs. Rajan emphatically, closing her eyes and nodding her head, "most Indians do not think about what it means to be Indian." Agastya wanted to slap her, very hard, and walk gracefully away to get himself another drink. "Go on," she said impatiently, nodding and blinking her eyes.

"I suppose being Indian means being born an Indian citizen and not wanting to change citizenship." That's got the bitch, said Agastya in silent triumph as he saw irritated bewilderment alter Mrs. Rajan's face. Just then Mrs. Srivastav arrived on her hostess rounds, like a long-awaited miracle, compelling Mrs. Rajan to re-alter her face. Agastya was determined to leave with her, if necessary, by clutching on to the edge of her sari. Small talk, while he silently finished his drink.

"Ask for refills for us too," said John's wife sweetly.

"He's been drinking steadily all by himself, has he?" asked Mrs. Srivastav.

On the way back from the temporary bar set up at the edge of the lawn, Agastya was called by Bajaj. Thank you, he said silently, as he went up. Bajaj was chatting with Srivastav's ex-bridge partner, who looked much fatter standing. The new prey of Srivastav's scowls was Gopalan. "Hello, Sen, when did you get back from Delhi?" said Bajaj. "Have you met Mr. Panda, our Deputy Secretary Industries, ex-Collector of Koltanga . . ." Agastya shook a warm, moist and sticky hand, and wondered if the fat man had been masturbating below the bridge table, to express, in secret, his real opinion of his bridge partner.

Bajaj said, "Sen, has Srivastav saab told you? We'll probably post you to Jompanna as Block Development Officer. It's a backward tribal area, and will be a rich experience for you." Agastya nodded and tried to look enthusiastic.

Panda said, "I think you're lucky to be a BDO in Jompanna. It'll be a wonderfully new world." He pushed up his spectacles and lit a cigarette. His voice was very slow and heavy, cultivated to enunciate profundities. He continued, "As BDO you'll see grassroots development," he smiled, he had brown teeth, "in a developing country. You'll implement all those programmes that you merely read about in the papers, Rural Development, Tribal Welfare, Family Welfare, it's a tremendous opportunity to learn." Bajaj nodded, sad spaniel eyes in a Don Quixote frame.

The thumri that was now playing was familiar, "The pearl has fallen from your nose-ring, my beloved." Shankar's song, Agastya had been recovering from a fever that morning, and Shankar had drunkenly asserted that all one needed to bear the world was to transcend reason. A man joined them, small talk, he turned out to be Sharma, the District Health Officer. Oh-ho, Agastya remembered, the proud user of the circus-jeep, with the painted wrestlers. He looked around for it, there it was, looking almost dignified in the half-dark. Sharma and Bajaj talked office for a while, then Bajaj tried to include Panda in the conversation. "An unusual situation. You know Baba Ramanna's Rehabilitation Home," Panda nodded very slowly, as though his obese neck precluded faster movement, "he has politely refused government assistance. He says he has managed without Government for forty years."

Panda said nothing, but looked wise. Hoping to prod him into pronouncement, the District Health Officer said, "I went there again this morning, but couldn't meet the Baba. I met his son though. He said that government aid unfortunately will be followed by government interference."

"That's quite true, though," said Panda, "but that man is really almost a saint. What a labour of love, this rehabilitation programme of his." Everyone nodded solemnly.

Agastya saw a red Maruti crunch up the drive. Sathe got out, looked around, and went to talk to someone at one of the bridge tables. Then Bajaj was asking him, "Sen, you've seen Baba Ramanna's Home, haven't you?"

"Uh...no, sir, I haven't yet had the opportunity," and wanted to add, I'm about as interested in him as he would be in me.

Bajaj looked almost aghast. "Really, Sen, whatever have you been doing during training?" He turned to Sharma. "When are you next going. Take Sen saab with you. He must see it, it'll be very educative."

"Some time next week perhaps," said the District Health Officer, nodding at Agastya, "I'll pick you up from the Rest House, will that be all right?"

"Certainly, thank you," said Agastya, relying on Sharma to forget, or on himself not to be in his room, or to be too stoned to hear the knock on the door. You should have counted, he said to himself, the number of times you heard the words "education" and "enriching experience," and their variants, used about yourself.

He said, "If you'll excuse me, sir, I have to go and talk to—" he realized that he didn't know their names "—the Englishman and his wife." It sounded awful. "Mr. Srivastav's orders. I have to chaperone them this evening."

He moved away, saw Mrs. Rajan still leaning forward and talking shit, and veered to meet Sathe, who said, "Why were you standing there for hours talking to that hippopotamus? So what if they don't eat human beings. Come on, drink up, we'll get refills, and move away from this circus."

They did, Agastya grinning in anticipation of the causticity to come. "Which complex masterpiece awaits the final touches on your easel, O painter?"

Sathe laughed, as always, with his body. "Did you ever see my Krishna cartoons? A set of twelve. Those newspapers are reluctant to print them, they say they are too blasphemous. Quite sad. I thought of using English captions and sending them elsewhere, but they really don't sound as good in English." They had moved away towards the cars, and finally settled against the bonnet of the circus-jeep. "In one I have a politician telling Krishna at Kurukshetra, with sacks instead of bodies all around them, the sacks reading 'Black Money,' 'Corruption,' et cetera, 'The mind is restless, O Krishna'"—Agastya started. The words were too familiar, this was a commingling of two worlds, surely those words were not the subject of a cartoon—"and Krishna gives him two digestive pills and asks him to call him in the morning." Sathe waited for Agastya to laugh. "Your fine Anglicized mind didn't understand? Well, it does sound much flatter in English. You know, for a politician, the mind and the stomach, they're more or less the same."

"No, no, I did understand, it's really a good joke, I was just thinking of something else." Of a surreal silent room a few minutes from here, of fretting on a white bed under a ghostly mosquito net, the restlessness of the body mimicking the disquietude of the mind.

There was a stir around the bridge tables. "Those idiots are changing partners again." Sathe took a swig from his glass. "Have you met our Englishman and his wife?"

Agastya saw that Mrs. Rajan had left to look for other prey, and said, "Shall we go and talk to them. I have orders to chat with them all evening."

"Certainly, and let's fill up on the way." He finished his glass. "I wouldn't've thought the English could be so... sentimental, unless dear John's real purpose here in India is to look for karma, or try and arouse the shakti at the base of his spine, and he's too embarrassed to admit it."

You are doing well, said Agastya to himself, with your ignorance; even Sathe seemed to know what John and his wife were doing in Madna, no doubt he would also know who and what Baba Ramanna was. His this precious protection of his ignorance was so childishly exciting—it reminded him of the secret thrills of the early years of school, of the boarders conspiring to eat a day scholar's tiffin, and waiting with quickened breath and knees pressed together with tension for the sucker to discover that he wouldn't eat that day—a similar feeling. You certainly have regressed, he smiled, for your kicks.

"Make both double, Ganesh," said Sathe to the bartender.

"Oh, of course, he's your man," smiled Agastya, "when Srivastav asked you for help for this party, I thought you'd have sulked and refused, or asked for the Club's booze licence in return."

"He didn't ask me, he asked my brother," laughed Sathe. John and his wife, Agastya was pleased to see, looked a little drunk. "Hello," said Sathe, "you both still in Coventry, isn't that the term?" Everyone laughed. "Have you ever met Sen, the Pride of Madna?"

"Yes," said the wife, "he was on duty here, but deserted when Mrs. Rajan arrived."

Sathe nodded his complete approval of the move. "When do you leave for Jompanna?"

"Tomorrow morning, I think," said the Englishman, "I'll have to check with Mr. Srivastav. He's been kind enough to loan us a jeep."

"He's a very good Collector, by the way," said Sathe most unexpectedly. "Behind those scowls is an excellent administrator. You could do worse than talk to him for a while. I heard somewhere that Agastya here is going with you to Jompanna."

"So did we," smiled John, "he is the friend, philosopher and guide."

"I'm being posted there, in fact, in a few weeks' time," said Agastya, "as BDO," and added to John, vaguely, "I'll have to manage development."

"God help Jompanna," said Sathe, "if you develop it as enthusiastically as you sound. It's a wonderful place, once the best forests in the district, and one of the best in India. I went there with my father once, about twenty years ago, tigers still abounded then. Now, of course, they must've built roads and dispensaries—development. The Naxalites are there, too, trying to get the tribals to think, instead of wasting their lives drinking, and killing one another for their wives and watching their children die, and waiting to be overworked and exploited by forest contractors, like my father was. I think the tribals find thinking more difficult." Sathe turned to John. "You don't know what a Naxalite is, do you? They are as much a part of the story of Bengal as Bankim Chandra and roshogollas—"

"They are a violent and militant political group," explained his wife to John.

"You make them sound like terrorists," said Agastya.

"There protests the true son of Bengal," laughed Sathe, "anguished at this desecration of a great Bengali apotheosis. Naxalites terrorists! You might as well have said, Sita, that if Tagore's songs could be somehow transformed into pills, they would blast all other soporifics out of the market." Sathe looked at Agastya with benevolence, "You are so shamefully Bengali, Agastya, haven't you ever spared a thought for your mother?"

Then, at last, dinner. A bustle on the lawns as the groups broke up. The men slowly approached the women, to be gallant after ignoring them all evening. Mrs. Srivastav and Sathe's sister-in-law shepherded the guests to the tables. The clink and clatter of plates. The bridge players, expectedly, continued their post-mortem of the last game, and of previous games, and seemingly of all games ever played, over their plates of food, partly to impress the non-bridge players with, "Look, we have been exercising our minds while you've been getting drunk and wasting your time," and partly to talk so as not to have to listen to the views of other bridge players. By virtue of his position in the district Srivastav won all his arguments and looked around in triumph for other victims. Agastya was thankful that he was seen by Srivastav at his duty post (he was faintly amused by their names. As a couple, they were neither here nor there, neither Ram and Sita, nor John and Mary). "So," Srivastav smiled at them, "had a good evening? What is this?" mercurial alteration to scowl, looking at Sita's plate. "You are a vegetarian?"

"We thought of leaving tomorrow morning," said John, "if the jeep will be available then."

The furrows on Srivastav's brow smoothened. "Ah, yes, of course. Sen will go with you. You are going with them, aren't you?"

"Yes sir."

"See what Jompanna is like. If you don't like it then I'll try and get you to do your BDOship somewhere else." He turned to John, "So, did you get anything else of interest in the Record Room?"

"Yes," John smiled, quite genuinely this time, "some of my grandfather's inspection notes, his official tour diary, judgments in a variety of cases. I've photostated a few things."

Srivastav nodded. "The Record Room is in a mess, but perhaps that's why you could get so much. If it had been cleared up and organized, then some of that would doubtless have been thrown away." Then, "Sen," suddenly, with a scowl, "which Department are you attached to now?"

"The District Industries Centre, sir, this one week."

"Oh, a rubbish place, you can easily miss that. You've been reading the *District Gazetteer* for months, no," to John, "He'll explain anything you don't understand," to Agastya, "I've told

Joshi to give you the Small Savings jeep. You remind him tonight before you leave."

Over dessert, Agastya encountered Rajan, the Collector of Paal. He was stunned to discover that Rajan was as lethal as his wife (and they recalled Madan, "I feel quite happy when two really fucked people marry each other—the world begins to look organized"). Rajan was aggressive and open, and given to continual self-revelation in the conviction that he fascinated his listeners. He had taught Physics, somewhere in America, "with some Nobel laureate physicists," pronounced fissicists. From a twenty-minute monologue Agastya learnt that Physics had led him to Kant who had led him to the Indian Administrative Service. "Even among those fissicists there were petty jealousies. I was getting nowhere, I felt. I was restless—"

Et tu, Rajan, smiled Agastya.

"Why are you smiling?"

"No, nothing, sir, do go on." Rajan did. In ten years, perhaps I'll be like this, thought Agastya, with a wife like Mrs. Rajan, chatting with a stranger about restlessness as though it was the price of petrol.

He reached his Rest House room well after twelve. John had wanted to leave at seven the next morning; Agastya, thinking of his exercise, had suggested eight, and had convinced them that it wouldn't be uncomfortably warm.

The soft blue light, the cloying smoke from the coil of incense that he had lit in the evening to keep the mosquitoes away. He stood at the door looking in. How many nights. He switched off the tube-light on the veranda. No, now the room was black, like a tomb. He switched on the light again and began the familiar journey through the room, around the bed, past the table and the dressing-mirror, where his reflection looked spectral, the wraith that he had always jested with, the only listener of his silent laughter. There were the same cassettes on the table, the books on the shelf. He remembered Sathe's description of his Krishna cartoons. He picked up the books and read aloud in the glow of the tube-light. "'Strong men know not despair, Arjuna, for this wins neither heaven nor earth.'" His voice sounded strange, like someone else's. "'Death: a release from impressions of sense, from twitchings of appetite, from excursions of thought, and from service to the flesh.'" Standing in front of the mirror, with his reflection soothing him, he wrote in his diary: "When I am with people, when I talk to them, I feel all right, but when I am alone." Then he gave up, and allowed the pen to trail aimlessly across the page. It felt nice, as though he was letting the pen do what it wanted. He read some of his earlier entries, and then, holding the pen lightly, let it crawl across the words, like an injured ant.

HE WAS ready, exercised and bathed, by a quarter to eight. The jeep was punctual, too, driven by his old friend who had never been able to tell one district office from another. Sita was in jeans and John wore a sola hat. "Just in case the heat and dust get too much?" asked Agastya, with what he hoped was a winning and disarming grin.

John smiled embarrassedly. "A family heirloom, actually. My grandfather wore it on his rounds. I brought it along because I was dying to wear it. Now I can look a pukka burra saheb."

They moved out, on the road to Mariagarh, at the end of which, on an earlier occasion, had been a blue film with a Superintendent of Police in a Rest House into which that Tamse had tried to squeeze an entire country. This trip promised to be equally strange, accompanying an Englishman and his Indian wife on the trail of a grandfather who had been mauled by a tiger two generations ago. To Agastya the world seemed infinitely bizarre.

Sita and Agastya sat in front. "You sit in front if you like," he had said to John Avery, "it'll be less bumpy."

"No the back's perfectly all right. I can sprawl here," and he did.

"It's really very nice of Mr. Srivastav to give us a jeep for this journey," shouted Avery over the roar of the jeep's diesel engine.

Agastya wished he wouldn't be so formal, and shouted back, "One of the reasons I'm going with you is to make this trip official. Then the jeep's log book can read, Assistant Collector Under Training on tour to Jompanna."

The noise of the jeep made sustained conversation impossible, for which Agastya was happy. He could slide down in his seat till his neck rested against its back and, without chafing, allow his mind its restlessness. In a jeep, he would smile and argue with himself, you can do nothing about your mind or your future, not until the journey is over. In a moving jeep he was not vexed by the onus of thought. Later in the year he would like being a BDO for much the same reason; the job entailed long jeep journeys in which he would be at rest, watching the miles pass—village boys on a tree, a hut of a post office, the sky amber at sundown—while his mind roamed, when he would dread the end of the road because then again he would no longer be free.

The town looked so ugly that he wanted to laugh. He realized that if he liked Madna at all it was because of its horrifying unpretentiousness, its greetings-from-a-cesspool-we're-all-in-it feeling. The adults defecating modestly behind bushes, the children, lords of innocence, waving to the jeep while shitting beside the road, cows and stray dogs, even, inexplicably, a camel, and people, people, burgeoning like a joyous cancer. "A sense of national or social sanitation is not a virtue among us. We may take a kind of a bath, but we do not mind dirtying the well or the tank or the river by whose side or in which we perform ablutions." Of course they had all heard of Gandhi, the Father of the Nation (but to some, Agastya remembered with a laugh, he was the Uncle—it must be so confusing, that Nehru's progeny were also Gandhis), the twentieth-century superstar (especially after the film, the Hindi version of which at least a few of these defecators had seen and enjoyed in a packed cinema house, jabbing their fingers joyously at the stars of their Freedom Struggle, "See, there's Patel!" "Nehru! Nehru!" and it had made them feel good to see that their great leaders, after whom they had renamed everything in sight, had got together and chatted so often), whose birthday was a national holiday. But half these defecators were illiterate, and those who weren't would never read Gandhi, much less implement him; they wouldn't step beyond the *Dainik* and the spice of a BDO's supposed love affair with a Collector. And those who did not defecate in public and could read had been blinded and their noses clogged by their familiarity with excrement on the road. Besides, it was always much easier to deify a hero than to understand him. But these shitters would never learn unless taught; Agastya was oddly reminded of the night before, and Sathe saying that the Naxalites around Jompanna were trying to get the tribals to think; it seemed then that the to-each-his-own outlook was inadequate—some people were compelled to obtrude in the affairs of others, sometimes just to remind them that they too had minds.

The jeep raced through the miles of paddy. The harvesting had begun. "What are all these fields?" asked Sita into his ear.

"You ought to be ashamed of yourself, city slicker," shouted Agastya, "that's paddy." Sita laughed.

He looked at her, whorls of down on the side of her cheeks, faint crease-marks on her brown throat. They had probably met at one of those English universities—(then his mind began to wander) or maybe in some English town, during a race riot; maybe John Avery wore a wig and was actually a skinhead, and she had married him because beneath the formality slumbered a master of kink. He wondered again at their presence in Madna. "Why are you smiling?" asked Sita, again into his ear.

"I'll tell you when this jeep stops," he shouted.

The level crossing was again down. The same disorderly row of overloaded trucks and other jeeps, the drivers smoking and cursing one another to pass the time. On the last occasion Kumar and he had chatted while piddling. They all got off. Everyone stared at Avery.

"It's your sola hat," said Agastya, "they haven't seen an Englishman and a sola hat together since 1947."

"Yes, it is a little absurd," said Avery, took it off and put it on one of the back seats.

Agastya watched with envy the driver stroll away to the bushes that bordered the fields. The presence of his companions was constraining. But it was another forty-five minutes to the nearest Rest House. He said, "Excuse me," and went after the driver.

Avery followed him. From behind a bush Avery laughed and said, "When in India..."

A few kilometres later, they could see the forest, a sash of dark green on the horizon. Then they turned left at a fork. The driver pointed, "The State Highway goes on to Mariagarh, sir, and later, joins the National Highway to Madras."

They entered the forest imperceptibly. A few isolated teak trees, like a disorderly vanguard. But this was no virgin forest, thought Agastya; everywhere there were symptoms of desecration, tree stumps, clumps of decaying bamboo, gaps in the trees that were sometimes small fields, too many new saplings planted by an assiduous Forest Department, and the road itself, new and black (from which, Kumar had said, the engineers had made lakhs), an interminable cicatrice on the flesh of the forest.

Villages, fields, patches of scarred forest, bridges over nalas, bus-stops, squatters on the road, the jeep moved on. Agastya felt a nudge on his shoulder. Sita had fallen asleep, her head had lolled. He looked back. Avery was asleep too, uneasy with his sola hat as a pillow.

They stopped for lunch at a Rest House at an insignificant small town called Tilan, a few shops, a bus-stand, a post office, another statue of a deformed Gandhi, a petrol station, vegetables being sold by the squatters on the road, curious eyes, dust. They met the tehsildar of Jompanna on the veranda of the Rest

House. "You'll reach Jompanna by about five, sir. You will have to make a night halt at Jompanna, sir. I have made arrangements. Then you can proceed to Marihandi tomorrow morning, sir, only forty-five minutes by jeep. Lunch is ready, sir," a hand moved almost involuntarily, a few inches towards the dining room, "and they have also boiled water, sir, to drink, for..." With his chin and a wriggle of his eyebrows, the tehsildar indicated Agastya's companions.

They all felt too dry, tired and dull to talk. Lunch was lavish, from chicken drowned in oil (called, in officialese, a Revenue Chicken, that the subordinates in the Revenue Department arranged for their superiors when they came touring, and for which they were always inadequately recompensed) to grapes. The tehsildar and his minions hovered around the table, beaming.

"Won't you eat with us?" asked Agastya perfunctorily.

"No, sir, for me only two meals a day. Otherwise I cannot function efficiently."

"That's begging the question," murmured Agastya.

They began lunch by finishing a jug of water. "I suppose this really is boiled?" asked Avery, after downing two glasses.

Agastya laughed, "Not to your desire, I think. You should have brought along with you an Indian stomach." Neither of them laughed. They ate little, and Agastya gorged, for not everyone in the district cooked like Vasant.

Immediately after lunch the tehsildar suggested tea.

"No," said Agastya firmly.

"But it is ready, sir."

"OK," said Agastya.

They sat in the veranda for tea, looking at the world through green lattice-work, the tehsildar drank from the saucer. Avery and Sita refused tea vehemently and instead looked ill. "We should start immediately, I think," said Agastya. His companions looked dead to all suggestion.

The tehsildar wanted them to sleep. "The rooms are all ready, sir."

Agastya called the driver. "Should we start right away?"

He nodded, "Better to start now, sir, then we can get to Jompanna while it is still light."

Agastya turned to the tehsildar, "Thank you. How much for the lunch?" Eyes and mouth round in protest. They fought for a while. Avery got up to join them. They moved to the jeep after they had pushed a fifty-rupee note into the tehsildar's shirt pocket, among the spectacle case and pens.

"Rather nice of the tehsildar to be like that about the lunch," said Sita, as she got into the jeep.

Agastya smiled cynically. "Well, if we hadn't paid, then in a few days they would be saying, Sen is like all the other officers, never pays. Most officers pay, of course, but never fully."

"I don't follow," said Avery.

"Setting up that lunch wouldn't have cost less than 100 rupees," said Agastya, "we paid fifty. The tehsildar didn't spend anything, of course. There are too many small-time businessmen in his jurisdiction only too happy to spend some money on his behalf, owners of small rice mills, petrol pumps, that sort of thing. Everyone is happy with this arrangement." They looked a little awed and surprised at Agastya's knowledge of the world. So did Agastya.

Then they were silenced by the starting of the jeep. They half-dozed through a similar landscape to Jompanna, but Agastya noticed that the forests were gradually growing thicker.

They reached after five, lulled by the jeep into a languor that clutched their bones. Violent-green weeds hemming the drains, shacks, the chaos of the weekly bazaar, tribals in clothes of many colours, bicycles, merchandise on the road, grains, sugarcane, raw tobacco, trinkets for the woman, baubles for the child, cloth, Agastya inhaled the whiff of hashish. They chugged slowly through the bazaar, three double-storeyed buildings, one video shop. Jompanna wasn't a town, but a large village, with a population of about twelve thousand, half of whom were tribals. The Rest House was new, built, with other offices, on the immensity of red sand on the edge of town. Red sand till the forest on the horizon, its awesome monotony merely accentuated by the buildings, roads, the bushes and trees. Government had come to Jompanna but recently—three years ago it had merely been one unremembered outpost of the district of Madna.

"God, what an ugly Rest House!" exclaimed Sita. It was. Bright pink and green, the shades of a cheap pastry, with white iron grilles, a psychedelic cage, gleaming new, with none of the compensatory dignity of age. A welcome party on the veranda, and a few idlers who had gathered to see an Englishman. "Myself MumbledName, sir, I'm BDO of Jompanna, yes, sir, I shall hand over charge to you when you come for your training. This is MumbledName, sir, the Sabhapati here, and that is the Revenue Circle Inspector, who will be with you at Marihandi tomorrow. Tea, sir?"

The rooms were as usual furnished like houses. The bathrooms had tiles and taps but no tap water. "We're ready for the water connection when it comes, sir," explained the caretaker, a thin voluble man in khaki shorts, "till then we use the well."

"You're also the cook? We're all vegetarians, you know that, no?"

"Vegetarians! Even that—" He jerked his eyeballs towards the next room.

"He most of all," said Agastya, welcoming a familiar feeling, "he was a Christian once, bloody beef eater, but he fell in love with India the moment he arrived, and converted to Jainism—a Digambar, too, in England he roams around naked." The caretaker looked suitably sceptical.

Tea on the veranda. Avery and Sita didn't emerge for a while. The sabhapati looked like a politician who might have taken his doubts to Krishna in a Sathe cartoon—fat, in white dhoti and kurta, fat moustache hiding his upper lip, eyes old with petty intrigue. Later, Bajaj was to warn Agastya about this president of the local political body. "Watch out for him," Bajaj would say, "he has Jompanna in his grasp. He is almost single-handedly responsible for the absence of tribal development in the block."

A clean orange sun in a fading sky. Below it a beautiful one-storey building, in grey stone, incomprehensibly long, contrasting almost vulgarly with the rest of Jompanna. "What is that?" asked Agastya.

"The new hospital, sir," said the BDO, "built by the Dutch last year."

Agastya wanted to laugh.

"You are going to Marihandi tomorrow, Sen saab, to see where that Mr. Avery was killed by a tiger?" The sabhapati spoke English slowly, but fluently.

"Yes."

"But there are no tigers there now. A tiger was last seen in this area about twelve years ago."

"We haven't come here for shikar," smiled Agastya, "just to see the place."

"This Mr. Avery travelled 8,000 kilometres just to see Marihandi?" asked the sabhapati.

Agastya wanted to laugh again, absurdity after absurdity.

They finished their tea and put down the saucers. The sabhapati asked, "When are you coming to join us, Sen saab?"

"Soon, I'm not quite sure of the exact date." They got up.

The BDO said, "We'll meet again tomorrow, sir. Now we'll take your leave, sir," and did.

Agastya was amused, among innumerable things, by officialese. No officer ever left, he always took his leave. None of them ever stayed a night somewhere, they always made night halts. Perhaps leave was actually a euphemism for arsehole, thought his irrepressible imagination: we shall make a night halt, sir, and there I shall take your leave, sir. He laughed loudly, making the idlers look up. He was again assailed by that sense of the unreal. *Now* what was he doing, here in the obscurity of a place called Jompanna, on the veranda of an incredible Rest House, with a hospital out of Holland on his right, and ahead of him a few idlers of a large village relaxing on red sand under a banyan tree, waiting to see an Englishman—and tomorrow with the Englishman he would travel even further into the remote, only to see a clearing in some clump of trees, just because more than fifty years ago, at that spot, a tiger had got a man before the man could get him. And soon the Englishman and his Indian wife would appear beside him, for four hours of kill-time conversation, and all the while the world would have continued to swirl in its uncaring way. Eighteen train-hours away (no, more, this was not Madna, from Jompanna it would be about twenty-six), in Delhi, his uncle would be setting out for his evening stroll, and Dhrubo and Madan would be two of thousands homeward bound from their offices, in clothes that irked their skins; and twenty-two hours away, but to the northeast, in Calcutta, his father would have finished another slow ceremonial day, and was perhaps at this moment strolling on the lawn, wondering about his son, and Neera would be out on a beat, or downing her nth tea in a crowded café with her journalist friends.

The sun slipped into the forest. Dots of light began to appear in the blackness beneath the grey-blue. The sugarcane stalls beyond the Rest House gate switched on all the lamps on their rickety tables, and the lights from the naked bulbs were transformed by the carved earthen shades, the handiwork of exploited tribal potters ("ethnic," Dhrubo would have dubbed these shades, with a delectable sneer). The idlers melted away. From the veranda the stalls looked beautiful, even romantic, like a terrace restaurant in one of Delhi's new hotels (which would have a fancy Indian name murderously pronounced by alien tongues, and where coffee would cost as much as the shirts Madan usually wore), a radiant transformation just because the sun had set—the glow of the lamps could create this illusion that squalor was grace in a softer light.

Then the stalls began the music, just one speaker but Volume on full. Hindi film songs, as always, no matter that only half the population could speak the language, and that with difficulty. "Spring has awakened with me/ I seem to see its wonder with new eyes." A languorous rhythm, a voice clear like one's vision after the rains, and he remembered where he had heard the song before. Darjeeling, he and Prashant had been walking on the hill roads, the last year of school, a clean summer evening; Prashant had been pensive—hesitant revelations about his homosexuality, which had for some reason impressed Agastya tremendously, Kanchanjanga bright and two-dimensional, like a photograph, and a group of Tibetan girls had passed them by, on nimble hill-feet, softly singing this song, happy to be what they were, the off-spring of aliens in an apathetic land. And Agastya was again overwhelmed by the conviction that there was a method in his past, Kanchanjanga in Darjeeling, and its photograph in Mariagarh, Durga in Delhi and Jagadamba in Madna. He would thus always try to organize his past, to force order into it, and it would continue to mock him with images of worlds lost, and semblances of a pattern.

A movement behind him on the veranda, making him start—the Averys. "We just dozed off," said Sita, with a laugh. Distinctly a post-coital laugh, thought Agastya, and again noticed how much easier it was to be in company, how in seconds his mind moved from the sombre to the frivolous.

The new song had a fast beat, happy and foot-tapping. "There's no lover like me under the sky/ I shall follow the sway of your hips to the horizon." He watched the Averys settle down in their chairs like dark shapes. Beneath the song the evening was soothing, the creak of a passing bicycle, a distant jeep, muted conversation from the caretaker's house, some-where, laughter in the gaining gloom.

"It's so peaceful, isn't it," said Sita suddenly, "and so ab-solutely different." Agastya could sense her turning towards him. "Didn't you find all this a little strange when you first arrived, after Calcutta, I mean? Even though Calcutta is simply awful."

"Do you want to get into a Bengal versus the Rest of India fight?" asked Agastya, "Calcutta has *soul,* soul even oozing out of its—" He stopped before he could say "tits," and then Avery startled him by speaking, he had expected him to continue to be silent and look mildly confused for the two remaining days.

"You were right, Sita, this place is not a bit like Grand-father's letters. I didn't expect it to be really, but still, it's sort of surprising."

Agastya tried to look solemn in the dark. With Sita he could be flippant, more at ease, because they came from the same stock, megalopolitan Indians, who ate hamburgers and knew who Artoo Detoo was. But Avery was different, almost another species. They had nothing in common, not even a language, leave alone the accent. Agastya remembered Sathe, many months ago, in front of his easel, saying that each language was a culture. And two generations ago an English Collector and District Magistrate had written letters home from an obscure town in India. And John Avery had read them fifty years later, and heard stories about his grandfather, had met an Indian girl, and sensed a country through the books and films of other climes, and had been moved to take a passage, only to be a little bewildered, and perhaps feel a little foolish.

But Agastya said nothing. The dark was dissolving Avery's stiffness, and Agastya sensed that a word from him could ruin the mood. "My grandfather wrote home almost every day," said Avery, "his letters are delightfully detailed, the district life, the Club, whom he had met, who said what—all interspersed with things which now seem even historically significant—he wrote, for instance, in quite a few letters, that all you're reading about in the newspapers about Non-Cooperation and the burning of English goods could be happening in some other country, not a whisper of that in Madna. He wrote well—he liked this place, and his work. He wrote his last letter from here, Jompanna, from an inspection bungalow. But I can't place him here," Avery's arm drew designs in the dark, "I can't relate this place to his letters."

"Your grandfather wrote of the Madna Club? Have you two been to it?"

"Yes," said Avery, and all three began to laugh.

"It's such an *instantly* depressing place that it's quite interesting," said Sita.

"I think if my grandmother had been alive, she'd have wanted to come too," said Avery. "Sita and I were coming to India anyway, to Bombay."

Sita laughed unexpectedly. "I think we should tell this young man, John, he won't be very shocked." She turned to Agastya, "John and I aren't married yet, but are going to be soon. We went to Bombay so he could meet my parents, and so that I could convince my mother that he wasn't what she calls a Pakibasher," she giggled adolescently, "then Madna was just a train away, so he wrote to the Collector, and here we said we were married because that was much simpler. John was really born two generations too late—he would've fitted in so well in the Raj. I kept telling him Madna would be a waste of time, not at all like what he expected, now he's regretting just everything, no, John?"

"No, of course not," Avery mumbled. He was put off, perhaps by her frankness about themselves, but there was something else, too. In the dark Agastya could feel a tension between the two of them; perhaps they had quarrelled about something, or perhaps, and his stomach heaved with silent satirical laughter, India had got to them, too.

They could see him convulse; hurriedly he asked, "Why don't you tell me a little about yourselves, where did you meet?"

A short silence, then Sita said, in a curiously defunct voice, the teasing and the laughter gone, "In London, where else? I'd gone to the London School of Economics for a Ph.D, from Elphinstone. John was there, too. Now he's joined the British Council." All that Agastya knew about the British Council was that in their early college years he and Madan had gleefully stolen books from its library.

The caretaker crept up behind them and switched on the light. "No, no, switch it off," said Agastya irritably. He did, and asked them whether they wanted anything, tea, perhaps. But the one flash of veranda light had befuddled them, and ruined the intimacy. "I want sugarcane juice," said Agastya, "will you two have tea?" Sita also wanted sugarcane, Avery would have nothing.

They talked on, Agastya and Sita, desultorily, with Avery intermittently contributing a sentence, through the sugarcane juice and dinner, both of which were good ("I'm glad you told him we were all vegetarians," said Avery, "another meal like that lunch and I'd've been dead"). Agastya would have liked Avery to talk more, but didn't know how to get him to do so; and he wondered how Avery had survived the train from Bombay to Madna—on a train everyone wanted to know about everyone else. Perhaps Sita had parried the queries, while he had looked out of the window.

Agastya's first night in Madna in another room. This one had no false ceiling. The caretaker cooked well, it wouldn't be so awful here, he thought, as a BDO. He remembered his very first evening in Madna, when he had been awed by the foulness of Vasant's cooking. Just simple good food could make one happy, he thought, how nice and animalish. Food had been one of the first shocks, then mosquitoes and the heat. It had been too tiring a day, perhaps, but that night he slept well.

Early next morning, he and Avery with teacups on the veranda, looking out at the softened shabbiness of Jompanna. "In your grandfather's time," said Agastya, "the forests would have been much much closer. You cut the forest till you see red sand. Then you build on that red sand till you get a video parlour."

Sita wasn't too well, Avery had said, she had suggested that they go on to Marihandi without her. She was down, Agastya presumed, or it was PMT. He remembered, when Neera had first told him, many years ago, about pre-menstrual tension, how impressed he had been, in an obscure way, with womankind.

"Yes, I really wouldn't have imagined a video shop here," said Avery.

"The entire district is full of surprises," said Agastya. "On my first day here, Kumar, that's the Superintendent of Police, invited me to see *Amadeus* and films like that, on his video." Avery looked suitably surprised. "But here in Jompanna, of course," Agastya added, "the more popular things would be Hindi films and secret screenings of something bluer." They looked out at the sugarcane stalls, strips of pilfered bamboo and teak, empty and squalid.

"It's amazing," said Avery again, abruptly, "a video here."

"Yes, it is." That Avery felt a kind of absurdity at the incongruities of Jompanna faintly irritated him. "About sixty-five per cent of the population of the block of Jompanna—a block is roughly one-sixth or one-seventh of a district—is illiterate. But one doesn't need to be brainy or literate to watch a blue film on video. Your real surprise is just the..." he looked for the word, "juxtaposition, isn't it?" and then he was galled by Avery's solemnity (and so began, in Madan's phrase, to "finger" him), "but that's because India is a land of sublime and fascinating contradictions, where the Himalayas of the soul arise out of dung, and dance hand in hand with the phallus of Shiv." Avery looked at him with a faint Srivastavean scowl.

They left for Marihandi soon after, Avery carrying a small faded-canvas bag. Sita came out to wave them off, "See you this evening." An hour's drive to Marihandi, some of it on the rise. The forest was less desecrated but still unimpressive. Marihandi was just a village, naked children, and dung-smoke against the sky. The Revenue Circle Inspector of the day before was on the veranda of the Inspection Bungalow, light-blue shirt on a cream dhoti. The Inspection Bungalow was a late-1940s building. "Nothing survives of my grandfather's time, I suppose," said Avery.

The Revenue Circle Inspector explained (standing, while they sat on the veranda and had tea) and Agastya translated. The place where Richard Avery died was about an hour's walk away, not a very difficult walk. It had in those days been a kind of watering-hole for tigers. Now, of course, there were no tigers there, no water either, in some places no trees. Fifty years, said the Inspector, is a very long time for a forestscape. But the place of the attack was marked by a memorial, they could perhaps look at that first, and then anything else that the sahebs might want to see. They left after tea, Agastya feeling futile. With them were the Inspector and as guide, an adolescent tribal male, lean, with the hipswinging, vaguely erotic, walk of one used to miles. Perhaps Avery sensed Agastya's mood, for he said, "I don't think we're going to see anything particularly exciting, just a stone. But it would be like the end of a journey. Though you could say that that was at the Ross cemetery in town on my first day here. Did you know it was called the Ross cemetery? I asked about the Ross, no one seemed to know."

They walked through part of the village, dust that the rains would turn to mud, foreboding glimpses of the insides of hovels, a Government Fair-Price Shop, everyone staring, some giggling, a few salaamed the Inspector, some asked the guide questions that led to laughs, the ubiquitous children followed them. The mid-autumn sun felt pleasantly warm on their shoulder blades. A few moments later Agastya sensed that Avery had been talking to him, and looked up from the rhythmic fascination of once-white canvas shoes falling on light brown dust. Avery was gently sweating.

"Why did you leave your sola topi behind?" asked Agastya.

Avery smiled, "Perhaps a tiger would've got me, too."

They moved across the fields, the guide always having to slow down for the guided. "What have you and Sita been doing since you came to Madna?" asked Agastya, feeling vaguely guilty about his earlier inattention.

"On the first day, apart from the cemetery, I looked through the records at the Collectorate, to try and get something on my grandfather. What I got most was another perspective, really. Then on the second day we went to Gorapak, Sita and I," Avery laughed suddenly, "my grandfather mentioned Gorapak quite often in his letters. If he wasn't coming to Jompanna to hunt, he was going to Gorapak 'to relax.' Relaxation watching those temple walls. But I liked my grandfather even more after I saw the place."

They crossed fields of stubble, huge mango trees at strategic points around them like giant chess men at the end of a gruelling game; a few hundred metres ahead the beginning of scrub that gradually became thin forest. The Inspector turned to them, "Sixty years ago all this could have been good forest, sir. Now, of course, no one comes here to hunt, and the animals are all gone, so I don't think anyone here would be able to point out the route the saheb's grandfather might have taken. And now the remaining forest has thinned considerably, and there are many tracks through it that the tribals of the surrounding villages use to reach Jompanna. New tracks are being made almost every day. The saheb must not think that a track we will walk on could be one his grandfather might have used." Agastya translated. The Inspector was fiftyish, and looked maroon with exertion. Poor man, thought Agastya, his immediate boss the tehsildar would have left the success of the expedition to him, and so he had to sweat on a meaningless jaunt—but there was no one to blame, least of all Avery and Srivastav, one had been romantic, and the other gracious.

"On the first day we visited the Club, too," Avery smiled at Agastya, "some club. In my grandfather's letters it was a place for family parties—and dances and plays." He continued after a while, "At Gorapak I met some Forest chap who knows you, Dubey—" and suddenly Agastya remembered that two evenings ago he had promised Mohan that he would meet him before he left for Alwar, and Mohan must've waited all evening while he had been musing on a veranda in Jompanna, and then he might have telephoned the Madna Rest House to find that Agastya had left for Jompanna without a word. He felt deeply ashamed of himself, he would leave behind a letter for Mohan with the foresters, and no excuses in it, just grovel—"is so good artistically one can't help feeling that it's not just smut. Sita had nothing to say on this—you know, she knows very little of the country outside Bombay—and Dubey was a little vague. He said that sex is part of the Hindu," Avery used his hands to express some philosophic indefinable, "*thing*, and joy is part of Hindu thought, and . . . all that—you haven't been listening?"

Well, he'd just missed a chunk in the middle. "I think that's a metaphysical gimmick to attract the foreign tourist," he laughed, "no, you're not a typical one. No, I really don't know why there's so much sex in a Hindu temple, but great fun to watch, no—doubtless your grandfather would've agreed. Apart from this Hindu joy business, another theory is that the craftsmen were just sort of showing off their skill, and no one minded because they sculpted so well, ha, ha. No, as far as I know, there are no conclusive explanations for it."

Into the forest, young sal and teak, bush and unspectacular shrub, clearings where the tribals had burnt down the trees to create a field, the sun's patterns on the tracks, they passed a group of tribal women, startled-eyed and black-bronzed; the guide moved on, untiring grace. Occasionally a bizarre rock-formation, or a patriarchal banyan, monstrous and ageless, four storeys high and five houses wide. They changed tracks often. Then the tribal stopped and pointed to a small stone a few feet away from the track, in the shade between two trees. "This is it," he explained. Grey-white stone, as though it had been washed often, looking patient and pretty.

In memory of Richard Avery, Collector and District Magistrate of Madna, 1917–1923, who was attacked, here at this spot by a tiger on the night of 22 August 1923 and later succumbed to his injuries. He now lies buried in the Ross Cemetery in the town of Madna. A just and sympathetic administrator, he loved the land wherein he lived. May his soul rest in peace. This Memorial Stone erected by the Civil Administration of the District of Madna, 1923.

Avery took out a camera and began clicking away.

"You are a hick tourist, after all," said Agastya.

"What else did you think I could be carrying in this bag?" asked Avery, as he moved to freeze with a click Agastya, the Inspector and the grinning tribal.

"Oh, lots of things. Anti-dysentery pills, anti-sunburn lotion, an inflatable sola hat, maybe a cricket bat, a cup of tea, a picture of the Queen, or maybe Diana."

Avery laughed and continued to click away. "Once I start I can't stop. That's why I didn't take a single shot on the way."

The orange sand of the track, a few trees, sal and teak, a few yards away another ancient banyan, dead leaves, tree stumps, scrub, one luxuriant explosion of bamboo, a few tribals passing by, graceful and open-mouthed, the sky—the end of the road for two Averys.

"No chance of any tea here, no?" asked Agastya wistfully.

"No, sir," said the Inspector firmly, "we can rest here for a while, sir, then on the way back a short detour and we can see what was once the watering-hole."

Avery sat with his back against the stone. The sounds of different birds, shade and sun, wind and forest rustle. "My grandfather was quite happy in Madna," said Avery to the sky.

Agastya said, "And now that you've seen the place, you wonder how."

Avery laughed. He twisted to touch the stone, then he read aloud the inscription, half to himself. "But in his letters, I realize now, despite all that detail there is no sense of a *living* place. In fact all that detail somehow further deadens it. There was apparently a big clock in the dining room, and most of his letters would begin, 'It has just struck four and Baldev has brought in my tea,' 'It is now seven thirty and Natwar, the one who can never get my boots right, is at the door asking about dinner.' Everything is static, as though Richard Avery would always remain here in Madna, contented, with his servants, and the Club, and the hunting near Jompanna and the relaxation at Gorapak. As though nothing would ever change—the letters are like photographs, that's really why I was so curious."

More cautious revelation about grandfather and self; then the waterhole, an indistinguishable undulation, the walk back across the fields and through the village, now somnolent, tea at the Inspection Bungalow, expressions of gratitude to the Inspector and the guide, met with genuine grins ("Should we tip?" whispered Avery. "Certainly not the Inspector, he'd be very offended, the boy, yes"), they woke up the driver and left for Jompanna, and reached there after three. Sita was on the veranda, with *The Illustrated Weekly of India* and tea. Avery enthusiastically described everything to her, and they decided to miss lunch altogether because it was too late.

That evening, again on the veranda, Hindi film songs from

the sugarcane stalls, lamps and a romantic glow, Sita suddenly asked Agastya, "How's your wife now?" and he, after his sleep, feeling too relaxed, the rare jeep-journey feeling, to wonder at the question, or to lie, said, "I'm not married yet."

Ahmed, Deputy Collector (Direct Recruit), had told them the story—he had been their guide to Gorapak. "An odd person," said Sita, "he always seemed to smile at his forearms when anyone else said anything, and we were a little confused—he talked of you endlessly, and it seemed that your mother and your wife were both English, but your mother seemed to have died of cancer *during* childbirth, and she had simultaneously been a Goanese fisherman's daughter, whom your father had torn away, to use Ahmed's phrases, from the bosom of her family. All that was clear was that she had been a Christian, that seemed to have impressed Ahmed a lot." Ahmed went up many notches in Agastya's estimation. Sita said, "So I thought you were an Anglo-Indian, you know," she giggled in the gloom, "whom in school we used to call 'Ding' or 'Dingo.' Bombay was full of them."

"And Calcutta, and Bangalore, and the schools of Darjeeling," said Agastya, "but not only Anglos, I think, almost all Christians were called Dings. For many years I was called, among other things, Half-Ding and Single-Ding because of my mother, and amazingly enough, all the Anglos were very good at sports, and simply nightmarish at studies, and the fairer they were, you know, the more sort of Caucasian-looking, the more rapidly they went off to Australia, and the ones who looked sadly and unmistakably Indian, like my mother's cousins, became sadistic teachers of the junior classes in convent schools, hopelessly brainless, but incredibly tough and mean—"

"Oh, yes, yes—" Sita was laughing helplessly, head and cheek against the back of her chair, shaking; what Agastya had nudged in her was a common chord, a common memory, a cause of joy because it was shared. He again sensed that these two, an Avery and an Avery-to-be, much more than other couples, had pasts which the other could not grasp—but perhaps for them their pasts were not significant, and maybe just their London years could provide a sufficiently stable foundation.

They returned to Madna the next day, Agastya happy because he had again managed a clandestine exercise in his room. They went to Srivastav's house in the evening, Agastya to report and eat, Avery and Sita to say thank you and goodbye and also to eat. Srivastav looked happy and was terribly inquisitive; Agastya answered more heroically than knowledgeably ("Did you see signs of drought there? Even though we had very good rains this year, Jompanna Block has always been prone to drought, you see, the catchment area is small, and the water table low, so when you are BDO you must be particularly careful about the scarcity of drinking water..." to all of which Agastya answered, "Sir") and, remembering the food at Jompanna, said, yes, he would like to be a BDO there.

They talked of the house itself, what it must have been like in Richard Avery's time, what, from his letters, his furniture had been like, which Collector in which year had granted how many acres of the compound away to benefit what institution; of the Indian Civil Service and the Indian Administrative Service, and the difference between English and Indian members of the Indian Civil Service, and the exceptions to the norm—the Richard Averys and the Madhusudan Sens. Srivastav, of course, talked the most; surprisingly Avery was quite a close second.

John and Sita were leaving early next morning, by the five-forty train for Bombay. So early farewells after a heavy dinner. Srivastav said, "Sen, will you wake up in time to see them off at the station? Don't say no, they are guests of the district." On the way out, on an impulse, Agastya stole his Collector's car keys.

Well, Srivastav had been far too jolly all evening, and Mrs.

Srivastav had been wearing her black bra; and in the jeep all the way from Jompanna, he had thought of his Delhi visit, just three days old, but light years in the past—images ephemeral as coalescing mist, Dhrubo's mother kissing him on the cheek at Delhi airport, an old photograph that he had unearthed of Neera and he stoned in front of the Victoria Memorial; he had returned to his Rest House room and his mirror had again been blurred by dust. And he had felt guilty (unreasonably, he thought, which had irritated him all the more) about Mohan. Avery had looked happy, mission accomplished, Sita had looked happy, she was going home. And the blackness had arisen out of the fathoms, and he had again wanted to dislodge the order that surrounded his despair, that incapacitated him from action, but had not the solace of profundity. All evening, companionship galled him, the conversation and laughter, the children; he had felt even more alone and had crawled into himself. The keys had been on a wooden tray on a side table, he had picked them up, thinking, now there would be fruitless hunts and accusations of carelessness, and he would have ruined the evenness of at least one more life. Walking back to the Circuit House with Avery and Sita, he laughed silently at the meanness of his actions.

He laughed even more in the tube-lit silence of his room. Five keys, it sometimes felt so good, to concentrate all one's faculties on acts without reason. Srivastav would shriek at the driver and the servants, ignoring Mrs. Srivastav's gibes that he had misplaced the keys himself. One key for the car, the second for the petrol tank, perhaps a third for the garage, then at least two keys, hopefully, to two steel almirahs that would contain everything important that the Srivastavs could ever want, the duplicates to which Mrs. Srivastav would have locked inside the almirahs themselves, and Srivastav would shriek at this his wife's senselessness. He got out of his clothes to the music of Keith Jarrett and lay down naked with the keys.

The car keys were called Usha and Union (that amazed him for a moment, the possibility that someone somewhere in the country was being paid for thinking up names for car keys, and then he reasoned, that this, like the Hindi radio news read at slow speed, was just one more act without explanation), and their bottom edges were irregular but graceful, ridged exactly like distant mountains, they looked smooth and worn, at least they had a purpose. Srivastav would probably not have the duplicates with him, and the driver certainly wouldn't. They would probably be in the office. He laughed, he would be ably supported by Chidambaram's incompetence in locating them. Well, then, at least one day of acute discomfiture.

He had been the last to move out of the drawing room; the children had left at nine, had either gone to bed or, he had thought, to examine each other's privates (and thus, again that dark humour that did not ease, that he shared only with a mirage, a looking-glass companion). Sita and Mrs. Srivastav had smiled inanely at each other while waiting for Avery and Srivastav to stop talking about the Record Room. He had again felt impotent with rage, and for not being master of his time, had wanted to explode. Now he picked up the keys and kissed them, his stomach convulsing as though vomiting out the laughter. An insane revenge, but fitting—the only answer to a world in which a bullock's tail could flick dung on to you if you weren't careful, in which a sulking District Judge could ring you up to tell you that he was not inviting you to dinner, where you hungrily scoured the offices of subordinate district officials to coerce invitations to any meal, because you suspected that your cook might be feeding you his excrement. He laughed well into the night, and slept heavily.

AGASTYA on his way to the office of the Superintendent of Police, to pay Kumar for his train ticket to Delhi. Past the ponds and buffalo, the crowds outside the Collectorate, still waiting, the wild cannabis. Kumar was in his office, breathing threats into some machine on his desk. "Hann bhai Sen, your Englishman has left?..." Casual talk "...You come for dinner some time, yaar, and meet my wife..."

Agastya took out the 450 rupees. "For the train ticket, sir."

Kumar beamed, and took from Agastya's hand one 100-rupee note, "when you begin service you don't get paid so well yaar, I know. You cannot afford more than second class, so I'll take from you only the money for second class." His face added, What a darling I am, no? Then more small talk.

Walking away from the police office, Agastya wasn't sure whether Kumar had been unnecessarily generous or incredibly base. Kumar would have sent a police menial to buy those tickets, and given his style of functioning, would not have paid the menial any money in advance. And after buying the tickets the menial would not have had the guts to ask someone like Kumar for the money. If he was going to pay the menial 900 for two train tickets, he would hardly pay more than 300 for Agastya's ticket out of his own pocket. Perhaps Kumar would repay the menial with a favour (a desired posting, or the stoppage of a transfer), and had smoothly pocketed for himself Agastya's 100. In his place, smiled Agastya, I'd've taken much more. Maybe it was a sort of deposit towards future blue films, and he smiled again, anarchistically, this was certainly a scoop for the *Dainik*, especially since it was all conjecture; he thought about this for a while, but there was no way of getting the story to the *Dainik* without getting himself into a mess.

He moved towards the Collectorate; a few things to do there, check for letters that the idiot peon Digambar might have missed, collect his pay cheque, and like a good officer, meet other officers, have tea and waste time. Through the crowds, the incurious eyes—a few struggled to their feet to salaam him, for they had seen him somewhere before, where, they couldn't quite remember, but perhaps he was important though he didn't look it, yet better to give him the benefit of doubt.

Salaams also from the peons in the corridor of the Collectorate. Srivastav hadn't arrived yet, Chidambaram wasn't in his hole either. "He's gone to look for some car keys," said the bewildered clerk substituting for Chidambaram, sweating with the strain of receiving phone calls for the Collector. Agastya's smirk disappeared when he found out that his pay cheque, for reasons unknown, hadn't yet arrived from the District Treasury. The clerk was too delirious with the strain of doing another clerk's job to answer coherently his questions about his pay cheque. He went to Joshi's room.

Where he seemed to interrupt the second of the six (or so) tea breaks of the day. Life was a leisurely affair in Madna. Various ageing fat men in the room, the denizens of the Collectorate, who shuffled at seeing him and sat down demurely. Joshi beamed at him, "The Collector has lost his car keys," and waved his pale hands to suggest the consequent chaos. The District Supply Officer was there too, Agastya remembered him best from his first morning at the Collectorate. He was still sweating, as though Srivastav's shrieking months ago had permanently damaged his delicate metabolism. Agastya felt happy to see such placid faces. He sat beside the Supply Officer, who smelt like a scented eraser out of a geometry box, to possess which, sixteen years ago, he and his schoolfriends would have done just anything. Tea was served first to Joshi, and then to Agastya. Silence, murmurs, clinks, and slow contented slurps over saucers. Then the Supply Officer made two paans, the second one for Joshi. His fat hands moved slowly, with care and grace. He worked like an artisan on the paans, for him time was not important. When he and Joshi pushed the paans into their mouths, they looked only at the inanimate, at table tops, files, wall calendars. Tea in the RDC's room was a ritual, and Agastya was reluctant to disturb it.

But Joshi, paan in mouth, and empty cup pushed to one side of the table, beamed at him again. So Agastya said, "Joshi saab, my salary cheque hasn't arrived yet from the Treasury. No one here seems to know why." Behind his spectacles Joshi's eyes became orbs of concern. He picked up the intercom, his tongue manoeuvring his paan into some unobtrusive crevice. Some conversation, a clerk came in, entry legitimized by the files in his hand, someone was dispatched to the Treasury, eventually Agastya was told that he'd get his cheque the following day. Then Joshi beamed again. Then more desultory conversation, and Agastya was shocked to hear that the Monthly Revenue Officers' Meeting was on the following day.

When he left Joshi's room (certainly not for the District Industries Centre to which he was attached that week, but for his room, to stone a few hours away), he was worried about the Revenue Officers' Meeting. It would be slow death. He had survived four such meetings, but now felt too anarchic. The theft of the keys seemed to have liberated him. When he got into the jeep he was saying to himself, approach the problem of the Meeting as a problem in science—like those Physics numericals in school that he had so enjoyed, and which had sent Prashant's and Dhrubo's pupils, frantic with ignorance, to the edges of their eyes, seeking out wisdom at other desks—therefore use against it logic and method, and you will also waste more time that way. He started laughing. The driver grinned in sheer sympathy, for he liked the sounds of happiness. The obvious course was to pretend to fall ill, but illness had its disadvantages, the most acute of which would be Srivastav's visit. And Srivastav might catch him masturbating or smoking a joint or both. Thus, to make out a strong case for illness, he would have to send for Dr. Multani. He smiled to himself, he was proceeding well, yes, definitely logic and method.

The jeep churned its way down the untarred road, making more noise than progress. He was again overwhelmed by the unsettling but exquisite feeling of the night before, that arose out of concentrating all one's faculties on acts without reason, and he found all this much more enjoyable and challenging than the real life. He laughed again, and hoped that the Government of India would never find out just what kind of officer it was training in the district of Madna.

And to Multani, of course, he'd say that his stomach was upset. But what if Multani asked him for a shit sample? That could be awkward, particularly since he'd been shitting so well of late. Or he could steal someone else's shit, Vasant's, perhaps, in whose case all he had to do was steal into the kitchen and delve into a vat. That would be quite a scoop for the *Dainik*: "IAS Officer caught stealing cook's condiments."

Shankar's door was open and welcoming. No, he said to himself sternly, solve this Meeting problem first. Yes, steps one and two were definitely illness and Multani. A fever, perhaps? He bolted his door and contemplated the rolling of a smoke. Then he checked himself, no, don't think of so many things at one time, and smiled at the checking. But many-branched and endless, Arjuna, are the thoughts of the man who lacks determination, he remembered, and started laughing again. He began the preparation of a joint.

In school an extremely popular myth had been that an onion in the armpit could bring on a fever. Some like Prashant had sworn by it ("Bets! You have bets with me on this!"), but Agastya had never actually *seen* anyone with an onion in his armpit. Besides, he didn't want a fever at all, all he wanted was to bunk a meeting. Then he wondered if he should shave off his beard. Because if you are cleanshaven, he thought, you just have to stop shaving for two days to convince people that you are ill.

Well, he'd have to settle for weakness, then, and weakness that fell just short of a blood test. He smiled at the inch of ash on the joint that he had rolled. The ash leaned gracefully to one side, like Pisa's Leaning Tower, and from it a sinuous line of blue smoke. The ash was wrinkled and serrated; it could even have been human skin, infinitely creased by age and crumbling in winter, transformed by disease, leprosy or any other of those horrors to which flesh is unwilling heir, into this desperate greyness.

Finally he decided that he would see Multani at his clinic that evening, for which visit Multani would be as pleased as a pimp, and consequently much more amenable to Agastya's suggestions of mystery behind his weakness. And at the clinic he could hint and hint until Multani invited him for dinner. Now that he had concluded his cogitations, he lay down on the bed in celebration. He smiled, it had been so taxing, approaching the problem of bunking a meeting, armed only with logic and method. Stealing someone's car keys impetuously was just as effective, and so much easier. So it was no use, he smiled again, bringing to his existence some of that logic and method. Always the softer option.

He wondered if he should smoke again. In Delhi Madan had lazily said as though talking of a volcano in Colombia, that the police were getting stricter about smokers, that the best chance of escape, when caught, was to be caught by a constable who also smoked, and that the next session of Parliament was going to pass a really mean Bill against people like Somaram (Somaram was Madan's old friend, and favourite peddler in the Red Fort area). But, reasoned Agastya, it would be a long, long time, an eternity, before Madna would become Delhi.

Later, laughing continually at his choice of phrases, he wrote a note for Digambar to take to Srivastav. "Sir, I woke up this morning feeling extremely weak. I consulted Dr. Multani, who diagnosed the weakness as change-of-season exhaustion, and advised a few days' rest. Kindly excuse me from the Revenue Officers' Meeting. I shall call on you at home as soon as I am well."

He went to Dr. Multani's clinic after sundown. The address on the prescription read, "(near Friends Chemists)." At the bottom of the prescription was an advertisement two inches high:

Come one Come all
To Friends Chemists.

Like something out of Bangkok, thought Agastya, and Multani getting a percentage of the profits.

He walked, again through a Madna with which he was not familiar. Friends Chemists was on the main Market Road, the corner shop of an alley, Multani was down the alley. The waiting room seemed to have spilled on to the wooden boards above the drain running along the alley, dazed waiting-room faces, waiting babies and tired mothers. He quite liked seeing other people looking depressed. Multani had hired some kind of goonda to be his receptionist, red shirt with only the navel button tied, gold chain around his thick neck, the type, smiled Agastya, who behaves as though he's well hung. They all looked at Agastya, he didn't fit. "I'm a friend of Dr. Multani," he told the goonda, wondering whether Multani had hired the goonda because he buggered well, mouthing filth, and without lubricant or tenderness. He went through a wooden half-door and past a smelly green curtain, laughing.

Multani sat at a steel table peering into an adolescent's mouth, which he abandoned when he saw Agastya. Much joy and handshaking, questions to which the answers didn't matter. Multani finally asked him to sit against one of the dirty pink walls, beside a silent water cooler, sufficiently large to accommodate a city of rats. "I can't believe this is a social call, Sen saab, no one calls on me unprofessionally, yet you look perfectly well... If you give me twenty minutes I'll just finish my patients" (Perhaps he means kill, thought Agastya) "...then we can relax and chat..." Multani beamed once more and returned to the adolescent's tonsils. The adolescent continued to stare at Agastya past Multani's round pink head. With his stretched jaws he looked like a python momentarily distracted from devouring a piglet.

Multani's room looked so awesomely depressing that he found it amusing. It was like a caricature of a shabby clinic, something out of a TV serial that desired to be realistic. A hospital bed half-hidden by a green hospital screen, beside the bed a large cupboard with ointment boxes and strips of pills oozing out of it like toothpaste out of a split tube. On the walls, calendars from pharmaceutical companies, one showed a woman in a sari laughing while running beside a tonga, from which all her friends were looking down at her and laughing back. The company, Agastya read, made beltless sanitary napkins. (They remain in place, Prashant had maintained in the last years of his life, "because of the stickiness of pussjuice. Bets?") Between patients Multani sent the goonda for tea and a Thums Up and asked Agastya questions, giving him lots of time to plan his lies. Multani looked so pink and positive that he decided that he'd get dirty with him when they were alone, just to see how he would react.

He wondered what it would be like, to be a doctor in a small town, and come to a room like this every day, and look into people's mouths and breathe in their exhalations. So what if you earned 8,000 rupees a month for it, he thought, as Multani surely did, surely what was far more important was the quality of your life. He stopped there, because the argument against him was the contentment on Multani's face; well, to each his own, then, he concluded dissatisfiedly.

Multani took less than two minutes per patient; some, with a bashful half-smile at Agastya, he took to the bed behind the screen. He took five rupees per sucker and directed them all to Friends Chemists. Staccato conversation with Agastya all the while. Then the last man, tall and thin, about Agastya's age, looking almost tuberculous with exhaustion. He sat down opposite Multani and began coughing almost immediately, and Agastya instinctively stopped inhaling, another old habit of his, to stop breathing whenever anyone around him coughed. But the man wasn't a patient, but a salesman. He took out tubes of ointment and strips of pills from his sad plastic briefcase and displayed them to Multani, mumbling all the while about the virtues of various maxes and mycins. The salesman had buck teeth. He remembered, after the first rains in Madna, he had seen Shankar's wife, but she had bared only her canines, and had looked predatory. But the salesman's lips wouldn't quite meet over his incisors, and he looked just a loser. Multani acted tough, with an occasional sly side glance at Agastya. Yes, he'd see, he'd see, about this pill and that tablet. The salesman sweated, in anticipation of being effusive in his gratitude, but retained his fixed smile. Could he take a few orders? "No, not now, not now," said Multani. The salesman's eyes didn't move from Multani. Agastya's age, but he came from the hinterland, or the unfamiliar Madna beyond the offices. He vaguely wondered what a salesman's day would be like, perhaps just moving from one Multani to another, grovelling for orders. But after the contentment on Multani's face he was now reluctant to pre-judge and dismiss other lives. But equally true, that as the sales-man talked, he looked almost feverish with unhappiness. Maybe, thought Agastya, he was ambitious and just not satisfy-ing himself, perhaps he wanted to do much better and make enough money to set up some small business or something. Even the salesman must have concrete plans and a defined fu-ture, and happiness for him, perhaps, would be a clear matter of either getting more money or not getting it.

The salesman was so intense, with his fixed smile, a Dale Carnegie type, that Multani seemed to be wilting. He won-dered what the salesman would think of him, Agastya. Would probably just sneer, might even be envious, would say, a soft success story, the son of a Governor, Anglicized and megalopol-itan, now in the Indian Administrative Service, all you have to do is recline and fart to earn your money. And then if Agastya told him, I want to resign because I feel restless? He was sud-denly ashamed of himself, looking at the salesman, talking about medicines for twelve hours a day, his restlessness seemed awfully frivolous. The salesman made him feel both eerie and guilty—be happy you are not him, and how dare you behave so cheaply when you have the chance not to be him.

Then Multani was through and, over his Thums Up, beam-ing only at him. Agastya took long to describe the symptoms of his weakness, and then added, "I also have a rash in an embar-rassing place." Multani stopped beaming, began instead to look reassuring, asked him to lie down, and checked him out, throat, pulse, stomach. To Agastya on the bed, Multani's face above him looked grotesque, his cheeks sagged, looked like shaved buttocks, as though gravity was inexorably pulling his flesh down. "You seem all right," said Multani, puzzled, and then demurely, "perhaps your rash..." Agastya immediately took off his pants and lay down, eyes closed and left leg bent, like, he laughed silently, a Caucasian pin-up girl suntanning herself on some alien beach. He laughed even more when his nostrils caught the faint stench of smegma. Multani didn't go too close, murmured, "There doesn't seem to be anything..." and gave him an ointment, a tonic and some vitamin pills, all from the overflowing cupboard, left behind by other intrepid-despite-defeat salesmen. Agastya immediately checked the alcohol content of the tonic. Good, fourteen per cent. Then the usual doctor talk, "Nothing really wrong with you, you must sleep and eat well, your insomnia—"

"Oh, eat well. I can't," and he smiled bravely, "eat well while I'm staying at the Rest House..." Two minutes of that and Multani had invited him for dinner. He said yes, thank you immediately, and asked, "Perhaps I should just rest for a few days, no, until the season stops changing?"

"Yes, yes, of course," said Multani, a little absent-mindedly, perhaps startled by the immediacy of Agastya's acceptance, or by his diagnosis. "I'll just slip across to Friends Chemists, and phone home that I'm bringing a friend along. Just two minutes." On the way out he asked his goonda to get Agastya another tea. Agastya wandered around the ten-by-ten hole of a room, cupboard to hospital bed to steel table to cooler, wondering if he should steal anything. But there was nothing interesting except the money in the drawer, and Multani had probably counted that.

Multani's scooter was new and of some off-white shade, indeterminable in the dark. They watched the goonda lock up the clinic. Agastya was startled to discover that Multani rode his scooter in an insanely reckless manner, but Multani's face displayed no consciousness of this as he turned to him quite often in the course of an incomprehensible monologue that lasted the entire journey. Agastya could only shut his eyes and succumb to the strange excitement of a fortuitous throw-of-a-die with death—again the chance to burst into fragments of flesh, again that perception of an ultimate release, the profoundest renunciation of one's sentience, almost sensual in its bliss, that even one's death need not be one's own act. The scooter raced through the alleys of the town. On his eyelids flashes of the passing lights, and Multani's hair-oil scent in his nostrils; his was the generation, his father had said, that didn't oil its hair.

Multani stayed above a malodorous drain in a dark alley, or so it seemed. The scooter stopped outside a wall of blue wood. Multani knocked on it and part of it opened inwards. "Accommodation is a big problem in Madna," Multani began apologizing while ushering him in, "I pay 500 rupees rent for this hovel." The wooden box was really an enclosed veranda and Multani's drawing room, with quite a few people in it. "Sen saab, please meet my father... my children, Vinod and Apsara, say hello to Uncle, children..." (they didn't, and instead disappeared into the folds of their mother's sari, from where they peeked at him, trying to look cute) "... my wife... and this is Dr. Ghoshal, he works in the Civil Hospital."

The usual embarrassed pause; then, "Do sit down, Mr. Sen," said Multani's father, "as Darshan says, accommodation is a big problem here, but that ought not to prevent us from sitting down." Everyone laughed, and Agastya was surprised; he never expected any wit from old men, or rather, anything that he himself would call wit. Humour, unlike the sense of dislocation, was just too generational—Pultukaku, for instance, was supposed to have been some killer joker in his time (and when the entire clan congregated in Calcutta on rare Pujas, the aunts would still drift towards him and shriek with teeth-gritting laughter at any emission from his mouth), but Agastya remembered smiling (and only smiling) at only two lines of his in twenty-four years; conversely, nothing that he ever said to raise a laugh ever did so with his father, Pultukaku, or his aunts.

But he smiled at Multani's father. "Please don't call me Mr. Sen, sir, Agastya is better." Probably senile, he would've said if asked to describe the old man, watches TV all the while, even when it's off, belches very loudly, takes very long in the toilet, spends much of Multani's money on his medicines, is terrified of death. (From Delhi he had told his father over the phone, "Manik Kaku is looking more and more like a skeleton, maybe his granddaughter looks the same. Why doesn't he sell himself to a biology lab?" In his next letter his father had abruptly, without alluding to anything in any way, almost in the fashion of Marcus A, had talked of old age, but in a very sort of Indian way, of the obligation upon the young of revering it, if necessary, only because it was old age, "because the old need reassurance in the guise of respect more than the young.")

And there was evidence to support Agastya's dismissive summary of Multani's father; for TV hadn't yet arrived in Madna, so the father had been listening to the radio, a question and answer programme on diabetes, and sometimes his head did shake involuntarily.

"Agastya, a good name, an unusual name. Of course, you have no idea what it means," said Multani's father. Agastya had told his father once that it was best to be very young or very old, because then you could say marvellously rude things with no repercussions, and no one took you seriously, so you were ready for perfect irresponsibility, and between the two, it was much better to be very old, because if you were very young, then you were also obliged to be cute. Of course, his father hadn't laughed.

Before Agastya could say, About half an hour ago I stripped in front of your son so that I could show him my loins, the father said, "*Agam* is mountain. Agastya could be *agam* plus *asyati*, one who pushes a mountain. Or *agam* plus *styayati*, one who stops a mountain. We often have this ambiguity, an uncertainty about our names, their origins. It should also be linked to the Latin *augeus*, which means to advance. That is appropriate since the sage Agastya was also the wanderer who pined for

Benares. A good name, and for some of us names still matter, but for how long I don't know."

Then Dr. Ghoshal intervened, "A very Bengali choice of a name. Bengalis are very fond of lovely names. Take my own, Shyamalendu." No one did. Dr. Ghoshal was, indeed, very Bengali himself. Tall and thin, but with a large belly, fingers yellowed by nicotine and fish curry, bespectacled, large yellow teeth, black hair combed straight back. Agastya wondered what he and Multani had in common, apart from their profession. Like other Bengalis who elect to settle outside Bengal, Dr. Ghoshal blamed Calcutta for not preventing him from doing so. "But Calcutta has *Life*," he conceded. At that Multani's father, without saying a word, turned the radio on very loud. This (it was now the Hindi news, read at slow speed) prevented all conversation. Then Dr. and Mrs. Multani returned from the bowels of the house; he (in kurta and pyjama) very firmly switched the radio off and looked around with a so-everybody-enjoying-yourselves smile.

Small talk, shy questions about Agastya's father, they trying to put him at ease, convinced that he needed easing, and he delighting in being perverse and squirming and looking more and more uncomfortable (fingering them, in short); Dr. Ghoshal stuffing snuff into his nostrils, breathing noisily through his mouth, and hypnotically intoning the name of other Bengalis in high places, Ambassadors and Secretaries to the Government of India; tempting Agastya to disturb him with, I want to resign, fuck a djinn, smoke marijuana, read Marcus Aurelius in the sun, to watch his face for the incomprehension at each one of those acts.

Suddenly old Mr. Multani interrupted them with, "Mr. Sen, do you know Bengali? Fluently?" The question made Multani, his wife and Ghoshal look at one another surreptitiously. The old man, face almost belligerent, stared determinedly at Agastya.

"Why, yes."

The old man stared some more, then nodded, "I'm very surprised," but his tone said, You are lying of course. He continued, "Darshan only speaks Hindi, and to me it seems that no one born after Partition cares," Multani smiled bashfully, "and then sometimes I think that these things don't matter.

"I left so much behind in Lahore, when I came to settle in Madna, after 1947, and here I had to struggle, to send Darshan to study medicine at Indore." Old Mr. Multani spoke slowly, but with a kind of intensity, as though determined to talk even though he suspected that if no one interrupted him, it would only be in deference to his age, and perhaps because no one was listening, "I watched him grow," Multani looked both bored and embarrassed—certainly he had heard all this before, perhaps his father with the one kind of single-mindedness of age, spoke of little else, but he didn't see why his father should bore a stranger, "and, I thought, my son has seen nothing, it is good, he has not seen the British, he has not seen the riots of Partition, my entire generation suffered. Some time ago there was a riot here in Madna, too, but compared to the forties these riots are like firecrackers—hoodlums having their special brand of fun and organizing Integration Meetings. You, for instance, Mr. Sen, have never seen Hindus and Muslims at war?" (Of course he hadn't. In his second college year there had been riots in Old Delhi, and the university had closed down. They had immediately got on to a bus for Manali, to get something good to smoke and waste time with the hippie-CIA agents, and on their way out of Delhi, Dhrubo had complained against the Muslims, "Why can't they scream more effectively against the hypocritical secularism of India? If Sunday can be a holiday to please the Christians, then they should demand that Friday be a holiday, too, for them. Then we'll have a four-day week, see." The riots had been six kilometres away.) "Darshan is lucky, I would think, he has not been a refugee like me—wanderers clutching only our pasts—we had nothing else. But, then, what we have lived through, though it was awful, it was also momentous, and sometimes I feel that it is much worse to be the generation after."

The old man exhibited an irrational pride, a kind of anachronistic nationalism. He droned on about the terrors of Partition (Ghoshal asked Agastya in a loud undertone when he thought Calcutta's Underground would be completed), "... your generation has missed the most dramatically significant years, the first five decades of our century..." But nationalism and those fifty years had also passed Madna by, thought Agastya, so he had sensed many afternoons ago, when he had seen, with Sathe, an eternally somnolent town from a bridge. Multani's father had known the sufferance of colonial rule, but Agastya and Darshan Multani had not, and unlike John Avery, had not even been particularly inquisitive. Patriotism and its bloodletting had simply bypassed Madna—in his letters home Richard Avery had testified to that, and Agastya had just been born too late. He felt strange, both deprived and curious, what must it have been like, to wander the streets of Calcutta and not be allowed entry into the Calcutta Club, Natives Keep Out, "... and they have left behind cultural cripples, incapable of appreciation, so I used to think, but now I'm not so sure, because there is no fault anywhere—your generation is what it is, just like the English we speak, it is inevitable. That is why I was surprised at your name, and your knowledge of Bengali, I did not expect it." But just then Mrs. Multani tactfully suggested that they should eat, and they all moved towards the bowels.

Vegetarian food, but excellent, and Agastya gorged. The old man said little, but Ghoshal and Multani probed continually, Agastya's background, the Civil Services examination, the nature of his job, his reactions to Madna, his marriage plans, his other interests. At eleven he said thank you, and I hope we shall meet again, to everybody and sat down behind Multani for another dangerous ride. They stopped at a cigarette shop. The town hadn't slept yet. They had paans and Multani a cigarette. "I don't smoke in front of my father," said Multani sweetly. Agastya noticed that he didn't inhale.

HE STAYED in his room for the next three days, to exercise, masturbate, listen to music, stone, read slim books on philosophy, and live his secret life. In Delhi's sun the three days might have been terrestrial bliss, but in Madna he enjoyed his usual tepid insanity, the lizards chasing one another around Tamse's painting, an exhausting courtship. Then the dubious consolations of Marcus Aurelius, whose wisdom, at moments, he found infinitely amusing ("Do unsavoury armpits and bad breath make you angry? What good will it do you? Given the mouth and armpits the man has got, that condition is bound to produce those odours..."), yet who continued to fascinate him by his oscillations between disgust and a longing for the cessation of its causes. For three days he opened the door only for Vasant and Digambar. On two nights he walked along the rail tracks, for miles.

On the fourth afternoon he had just finished a joint when a very noisy jeep stopped outside the room. A knock on the door. A smiling stranger. Before he could say anything Agastya said, "I'm ill. I can't go anywhere." Behind the stranger stood the circus-jeep.

"Myself Adho Tiwari," said the stranger (two months later Agastya realized that Adho was not part of Tiwari's name, but actually ADHO, Additional District Health Officer). "Mr. Bajaj has sent me. You wanted to visit Baba Ramanna's Rehabilitation Home?"

"Certainly not." Tiwari (quite predictably) looked a little nonplussed at the vehemence of this answer. "But..." he began in reply, and of course, eventually Agastya lost the argument and sat in the jeep, and not totally reluctantly. For one thing, it felt nice, just to sit inside such a jeep, he felt a little like Yuri Gagarin. Then, he would be travelling alone, because Tiwari explained, Bajaj saab has work, and DHO saab also, and myself also, but Bajaj saab said you were so eager to see the Home, so I have made a ring to the Home and said Mr. Sen IAS is coming, and they have said welcome. But what was nicest was the completely purposeless journey, to go stoned to some unknown place, one more long jeep ride, to meet some unknown people. Hopefully the Baba was rehabilitating nymphomaniacs or prostitutes. And acceptance was much less strenuous than refusal, again, he smiled, the softer option.

On the road to Gorapak. Winter wasn't far, but an afternoon in Madna was still warm, and the town was asleep. Again through the East Gate, it was once used only by the elephants of a tribal king. The paanwala in the niche of the gate was now alone with his transistor; the Hindi film song, hopelessly incongruous as usual, a full female voice inviting a billion listeners to sex and passion, followed them through the shacks which seemed to stretch to the horizon.

> The night is alone
> The lamps are dimmed
> Come closer my love
> Into my arms.

The jeep chugged along, it seemed incapable of speed. "I'm used to driving slow, sir," confirmed the driver, a loquacious man, "so that when we pass, people can read the messages written on the jeep, sir." Agastya nodded wisely. Yet one more encounter with new faces, he thought, as he watched a tree and a cloud move past in slow motion, and eventually this one would also blur into the others; all that would remain distinct, perhaps, would be a few words that only he would deem significant, or an angle of face, which in turn his mind would link with other things, some oddity of accent, or some other words, confusing time and place and people to look for a pattern, some essence.

Almost an hour's drive. Then in the last half-mile the landscape changed. Smaller fields, bordered by wire fence and eucalyptus. Neat white huts, with grey asbestos roofs. "The Home, sir," said the driver. Long red-gravel drive, more trees, neem, middle-aged banyan. Long low huts, white and grey, around a central courtyard. No one in sight. Peaceful, occasional cries of birds, from somewhere the sound of a water pump. The Home, whatever it is, thought Agastya, looks cleaner and prettier than any other place in the district, looks like the *model* of a commune.

A woman, fortyish, in a white sari, came out from one of the grey huts, probably, Agastya thought, to wonder at the colours, sketches and messages on the jeep, and then remembered, of course, they must've seen it here at least a hundred times before. They walked towards her. Painted food-for-thought boards (in English, Hindi and the regional language) on the hut walls. The nearest one read, "Real leprosy is attached to an unclean mind: M. K. Gandhi."

The driver smiled and said something to the woman. She looked at Agastya expressionlessly and asked him to follow her. Ten steps down the side of a hut, and she stopped, and with a hint of a smile, pointed to a man approaching them from the fields behind the hut.

Agastya stayed at the Baba Ramanna Rehabilitation Home for Lepers for more than four hours, and quite enjoyed himself. The driver didn't, but he was paid either to drive or to wait, so he waited. Agastya didn't meet Baba Ramanna himself, who was seventy-seven, and whom fame, of a kind, had made misanthropic. But he met the son, Raman Karanth, the man who had approached them from the fields behind the hut. Karanth was short and thin, and wore extremely rough white khadi.

"What do you want to see here, Mr. Sen?"

"Uh . . . whatever you think I should see."

"You're in the IAS aren't you?"

"Yes."

"If I may say so, you don't look it."

"Yes." At which Karanth gave him a look.

Forty years ago Baba Ramanna, then with the less sagelike name of Shankaran Karanth, had had a lucrative medical practice in Bangalore. "He wasn't married then," said his son to Agastya, as he showed him the Home's vegetable gardens, "that must have made it easier. His parents were at Tumkur. My grandmother is still alive, by the way, she is ninety-six. Still at Tumkur." Karanth pointed out the plots of spinach, carrot, radish, cauliflower.

"Where do you get the water from, for these fields?" asked Agastya.

That was part of the Ramanna story. In Bangalore, forty years ago, with nationalism buzzing all around him, a bachelor doctor, making lots of money, had begun to worry about his future. His son told the story readily enough, and Agastya realized the rest. "Let us have tea first," said Karanth, "then I will show you around a little more." They moved towards a hut beyond the vegetables. On the door a painted sign said, "Dining Hall," and above it, "To look down upon fellow human beings, to condemn any community or class of men, is a sign of a diseased mind, far worse than physical leprosy. Such men are real lepers of society: M. K. Gandhi." "When I say he worried about his future, I mean he saw it only as a sort of predictable extension of his present." He objected, added Agastya silently, to the conventions of the cycle—the earning of money, marriage, the nurture of children.

Floor and walls of packed earth and cow dung, asbestos over their heads, paintings on the walls, mats on the floor. The paintings were landscapes, competent without being distracting. "These are much better landscapes than those put up in Government Rest Houses," said Agastya.

"Yes," smiled Karanth, "but the artist who painted these had lost all his fingers to leprosy, a very advanced case. He painted with a few remaining toes."

Beyond was the kitchen, the same packed earth and cow dung. Men and women, in white khadi, looked at Agastya and greeted Karanth. Agastya surreptitiously eyed their fingers and toes. They picked up cups of tea and walked towards the well. "Some of the most unlikely people are rebels," said Karanth, "sometimes against the unlikeliest things. My father, I think, was also attracted by the fun of the terrible unorthodoxy of the act." Shankaran Karanth searched for a place away from Bangalore, where he would not be pestered by the petty intrusions and criticisms of acquaintances, and where he would not feel the pull of the city. His only major regret in the early years seemed to have been that he had had to leave Bangalore, for he had grown to love it.

"Why did you want to visit this place?" Karanth suddenly asked Agastya. "Is it because someone said it's one of the tourist spots of the district?"

"Well, yes," he answered, "more or less."

Karanth laughed, a shrill uninhibited sound. The tea was strong and oddly sweet. Agastya realized after a moment that it had gur instead of sugar. They strolled towards a clump of banana trees. "This is a very big compound," he said politely.

It had, of course, been much smaller when Shankaran Karanth had first arrived there, to try and cure, physically and psychologically, a few destitute lepers. "God knows, Madna

Town was far enough from Bangalore," said Karanth, "and this place must have seemed beyond the ends of the earth. But land was very cheap here. Gorapak, perhaps because of the temple, had lepers to spare, and the water table in this plains area was high."

Agastya, for the nth time in his life, was glad that he was stoned. That lazy, pins-and-needles feeling behind the eyes and in the head distanced everything, made everything equally surreal and consequently equally acceptable; the banana trees, the five o'clock sun above a hillock and the short bearded man beside him seemed as real and important as the words he spoke and the images they evoked. Initially, to him, Baba Ramanna had seemed pleasantly mad and completely remote, a do-gooder out of a book of legends for children, a small-time Ishwar Chandra Vidyasagar or a male Mother Teresa. Later in the evening, in unsettling flashes, Baba Ramanna's achievement had seemed inhuman, almost monstrous; as Agastya stared at the fields and orchards, and the two wells, phoenixes that the Baba had helped to rise in triumph out of barrenness, he felt a little sick—at the immensity of a human ambition, but also at its nobility and virtue, at the limitlessness of the potential of human endeavour, but also the infinite patience and craft required to bring the endeavour to fruition.

"What do you know about leprosy?" asked Karanth. A few metres ahead were children on two see-saws and a swing. Agastya quite liked the Karanth beside him. He spoke well and explained intelligently. He didn't brag, but he was aware of the implications of his father's achievement.

Agastya laughed, surprising Karanth. "No, nothing really. All I know is that it's not contagious, and that in the early stages it can be quite easily cured."

"Then you are not the average Indian," said Karanth, as he smiled paternally at the children. Then he talked rubbish with them for a while.

Shankaran Karanth had at first found it difficult even to get the lepers to come to him; just as later Agastya learnt that the tribals of Jompanna had initially wanted the Naxalites to leave them alone. "The really important and difficult thing was their psychological rehabilitation, to convince them, after their flesh had stopped rotting, that they were not freaks, or monsters." Karanth waved at someone. "Also, getting them to work. Beggary is psychologically very damaging, it encourages a sort of fatal laziness." In the early years some of the lepers hadn't liked the idea that Shankaran Karanth wanted them to be independent, absolutely self-sufficient.

"You are Assistant Collector, Madna, you said?" asked Karanth abruptly, stopping outside a hut. Inside, a transistor was playing bhajans.

"No, not yet, I'm training here."

"That partially explains your willingness to listen," Karanth smiled cynically, "most district officials are deaf. Before some German organizations started funding us, none of them ever came here. Now it seems they can't leave us alone. They want to force a loan down our throats. Forty years later, they want to officially recognize the Home, which means interfere in it."

It wasn't his willingness to listen, Agastya guessed, that was encouraging Karanth to speak, it was also Karanth's own desire to talk to someone, anyone, prompted by the presence of an ear made sympathetic by a stoned head. Karanth was a doctor too, but he had been educated at Poona. His wife and child were in Hyderabad. His father, Agastya sensed, had grown more uncommunicative. At the Home he could only talk to the lepers he and his father had helped to cure, and their only topic could be the daily routine of their lives.

The board above the door of the hut said, "The weak became strong on Tolstoy Farm and labour proved to be a tonic for all." "The Health Department officials became even more excited when they saw these boards," said Karanth, with an attractive cynicism in his voice, "they must help us if we had the sanctity of quotations from Mahatma Gandhi. On the newer boards we've stopped writing M. K. Gandhi, and no visitor gapes at them. One Executive Engineer—I forget his name— offered to make us a statue of the Mahatma. He said that he had built quite a few, and seemed quite hurt when we refused. He didn't understand my father when he said that to build a statue is to forget the man, or is the first step towards a kind of idolatry. The Executive Engineer kept saying that we wouldn't have to pay anything for it."

They sat on the earthen steps of the hut and drank more tea. Shankaran Karanth finally got the lepers to dig a well and grow their own food on the land around them. He married a woman his parents had selected, but on the condition that she didn't object to his life. Over the years the lepers thought him a miracle, and called him the Baba, the Father.

Later, mulling over his visit, Agastya envied Baba Ramanna most of all for knowing, when he had been merely Shankaran Karanth, how to master his future. Karanth asked suddenly, "Do you want to meet my father?" and looked almost relieved when Agastya hesitated and said, "No." Not surprisingly, however, he accepted an invitation to dinner.

A shortened thumb, stumps in place of some fingers, three-toed feet, some slightly awry faces—dinner with the lepers; he could barely admit to himself that he found the novelty of the experience faintly erotic, like a burgeoning fist deep in his belly. The driver wouldn't eat, "He has a few old-fashioned ideas about lepers," smiled Karanth. The food wasn't celestial, rice, dal, spinach, curds, but Agastya decided that Vasant should turn a leper so that he could spend some time at the Home to learn how to cook. "You wouldn't believe," said Karanth, as they sat on the floor of the Dining Hall with the other residents of the Home, "that these people were once like the beggars you see all over India." At Howrah station, for example, where the colour and texture of their bodies were like their rags, grey and decaying, where they survived on trying to turn the apathy of the million passers-by into distaste or disgust, their visions of the universe appallingly simple, just a million tramping feet; the metamorphosis was miraculous, thought Agastya, as he watched a three-and-a-half-fingered hand ladle him out some more curd.

Generations of lepers; some stayed on to help the new entrants in the Home, others left to try for a better life.

"Do visit us again," said Karanth, as they walked to the jeep.

"Yes, I shall try," said Agastya, truthful for once, "but I'm to spend the next two months in Jompanna."

"You shouldn't have eaten sir," said the driver, worriedly, as they moved off in the dark, "they are lepers."

"You are right," said Agastya, "I can feel my fingers going numb. Look," and he held up his hand in the half-light from the dashboard.

Criminally frivolous, so Neera later condemned his attitude towards the driver's idea of lepers. But then, when they met in Calcutta a few months later, she damned many other areas of his mind, too. A mild winter, he was in bed and watching her large but comfortable body at the mirror. He irritated her terribly when he confessed that he envied Baba Ramanna and the Naxalites of Jompanna not their nobility of purpose, but their certitude in knowing what to do with themselves. She turned, ethnic blouse in hand, and tried to explain in her strident Marxist way that the tribals and lepers were where they were because of the "exploitation of the class" to which she and he belonged—"class nexus" et cetera. He laughed, enraging her even more, and said, "I don't give a shit—well, maybe a shit, but nothing more. I don't think Baba Ramanna and those Naxalites, the better ones, anyway, are doing all that out of a sense of guilt. They're doing it because they want to. To each his own, see, Neera. You can't really help anyone else if you yourself aren't feeling all right. Like Baba Ramanna's son, Karanth, I don't think he's feeling so splendid. He meets his wife and child once in six months, and he had once wanted to be a neurosurgeon, but he also loves the Home, so he's a little confused see, and eager to talk to any stranger who looks a good listener. And the driver of that circus-jeep, when you're feeling as fucked and confused as I always do, your mind revolves only around yourself, you can't be bothered about the opinions of others, or about educating them, the only way out is to crack some secret joke, and feel your belly shake silently." But she didn't understand.

"You don't understand, sir," shouted the driver over the noise of the jeep. "Leprosy is not a joking matter." Suddenly, over the black shapes of trees on his left, Agastya saw a very large golden ball in the sky, like something above an amusement park, some advertisement for frolic. For a moment he thought that they had covered the one-hour's drive in fifteen minutes, and that the ball was some space-age oddity of the Madna Thermal Power Station. It was almost apocalyptic, the beauty of this moon. A huge globe of amber, he watched it all the way to Madna. A black sliver of cloud across its face, giving it a hint of Saturn—our own Shani, yours and mine, Shankar had said. Distant trees silhouetted against its faint orange glow, as against a fire, cotton cloud banks tentatively touching its edges, red and luminous. It could have been, he thought, a planet aflame.

"So," ASKED Bajaj, "how was Baba Ramanna? Did he change his mind about the loan?" He and Agastya were in his office, surrounded by the complementing shades of brown.

"No, sir," said Agastya.

"He's sulking," said Bajaj and laughed. "He argues that Government wants to give him a loan only because he's now a celebrity. But bhai, we can only give loans to people who we know will make good use of them."

"Yes, sir."

"So? Off to Jompanna?" Bajaj leaned back in his chair and smiled sadly. "We shall meet quite often, and, anyway, there'll be a Development Officers' Review Meeting every month. But your posting seems to have upset a few people in Jompanna. The sabhapati, you've met him once you said, came here, tried to get me to cancel your posting order." Agastya showed his surprise. "Then other politicians too, but I put them off by saying, look, it's only for two months, and Mr. Sen is an IAS officer, he will not let the IAS down." Just you wait, said Agastya silently.

Bajaj slowly scratched an armpit. "Half the population of the block of Jompanna is tribal, try and help them as much as you can. The main fear of the politicians there is that you will." The afternoon sun from the windows behind Bajaj's head lit him up. His ears glowed red, and Agastya could see the down on their edges, gleaming golden. "There is no caste war or anything like that in the area," Bajaj spoke as though Agastya was following him, "it's simpler, just economics and politics. The tribals there have been ignored for decades, primarily because most of them stayed in those inaccessible hill forests. The money that was pushed into Jompanna was directed by the politicians to benefit the non-tribal population of the plains, you know, primary schools, dispensaries, roads, wells, bank loans—in return the same politicians were voted back to power in the local political body, the Block Panchayat. Your sabhapati, for instance, has been President of that Block Panchayat for almost thirty years." The phone rang. Bajaj argued for a few minutes in a mix of the regional language and Hindi. Then he returned to the pep talk. "Hahn Sen, so what was I saying? Yes, Government cannot really be blamed for the—" his hands seesawed in the air, "skewed development of Jompanna. You see, until a few decades ago the tribals were practically invisible. Sometimes I feel sorry for them, they've never been touched by the Indian mainstream. What do the tribals of India have to show for these decades since 1947? Just a few photographs with Nehru." Bajaj shrugged sadly and Agastya shifted in his chair. "The tribals began to leave the forests only after the forests were too ruined to sustain them. Of course, there have been critics," Bajaj nodded at Agastya, who quickly nodded back, "who say that what the Government has really done with its policies since 1947 is to ruin distinctive tribal cultures without providing any real compensations. And that is, as usual, because the critics have no idea of what they are talking about."

A peon entered with four o'clock tea. Agastya whispered loudly to him that he wanted another cup. "As BDO," said Bajaj, in a more conversational tone, "tour the Block as much as you can, see villages, meet villagers, it'll give you a much better idea of the job. Of course, even now there aren't many all-weather roads deep in the forest." Bajaj, over his cup, eyed Agastya sadly, perhaps disappointed with him for not asking any penetrating questions, but also because it was his natural expression. "You will ask why there are so few all-weather roads. So will the critics, out of ignorance. What is the population of a tribal village? Some have as low a population as fifty. Remember that till a few decades ago many were nomadic, moving from one part of the forest to another. So their villages are scattered. So what do they expect, that we build a road to benefit a group of just fifty tribals? Absurd." He finished his cup and leaned forward to put it on the table. "A road, like any other development programme, has to be economically viable, no? So we say, here, if you group these villages together, ask them all to shift to one or two spots, then we'll help to develop the area, build their houses. Then the critics start wailing, you're ruining tribal culture! Leave them alone! But show me one tribal who wants to be left alone, who is opposed to development as we understand it. Dispensaries, schools, roads, access to markets, bus services, bank loans, of course the tribals want all that, but for that they just have to live together in larger groups. We are a poor country, we can't have one road and one dispensary for every fifty tribals."

Agastya finished his second tea, and looking down at the beige carpet, tensed himself, preparing as it were, to leap out of his chair, thank Bajaj crisply, say that he would not let him down, sir, and walk out of the room with a heavy grace, dignified despite the burden of the development of a microcosm. Meanwhile Bajaj continued to look at him sadly, as though seriously doubting his usefulness to the Government of India.

Agastya looked up, the first movement of the exit that he had planned, and Bajaj said, "Chipanthi. You must visit Chipanthi. It's a central tribal village in a group of villages spread over a vast area. And scarcity. Jompanna is a terribly drought-prone block. Everyone will be complaining to you about the scarcity of drinking water from the first day."

Agastya was at the door when Bajaj said, "Oh, Sen, I forgot to tell you something interesting. In some village near Chipanthi,

I think, there were rumours about two years ago, of a human sacrifice."

Packing for Jompanna. Vasant came to watch and criticize Digambar. Agastya remembered his first day, the train had been four hours late, and he had felt as though he was living someone else's life. Then on the first morning he had been charmed by Tamse's painting and had wondered whether these walls would grow on him too. Now two months in Jompanna, then end of training, and he'd take a break in Calcutta before he returned to be Assistant Collector somewhere, it could be Rameri, because he'd heard that Menon was about to be transferred; bleak, isn't it, he said silently, smiling at his cassette recorder, to hanker after this room. "I shall be coming to Madna at least once a month for meetings et cetera. Try and keep this room free for me," he told Vasant.

He should've told Sathe that he was keeping his *Gita* a little longer. He should've left a letter for Mohan with Bhatia. Even though he had smelt hashish at the Jompanna weekly bazaar, he should've picked some more cannabis. He should've stolen something from Bajaj's office that day.

The BDO whom he had met on the veranda of the Jompanna Rest House and whose name he hadn't caught arrived at about six in the evening.

"You didn't tell me your name last time," said Agastya pleasantly.

"Patel, sir," he said, smiling. Patel apparently had come to warn him about his office. "The sabhapati always wants to use the office jeep for his private trips, sir. But you are IAS, sir, you can stop that. And the Office Superintendent is a most dangerous man, sir." Agastya thought of a light-eyed man with a shoulder-holster.

He went to the Srivastavs' that evening. Srivastav concluded his lecture with, "You're beginning the best part of your training. Do it well." Next morning, his suitcase, hold-all and grip in the jeep, and he left for Jompanna, Vasant's children raced the jeep to the Rest House gate. A third trip down the road that he had traversed before with Kumar and then with Avery and Sita, but for the first time he was alone. The level crossing, lunch at Tilan. The driver drove slowly and carefully, and his middle-aged face was mildly cynical. Look, there is no need for urgency in driving, or in any other government work—he had that kind of face. They reached Jompanna at dusk, but the half-light could only marginally lessen the ugliness of the Rest House. The caretaker gave him the room he had earlier given Avery and Sita. Tea on the veranda, the lamps were switched on at the sugarcane stalls, and the driver said, "I'll go now, sir, and come tomorrow at ten?"

The driver was at the jeep when Agastya said, "Oh... Chandram." The driver turned. "When Mr. Patel was BDO the jeep must've stayed at his house at night, no."

"Yes, sir," said the driver.

"Then where are you taking the jeep now? Shouldn't it remain with me at the Rest House?"

The driver's voice then changed faintly, an inflection of lessened innocence. "The sabhapati has asked for it, sir."

Agastya thought it over. "OK. Ten tomorrow." The jeep left. He went in to rearrange his room. Then *déjà vu*, as he argued with the caretaker about the extra furniture. "Look, I don't need this sofa and these two armchairs and that dining table."

"But it's not a dining table, sir, it's a writing table."

"Just take it away. And remember, boiled water. Let the water boil for five minutes, that is, count five minutes after the water has begun to boil..."

After dinner on the veranda, night sounds, and night music from the stalls. The caretaker surprised him with excellent coffee. A few lights on at the Dutch hospital, he wondered what Avery and Sita were doing at that moment, two months here in Jompanna, and a job about which he knew nothing.

NINE THIRTY in the morning, and the caretaker, an astoundingly opinionated man, said, "You should have lunch now. Then when you come back from work in the evening, you can have dinner. Two meals a day, that's what all officers have, it keeps you fit."

"And if I feel hungry in the afternoon?"

"You shouldn't. Officers don't. And if you do, eat bananas. They are good for the health, and for the stomach. Anyway, you come and have lunch now, I've already prepared it."

The Block Panchayat office was a five-minute drive away, beyond the Dutch hospital. As the jeep skirted the hospital, he again marvelled at its incongruity. Here on this red sand, which nurtured only wizened trees, ugly Rest Houses and squalid shacks selling tea and juice of sugarcane, were these acres of green lawn and dignified grey stone. He wondered at motivation: what had induced the Dutch to build a hospital of charity in an obscure corner of India, or the Germans to fund an Indian curer of lepers? But he was greatly amused, a few weeks later, to learn that the Dutch missionaries at the hospital were converting tribals to Christianity. But his laughter at the news wasn't cynical, it was mildly incredulous, because it sounded so *absurd*, that in this age of AIDS and the atom, some missionaries were converting the heathens to the Lord's Path before healing them. God, he laughed, when will these Christians ever grow up? And even the bubble memory of his mother didn't embarrass him. From then on the hospital, by its very elegance and beauty, began to look a little ridiculous. Lakhs of rupees just to seduce a few tribals, to make the sign of the Cross over some sick, illiterate and bewildered individual called Anganagla, or something like that, and insist on a David or John before or after his name. Maybe, he sometimes thought when he passed the hospital, they had a red phone, a hot-line to the Vatican, and had to send in daily reports, "Your Highness," (but what did they actually call him? Maybe George Ringo I) "four more heathens captured today. Two unsuccessful cases were Muslims. They were very very angry and snatched the medicines out of our hands and left."

The Block Panchayat office was also on red sand, shabby-yellow and one-storeyed, with aimless lazy groups under the trees outside it. Their faces recalled those that he had seen every day outside and in the corridors of the Collectorate, the faces of dawdlers, and some glazed with waiting. He himself had smoked in the morning, as usual after his clandestine exercise and before his bath, and as he got out of the jeep, he wished, again as usual, that he had smoked a little more.

Everyone looked. For those who had to wait outside the Jompanna Block office, the arrival of a jeep could be an immensely exciting experience. He said, "Oh, Chandram." The driver turned, his face showed that he had begun to distrust Agastya's tone of voice, high-pitched and polite. "Give me the jeep keys, will you. I think I'll keep them." He was to love the pettiness of the struggle against the sabhapati over the jeep.

A blur of welcomers in the corridor, they directed him to his room, mumbling their names and designations. A short fat man in the forefront mumbled the most. His room was at one end of the corridor, pink walls, with photographs of Gandhi and Nehru above the windows. He was dismayed to see about twenty chairs, in three rows facing his desk, because they indicated that it was quite possible that twenty people could come to meet him at one time. A fridge between the windows, he immediately went to open it. It had napkins, a box of chalk, a few rolled-up maps and three pen stands. But his chair was extremely comfortable, one of those office things that swing at many angles in all directions. He was swinging in all directions when the door opened and a crowd (or so it seemed; when they sat down, they were only seven) walked in. It settled down into one politician and six groupie-goondas.

The politician was very important in Jompanna; at least his tone said so. Crimson eyes and a five-inch moustache—Agastya caught neither his name nor the reason for his importance. "I shall speak in Hindi, Sen saab," said the politician, "for your benefit. If I speak in our language then you will not follow." Raucous laughter from the goondas. "No, I will," he said brightly, "and you must teach me by speaking to me only in your language." Raucous laughter again. One-all, said Agastya to himself.

The politician had come to say hello to the new BDO saab, and to talk about himself for the next twenty minutes, also to explain to the new BDO saab the gravity of the problem in the Block of drinking water, and finally to complain that a bore, in some village the name of which was one of the million things that escaped Agastya, was not working.

"Bore?" said Agastya cautiously. "You mean borewell."

To which the politician looked startled, "Of course. Before you came I just—" his hand gestured towards the door, "met the EO who says that the bore was repaired two days ago, but the villagers say it wasn't."

By the end of the first day Agastya had found out that EO was an Extension Officer; by the end of the second day, that the office had at least ten of them; but what each did remained dark for weeks.

He rang the bell. The peon appeared, for some reason, smiling; that greatly nonplussed Agastya. "Call..." he wondered, perhaps he should call that short fat man who had mumbled the most in the corridor, he had seemed very bossy and authoritative, anyway, he couldn't call anyone else, he hardly recalled another shape, but surely that short fat man had had a name and a designation "... call that short fat man who mumbled..." he waved weakly at the corridor. To his immense surprise the peon nodded smartly and left. Perhaps everyone called the short fat man exactly that, thought Agastya for a hopeful second. And he took almost a week to grasp peon tactics. The peon principle was to see your boss as seldom as possible, and for the briefest of periods. All the peons nodded smartly at whatever he said and left the room immediately. He quite admired them.

The peon returned with the short fat man, not because he had deciphered Agastya, but because the short fat man was Malik the Office Superintendent, and therefore likely to understand Agastya's demands and thereby lessen the peon's work. Malik saw the politician, mumbled something, and left the room. Agastya smiled at the goondas. Malik returned with another man, dark and scruffy, who chatted excitedly with the politician for a few minutes. Both ended with dissatisfied faces, then abruptly the politician said that he would take Agastya's leave. Outside the goondas chortled.

Endless, the line of people who came to see the new BDO. For the first few days he dreaded every visitor; he felt distinctly ill every time the door opened. The second visitor on his first day was an old bespectacled woman, who mumbled something, sat for a few minutes, mumbled something again, and left. He never knew why she came. Perhaps it had been something important for her, perhaps she had asked him a question and had expected his answer to be yes, had waited, and had left interpreting his silence to mean no. He rang for the peon and asked him, stupidly, what the old woman had wanted. The peon said, airily, "She? She didn't want anything," and left.

After that he asked Malik the short fat man to sit with him. Things were equally bewildering then, but in a different way. For Malik explained carefully to him the purpose of each visit. One wanted a bank loan, another wanted to be transferred to some other place. Two bespectacled doctors reported on some vasectomy and tubectomy camps being held somewhere (Bhatia, he remembered, had called them "your cunt- and cock-cutting camps"). Four politicians came to ask for the transfer of seven teachers in two primary schools to three other primary schools. One old ex-soldier, black with indignation, came to complain of some political body in his village that was planning to change the name of the village against the wishes of the ex-soldier and other like-minded villagers. Some visitors had demands and requests which even Malik couldn't comprehend. These he soothingly directed to other offices—"Oh, for that you have to go to the tehsildar." "No we can't do that, that will have to come to us through the Divisional Forest Officer at Madna." And Agastya could see these rejected petitions moving from one ignorant official to another unhelpful one, the black creases on each petition marking its tortuous journey. And he also remembered his first day at the Collectorate, Srivastav's room, the ease with which he had seemed to assure (and not merely manage) those who had come to see him.

Malik had the face of a petty villain in a film, the kind who, in the last reel, is not butchered, but instead, chastened and scared, goes to jail for many years. Soft flesh and dead eyes, he wouldn't ever murder, thought Agastya, but he would probably blackmail—trapped between his face and my incompetence, I feel sad for the development of Jompanna.

For the visitors who could be understood, he summoned the concerned corridor mumblers. Then they chattered, and he sat back (resisting the temptation to swing in all directions), not following a word, but quite pleased with himself for having organized what sounded like a purposeful dialogue. But he wasn't pleased for long, because the dissatisfied faces of the suppliants, and their frequent appeals to him, indicated only too clearly that the dialogue had not been useful. In a few days he could see that the corridor mumblers, almost all his subordinates, disliked work, but it took him only a few hours of the first day to sense that most of them were also naturally unhelpful, and to begin to scowl, at both obtuse petitioner and evasive officer.

Development is as major a leitmotif in the Indian story as are the goulash of cultures, and the other legacies of a long and complex history, but development would never be fashionable or glamorous in Jompanna. Jompanna was Indian oblivion; life for most was slow and unheroic there. No First Page politician had ever gone there, and the visits of those who had, had been quinquennial, to make the promises and get the votes. And certainly, no one ever came to *stay* in Jompanna, except Caucasian missionaries, with Malayali nuns in their wake. The superficies of development were visible elsewhere—in the skyline of a thermal power station, in the dead saplings edging a road, but here it seemed a mere word in a government file. To Agastya, many months ago, Madna had been a slice of the country hitherto unexperienced—but Jompanna was to be transcendental.

A one-hour lunch break, but extendable to four. Agastya was ravenous, and looking out of the windows, slowly ate six bananas. He could see half a tree, the capped heads of a few dawdlers, and beyond them flat red sand, a few more trees near the road, an occasional vehicle, a jeep, a cycle, a bullock cart (which took minutes to pass his two windows), a corner of the Dutch hospital, shacks, and the inch-high forest in the distance. For two months he saw these things, unchanging except for the angles and intensity of light, and they gradually became for him the enduring contours of under-development.

During lunch on the first day the driver sidled in while he was on his fourth banana and asked for the jeep keys. "Diesel to be filled, sir."

Agastya silently applauded the sabhapati for the neatness of the tactic. However, he asked, "Why?" and began his fifth banana.

"But sir..."

"I'm not going anywhere now, am I? We'll fill up later." When Malik returned after the lunch break (face further softened by the stomach's satiety), he asked him, "What are the rules on a sabhapati's use of the office jeep?"

Malik smiled like a fat rat in a cartoon film. Then he explained, as usual not looking Agastya in the face. A sabhapati could use the office jeep for any official purpose, for visiting the site of any development programme, or to attend any official (as opposed to political) meeting—that kind of thing.

Petitions, applications, requests—he didn't receive them only by hand, they also came by post. The daily post was a large fat file, sheets and sheets of incomprehensibilities. He read the ones in English, and blindly signed the others, reasoning (very astutely, for such a fucked officer) that if anything was important, he would get to know, anyway. Not that the English letters made more sense. A fat thing, for instance, a kind of bilingual novella, from the Bank of India branch at Tilan, which began: "We are returning your loan proposals after having disqualified them for the following reasons..." followed by pages and pages of stamped documents, figures and something which he could only take to be handwritten confessions of many ghastly acts. What did they mean? and sometimes he whined (but quite enjoying himself), why me?

And the files. The mountains on his desk easily rivalled Srivastav's, and he now understood the pleasure in throwing them on the ground. His files also landed, depending on their weight, with dull thumps or sharp claps; they also lay on the stained rug like corpses on a battlefield, giving him the illusion of some obscure victory.

The files were of flimsy brown, or thick yellow, paper. All

seemed to be marked Urgent. His mind blanked out on the first page of each. He was supposed to sign somewhere, he would reason logically, otherwise the sonofabitch wouldn't be in front of him. After a search he would find the place for his signature, just above the stamp reading "Block Development Officer, Jompanna," and a little cross by the side of the stamp, the cross plainly saying, Here, Idiot, sign here. On each file he spent, he felt, more than enough time and effort just to find this place for his initials (with some files this search devolved into some intricate treasure hunt—the stamp and the cross were at times tucked away in the third or fourth folds of huge sheets that opened out like maps). He would be an exhausted wreck, he was convinced, if he also had to toil to study what he was signing. Thus he finished his files and threw them on the floor, and between files he swung a complete round in his chair, but that didn't faze Malik. Of course he often wondered at the contents of the files, but he would push only one or two across to the Office Superintendent (on the second day he began calling him "OS" instead of Malik, it made him feel more efficient), saying, "Here, explain."

Malik would lean forward in his chair, his flesh exhaling a redolence of snuff, sweat, paan, hair-oil and cheap talcum, and say, "Yes, sir," (reassuringly) "that is the Advance Increment for the Extension Officers, Animal Husbandry," and "That is the reply to the DDO's DO letter on last year's kharif campaign." One file, on some illegible aspect of Health, contained pamphlets in English from the Health Ministry. Agastya idly opened one, and read "... place the rubber mat carefully underneath the buttocks..." He sat up. Porn, this was porn, was the Health Ministry secretly sending porn to 5,000 BDOs all over the country. He flipped back to the cover of the pamphlet: *Instructions to Rural Midwives.* Oh, what a fall, but he read through it, anyway (desultorily wondering why it was in English).

While he was nodding intelligently at a visitor, or throwing uncomprehended files on the floor, subordinates often whizzed in through the door and pushed out a paper or another file at him purposefully. With taut index fingers they jabbed at the here-Idiot-sign-here cross. And he paused with his pen in the air and demurely asked, "This is to do with...?" They mumbled a reply, he nodded, satisfied, and signed (and in his mind, saw them doubling up with laughter outside). In the first few days, he felt, they could have got him to initial just *anything*— "I certify that my nose has begun to look like a dildo," he could easily have signed that too, with a flourish.

Eventually, of course, he learnt to see the pattern, how an incomprehensibility in the post became, in a few weeks (things moved even more slowly in Jompanna than in Madna), an incomprehensibility in a file—the passage of a petition, or a request for redress, from desk to desk, gathering around it, like flesh around a kernel, comment and counter-comment, and irrelevant comment, till it was fat enough to be offal for the rats in the office cupboards.

Office closed at six, some slipped away like shadows at four. At seven on the first day he was on the veranda of the Rest House, completely but pleasantly drained, and idly wondering how to get a drink. The jeep was parked under a tree. The stalls were playing a familiar Hindi song,

> You do not disappoint me, Life
> You astound me

a recent super-hit that he had heard at a hundred other places.

He gave up trying to comprehend and enjoy the job on the fourth day, at the General Body Meeting of the Block Panchayat. Four hours. But he couldn't write letters, or while the time away in shifting his buttocks on wood and clandestinely flicking his sweat on to his neighbours. He had to concentrate, and answer questions, on the transfer of primary-school teachers, on the scarcity of drinking water. The sabhapati, who had lost the fight over the jeep, was particularly vocal and unrelenting. Not that Agastya made a mess of the answers (in fact, prompted by Malik, he reacted to most topics with competent bureaucratic vagueness—"Yes, I'll look into that," "That's a good point, OS, make a note of that").

But he had come to Jompanna with a vague hope that somehow, in some obscure way, things would be better. He would settle down to the job, everyone had said that it would be challenging, involving, and perhaps his restlessness would dissolve in action. But at the meeting he sensed, as he parried questions and encouraged distracting debate, surrounded by noisy politicians and tranquil Extension Officers and clerks, that he *would*, eventually, settle down to the job, but that it would not involve him, that his restlessness would not lessen, it would merely get a little cramped as it made room for the trivia of his new life, the problem of someone's bank loan, or the organization of some Family Welfare Camp. So he brought only half his mind to his work, while the other half worried him, like a mild headache. He picked up a few habits of the district officer, of eating two stupefying meals a day, of bringing some files back to his Rest House room in the evenings, where he tried to comprehend them to the music that drifted in with the mosquitoes through the open windows. Sometimes he felt, for reasons unknown, that for him a downward journey had begun, but from which crest to which abyss he did not know, or particularly care.

SOME TIME in his third week in Jompanna. A tribal woman, thirty-fiveish, in front of him in his office, and he hardly listening to her, revelling in a rare uncontrollable erection. The woman was strong, veined forearms and lined tragic face, aquiline nose, eyes darkened by a contemptible life, she even smelt of the years of squalor, hard buttocks the size, he thought, laughing silently, of the fucking moon. She had to repeat herself many times before he understood her.

She came from Chipanthi, she said. The men had told her not to come, that it would be no use, but she'd heard that a new officer had come, perhaps he would help. There was only one well in the area, and it had dried up, it needed to be cleaned, they had complained to the earlier officer, but no one had done anything. Not taking his eyes off her, Agastya rang up the Deputy Engineer, who was new, keen and envious of the IAS. The Deputy Engineer protested feebly that Chipanthi was the heart of the Naxalite area and quite dangerous, to which he retorted (surprised at the cleverness of his answer), that even Naxalites needed water. He then told the woman that he would himself go to Chipanthi and have a look, soon, in a few days. He smiled reassuringly at her, her face softened a little, and he almost came.

He and the Deputy Engineer did go a few mornings later, in two jeeps. ("You needn't take your jeep, Chaudhri saab, why waste government petrol?" But the Deputy Engineer mumbled something unintelligible, about having to go somewhere else from Chipanthi. The matter was simpler, Agastya knew, it was, in officialese, a "prestige issue." The most important person in a jeep was known by where he sat, in the outer left seat in the front, perhaps because it was the most comfortable. If Chaudhri and he travelled together, then Chaudhri would have to concede that seat to him. Agastya marvelled at his pettiness.)

Thus he journeyed into the forest in a convoy of two. Two hours to Chipanthi, kilometres of desecrated forest. Chipanthi was at the base of the low hills that had once been heavy with timber. Now the trees brought less rain, the tribals had ruined the jungle as a changing world had ruined them. Generations ago they had been kings capable of founding townships, now they were emasculated, relying for succour on government largesse.

The last few kilometres of the road to Chipanthi were untarred, and the last stretch seemed just bumpy hard red sand. But the forest remained ravaged, tree stumps, burnt clearings, a coarse red dust. Around them the hills, low and ugly, their green also broken by scars. Chipanthi appeared, a few huts of mud on burnt earth. The jeeps stopped. He got out, feeling stiff. The silence was startling. Even the forest seemed deadened. An uneven clearing of red sand, scrub, then the scraggy trees, yet Bajaj had said that he must visit Chipanthi.

They saw no one around the huts. No naked children, noisy and curious, advertisements for malnutrition. Just a noon silence and a warm late-November sun and the crack of twigs beneath their feet.

"Where's the well?" asked Agastya.

"Beyond the huts," said one of Chaudhri's gang. Then a young man at the door of the first hut, lean and sullen.

"What is the population of Chipanthi?" asked Agastya. No one seemed to know. A few more faces, dark and somehow strange. He saw the woman who had come to the office. She looked different, more confident.

"This way," she said.

He was relieved to see more people around the well, who turned at their approach. But something was odd, and he realized in a moment that it was the muteness of the village, there seemed to be no laughter and no conversation. The village did have children, but they were all busy. Women were tying them to ropes and letting them into the well. After a while the ropes were bringing up buckets. He went closer. The buckets were half-full of some thin mud. The only sounds were the echoing clang of the buckets against the walls of the well, and the tired snivelling of a few children on the side. He looked at them. Gashed elbows and knees from the well walls, one child had a wound like a flower on his forehead. The woman who had come to the office was looking at him in a kind of triumph. He looked into the well. He couldn't see any water, but the children were blurred wraiths forty feet below, scouring the mud of the well floor for water, like sinners serving some mythic punishment.

Chaudhri peeped into the well. One by one, they all peeped, and came away with suitable expressions of horror. The numbers around them had increased. Agastya spotted a thin middle-aged man in khadi, he didn't fit in with these hard half-naked bodies.

"Very sad situation," said Chaudhri, looking at his watch.

"Yes, what are we going to do?" asked Agastya. The woman who had come to the office and the man in khadi sidled up, sensing a conference. The khadi-man really didn't fit, thought Agastya again, disconnectedly, with his beard and large nose, he looked like a university professor of some subject which would give him immense scope for talking shit—Sociology or Comparative Literature, something like that.

"We'll send around a water tanker immediately," said Chaudhri.

"How soon is immediately?" asked Agastya. Chaudhri

looked at him, a little startled by his voice. The khadi-man waved away some of the other tribals who were beginning to look interested. Agastya rather liked that. Almost automatically the four of them began to move towards the jeep, with Chaudhri's gang following them.

"Uh—a few days, I think. One tanker is out of order, it's being repaired at Tilan, another tanker is leaking very badly, by the time it gets here, there'll be no water in it. And the third one is at Chhopa." Agastya looked at him with distaste. "Chhopa is the sabhapati's village, isn't it. It's probably as wet as—" He was going to say, the sabhapati's puss, but checked himself in time. "No, let's do it my way." He smiled wickedly at Chaudhri. "It's good that you brought your jeep. You go back in that jeep, take everybody with you. You'll reach Jompanna by about two thirty, I think. Arrange for one tanker, and your—" he stopped, wondering what they were called "—gang that cleans up wells to come here. I'll wait here for them, to sort of ensure that you—" he paused, and then decided to be recklessly truthful "—you do some work about this when you reach your office."

Chaudhri didn't follow; when he did, he laughed shrilly, irritating Agastya a great deal. When he next met an impressed Bajaj, he explained, "I thought it was the only way to get them to work, sir. If I'd gone back that afternoon to Jompanna, I would've been distracted from this business by the usual office routine, and those Junior Engineers would've turned up one by one, to explain what was wrong with the tankers, and why the well couldn't be desilted until a month later or something like that, their usual arguments—you know, sir, their laziness hidden by jargon—and I'd have agreed, because sitting in the Block Office at Jompanna, Chipanthi and its problems would've seemed remote, and everything would've been postponed."

Chaudhri and his entourage of subordinates were not used

to inexplicable behaviour, but Agastya remained aloof and adamant, simultaneously wondering if he should provide them the other reason, that he wanted to get away from the office for at least a few hours to a new world where he could eye some sexy women. The jeep left, bumping gracelessly over the red sand, crowded with glum and confused men. He and the tribals watched it career into the forest. He was feeling heroic and foolish.

He looked around. The tribals stared at him blankly. A pleasant afternoon sun, and a light breeze. The familiar unreal feeling asserted itself, here, in a barren patch in a decaying forest, amid mud huts and strange tribals, with children being wounded in a well—what was he doing here? He looked at the faces. A woman suddenly giggled, and hid her face behind another's shoulder. A young man smiled, hesitantly. The man in khadi asked, "Perhaps you would like some tea?" He spoke in awkward Hindi.

"Who are you?" asked Agastya, because half of him was still feeling tough.

"My name is Prakash Rao," said the man.

They began walking back towards the well. Some of the tribals moved ahead, with a bestial grace that recalled a guide, a tired Revenue Circle Inspector, and John Avery. Near the well they brought out a charpai for Rao and Agastya. "At the earliest the tanker can only be here by sundown, no?" asked Rao.

Agastya sat down on the charpai, Rao continued to stand. Their presence distracted some of the tribals at the well. Some of the children forgot their bruises, and, snivelling absent-mindedly, gazed at them. The tea is going to have that well water in it, he thought, and then felt so ashamed of himself that he grinned. But Rao was staring at him, so he just said, "Yes, uh, yes." He was now feeling quite happy, at having escaped the office in such a delightfully bizarre way, at the thought of an afternoon spent in watching taut female bodies struggle to extract water out of a well of mud. He tried to make his face look less lustful.

Rao was saying something again. "When Para returned from your office that day, saying that you had promised to come, the rest of us were quite sceptical." From close, Rao looked older, about fifty. He was obviously an outsider, but as with Avery at the Collector's party, he was determined not to find out what he was doing at Chipanthi. Rao couldn't be a Naxalite, he thought, or could he? His idea of Naxalites, as about many other things, was very vague. Para came towards them with the tea. Her thin sari outlined her full hard thighs. When she bent down to place his tea beside him he saw the veins blue beneath the skin on the inside of her upper arm.

Suddenly a loud gasp from a woman at the well. The knot around a child had abruptly come undone, but the child was still holding on to the rope. Everyone crowded the woman as she slowly began pulling at the rope. Others shouted encouragement into the well, which boomed back. The child scrambled against the wall for a foothold, like some monstrous broken spider. After eons his terrified face appeared above the darkness, paler than the sun. Hands helped him out. He sat down on the damp sand and began to blubber. The women tried to soothe him.

Agastya wanted to protest, against the people who led such lives. For a ghastly second he thought that they were putting on a show, intending to make him feel, yet again, absurd, or guilty. They irritated him, almost to the point of anger; and later, nothing could convince him, none of the angry arguments of the other Naxalites, or the more sober theorizing of Rao, that the tribals were compelled to live like this, risking the lives of their children for half-buckets of mud.

After their teas Rao suggested a stroll. Past the mud huts, up a gradual slope. "This place is almost as clean as Baba Ramanna's Home," said Agastya. "Ah, I've never been there, but I've heard of it, of course. Yes, most tribals have very clean habits. That's one thing they don't have to learn." They walked slowly on the tracks in the forest—grey-brown trees and puckered fallen leaves.

Rao was a Naxalite, after all. "I'm from Telengana," said Rao. Then, with a side glance at Agastya, "What do you know about the Telengana Agitation, Mr. Sen?"

"Nothing, really." About as much as I know about sex on the walls of a Hindu temple, or the significance of the fall of a pearl from a nose-ring, nothing. "It was against rural exploitation, just like the original Naxal movement in Bengal. That's about all, I know none of the details, and please call me Agastya." Or English, he thought, or Ogu, or August. His names seemed like aliases, for his different lives.

"Rural exploitation," Rao smiled sadly. He, like the tribals, faintly irritated Agastya. "It's a phrase that now has no meaning, that actually hides the horrors," Rao pointed dramatically at some tribal women approaching them. "They are beautiful, aren't they, Mr. Sen?" They were. The women neared them, smiled at Rao, chattered to him in the dialect, passed them. "As late as ten years ago, in the more remote areas of these forests, especially towards—" he seemed to point at a treetop— "Pirtana, these women did not cover the upper half of their bodies. That was their custom." He looked at Agastya as though he expected to see a hard-on on his forehead.

"Yes, and various people must've," he wanted to say, fucked, but he restrained himself, "taken advantage of their innocence, various minor district officials. Range Forest Officers, and Revenue Circle Inspectors, Head Constables."

"Not only minor, but more respectable officers too." They crossed another barren clearing, rocks, scrub and red sand. There was a snake's skin beneath a bush. Agastya picked it up. Grey-white and brittle, it caused on his flesh the excitement of repulsion. "At Pirtana the new Assistant Conservator of Forests, too. A man called Gandhi, even he abused the honour of the tribal woman who cooked for him. The men of her village were very angry. They visited Gandhi three nights ago, and surprised them both. In revenge, and as punishment, they cut off his arms."

A light breeze, forest whispers of leaves and dust, the faint discomfort of damp at the armpits, something crackling in his hand, and some warm fluid seeming to flood outward from the base of his spine. Mohan.

"...goes totally against all that we've been telling them, but," Rao shrugged, "it was impossible to stop them."

SUNDOWN. The forest had turned cold. A sharp and clean night sky, slowly beginning to emerge with the stars. They still waited for the water.

Rao's other friends had come, three of them, from the villages in the hills. They had heard, they said in harshly accented Hindi, of an IAS officer who had come to Chipanthi because he was greatly interested in tribals. They all looked similar, thin, dark, bearded, all in guiltless khadi. Agastya asked them about Mohan, but none of them knew any details.

The initial shock had long passed, so had the disbelief that had followed it. All that remained was a remoteness and a mild horror at these men of an incomprehensible anger. He hadn't told them that Mohan was a friend of his. Somehow he couldn't. In any case Rao and his friends didn't want to listen, they only wanted to talk, to explain, to justify, to clear their heads. For them Mohan was worth only a two-line aside. Quotations from Mao tumbled out of their mouths alongside excited analyses of the tribal dilemma. These tribals needed help to think, they said, because they felt anchorless in the new world. "Look at the way they struggle for water. You have seen how simple they are."

They were at their sixth round of tea in Rao's hut. A kerosene lamp, and a bed in the corner, clothes hanging from nails on the wall. Para served them tea. Her ease, her familiarity with the hut suggested to Agastya that she stayed there.

Suddenly he was laughing loudly, wondering why these guardians of honour did not cut off Rao's arms too. Her presence irritated him, and he said, "Don't keep calling them simple, your attitude is condescending. They are not merely simple, they are also extremely violent, something you seem to have encouraged. Don't say they are simple, say they are different, that's all." Para didn't understand Hindi, but his tone startled her. "If Gandhi seduced a tribal woman, surely it was equally true that she liked the seduction." He stopped, out of a kind of bewilderment.

No, they said agitatedly, sex was part of the larger exploitation, so it could not go unpunished. He watched them gush on, purple lips and white teeth, on their faces the play of violence and the passion of zealots, chiaroscuro skins in the lamplight, the tang of kerosene in the air, and around them the gloom of mud. Even more monstrous, that it had been Mohan who had suffered in this manner for his lust, he had needed no physical agony to quell his mind. In this sea-movement from one condemned spot to another, the only distraction seemed these flecks of insanity.

Later he smoked tobacco the tribal way. A dried and neatly rolled tobacco leaf, which hit him almost like marijuana, that familiar anodyne. After that even Mohan seemed to fade and he had to listen only intermittently to Rao and his friends incoherently explaining the kinds of exploitation, of the forest contractors who didn't pay the tribal enough for the oil seeds and tobacco leaves that he collected for them, of the timber smugglers who ruined the forests much more than the tribals did, but foisted the blame on them by bribing the Range Forest Officers. "The tribals are trapped, and your government development can't save them because sitting in those big cities, you have no idea of how they live."

"I can't believe that they are *forced* to live like this." It was easier to talk than to listen to them, and he disliked Para for the way she sat a little behind Rao, face relaxed and distant, but eyes flicking continually, trying to follow the conversation by the tone of the voices, and he wanted to make a token protest, against her conviction that what men like them said was always worth listening to, against a world of action through belief. "For one thing they can shift from Chipanthi to some place where water is more easily available. There are many places like that in the forest. Of course, it isn't easy, but nothing important is, see, except maybe cutting off someone's arms. They were nomads once, and Chipanthi is no place to be attached to. If you are teaching them to distrust the world outside this forest, why don't you also teach them to be self-sufficient. They fear exploitation, and they are all illiterate, but they can walk miles to catch a bus to see a Hindi film on the video at Jompanna. Yes, yes, I know, self-sufficiency is not easy and neither is thinking, but both are more valuable than anger." The tobacco liberated him, and he matched their incoherence with his.

He was an honoured, though unexpected, guest, so later, around a huge fire near the jeep, the tribals danced for him. The men drank some kind of tari. "They used to drink all day," breathed Rao hotly into his ear, "before we came. Their children began drinking it at six months. They didn't *know*." Agastya drank too, it was extremely potent, and he was soon uncontrollably high. The women danced, arm in arm in one row, a slow monotonous shuffle to a single arrhythmic drum, one step forward, two steps back, always one step forward, two steps back.

He watched them, an orange sheen on black skin, shy smiles at one another, faces turned to their feet, and he dreaded their innocence, for it was dangerous, so tempting to corrupt.

The lights of two tankers were seen in the distance. The dance broke up with drunken yells of joy.

"HE GREW very lonely, I think, and he was always a very physical sort of person, and Rohini hadn't gone to Pirtana, remember," Bhatia leaned forward to reach the ashtray. "I met him twice or thrice when he came to Madna for some work or the other. He would say that Pirtana was very boring, and then laugh."

An evening at the Madna Circuit House. Agastya had travelled all day from Jompanna for Bajaj's Development Meeting the next day. Vasant had looked happy to see him, had smiled and said that his old Rest House room was occupied. He was staying the night in the room whose curtains had small red aeroplanes on a green background. He had telephoned Bhatia as soon as he had arrived, and he had come over, again with a half-bottle. A fortnight ago, on the morning after his visit to Chipanthi, he had tried to contact Bhatia on the phone from Jompanna, but he hadn't got through. Later, when he had, Bhatia hadn't been in office.

"The Rangers at Pirtana must have known about Mohan, they themselves do the same all the time, but I don't think anyone here in Madna knew. Now of course no one can talk of anything else." Bhatia lit another cigarette. He was smoking more since Agastya had last seen him.

Talking about Mohan was almost a duty (if Agastya hadn't telephoned, Bhatia would have later said, "Some friend you are. You came to Madna and didn't drop by or telephone, not even to ask about Mohan"). Besides, a fortnight had passed, and he was a little startled to realize that in time even the most horrifying news that doesn't concern oneself directly, can turn a little stale. But once Bhatia began, a ghoulish curiosity returned, making him feel guilty. Bhatia looked excited and important, as the purveyor of a first-hand report of a catastrophe that was close to them. "Gopalan and I went to Pirtana as soon as we heard the news, some time in the middle of the night." A tragedy is never a tragedy for long, thought Agastya, until it happens to yourself, and when it is a friend's, it is, in some obscene way, almost stimulating.

"Pirtana has a small and really lousy Primary Health Centre. Mohan was in a state of shock. The doctor, he seemed OK, didn't let us see him. The chowkidar was there at the Centre, he was the one who had called the police. He told us the story. Neither Gopalan nor I believed him, that Mohan had been fucking his cook on the sly."

Perhaps it was the drink, or Bhatia's use of the word "fucking," or some grotesque reaction to the inglorious horror of the story, or a secret relief that it was after all someone else who had suffered retribution for his sins, but suddenly both of them started laughing. They were deeply shocked at themselves, and that somehow made them laugh the more, in a kind of panic. Agastya switched on the ugly bedside lamp and switched off the tube-lights. "That's better, laughing in soft light." Bhatia drank from his glass and his laughter turned to choking.

"I had to send the office telegram to Alwar. What could I say? Anyway, I sent, 'Mohan seriously hurt in accident. Come soon.' Then we tried to keep the story from spreading, but that didn't work. That *Dainik* is really a disgusting newspaper. One Range Forest Officer at Pirtana also said that some journalist used to visit Mohan quite often at the Forest Rest House. He thinks the journalist might have been blackmailing Mohan but I think that's all rubbish. The doctor said Mohan shouldn't be moved, but Rohini and some elder brother came, they flew to Delhi and then probably drove to Alwar. I haven't heard from them since."

Agastya was a little less drunk than Bhatia; Bhatia had a story to tell, and as raconteur it seemed only appropriate that he should drink a little more than his listener, pause whenever he thought fit, sigh often and look reflectively at inanimate objects. "I didn't like meeting Rohini at all. The three of us had become good friends while staying together. You saw that, I had dinner with them so often. She looked so scared when I met them at the station. I felt guilty at having called her a sexy rustic and other rubbish like that. I just felt guilty about everything, as though Mohan had been my fault, I had been in the same district when it had happened, and so it was my fault, that's what I felt. It's sickening, that feeling of irrational guilt. She was noticeably pregnant too, and sexy in a tender pregnant kind of way, and I felt guilty about that too, you know, how you feel horny in the strangest of circumstances? And Rohini kept asking, Mandy Bhaiya, what accident, how is he, he's all right, isn't he. And for a moment I wanted to say something like, oh, that telegram was an April Fool joke." Bhatia got up unsteadily, and said in a quicker, less sombre voice, "I'm very drunk. You?"

Agastya went through his cassettes for music that would please Bhatia. He had none. Slyly, half-sure that Bhatia wouldn't notice, he put on, softly, the songs of Nazrul Islam. "Don't play sick Bengali songs, please," said Bhatia immediately. "No, let it be," argued Agastya, "we want some incongruous background noise for your depressing story."

"Gopalan, the bastard, didn't have the guts to tell them the truth. *You* tell them, he told me and then, you'd *better* tell them. So just before we left for Pirtana, I told the elder brother. He was a little weird. He always looked preoccupied, as though he'd forgotten to turn off a gas cylinder in the kitchen, or left

the taps on. I told him that the tribals had very wrongly suspected Mohan of fooling around with one of their women. I
went in with them to see Mohan. He was looking white and
dead. He didn't speak. He looked at us, and looked away, then
looked at us, then looked away again. There was one really horrible moment. He looked so awful that Rohini sort of instinctively reached under the cover for his hand. Then she broke
down, and he sort of grimaced."

"Mohan *was* fucking that tribal woman on the sly, wasn't
he?" asked Agastya. This time it didn't sound funny, but terribly
unreal; perhaps because Mohan had been a friend, and unexpected acts from friends are doubly startling, making one feel
as though one didn't know anything at all—he remembered
Dhrubo's rage on Delhi's Airport Road, when Scott Joplin had
mingled with the whizz of passing cars, at hearing of Agastya's
mad plans, and wondered whether that rage had been partly
due to his not conforming to Dhrubo's idea of him, an IAS officer who looked like something out of a kinky film, who
would get hazaar fucked in a small town, but surely wouldn't
do anything about it other than write virulently funny letters.

"Yes, he must have been. The chowkidar said that the woman
was some kind of whore, as loose as a tooth about to fall, and I
suppose Mohan missed Rohini or something like that."

"Don't be silly, Mandy, you and I have been lonely and
horny too, here in Madna. But you wouldn't fuck your cook,
not even if she looked like Khajuraho and sat down beside your
plate while you had lunch and shaved her puss in front of you."

"Oh, well, I don't know, I suppose we didn't know Mohan
well enough. Those four tribals and that woman are on the run,
somewhere in the forests around Pirtana. For once we are
happy that the forests have been thinned by the smugglers and
the tribals. The police'll get them, I think. They'll also clean the
Naxalites out of the area. It's quite true that this would never
have happened if those Naxalites hadn't been staying with the

tribals for months, one bunch of bastards trying to get another bunch of bastards to think."

They emptied the half-bottle, last drinks. Agastya switched the cassette to side B. "The *Dainik* and this town haven't had so much fun since that story of Srivastav and the female BDO. And Sathe is quite mad. Suddenly he said, 'I could get quite a cartoon out of Mohan.'"

"Shall we repeat that day, go to Dakshin, buy another half-bottle, and stooge a dinner off Sathe?"

December, yet the alleys were still warm. The goats were still there, sentinel statues outside a blue door. Bhatia asked, "Any news about where you're going to be posted as Assistant Collector?"

"No, not yet." Dakshin was the same, bright and noisy. At one table the man with leukoderma was still gobbling up idlis from a sea of sambar. Bhatia, a half-bottle under his arm, again argued with the rickshaw-wala outside Sathe's hotel. "For the first time now I feel I need some continuities"—Agastya suddenly remembered that line from his past. He had read it, or heard it somewhere, perhaps in Delhi? But he couldn't remember.

Sathe wasn't home. They walked through a few doors into the hotel, met Sathe's brother, ate a lot, and gracefully acceded to the brother's request that the meal be on the house.

The meeting took all of next day. Bajaj yelled almost as much as Srivastav. In the evening Agastya went to Srivastav's house. Srivastav said, "Bajaj says you've been doing good work in Jompanna. Good." Mrs. Srivastav said, "See that you don't misbehave with any tribal woman." Then they discussed Mohan.

Seven the next morning. He, exercised, bathed and stoned, was about to start for Jompanna, when from the Rest House, he saw a fat figure waving his arms and stumbling towards him. "Ho, Sen saab," Shankar began yelling from a distance of forty yards, "Vasant told me you were here, so I thought we must meet again before I go, at least once." He wheezed, and spiced the morning with his unique effluvium of whisky and sweat. "I have again sung all night. Soft, controlled singing." He leaned forward, and shaking his head, rolling his eyes and wriggling his ears, breathed tunefully into Agastya's face,

> Allow me to stay
> In the shadow of your eyelashes.

Then he straightened. "Incomparable thumri, Sen saab. And I have been singing not in sorrow, but in celebration. But," he stopped smiling, and his face creased with a kind of petulancy, "I wasn't really satisfied with last night. I sing much better when I'm sad. Where are you going?"

"Back to Jompanna."

"You have time for some tea with me?"

"Oh, yes."

"Ah, I knew you would." They began walking towards the Rest House. "How many times I have told you, Sen saab, that we are similar? We are men without ambition, and all we want is to be left alone, in peace, so that we can try and be happy. So few people will understand this simplicity. Any other person would have said, no, I don't think I have time for a cup of tea, I'm already late, I have so much work waiting in Jompanna. Work? That kind of petty work never ends. But you look different, Sen saab, more silent somehow."

"I think I'm growing up." At that Shankar neighed so much that he farted loudly. Vasant appeared, still looking like an unshaven lunatic. They sat on the veranda, from where, on so many mornings, he had seen the trains rush past. "I've been transferred, Sen saab, to Koltanga. I leave this afternoon."

Oh, well, he thought, just one more human on one more journey. "Did you have to pay your Minister?"

"No, no, so many times I have told you to believe in Jagadamba. Why will you not listen." Behind Shankar's head the Ernakulam Express glided by on its way to Calcutta.

"I do, I mean, I did once, in Delhi. Pray to her, Jagadamba, as Durga, I mean. Almost pray." He stopped, embarrassed. He could never have said this to anyone else.

Vasant brought tea. "You are coming back from Jompanna in a few weeks' time, aren't you? Next time I'll keep your old room for you." Shankar drank from his saucer, and sang,

> Allow me to stay
> In the shadow of your eyelashes.

He was in an irrepressible mood, and full of his own joy.

THE REST of the months in Jompanna passed, the same routine, office and Rest House, two vegetarian meals a day, exercise on the three feet of jute carpet between bed and desk, in the evening files in his room to the music from the stalls. The stalls had stopped selling sugarcane. Now they sold the juices of carrot and orange, apple and grape. Contrary to warnings, Malik at the office turned out not to be dangerous, but merely exceptionally lazy, lazy even by the standards of the office. After Chipanthi, he toured even more, to keep away from his desk, and to enjoy the tranquillity of the long jeep rides. He visited Primary Schools and Primary Health Centres, saw his first midwife, organized three sterilization camps, where he watched men and women being paid to turn barren, and where he wondered what it would be like for a heterosexual to be a doctor at a Primary Health Centre, seeing a hundred different male crotches a day. The sabhapati was, reluctantly, impressed by him. The Block also thought him extremely efficient, and its people said to one another, "IAS, after all." He did work reasonably hard, there wasn't much else to do there; but when he made his night halts, he stared for many night hours at different ceilings in the different Rest Houses of Jompanna.

Srivastav telephoned him in his last week. "Collector on the phone, sir," breathed Malik nervously. "Hahn Sen," Srivastav managed to make his voice sound like a scowl, "You're coming back on Friday, aren't you? Come back a day earlier, so you can attend Joshi RDC's farewell. He's retiring, no, at the end of the month. And your posting order has come, you're going to be Assistant Collector at Koltanga."

He put down the phone and looked out beyond two suppliants through the windows. A late-afternoon sun on the heads of the dawdlers, the red sand and the trees beside the road, the mild light softening the tableau of under-development.

Then he said goodbye to Jompanna. The Block Office organized a party to send him off. Chilli pakoras, burfi, testiculate gulabjamuns and tea. He, the sabhapati and two other politicians made speeches. In all the speeches he emerged as a kind of Indian Albert Schweitzer. An exceptionally ugly parting gift, a timepiece in bronze, Krishna and Arjun in a chariot, and the face of the clock in lieu of torsos and legs, and pencil batteries where their feet should have been. Agastya tried to look grateful. He packed slowly, as usual. Everyone came to the Rest House to see him off, and waved.

He reached Madna late in the evening, but Vasant had kept his old room for him. The extra furniture was back. "I'm here for only two or three days, but it'd be very nice if you remove this stuff once more." Vasant said OK, and called a few others to help. The frog was revealed under the sofa, startling everyone but Agastya. He went to Srivastav's house to say hello and eat. Srivastav told him that Joshi's farewell was fixed for five thirty the following evening, and that it would be followed by dinner, and he said that he wanted to go to Calcutta for a few days before he joined at Koltanga.

He returned from Srivastav's house after ten. Srivastav slept early, for he got up early, to play badminton at the Club. Past the Industrial Training Institute and the Madna Club, thinking about Koltanga. He brought a chair out to the veranda and switched off the tube-light. Shankar's room was silent, locked. He didn't want to be alone just then. He walked across to the

Circuit House, but the room in which the phone was kept was locked. He walked to the Madna International Hotel, across the bridge below which the beggars were settling down for the night, past the dark offices. But Sathe had gone to Hyderabad. From the hotel he telephoned the Forest Colony. A chowkidar picked up after many rings. Bhatia was at Mariagarh. He had a drink with Sathe's brother, and walked back, past the Circuit House and towards the rail tracks.

This time not the tracks that touched the horizon, but the tracks that curved away to the thermal power station. The pad of rubber soles on wood and stone, a truck horn somewhere shattering the dark, distant laughter from a paanwala's shop. He had to think. He couldn't go to Koltanga and start all over again, reorganize furniture in a house, attend an Integration Meeting, without thinking.

A long walk, he didn't know how long. Time had never mattered on his night walks. The moon was almost full, and in its blue-white light, everything—the houses and shacks, the trees and scrub—looked black, with no shape or outline, black squat blobs, one with their shadows. So must he, he thought, look like a blob to someone watching from a distance, a moving blob, terminus unknown.

Open country, miles of freshly planted fields. And the power station against the sky, blocking the river. Points of light connected by steel, like the model of a constellation in a planetarium. He stood there for long, feeling the night breeze cold on his skin, thinking, I should've taken the other tracks. Then he turned back.

It was almost two when he reached his room. He switched on both the tube-lights and the lamp on the table, and put on Ella Fitzgerald on his cassette recorder. He sat down on the stool in front of the dressing-mirror to take off his shoes. The frog crouched in the shadow of the dressing table, black-green and at rest. He reached out to touch it. For a second he felt with his fingertips a cold clammy skin, before the frog bounded past his shoulder and hid behind his suitcase.

He would have to unpack, just a few things for these two or three days. "I love Paris every moment," sang Ella. He switched off the cassette. Then unpack, more elaborately, in Calcutta. But just a fortnight there, before he stuffed things into his suitcases and hold-all again. Then Koltanga, for at least two years. He switched off the tube-lights, but left the lamp on, and lay down in his jeans to watch the ceiling.

HE WOKE up early, six o'clock, feeling awful. Not yet day outside the windows, the light from the lamp was a hot yellow dot on the table. He couldn't move. There was a brown stain on the pillow an inch away from his eye. He watched it till the door handle rattled. Vasant with tea. "No, no second cup today." He finished the cup hurriedly, standing. It was hot, so he drank half the tea from the saucer. Vasant dawdled in the veranda, lazily viewing the world. "I'm not feeling too well today. Don't bring my breakfast until I ask for it." Vasant looked at him sceptically. He waited at the door until Vasant left with the cup. Then he went to the bathroom and out through the outer door, turned the corner, slipped past his windows, and came to the front. No one around. He locked his front door from the outside and returned to his room from the bathroom. He closed and bolted the opaque windows. Now just the faint light from the ventilators, and the lamp looked even brighter. He lay down again.

A late-evening feeling, around him an embalming gloom. But even complete physical rest was impossible. He would have to get up, sooner or later, for something or the other. He joined his palms together and looked at them, mounds and lines, long thin fingers. He wished that he had believed in palmistry, believed in anything beyond himself. He tautened his fingers and let them collapse, again and again. Through them he could glimpse, darkly, fragments of two sunsets, and boatmen in Japanese conical hats.

He had met so many people in Madna, but not Tamse. But, then, he hadn't really wanted to meet him, just as he hadn't wanted to meet Baba Ramanna, they might have proved disappointments. He had liked this Tamse of 1962, but how ridiculous the later Tamse had become, the government artist, who created statues and Rest Houses for people whose idea of art could be found in the drains. Tamse had to learn, he thought, that to be lonely was not enough.

Early-morning sounds, but he felt safe behind the locked door. Bicycle bells, the chatter of Vasant's children, then conversation on the veranda, scaring him by its proximity. The room in which Shankar had stayed was unlocked noisily, someone was moving in. He waited, tensed, for more sounds. Through the wall he heard laughter, voices, the dumping of suitcases, the dragging of chairs. Someone asked Vasant for tea. Then the thunder of water falling in an empty bucket.

A lizard fell on to the carpet with a sharp plop and scurried away towards the wastebasket. Menon would be there too in Koltanga, in his new post of District Development Officer, continually reminding him of what he ought to be. He felt a faint dull fever, about which he knew Multani could do nothing. He pulled the blanket over his head and breathed his own exhalations. That felt diseased, and nice, and he smiled. If he went to Multani's clinic, he would meet another salesman, whose tired face would again make him feel guilty. He had had enough of the mockers of his restlessness, Sathe's cartoons, Shankaran Karanth's dedication, a Naxalite's fanaticism.

Digambar's voice outside, asking Vasant where he was. He tensed again. Vasant murmured something. Sounds, as they settled down on the steps of the veranda to smoke Digambar's bidis. The blanket teased his nose and beard. He curled up on to his left. Beside his pillow was the napkin a naib tehsildar had bought him in late summer, for his protection from the sun. Now it lay starched with dried semen. He crumpled the cloth in his fist and laughed into his pillow.

The ventilators brightened as the sun rose. He ought to get up and exercise, perhaps slowly, to devour more time. Sounds from the veranda, as Digambar left. The whole day was a blank, except for the party for Joshi in the evening, where he would meet Ahmed and Agarwal, and the District Inspector of Land Records, and perhaps they would all probe his aliases. Half-laughing, he tried to masturbate, but he couldn't concentrate on Neera.

He got up and placed his recorder next to his pillow, above the napkin. He removed Ella Fitzgerald but didn't know what to play. Tagore's infinite gentlemanliness was hopelessly inappropriate for his mood, Vivaldi was too remote. For Shankar there had been his thumris and ghazals, he could conjure up exquisite nose-rings and eyelashes for consolation, and Dhrubo, too, had ragtime and his fashionable jazz, but his own taste had no continuities—merely a sad mongrel hybridity. He switched on the radio and tried to catch Hindi film music. But he couldn't—too early, or too late.

He got up again to roll a joint. He kept his marijuana behind his books. Getting stoned meant that he wouldn't exercise, not for a few hours. The *Gita* reminded him of the joker of Madna. "If thou wilt not fight thy battle of life because in selfishness thou art afraid of the battle, thy resolution is in vain: nature will compel thee. Because thou art in the bondage of Karma, of the forces of thine own past life." Suddenly Sathe seemed disgusting, who had found this as comic as the hacking off of a friend's arms.

He slipped out of the bathroom door after tea, slithered round the corners, unlocked his front door and went to ask Vasant for breakfast. Vasant was sitting in the sun, thumbing the dirt off the soles of his feet. "I thought you weren't having breakfast, we've cooked the tomatoes for ourselves," said Vasant, looking up at him, one hand warding off the sun.

"Then give me the potato, and egg, and milk."

He felt strange looking around at the Circuit House, Vasant's wife, the stray dogs, the world that had revolved so ordinarily while he had played out his secret life.

He was sucking at the hole in his tin of condensed milk when Sathe asked him from the door what he was doing, and whether he was practising for sex. "O, hello," said Agastya, "I didn't hear you slink up. Have a suck."

"You didn't hear me because you were busy mouthing that hole, and because the Maruti is a silent twenty-first century car. And no, thanks, to your magnanimous offer of that tin. Why's the room so dark, does sunlight scare you?"

"Sit down somewhere," said Agastya. He felt odd, seeing another person in the room, and talked out of a kind of nervousness. "The condensed milk is my only friend. I suck it thrice a day, after every meal, in gratitude for its existence. The cook here has what in officialese is called standing orders to bring the tin from the fridge along with every tray. Do you want tea?"

"Why is the milk brown?" asked Sathe, examining Agastya's breakfast tray with distracting intentness.

"The cook probably used his shit instead of sugar. Or it's the dirt from the tray. You see, he doesn't have hands like rock, or a steely grip, and so on. The tray dances in his hands like Uri Geller or something, and the milk slops over. Then he slops the milk back into the glass. I went over last night, your brother said you'd gone to Hyderabad."

"Yes, he told me. I came back this morning." And he was leaving the same night, for Bombay and Poona, to argue about his cartoons. "But I thought we should go out to Gorapak for the day, to relax over beer. Bhatia's in Mariagarh, the industrious fool. I rang up the Collectorate, and Chidambaram said that you were back from Jompanna. Now don't say you can't come."

"Of course I can, but not if you're wearing that shirt." Sathe's shirt *was* objectionable, small green and yellow flowers on a white background, like a shower curtain. Sathe laughed. "It's a lovely picnic shirt. Besides, this is Madna, August, no one will mind."

For a second something flickered in Agastya's mind, a memory, that he had once argued, or had wanted to argue, with someone about the standards of taste in Madna. Then he said, "Wait a while, I'll just get the scum off my loins." He closed the bathroom door on Sathe's laugh.

Sathe was standing beside his books when he came out, laughing, holding aloft his polythene bag of marijuana. "We must take this along. It'll ignite the beer."

"*Et tu*, Govind."

"Why, it's a great Indian tradition. It's one of the reasons why I like Madna, it's easier to get here than cholera." He laughed again. "You are as unlikely a bureaucrat as you look. I suppose Bhatia also smokes."

"Half the college smoked. It was quite fashionable. And Bhatia's lungs have probably turned grey-green. I'm sure if we chopped up his blood vessels and smoked them, we'd get high. I owe you a *Gita*."

"Keep it, please. I've several other translations to steal from. And these Bengali tomes, what are they?" He touched *Pather Panchali* and *Gora*.

"Oh, they're somehow very remote, one is about being a revolutionary, and the other's about being poor, in Bengal. But both great novels, though."

"Of course, Bengali, aren't they?" Sathe laughed. "But you surprise me, I didn't know you could read Bengali. Your father, I presume. He didn't want you to end up knowing only the English of the Bombay Goans." He watched Agastya change. "For someone who leads such a dissolute life you're in reasonably good shape."

"I was a marathon man in my college days." Agastya laughed as he put on his shoes. "I exercise quite regularly even here. It," he waved his hands at the wall, "seems to give the day some shape."

"One day, when you turn sensible, you'll stop." Sathe laughed, and sat down on the bed, beside the cassette recorder. "You'll learn the complete unnecessariness of any excess physical exertion. I know why you do it, to feel sexy," his legs left the floor as he see-sawed with laughter, "but sexiness is in the mind, ask me. And as an Indian, you should live the life of contemplation, what, does the *Kamasutra* recommend push-ups?"

At the car Agastya remembered. "Oh, there is some kind of party for Joshi this evening. I was to have attended that." He smiled at Sathe. "This is *déjà vu*, do you remember the first lunch at your house? Will you wait a second while I make the excuses." From the Circuit House he telephoned Chidambaram and told him that he was ill. Back in the car he told Sathe, "If Srivastav comes enquiring after my health, he'll find a locked door and that cook will tell him that the patient left at eleven in the morning in a red Maruti."

Then his last drive through the town and beyond, and the best one, in a silent car; with the windows up, the heat and dust were at bay, and the cycles and rickshaws and fruit-juice sellers looked like part of a film, distant and comfortable. Sathe sat easily, paunch hiding his belt, thick lips pursed in a soundless whistle. The shitting children were as excited about the Maruti as about a new toy—it was red, and not much higher than they, and a tap could dent it. "Can you poke your head out and glare at them?" asked Sathe.

Then they left the town behind and Sathe relaxed even more. "When last I saw these shitters," said Agastya, "I remembered that Gandhi line about how we lack a sense of sanitation. It sounds so simple, dig a small hole before you shit."

"But that's just extra physical work," said Sathe, "always the easier way out."

Far away in a field was a farmer behind two oxen, plough-ing, three slow spots in a landscape of brown and green. Agastya looked at him and thought, too many worlds, concentric, and he a restless centre. Madna, and within it Jompanna, Chipanthi, Gorapak, Mariagarh, like names out of magic, strong with an idiosyncratic tang, still reeking of the tribals that had once been their only inhabitants. And the megalopolitan world of Delhi and Calcutta, the bewitching, because elusive, alternative. Beyond which was the hinterland that countless trains tore through every day, with its dots of Ratlam and Azamganj. And stretching out to the infinite was the *Time-Life* world, from which John Avery had come, to which Dhrubo's Renu had gone, only to feel dislocated. Movement without purpose, an endless ebb and flow, from one world to another, journeys and passages, undertaken by cocoons not for rest or solace, but for ephemerals. The flux of the sea now seemed the only pattern, within and beyond the mind—mirrored even in his encounters with the myriad faces, on some of which he had tried to impose an order by seeing them as mirror-images, facets of his own self, but now that longing, for repose through the mastering of chaos, itself seemed vain. Perhaps it was true that he had first to banish all yearning, and learn to accept the drift, perhaps it was true that all was clouded by desire, as fire by smoke, as a mirror by dust, as an unborn babe by its covering.

The car slowed down and honked timidly at a few squatters on the road. He turned to Sathe, "I don't think you know. I've been posted to Koltanga. Where the company of Shankar will be far outbalanced by the presence of Menon."

Sathe, expectedly, laughed. He was an unsympathetic man. "Koltanga. The town is one-tenth the size of Madna. No indus-tries, no hotels, nothing, just rickshaws and a video parlour. I don't think I've met Menon, but I've seen him, he's pink and shrill, isn't he, and always makes you feel vaguely unclean?" Sathe played a tune on the horn. "And Shankar wanted to be posted to Koltanga, anyway. He must've paid over fifteen thousand for the transfer." He smiled, but without humour. "Shankar's is a sick story. he wanted Koltanga because he was genuinely homesick, unlike other engineers who bribe everybody in sight to be posted to places where they can make money. Shankar paid the Irrigation Minister 10,000, and the Minister did nothing. Shankar was powerless because he has such a record for incompetence and inefficiency that he can be suspended at any moment. If anyone is really so out of place in his job he ought to resign. Everyone was laughing at Shankar— see, the Minister took your 10,000 and farted in your face. And he is a comic figure, all that booze and music and astrology. Then he paid some more, and got his transfer. It's a sick story, he should've stuck to music and kept away from everything else. I heard him years ago, when he was fresh and hopeful. Now he sings only in memory of his other self, requiems for what he might have been."

They reached Gorapak in under two hours. They took out the food and beer. Sathe said, "My brother's children wanted to come. I tried to convince them of the virtues of attending school instead. Terrible if they had come. They'd have run around aimlessly and shrieked, cried if we hadn't played cricket with them. The whole day would've gone in trying to get out of the game by losing ball after ball."

The urchins followed them through the trees and over the excrement to the gate of the temple, half-heartedly clutching their clothes, lightly pinching their skins for alms. They cursed the urchins and smiled, the urchins cursed and smiled back. The gate was blocked by a supine beggar who listlessly raised his hands for display. "I think he'll be hurt if we don't shudder at his putrescent fingers," said Agastya. "He isn't too far gone, why doesn't he go to Baba Ramanna's?"

He stooped a little and repeated the question to the leper, who looked at him with faint dislike. A broad flat nose and small fidgety eyes. The leper rubbed his forearm against the side of his belly. "Probably can't speak anything other than his obscure tribal dialect," said Sathe as they entered the temple, "and probably dislikes Baba Ramanna for making them work and be independent. Each of us has his own view of things, no."

The courtyard was quite deserted. No chant from within the temple. Memories of his last visit, a second of lust for Rohini, a lascivious Kumar, stoning with Mohan and Bhatia in front of the incarnations of Vishnu. "We should go down to the river," said Sathe, "there is a nice place down there." The river had waned to its early-winter size, there were fewer boats on the water that moved timidly among the large grey-sand islands.

Sathe led the descent down the uneven rock steps. Scrub on either side, a few goats placidly standing at impossible angles and chewing, the sharp tack of Sathe's heels on stone, and soft murmurs from the village women on the beach. Sathe was panting audibly. The women watched them pass across the sand and into a glade, which evidently was where the villagers had been defecating for decades. "The place I know is further on," said Sathe, huffing and laughing. Five more minutes across more naked sand, and they reached a small shaded pool.

"What an ideal place for villagers to shit," said Agastya. "Why don't they?"

Sathe laughed. "Thank God for obscure legends." He put down his basket and wiped his face and neck, which exertion had crimsoned. "For the villagers this spot is holy, and so cannot be defiled."

He collapsed on a flat stone. The pool was about thirty feet wide, its water was still and clean. Pale green sunlight through dateless gnarled banyans. Blocks of brown stone lay scattered around the pond, like broken beads from some giant diadem. "These are from the temple," said Agastya, "same kind of stone.

Especially that hut." The stone hut was on the other side of the pond; its walls were also intricately carved. "Must have been some kind of retreat for the kings, for sex or something." He looked around. The trees hid both the beach and the river, clean and quiet, but for the whisper of leaves and the cawing of distant birds, almost menacing. Surprising, too, the lushness that existed in the most unexpected places.

"From the temple this place just looks like another shit zone." Sathe had recovered and was unpacking the beer. "I discovered it more than twenty-five years ago with my father. The only place in the district I can think of that hasn't been ruined by the years." He stood two bottles in the water. "Cools much better than a fridge." While Sathe talked Agastya hopped from stone to stone. "One old and phenomenally boring sadhu lives in that hut. I hope he isn't around. He would disapprove vastly of our compounded desecration. Beer and beef and marijuana." Sathe called after Agastya, "You do eat beef, don't you?"

He paused on his toes on a stone. "As long as my aunts don't get to know." He felt wonderful. "My oldest aunt, my father's elder sister, says if you eat beef you eat the flesh of your parents." He began hopping again. His voice came to Sathe in snatches, from a thin bearded figure gavotting on stone. "My father eats beef too. He's amazing," he laughed, "he eats corned beef sandwiches and wears dhotis and reads the *Upanishads* in Sanskrit. He irritates my aunts continually. Every time I returned to Calcutta from Darjeeling for the Puja holidays, to eat myself sick at my aunts' houses, my father was in Delhi then, I had to swear that I hadn't had beef, I used to swear and they'd give me presents." He had reached half-way around the pond. "And in school I had an Anglo-Indian classmate called Peter Martin, whose parents also stayed in Darjeeling, they called it Darge, tea-estate types. He used to get food from home all the time, lots of beef. He told me when we were in the sixth, I was eleven and he must've been thirteen, the bugger used to fail like others used to pass, he told me," he began hopping back, "'Hey, English,' he said, 'if you want to be an Anglo-Indian you have to eat beef, but you'll still go to hell.' The fool thought that would stop us from attacking his food."

The last hop brought him to the stone on which sat Sathe, munching a sandwich. "Why don't we smoke some of your ganja first?" asked Sathe.

Agastya sat down on the ground and leaned back against the stone. "If you stayed here for months you could improve your eyesight or something, it's that kind of light. It's silent and green, like being under water." He looked across at the hut. "If the sadhu is here, maybe we should call him. I'm sure he'd love to smoke. The one person whom we shouldn't meet is perhaps Dubey, the Assistant Conservator here, probably an orthodox Mithila Brahmin who'd be aghast at this desecration."

"Well, I'm a Brahmin too," laughed Sathe, "Chitpavan to my toes. That's how I first met the sadhu. About five years ago. I'd come here alone. I was smoking a cigarette when he emerged from somewhere and gave me hell. Saffron robe and grey long hair, huge and tough, I was tempted to ask him whether he lifted weights. I said I was innocent because I was ignorant, and I couldn't have meant to be impious because I was a Brahmin. Then I showed him my janau." His laugh again jarred the stillness. "I've met him quite a few times since. He's an extremely talkative man. I suppose with the villagers he has to be solemn and silent. He's some kind of self-appointed guard of this place." Sathe pushed the sandwiches across to Agastya. "It's a great legend, all about irresponsible lust and illegitimacy. Some obscure tribal chieftain had a bastard child. He disowned both the woman and the son. She committed suicide in this pool, and the waters turned red. Lovely, isn't it? But nice irresponsible behaviour, because she abandoned the child on one of these stones. I asked the sadhu, *which* one of these stones. He was a little irritated, quite rightly, I think, and said that all the blocks were holy. Somehow the child survived in this 1,000-square-yard oasis. That's the best thing about myths, in them staying alive is such a simple matter. I wanted to ask the sadhu, where did the child shit? Equally wonderfully, the child hadn't seen the river or the sand. That was a great idea, someone just lived in this rich greenness without having seen any dirt and dryness to compare it with. But the waters remained red, and they wouldn't turn normal until the chieftain said he was sorry. Then there was a great drought, a good Third World touch, I thought, and there was no water anywhere but here. Everyone went to the King and said, Help. He came here and was hit on the head by lots of guilt. He renounced his kingdom to his legitimate children and came here to stay. So father and son stayed together, the father turned holy and taught the son about the wicked world, meaning himself. The waters turned clear, and thousands of fish bobbed up in this pool. Thousands," Sathe pointed languidly at the water. "Drop some bread into it and see. No one ever fishes here, even the fish are consecrated. And it's true that the pool never dries in the peak of the worst summer, obviously some secret underground source, and no one takes a drop of water from this place."

Agastya picked up the bottles from the water. "Cold and lovely," he said. He tore off some bread from his sandwich and threw it into the pool. Suddenly spasms in the water, startling after the stillness. He couldn't see the bottom for the turbulence and the darting silver fish. Then abruptly, the old silence, but now false, as though merely a veil.

BELCHES of meat and beer. Agastya said, "I don't think I'm going to Koltanga. I'm going to go home and think. I need to think."

Late afternoon, Sathe was flat, watching the sun gild the leaves of the banyan above them. He said, after a while, with sleepy sarcasm, "Yes, you could stay in Calcutta and translate my cartoons, for the Bengali newspapers."

Agastya hated him then. He got up and went and sat by the edge of the water. Watching the bed of the pool he said, "I feel confused and awful. Journey after journey, by train and jeep, just motion. Integration Meetings, Revenue Meetings, Development. First the job didn't make sense, and I thought then, when it does, I'll settle down. When it did, it didn't help, I'd always be wandering, thinking chaotically of alternatives, happy images of my past, mocking. Most of the time I felt guilty. At Chipanthi I thought, if my mind wasn't so restless, if it cohered somehow, then I'd be working, getting water to a village, something concrete. Even at Baba Ramanna's I felt guilty, immersed in myself, while a doctor had worked a miracle."

The afternoon sun seemed to yawn over the water. On its surface, in that washed light he detected a face. The sound of movement, and suddenly Sathe touched his shoulder and sat down beside him. After some moments, he laughed, abruptly, "Years ago. My father couldn't believe I wanted to be a cartoonist. That's no way to live. I don't think yours is any way to live either, I had said. He'd made a lot of money for us, but he'd had to work for it, in what I thought was an inhuman way. Days and sometimes nights in the forest, bribing the Forest officials, underpaying the tribals, beating others like him to a timber contract. He had wealth, but no dignity, which he must've wanted from us. He was outraged with me, I can see why. No one takes a cartoonist seriously, the joker of Madna. He must have thought I was laughing at the way he had lived. Of course I wasn't. Because of him, money would never bother me. I was grateful, of course I was grateful. But if I chose differently, it wasn't a *fault*, it was just a different choice." Sathe looked at Agastya's profile. Somewhere a bird cawed, mournfully. Sathe got up and returned with the leftover sandwiches.

He slowly threw bits of bread into the pool, and they watched the water writhe. "On the first day, in Kumar's office, you asked me what I was doing in Madna. Where you've grown up, it's different, isn't it, everyone pronounces 'epitome' correctly and doesn't use 'of' after 'comprise,' and behaves as though these things matter. But Madna is home for me, August, in Bombay I felt lost. My best years, my past, is here, bittersweet because it is gone. Whatever you choose to do, you will regret everything, or regret nothing. Remember," and Sathe laughed softly, "you're not James Bond, you only live once."

Later they hopped across (Sathe laughing helplessly at each stone) to the hut. It was absolutely bare, a clean earthen floor, and slits in the stone for air.

"You're sure the sadhu actually stays here?"

"What did you expect in here, a video?" They admired the sex on the walls. "Wonderful. It must have been an amazing sight," said Sathe, "a dozen sculptors chipping away at stone so that huge breasts and thighs could emerge."

"John Avery asked me why there was so much sex in a Hindu temple. I told him there was no satisfactory explanation."

"John Avery, I'd forgotten the pilgrim." They began hopping back. Sathe paused on one block to ask, "How was Marihandi with him and his sexy wife? I felt vaguely sorry for them, she was so removed from the Collectorate and the Club. She is your type, isn't she, I'm sure she doesn't oil her hair either. She must have been surprised by Avery's curiosity." They began packing up the bottles and napkins. "For her the best slice of the country would be Bombay—a flat in Warden Road, and afternoons at the Jehangir Art Gallery. I don't know if she sensed, when she came here, that she had nothing to offer, no oddities to catch the interest of anybody—Tantric rites, or the Raj, or Gandhi, no past, really. And Avery looked quite bewildered, didn't he, surely not his usual expression. Sita didn't care, and those of us who are at all conscious of our history are masochists with it—I wonder if he sensed that." They began walking. "But how can we blame Avery for not being interested in Sita's world, or yours." Sathe laughed. "You see, no one, but no one, is remotely interested in your generation, August."

Agastya looked back. "Would be nice to come here again."

"You'd probably meet the sadhu, he'd tell you all about the origins of your name."

There was a chill wind on the sand beyond the trees and the river looked dark and dying. The village women watched them pass, loose shirts and tight jeans in the twilight. They stopped a dozen times on the steps. The river was a dark mirror, the sky grey and sullen. "Some scenes," said Sathe, between gasps, "stick in the mind, don't they," he waved his arm. "They are pretty, and sometimes you find them in the most unexpected places. Or you think they are significant. From the Madna bridge, over the years, I saw the thermal power station grow towards the sky. Somehow that seemed momentous." The temple was deserted. A single bulb over the gate. The leper was no longer there. Near the car Sathe said abruptly, "You've heard about Mohan. I wanted to laugh. He seemed so sensible, how could he have been so sentimental about lust. That woman was just a tramp. And he made me feel odd, that it could happen to any of us if it could happen to him."

They reached Madna at eight. Agastya unlocked his door and stepped on a letter. Neera.

Dear Ogu,

To my closest friend, I'd like to say that I lost my virginity last week. How do you like my formal announcement? I haven't yet told anyone else but I was bursting with the news all these days. And oddly, my main feeling is one of great relief. It was like shedding a burden. (!) Unlike the sense of loss a lot of girls told me they felt. My other feelings are very confused but I am, unequivocally, relieved. I've taken the plunge, so to speak. And of course it really makes no difference at all. My life is as dull as ever. I wish it could have been together with being in love but one can't have everything. You haven't met him, but you'll dislike him a lot. He's also a journalist (*Telegraph*), bespectacled, bearded, he wears kurta-pyjama and has wet dreams about Marx. I can just see you laughing at me. Please don't. As it is I feel so odd. I'm going to Madras to attend Munu's wedding. But I'll be back to see you in Cal.

With much love, Neera.

Oh, Neera, you darling bitch, laughed Agastya as he walked around the room, letter in hand, here for sex I have been masturbating into napkins and stripping in front of doctors and glimpsing peons buy aphrodisiacs at bus stations, and in Calcutta you've been humping a mouth spewing historical inevitability, with spectacles above it.

Vasant's dinner would be a loathsome end to the day. So he went for his last walk through the town. He passed the house of the District Judge, one tube-light on in the veranda. Tomorrow and the day after would pass in the goodbyes, Bhatia, the Srivastavs, Kumar, Bajaj. Shankar and now Sathe had already gone out of his lives. Lunatic hammering from the garages annihilating the pseudo-ghazals from the music shops. The mechanic crouched over some dark mass. His arm, hammer in hand, flashed up and down against the light from his shop behind him. It looked like a very badly done brutal murder on stage. He would leave a job because he felt that he had to think—a mad act, irrational to all but himself, like running in a field at two in the morning, like deliberately nicking his index finger with a knife. Under a streetlight behind the juice-sellers, he saw an advertisement for a film, *Kanchanjanga.* He had once dreamed of regression, into the mild warmth of an autumn sun. But now reflux appeared to be impossible. The only movement seemed an onward, camel's-back undulation. Dakshin was harshly lit and bustling, as usual. He ate idlis in a sea of sambar, listened to the Hindi disco songs from the speakers, and hoped he wouldn't meet anyone he knew. He was back at the Rest House by nine thirty. He looked into his room from the window, like a voyeur. In the blue glow from the tube-light, he saw an untidy bed, a cassette recorder on a napkin by the pillow, cassettes and an opened letter on the table, a few books on the shelves.

On his last day in Madna he wrote to Dhrubo, "You must be dying while studying for the Civil Services exam. Meanwhile, I've become your American, taking a year off after college to discover himself." His aunts were outraged; one tried to relate his behaviour to the original sin, the marriage of a Bengali Hindu to a Goan Catholic. Pultukaku's reaction was expectedly unconventional. "As long as that idiot doesn't join Tonic," he told Agastya's father on the phone.

The last false promises to the Srivastavs, and Kumar, of looking them up from Koltanga, then the last train journey.

Opposite Agastya sat a bald man eager to talk about his stomach. To avoid him he opened Marcus Aurelius. "Today I have got myself out of all my perplexities; or rather, I have got the perplexities out of myself—for they were not without, but within; they lay in my own outlook." He smiled at the page, and thought, He lied, but he lied so well, this sad Roman who had also looked for happiness in living more than one life, and had failed, but with such grace. He watched the passing hinterland and looked forward to meeting his father.

GLOSSARY

almirah—cupboard

arrey—an exclamation, like "hey!"

ayah—a maid, especially one who looks after children

bhabi—elder sister-in-law

bhai—brother, but its use need not denote a blood relationship

bhajan—religious Hindu song

bidi—tobacco rolled in leaf instead of paper; very common in India

burfi—a common sweet

chapati—flatbread made of wheat

charpai—string cot

chhang—Tibetan intoxicating drink

chhee—exclamation, a sort of stronger version of "tch tch"

chowkidar—watchman

dal—lentils

dhaba—roadside eating place

dhoti—traditional single-piece cotton garment for Indian males, covering waist to ankle

dosa—traditional South Indian fried rice and lentil preparation

feni—intoxicating drink, most commonly associated with Goa

ghazal—Urdu song

goonda—rogue

gulabjamun—a sweet

gur—molasses

hahn—yes, but used more in the sense of an exclamation

halwa—a common sweet, generally made of milk and flour

hayn—exclamation, generally in the interrogative sense

hazaar—a thousand, but used generally in the sense of a lot

ice-pice—a corrupted form of "I Spy"

idli—traditional South Indian steamed rice preparation

janau—sacred thread, to be worn by Hindu Brahmins

kabab—traditional grilled meat dish

karma—a complex Hindu concept of salvation through proper action and duty

khadi—homespun cloth

kharif—one of the major Indian agricultural seasons, approximately June to October

kheer—a sweet, generally made of thickened and sweetened milk

kurta—traditional Indian upper garment, a kind of long loose shirt

kya yaar—exclamation, literally "what friend"

lakh—one hundred thousand

lungi—traditional Indian single-piece garment, wrapped around the waist

maya—complex Hindu concept of the world as illusion when compared to the ultimate

mithai—sweet

naib tehsildar—a minor Revenue Department official in the district, subordinate to the tehsildar

nala—generally open drain; also any conduit for water

namaste—traditional Indian greeting

nimboo pani—lime juice

paan—betel leaf with a variety of nuts, etc., in it

paanwala—seller of paan, cigarettes, etc.

pakora—traditional fried Indian snack, made of chickpea flour

paratha—fried chapati

patil—a minor village official

pukka burra saheb—literally "absolute big master." A phrase connected with the Raj, and used of the English in India, and of Anglicized Indians

rickshaw-wala—a driver/puller of rickshaws; a rickshaw is a very large tricycle and a common mode of transport

roshogolla—a traditionally Bengali sweet

saab—literally Master, also has Raj connotations

sabhapati—President of a village committee

sadhu—a holy man

salaam—greeting

salwaar kameez—traditional North Indian female dress set

sambar—traditional South Indian curried lentil dish

samosa—traditional Indian fried snack, usually stuffed with potatoes

sati—obsolete Hindu custom of widow immolating herself on pyre of husband

shakti—literally strength, power; also a complex Hindu concept of spiritual and metaphysical force innate in every individual

shamiana—a large tent for open air functions, like a marquee

shikar—hunting

shivaling—the phallus of Shiva, an object of worship for Hindus as the source of cosmic force

sola topi—hat, associated with the Raj, since most often used by the British in India

taluka—an administrative unit of a district

tari—an intoxicating drink made from the date palm

tehsil—same as *taluka*

tehsildar—the Revenue official in charge of a tehsil

thumri—a song, part of the repertoire of Hindustani classical music

tonga—a horse-drawn carriage

yaar—friend

TITLES IN SERIES

CHARLES DUFF A Handbook on Hanging
J.G. FARRELL Troubles
J.G. FARRELL The Siege of Krishnapur
J.G. FARRELL The Singapore Grip
M.I. FINLEY The World of Odysseus
EDWIN FRANK (EDITOR) Unknown Masterpieces
MAVIS GALLANT Paris Stories
MAVIS GALLANT Varieties of Exile
JEAN GENET Prisoner of Love
P. V. GLOB The Bog People: Iron-Age Man Preserved
EDWARD GOREY (EDITOR) The Haunted Looking Glass
OAKLEY HALL Warlock
PETER HANDKE A Sorrow Beyond Dreams
ELIZABETH HARDWICK Seduction and Betrayal
ELIZABETH HARDWICK Sleepless Nights
L.P. HARTLEY Eustace and Hilda: A Trilogy
L.P. HARTLEY The Go-Between
NATHANIEL HAWTHORNE Twenty Days with Julian & Little Bunny by Papa
JANET HOBHOUSE The Furies
HUGO VON HOFMANNSTHAL The Lord Chandos Letter
JAMES HOGG The Private Memoirs and Confessions of a Justified Sinner
RICHARD HOLMES Shelley: The Pursuit
WILLIAM DEAN HOWELLS Indian Summer
RICHARD HUGHES A High Wind in Jamaica
RICHARD HUGHES The Fox in the Attic (The Human Predicament, Vol. 1)
RICHARD HUGHES The Wooden Shepherdess (The Human Predicament, Vol. 2)
HENRY JAMES The Ivory Tower
HENRY JAMES The New York Stories of Henry James
HENRY JAMES The Other House
HENRY JAMES The Outcry
RANDALL JARRELL (EDITOR) Randall Jarrell's Book of Stories
DAVID JONES In Parenthesis
ERNST JÜNGER The Glass Bees
HELEN KELLER The World I Live In
MURRAY KEMPTON Part of Our Time: Some Ruins and Monuments of the Thirties
DAVID KIDD Peking Story
ARUN KOLATKAR Jejuri
TÉTÉ-MICHEL KPOMASSIE An African in Greenland
PATRICK LEIGH FERMOR Between the Woods and the Water
PATRICK LEIGH FERMOR A Time of Gifts
D.B. WYNDHAM LEWIS AND CHARLES LEE (EDITORS) The Stuffed Owl: An Anthology of Bad Verse
GEORG CHRISTOPH LICHTENBERG The Waste Books
H.P. LOVECRAFT AND OTHERS The Colour Out of Space
ROSE MACAULAY The Towers of Trebizond
JANET MALCOLM In the Freud Archives
OSIP MANDELSTAM The Selected Poems of Osip Mandelstam